PUR

The battle between Swift security forces and the Black Dragon's robots raged, with Tom Swift and the Hardys caught in the middle. "Don't think you've won!" the Black Dragon snarled at them.

At the same instant a column of blinding purple light erupted. Frank saw one of the robot attackers hit and incinerated.

The pulsing column of light was expanding. Security people and the intruders they'd been fighting moments before now all raced away from the underground complex. As Tom pulled Frank, Joe, and Sandra to shelter, the ground seemed to ripple under their feet.

A deafening roar flung them face-first onto the grassy lawn. The air around them seemed to glow purple, then went black. Sandra gasped. "What's going on back there?"

"Laws of nature were broken, and anyone too close is being punished for it," Tom said. "Punished with certain death."

Books in the Tom Swift® Series

Available from ARCHWAY Paperbacks

TIME BOMB

FRANKLIN W. DIXON

AN ARCHWAY PAPERBACK
Published by POCKET BOOKS
New York   London   Toronto   Sydney   Tokyo   Singapore

AN ARCHWAY PAPERBACK *Original*

An Archway Paperback published by
POCKET BOOKS, a division of Simon & Schuster Inc.
1230 Avenue of the Americas, New York, NY 10020

Copyright © 1992 by Simon & Schuster Inc.

Produced by Byron Preiss Visual Publications, Inc.

ISBN: 0-671-75661-3

First Archway Paperback printing August 1992

10 9 8 7 6 5 4 3 2 1

Cover art by Romas Kukalis

Printed in the U.S.A.

TIME BOMB

Particle detectors ready, Rob?" Tom Swift asked his robot assistant. "We have cosmic rays incoming in less than fifteen seconds."

"You're sure cosmic rays will land right here?" Rob's metal face couldn't show puzzlement, but the seven-foot-tall robot did stare at Tom.

"When our newest satellite is right overhead, a powerful electromagnet snaps on—powerful enough to deflect any passing cosmic rays," Tom told him. "As the rays hit the atmosphere, they—and the particles caused by their collision with air molecules—will land right here."

The young, blond inventor gestured at the array of particle detectors that were spread along the ridge they stood on. Sixty metal cylinders, each five feet wide and five feet high, were scattered in seemingly random patterns. Inside each of the big metal cans was a telescope mirror and a set of phototubes sensitive enough to catch the faintest glimmer of Čerenkov radiation given off by slowing subatomic particles.

Rob's glowing eyes gazed into the evening desert sky. "Why did we power all this up so far in advance of the particle stream?"

"I want to catch some particles coming *ahead* of the rush," Tom explained.

"But cosmic rays move at the speed of light."

"Tachyons are particles that move even faster," Tom said. "They'll show up twenty milliseconds before anything else."

"*If* they exist," Rob pointed out.

"In theory they do," Tom said. "Now we'll see if the universe is a democracy or a dictatorship."

"You've lost me, Tom," Rob said.

Tom's lean face lit up with a grin, and his blue eyes twinkled. "Either everything that's possible is *allowed* to happen—or everything possible *must* happen."

He glanced at his watch. "We'll know in a second. Ready?"

"I've patched myself into the detector links," Rob said.

They stood silently as Rob read the data flying along the computer linkup. "I've picked up several particle anomalies in advance of the air shower created by the cosmic ray collisions."

The robot was silent for a moment. "It's as if the tachyons arrived *before* those collisions. Does that mean they traveled through time?"

Tom shrugged. "We all travel through time, Rob. What makes tachyons interesting is that they move in the opposite direction from us." His eyes lit up. "And now we've managed to catch them doing it."

The gleaming robot suddenly interrupted. "You've got a phone call."

Tom stared. "What?"

"It's a new improvement I was trying out, building your portable phone into my circuits. Just talk. My sensors will pick up."

A second later, Tom Swift, Sr.'s voice came through Rob's speakers. "Tom, are you there?"

"What's up, Dad?" Tom asked.

"I'd like you to come to my office. A rather interesting package has arrived."

"We're on our way." Tom and Rob walked down the side of the ridge to the van parked on the road below. They drove through the California hills until they arrived at a valley sheltering a gleaming complex of buildings. The structures, clean and crisply designed, looked as brand-new as the rock around them seemed ages old.

This was the home of Swift Enterprises, the best invention Tom's father had ever created. Without this high-tech base, Tom's own inventions, like Rob the robot, would never have been possible.

As he pulled up by the administration tower,

in the center of the complex, Tom wondered what the package was that his father wanted to talk to him about. Well, he'd find out soon enough—after a quick elevator ride to Tom Swift, Sr.'s top-floor office.

Tom found his father at his desk. Mr. Swift took the wrapping from a flat box and handed it over. "What do you make of this?"

"It was sent by an S. Reisenbach." Tom frowned. "That's the name of the teacher you mentioned last night on that TV interview."

Tom's father nodded. "Ernst Reisenbach was one of the most brilliant scientists of this century and one of the fathers of nuclear physics. During World War Two, he helped build the first atom bomb. Then Reisenbach was at Princeton for the next twenty years, teaching the next generation of scientists—including me."

Mr. Swift smiled. "He showed me that inventing wasn't just tinkering with your hands but with your mind. He turned the theories of physics into reality. When I told the TV interviewer that Reisenbach made me what I am today, I really meant it." He removed a letter from on top of the faded, dusty box in front of him.

" 'Dear Mr. Swift,' " he read aloud. " 'I listened with pride when you mentioned my great-uncle on "Up Front and in Person." We found this box, marked E. Reisenbach, while cleaning out the attic. My husband and I wondered what to do with it until we saw you on TV. We decided that Uncle Ernst would have liked you to have his work.' "

Mr. Swift looked almost embarrassed as he fiddled with the string on the box. "I'm almost afraid to open this. It could be anything from laundry lists to notes for—for almost anything. Reisenbach never explained why, but he stopped publishing papers in the midfifties."

"Whatever's in there has to be old science by now," Tom said with a grin. "I mean, you may find a design for color television."

Mr. Swift opened the box to reveal a pile of yellowed papers covered with intricate math. "These notes don't seem to be about color TV."

As Tom's father followed the equations, his eyes grew large. "Reisenbach was years ahead when it came to theoretical physics. This suggests a good dozen years before the theory was published anywhere else that subatomic particles are actually strings of energy. And here he postulates that besides the four dimensions we know—length, width, depth, and duration— there are seven other dimensions. Eleven-dimensional reality wasn't seriously proposed until the late seventies."

Reading on, Mr. Swift looked even more baffled. "Reisenbach's mathematical constants for the multiple dimensions are very different from anything being discussed today." His voice died away as he stared at the pages. "But here he seems to be saying that they were developed from *laboratory research*."

Tom stared. "How can that be?"

"I don't know, but these equations are for sending an object back along the space-time axis."

"That's ridiculous," Tom scoffed. "Unless he had a working time machine." He stared for a second, then dashed around his father's desk. "If Professor Reisenbach pulled *that* off, we've got to duplicate his experiments." Tom's eagerness faded as he sorted through the papers. "There's a lot of stuff missing—like all the design notes."

Tom's father was already at work on his desk's built-in computer. "My database search shows unpublished Reisenbach papers in libraries all over the country." He sighed. "That's what happens when people pass away without organizing their work—it gets scattered."

He frowned, tapping more keys. "Oddly enough, I don't remember any death notices. Reisenbach left Princeton in my sophomore year. He retired—but where, no one knew."

Tom's father shrugged. "Well, we can start at the Caltech library." He glanced at the screen. "'Uncatalogued scientific papers by Ernst Reisenbach,'" he read. "Probably nobody has looked at them since the day they arrived. Who knows what dynamite is hidden there?"

From the looks of the box that Tom finally found, it seemed that his father's guess was right. Tom's visit to the California Institute of

Technology had taken him from the library's computerized database to an old card catalog, and finally to the library stacks in a subbasement.

"Yes, this is the box you want," the young librarian said in embarrassment, blowing dust off the top of the sealed carton. "I guess very few people get down here. But in a few years, we'll have even this material microfilmed, if not scanned for computer retrieval."

Tom hid a smile. Librarians had probably been intending to do something with this stuff for the last twenty years. "If we can get this up to the research area, I'll take a look at what's in here and see if it's what my father needs."

Once upstairs in a comfortable study carrel, Tom sorted through the contents of the storage carton. It was a hodgepodge of paper, including personal letters, business correspondence, lecture notes, and research data.

Tom shook his head. Reisenbach had obviously been a genius of the first order. The papers speculated on theories other physicists had only begun to explore twenty years later. Here, too, were tantalizing fragments of math and notations that hinted at physical experiments in time travel.

A thick envelope had slipped down the side of the box. Tom discovered it only when he had almost emptied the carton's contents. When he got the flap undone, he found a different kind of paper inside—light, flimsy, and brittle with age.

Tracing paper, he realized, slipping the packet out. Of course. This came from the days before copy machines were part of every office. Reproducing a design meant doing it by hand.

Carefully Tom unfolded a sheet until it almost covered the counter in front of him. Faded blue pencil marks showed a huge, complicated electronic circuit. In one corner, almost illegible from age and crabbed handwriting, he made out the note, "Power circuit—time warp."

With growing excitement, Tom spread out the other tracings. This was it!

Elsewhere in the library, a man turned from a computer screen and picked up the telephone on his desk. He dialed a number, which was answered by a flat voice that said only, "Yes?"

"This is Compton at Caltech," the caller said. "You left standing orders to report any research by Swift Enterprises. Well, Tom Swift has been in the library, looking for unpublished papers by a Dr. Ernst Reisenbach. The stuff has to be a good thirty years old, but Swift senior made arrangements for the kid to take it all with him."

"You'll get a bonus added to your monthly stipend," the flat voice on the other end said. "And, of course, the sincere thanks of the Black Dragon."

2

We've come pretty far in only two weeks."
Tom let his gaze roam over the mass of equipment that had taken over half of the Swift physics lab. Copies of Reisenbach's original designs were tacked on the walls, sometimes altered or completely revamped.

"It's amazing what he did with sixties technology," Tom senior said. "Still, a working model of this thing would have taken up most of a house."

"By substituting microchips for transistors, we've shrunk it down to manageable size," Tom admitted. "But it seems like a lot of work for a time machine that works in only one direction."

"Reisenbach's notes just hint at that. The testing will tell." Mr. Swift grimaced. "If only we had more of his papers."

"I'm surprised so many university libraries could lose them," Tom said. "The stuff's listed in their catalogs, but it's not on the shelves."

Tom's father shook his head. "Maybe there's a lesson to be learned here. Before I get much older, I should organize my papers to keep them from being scattered to the winds."

"Right, Dad," Tom said with a grin. "Get on it before you become too feeble. But before you do, I hope you can spare the strength to get the bugs out of *this* contraption. A time machine that strands you in the past isn't much of an achievement."

"Reisenbach achieved a lot," Mr. Swift said. "His idea that other dimensions in the eleven-D universe are compressed into energy strings from our point of view is years ahead of its time. He suggests his machine can open one of those strings. Things should remain much the same, except that time would run backward."

"*Run* is the word," Tom said. "If the math's right, time moves like an express train."

"We can check that in a moment," Mr. Swift said, powering up the equipment they had set up. "Is the test material in place?"

Tom used a pair of tongs to set down a heavy lead bar so it was surrounded by the Swift-updated Reisenbach apparatus. "All set, Dad. Is Harlan ready on the other end?"

"He's personally standing guard over his office safe," Mr. Swift said, grinning. "And he's wondering why, since he knows the safe is empty.'' The smile faded. ''Let's see if we can change that.''

Tom joined his father behind a blast shield on the opposite side of the room. ''All circuits are working,'' Mr. Swift reported, checking a set of gauges. ''Energizing.''

The hairs at the back of Tom's neck prickled as if an electrical charge had filled the air. He stared as a purplish glow suddenly surrounded the lead bar. ''The field is forming,'' he said.

An indescribable sensation seized Tom, as if his body—or was it the world around him?—were being twisted. The air crackled with static. Then everything went blurry.

And the lead bar was gone.

Mr. Swift cut the power. From the expression on his face, Tom figured his father had also felt the same strange sensation. But Tom Swift, Sr.'s eyes glowed with excitement. ''Let's get over to Security,'' he said.

They reached Harlan's office to find him standing in front of his safe. ''Let's see the inside,'' Mr. Swift said.

''I know what we'll see.'' The head of Swift Enterprises security was both baffled and a bit annoyed as he worked the dial. ''Nothing. You made me remove— What the—?''

Harlan Ames whirled to stare at the Swifts. ''What's that lead brick doing in there? I've been standing here since I emptied the stupid safe.''

The Swifts grinned in triumph. They had sent the ingot back one minute into the past, aiming for the safe's space-time coordinates.

"Don't tell me," Harlan said. "You invented some kind of cockamamie matter transmitter."

Laughing, Tom shook his head. "Even better, Harlan—a time machine."

"I think it's better to call our machine a time trigger," Mr. Swift said. "The machine itself doesn't travel in time. It stays where it is but sends objects back."

Harlan shook his head. "I thought good old Albert Einstein's theory of relativity said that time travel was impossible."

"Not exactly," Mr. Swift said. "Einstein set up new rules of motion. But they work just as well with time moving backward instead of forward."

Harlan shook his head. "Sounds screwy to me."

"Why?" Tom asked. "In this world you can go back and forth in three of the four dimensions. Time seems to be the only one-way street."

"Seems to be?" Harlan repeated.

"That's the way things appear in our frame of reference," Tom said, "the three-D universe. If we could somehow step into one of the other seven dimensions, things would look very different."

Seeing the security chief's baffled look, Tom turned him so he stood with the door to his right.

"Let's play a little game, knocking one dimension off our universe. Here are the rules. There are only certain ways you can move. You can go up and down"—he jumped in place—"and back and forth. But when you go sideways, you can go only to the left. How do you get out the door?"

Harlan shuffled and bobbed for a moment. He went forward, he went to his left. Now he was farther from the door than when he'd started. At last he gave Tom a glare. "There's no way."

"You're sure?" Tom asked. "Here, I'll take your place. Okay?"

Tom let himself fall to the floor, landing on his left side. "Now my feet point at the door, so it's 'down' from me. That's a direction I'm allowed to travel." He squirmed across the office floor, grinning.

Harlan's face went red under his leathery tan. "You cheated!" he protested.

"I followed the rules and went left, but in a way that changed the dimensions around me. What was one way became a two-way street— or floor."

"This is a very popular experiment, Harlan," Mr. Swift said. "Most adults confronted with this challenge fail. But when children try to reach a treat placed in the 'impossible' direction, most find some way to bend the rules." He smiled. "Maybe kids have more experience with games or less rigid minds than adults."

Harlan frowned in thought. "You're saying

that Einstein's rules can be bent and that you've made a machine to do it." His voice suddenly got sober. "Do you realize what a security nightmare you've created, when people can beam things in anywhere, at any time?"

Two days later Harlan Ames still looked unhappy as he stared out the windshield of a Swift Enterprises hovercraft. The all-terrain vehicle had whisked across the beach at Laguna Pequeña, then out onto the waters of the Pacific Ocean.

"Mr. Swift," Harlan said to Tom's father, "you've come up with some pretty bizarre things in your time. But a time machine?"

"Time trigger," Mr. Swift corrected. "We're just seeing if we can duplicate someone else's experiment," Mr. Swift said. "Today we'll test the trigger's capability for long-range time travel. Anchorage Rock is perfect for that purpose. It's close to the California coast, but small enough so that no one has ever lived there. And according to our geological data, it was once considerably more low-lying than it is today."

"Is that why you had the team out there, digging a hole in the ground?" Harlan asked.

"We wanted to bring the time trigger as close as possible to the old, low-lying level," Tom admitted. "The further back we send the test module, the less accurately we can place it spatially."

He vividly remembered what had happened the day before when they deliberately sent back a metal slug about the size of a nickel to appear in the center of a solid boulder. The result had been a huge blast—and a big hole in the ground where the boulder once stood.

"I was afraid that would happen," Mr. Swift had said. "It's the old problem of two objects not being able to occupy the same space at the same time. If we're not careful in placing our time-traveling objects, they and the objects they coincide with will blow up, with one hundred percent energy efficiency."

That was why they'd chosen an isolated offshore location for their next experiment.

About six workers waved hello from the little U-shaped island as the hovercraft swung into a cove—the anchorage in Anchorage Rock. Tom noticed that Harlan also had lots of security people already in place.

Harlan Ames followed Tom's gaze. "I've got sensors covering the air and water around the island," he said. "This will be a nice, private experiment."

With the help of the workers and some security people, they unloaded the prototype time machine. Tom and his father had spent days finding new ways to make the apparatus smaller and sturdy enough to travel. Now they fit three modules together at the bottom of the pit dug by the workers and connected thick power cables.

"Set the test module," Mr. Swift said.

Tom swung down into the excavation, carrying a shiny metal container about a foot long and four inches wide. It looks like a giant bullet, he thought, about to be shot into the past.

He knew that most of the bulk was shielding. The module's heart was a tiny chunk of radioactive material, whose age had been determined as closely as modern science could manage.

Tom placed the module in the center of the time trigger, then climbed out of the way. If everything went right, the machine would generate a field that would twist the module into another set of dimensions. Then the module would be flung back into the past.

Tom's father warned everyone off. A purple glow came from the bottom of the hole. Tom noticed the upset looks on the workers' faces as the uncanny twisting sensation hit them. Tom had already experienced the stomach-churning effect twice, but nausea still blurred his vision.

Then everything was back to normal. The workers returned to the pit, some still rubbing their stomachs. The time trigger stood right where it had been placed, but there was an empty space where the test module had rested.

"All right," Tom's father ordered. "Bring out the metal detectors. Let's find where that module is buried."

The heavy time probe had moved in space, but not very far. They dug down to the level where it was now buried merely by enlarging their initial hole. "Got it, sir!" one of the workers reported from the pit.

A moment later the module was carefully

handed up. It was no longer a gleaming bullet. The metal surface was dull and pitted, as if it had been exposed to the elements for a long time before being buried.

Tom cleared away the crud of centuries from the nose of the module. He inserted a long, thin probe while his father checked a control panel.

"According to the radiation decay rate we've registered, the module is now three thousand years older than when we sent it off." Tom's father grinned. "Right on the mark!"

A worried voice cut off the celebration. "Sir! Our sensors—they've gone dead!"

Harlan Ames leapt to the portable radio he'd taken from the hovercraft. "Perimeter guards!" he yelled. "Heads up!"

Even as he spoke, Tom heard the *thwip-thwip-thwip* of rotor blades.

Some kind of helicopter, he thought, as he ran for cover. Although it sounds higher pitched than most I've heard.

A moment later the helicopter came into view. It looked almost like a scale model, its body barely six feet long. No human pilot could fit in there. Tom realized it had to be under remote control. Either that or the aircraft was a flying robot.

"Oh, no," Tom breathed. *"No!"* Only one man on earth built robots like that. The Black Dragon!

The minichopper swooped into a curve, and a

lance of fire darted from under its stabilizing wings. An attack rocket!

A deafening roar blasted across the island as the ship that had brought the workers to the cove vanished in flames. But as the minichopper turned toward the hovercraft, one of Harlan's security people knelt in the sand. The two-foot-long tube on his shoulder spat flame, and a miniature surface-to-air missile flashed upward to blow the intruder out of the sky.

An instant later the man tumbled back onto the sand, an ugly red splotch across his chest.

Tom whirled to see a figure rising from the water. He flung himself to take down his father and Harlan as the stutter of automatic gunfire filled the air. "Frogmen!" he yelled.

The workers and security guards dropped to the sands. Many of them, however, didn't move.

"We're being massacred," Harlan said tightly. He snatched a weapon from a fallen guard and began laying down cover fire. "Run for the hovercraft!" he barked, shooting to keep the divers at bay.

Tom never felt more naked as he ran across the sands, his father right beside him. Two guards joined them, firing as they ran. Only one made it to the hovercraft. Mr. Swift dove into the vehicle and started the engine. The hovercraft lifted off the ground on roaring fans.

"Where's Harlan?" Tom yelled, looking over the edge of the vehicle. The security chief was dashing across the beach, still shooting. A black-clad frogman rose from the water, scarcely a yard from the hovercraft. Harlan blew him away.

Even as he fell, the man tossed a bulky box into the craft's passenger space. A demolitions charge!

Tom snatched the thing up, hurling it as far as he could. Harlan jumped aboard, and Mr. Swift began piloting them away from the island.

Behind them, a huge plume of water shot up as the bomb went off.

Harlan lay on the floor, gasping. "I blew it, sir. If you want my resignation—"

"Don't be silly, Harlan," Mr. Swift said. "We were all caught off guard. And we'd never have made it aboard without your help."

Harlan rose to his feet, staring back at the beach and the still figures there. "What about the ones who didn't make it?" he asked.

"Either they're dead, or they've fallen into the hands of the Black Dragon." Mr. Swift's voice was bleak. "And so has the prototype time trigger."

3

Three thousand miles away, in the East Coast city of Bayport, Frank and Joe Hardy watched their father shake hands with a wiry man in a drab suit.

"This will be a different sort of case for me, Professor Drake," Fenton Hardy said, smiling. "Usually I trace criminals, not famous physicists."

"And usually I do not require the services of, ahem, private investigators to assist my research." Professor Drake's high, bald forehead gleamed as he peered over half-glasses. "Dr. Reisenbach became a bit of a hermit after he left Princeton. His later years are shrouded in, well, mystery."

"How mysterious could a sixty-year-old pro-

fessor get?" Joe Hardy's blue eyes gleamed imp-
ishly as he whispered to his older brother.

Frank Hardy ignored Joe's joking, a serious
look on his lean features. "You think there's
something mysterious in Dr. Reisenbach's
papers?"

The professor shook his bald head. "The mystery is where those papers are. Last week my
researchers found three boxes of Reisenbach material left in the warehouses of an academic pub-
lisher. Who knows what nonacademic sources you
might be able to turn up, Mr. Hardy?"

He handed a card to Fenton Hardy. "Here is
my phone number. Good luck, and good hunting!" Drake shook hands with the boys and left.

"Wow," Joe said, massaging his hand. "Who'd
think a stick like that would have such a grip?"

"Must be due to clean living, I guess," Frank
replied with a grin. He ran a hand through his
dark brown hair as he turned to their father. "So
where are you starting on this professorial paper
chase, Dad?"

"Why don't you start checking the electronic
grapevine?" Fenton Hardy said.

Frank headed upstairs to his room. "I'm on
it already." He soon returned with a sheaf of
computer printouts. "This guy *is* a bit of a mystery. He'd be ninety-something by now if he
were still alive. But nobody knows."

"What do you mean, nobody knows?" Joe
asked.

"Reisenbach's biography in *Americans in Sci-*

ence lists his date of death as 1965 followed by a question mark. His last communication was a telephone call with a Professor Lord, early in the morning on November ninth, 1965. Lord didn't even know where he was calling from."

Frank frowned. "There's something familiar about that date."

"Well, it was after the World Series. That was the year the Dodgers beat the Twins. Sandy Koufax was named the series' Most Valuable Player."

Frank gave his brother a glare. "Somehow I don't think pitching fits in with physics."

"Sure it does. Baseball teams have hired physicists to explain how curveballs do what they do." Joe would have gone on indefinitely if their father hadn't cut in.

"You've got more printouts there, Frank. What else can you tell us about Reisenbach?"

"The information isn't about him," Frank said. "It's about his papers. I scanned crime reports from 1965, just to see if perhaps he'd been the victim of foul play. Instead his name came up in connection with a series of recent library thefts."

"A ninety-year-old professor is knocking over libraries?" Joe said in disbelief.

"No, but someone is stealing Reisenbach's papers from libraries," Frank said. "Mostly university libraries have been complaining about the theft of rare books. The Reisenbach stuff is sort of an afterthought—another thing stolen."

Frank frowned. "The funny thing, though, is that the thief in all the cases seems to be the same guy."

Joe still couldn't get the smile off his square-cut, handsome face. "Let me guess—the thief is actually Professor Drake."

"No, the guy is short, fat, and pretty forgettable-looking, always the same description. In some cases he even used the same alias. I passed that on to the library association's network so they can alert other collections."

Fenton nodded. "I'll give Professor Drake a call as well. At least he'll be getting something for his money."

For three days the Hardys banged their heads against a seemingly solid stone wall. "The guy is all over the public record till 1964," Frank complained as he sat at his computer keyboard. "Then he retires from the university, sells his house, cashes in all his investments, and—*poof!*—he's gone."

"Guys don't go *poof!* from May of one year to November of the next," Joe said, looking up from his sports magazine. "Check for any money angles. You know what they say—Where there's a will, there's relatives."

"But I can't find any reference to a will," Frank said, staring at his screen. "Unless . . . relatives. Yeah, let's see if there's any reference to legal action by relatives."

The screen lit up, and Frank read eagerly.

"Aha! Reisenbach's brother did come looking for an inheritance. But the claim was filed in New York, not New Jersey." He frowned. "And the court records were sealed."

After hearing Frank's report, Fenton used his legal contacts in New York City. "The records are still sealed, but I got the name of the attorney who worked on the case—S. T. Charteris, of the firm of Charteris and Caldecott."

Frank went back to the computer. "That firm is still listed," he reported. "But S. T. Charteris passed away about five years ago."

"Still worth a try," Fenton said. "Give me their number." He dialed it on the phone, punching the speaker button.

"Charteris, Caldecott, and Pagliarusso," a woman's voice answered.

"I'm calling about a case handled by S. T. Charteris regarding Ernst Reisenbach," Fenton said. "It happened some years ago."

"Let me connect you with Mr. Charteris," the woman interrupted.

"What'll she do, hold a seance?" Joe wondered as they were clicked into electronic limbo.

A moment later a new voice came over the phone. "This is Stan Charteris. I understand you're inquiring about an old case of my father's?"

"It's in reference to the estate of Ernst Reisenbach," Fenton replied.

There was a brief silence, then the lawyer laughed. "That case goes back to my *grandfather's* time—ancient history. My grandfather set up a revocable trust for Ernst Reisenbach a good thirty years ago, and we're still paying out on it. In fact, it was one of the first responsibilities I was assigned when I started working here.''

"A revocable trust," Fenton Hardy said. "What does that mean?"

"It means that if he turned up tomorrow, he'd get all the money we've held in trust, plus the house in Canada," Charteris said.

"The house in Canada?" Fenton repeated.

"We've used the interest from the trust to keep the place repaired, cleaned, and protected. The trust agreement is very specific on that, although nobody has lived in the house since Ernst Reisenbach disappeared.''

"And where is this house?" Fenton pressed.

"It's in Niagara, Ontario. Forty-three Sir Adam Beck Road," the lawyer said.

"Sir Adam Beck!" Frank muttered.

Fenton Hardy finished the call, then turned to his son. "Sir Adam who?"

"The Sir Adam Beck power station in Ontario was the place where the Great Northeastern Blackout began—on November ninth, 1965," Frank said.

"Which is also the last time anyone heard from Ernst Reisenbach!" Joe added.

"The time and place are intriguing," Fenton admitted. "Would you like to check out the house?"

The next day Frank and Joe drove a rental car out of the Niagara Falls airport, heading for the Canadian side of the border.

"Guess we won't see the falls," Joe groused. "Everything's too foggy."

"The guy at the car-rental agency complained that the weather has been lousy for the last five days," Frank said. "Have you got the map? Sir Adam Beck Road must be near the river."

They turned onto a small dirt path that wound under a canopy of dripping pine trees. The trees opened into a small clearing, where a comfortably old-fashioned log cabin stood. It looked forlorn in the rain and was obviously not lived in. Frank noticed that the front lawn was cut, but the garden was overgrown with weeds.

He opened the car door. "There doesn't seem to be anybody around." He stepped over to the front window and peered in.

"But someone has been here," Joe said in a puzzled voice. He pointed at the damp ground in front of the cabin door. Frank saw footprints, tracks of a pair of stout boots heading away from the house.

"Well, whoever it was is gone now." Frank tested the door, which swung open. "And left us a way in."

He stepped inside with Joe right behind him.

Joe shook his head, staring around the living room. "This place is like a time capsule!"

"Or the set of an old sixties TV sitcom," Frank agreed with a grin. "I don't think they make lamps like that anymore."

A wall-to-wall green-and-orange tweed rug covered the floor, matching the color scheme of the floral slipcovers on the square, uncomfortable-looking sofa and chairs. From the spindly end tables to the oak-box television, the whole room screamed "old-fashioned."

"Mr. Charteris mentioned that his firm paid for cleaning." Frank ran a hand over the dusty surface of the TV set. "I don't think they're getting their money's worth."

Joe frowned, looking around. "What I want to know is, why did someone spend the night? It was raining today, so the ground was muddy and we saw the footprints. But it wasn't raining so heavily that footprints coming in would be washed away."

"So what are you saying? We've got a hobo? A squatter?" Frank looked around the untouched room. "It sure wasn't a vandal."

A stab of uneasiness passed through him. "Let's give the place a quick once-over."

Frank was in the crawl space under the roof when he heard Joe calling his name.

"What is it?" he asked, whacking dust off his knees as he joined Joe in the kitchen.

Almost hidden behind a large cupboard was a door. Joe, grimacing horribly, had it open. "Look down those stairs, if you dare," he said in his best spooky voice.

"I hope they've kept the cellar cleaner than the attic," Frank replied, not taking the bait.

"I'm not sure I want to find out," Joe said, flicking on a light switch. A dim overhead bulb lit the stairway. It looked as if the cleaning staff had never gone beyond the door. The dust of more than a quarter of a century lay on the cellar stairs.

But someone had been down there. Footprints showed in the dust coating. Frank began to feel uneasy. There was only one set of prints, left by someone climbing up the stairs.

He pushed the feeling away. "Stop acting like we're in a bad horror movie," Frank said. "There's a perfectly simple explanation. Whoever got in here didn't enter by the front door, but through some entrance in the cellar."

Joe relaxed a little, looking sheepish. "Of course. Let's go down and check it out."

They went down the stairs, which ended at another door. Joe tried the handle. "Locked," he reported. He squinted in the dimness of the overhead bulb, then whistled. *"Severely* locked. The locksmith who installed this baby was working with the top of the line back then."

He smacked a palm against the door, which didn't budge. "And this door is solid steel, about ninety times thicker and tougher than any of the doors upstairs." Joe glanced at Frank. "Maybe it's a fallout shelter."

Frank remembered reading about the terrible fear of nuclear war during the sixties. People had built shelters to avoid the deadly radioactive fallout from the expected atomic bombings.

"Whatever's in there, we won't get to it this way," he said. "Let's find the other entrance."

They went back outside and spent half an hour

circling the cabin but couldn't discover any entryways into the cellar, no doors, windows, chutes, nothing. Nor did combing the nearby forest reveal a secret entrance.

Frank stood in the drizzling rain, the uneasy feeling back in the pit of his stomach. "I'm beginning to think we'd better find the person who made those footprints."

It was easy enough to follow the trail in the dirt. When they reached the paved road, however, Frank and Joe had to cast around for a bit.

"Over here," Joe called from the opposite side of the road. "The same kind of boot prints are in the soft dirt at the side of the road. They're heading for town."

"I'll get the car," Frank said.

They followed the trail for nearly half a mile. Then the boot prints disappeared.

"Either the guy flew away or a car picked him up." Joe pulled up the collar of his jacket to cover his neck from the drizzle. Now he joined Frank in the rental car.

Frank considered their surroundings. "This isn't the world's most heavily traveled road. Let's head for town and see if we find any hitchhikers."

They stopped at a gas station for a fill-up and some information. The station owner shrugged. "I just got here." Then the man frowned as he got their change.

"Hey, Neil," he called to the young man coming out of the office. "Where did you get these?" He held up several American dollars.

The young man shrugged. "Guy in a blue pickup paid with 'em. Why? Aren't they good?"

"They're better than good," the station owner said. "These are silver certificates, worth up to five times the face value of regular bucks."

Frank felt that weird feeling coming back. Silver certificates went out of circulation a good twenty years ago. Yet here was somebody paying with those old bills. Maybe the money came from that sixties time capsule, the Reisenbach cabin.

"Was the driver alone?" Frank asked.

The young gas jockey thought for a second. "There was this geezer riding along. He paid." Neil laughed. "You should have seen his face when he saw what it cost."

"Can you give us a description?" Frank asked.

Neil shrugged. "Old. Baldish. White hair. Skin and bones."

Frank shook his head over the sparsely detailed description. Joe was more practical. "Did you notice which way the truck went?" he asked.

Neil pointed toward town. "I heard them say something about catching breakfast."

The Hardys took their change and headed for the nearest diner. "Who owns the blue pickup outside?" Joe asked as they stepped in.

A heavyset guy with a red face and a baseball

cap looked up. "If you've put another dent in old Daisy, don't sweat it, kid."

"We wondered if you just had a passenger," Frank said. "Dad sent us to pick up a friend, but we think he hitched a ride with you."

"Is your father's friend a skinny old guy?" the driver asked.

"Yeah, balding, with white hair," Frank said.

"Guy stared at my old clunker like it was the hottest thing on wheels," the driver said. "I got one of those digital speedometers. You'd think it was a computer or something, the way he carried on. He offered to pay for my gasoline, then I thought he was gonna croak when he saw the price of gas. Funny guy."

"The man at the gas station thought you'd be having breakfast together," Frank said, looking around the diner.

"Grandpa saw the prices and freaked out again. He left, saying he was going to the library, of all places."

Frank looked at Joe. "What do you say we catch up on our reading?"

They thanked the driver and headed for the nearby library. Inside, they found a thin crowd, mainly older people stopping by for a look at the newspapers. One member of the group, however, had no interest in current affairs. He sat in a corner, surrounded by encyclopedia yearbooks, almanacs, and coffee-table books on the sixties, seventies, eighties, and nineties.

The man put one book down to read another,

and Frank stepped back, staggered. That weird feeling was back in the pit of his stomach, backed up with a chill down his spine.

He'd seen that face before—in books on the history of science.

The man was Ernst Reisenbach.

4

This is crazy, Frank told himself. Ernst Reisenbach is dead—or at least ninety-something years old. He can't look the way he did in 1965.

Feeling as if he'd stepped into a bad sci-fi movie, Frank approached the library table. "Excuse me. Professor Ernst Reisenbach?"

The book dropped from the man's hands to land with a clatter. His thin, pale face went whiter than his hair. "Y-you know me?" Reisenbach's words were blurred with a slight German accent.

"I'm Frank Hardy, and this is my brother, Joe. A search for your research papers brought us to your house up here. But a better question is, what brings *you* here?"

Joe looked critically at the professor. "No

tan, so I guess you didn't just run off to South America. Unless the doctors told you to stay out of the sun after the plastic surgery. They must have knocked a good thirty years off your age."

The professor glanced at the book on the floor. When he looked up again, he had obviously come to a decision. "I haven't been to South America or anywhere—except the fourth dimension. I undertook an experiment in time travel."

"Sure. And you've got a time machine locked up in your basement."

Joe's outburst turned a lot of disapproving faces their way. "Let's get out of the library so we can talk," Frank said. His mind was reeling from what he'd just heard. What if Joe's sarcastic comment about what was in Reisenbach's basement was actually on target?

"What you said makes a weird sort of sense," he quietly told Joe as they went outside. "What do we know about Dr. Reisenbach? He pays with 1960s money, is fascinated with outdated technology, and is horrified by today's prices."

Professor Reisenbach nodded, catching up with them. "It was quite a shock to discover that every dollar I'd brought with me was worth only a quarter today."

Joe frowned, doubtful.

"When Professor Reisenbach stepped into his machine, baseball cards cost a nickel," Frank said. "Comic books were twelve cents."

Joe glanced at his brother. "You really believe

him?" he said. "I keep waiting for someone to jump out with a hidden camera and say we're on some crazy video show."

Frank shook his head. "Bizarre as it sounds, everything fits. This man has traveled through time." He grinned. "But if we're having trouble, think what Professor Reisenbach is going through. A lot has happened in the last thirty years."

Reisenbach nodded. "I never expected the Communist empire to crumble, the wars in the Middle East, or what has happened to the price of oil since 1973. The best futurologists of my time never dreamed of any of these."

"I'd say the near future is your concern right now." Frank smiled. "We can offer you a place to catch up with the present-day scene. All it takes is a call to our father."

For a second Reisenbach seemed reluctant. "I had hoped to complete my visit unnoticed," he admitted. "But things are so different. I could use some help. Please, call your father."

"Wait a second," Joe said. "Did you say visit? You're planning to go back through time again?"

The professor smiled but said nothing. Joe looked at Frank. Frank only shrugged. They walked on down the street.

Frank tried the first pay phone they came to.

"Brace yourself," he said when their father answered. "We didn't find Professor Reisenbach's papers. We found the professor himself."

"He's not dead?" Fenton Hardy followed that exclamation with a barrage of questions. He was astonished to hear Frank relay the professor's extraordinary explanation.

"Sounds incredible," Fenton Hardy said. "But this I've got to see. Catch the next flight down to Bayport. I'll see you at the house."

It was early evening by the time the boys and Professor Reisenbach arrived at the Hardy home, on Elm Street in Bayport. Fenton Hardy was already at the door as they got out of their cab.

"Professor, it's a pleasure to meet you," he said, advancing to shake hands.

"I appreciate your hospitality," Reisenbach responded with a smile. "And I can hardly wait to see what's happened to household technology."

The scientist was like a kid in a candy store. Color television, VCRs, and microwave cooking were all wonders to him.

"I apologize for the microwaved dinners," Fenton Hardy said. "Both my wife and my sister are away, so I'm afraid we're roughing it."

"I could have no better introduction to the future," Reisenbach said, laughing.

"Hey, Dad," Joe suggested, "why not show the professor your fax machine?"

They visited Fenton Hardy's basement office, where they were in the middle of demonstrating the machine when a heavy blast shook the house.

For a moment the Hardys and the professor were frozen. Then Fenton said, "Sounds like somebody just blew in the front door." He leapt to a storage cabinet set into one wall, unlocked it, and removed a pistol and a box of bullets. They heard heavy footsteps clomping on the floor overhead, and then a muffled voice shouted, "Look for the old guy with the white hair. Take *him* alive!"

His gun loaded, Fenton took up a position at the bottom of the basement stairs. Over his shoulder he said, "Boys, get the professor out through the cellar doors and into the yard. I'll cover you."

"But, Dad—" Joe began.

"Go!"

Frank grabbed the professor's arm, leading him to the exit Fenton Hardy had suggested. Still protesting, Joe followed.

A quick twist on the lock, and Frank pushed the cellar doors open on well-oiled hinges. He took a fast look around, then beckoned Joe. "Help the professor up. We'll make a run for the van."

Frank waited until Joe and Reisenbach reached the far side of the garage. Then he jumped back down into the basement. "Dad, come on!"

At the top of the basement stairs, the door from the kitchen erupted inward. Frank stifled a gasp as he looked at the man framed in the doorway. The intruder wore what looked like a space suit, with heavy metal rods bracing his arms and legs. Motors hummed in the suit as he smashed the door to bits.

Fenton Hardy popped from behind his office door and fired a warning shot. The man with the iron skeleton didn't stop. Fenton went for a shoulder shot, but his bullet caromed off.

That suit is armor! Frank realized.

Fenton Hardy fired again and again, but the intruder and the other armored invaders who appeared behind him were completely bulletproof. Frank stood frozen until the men swamped Fenton.

Then Frank had no choice. He turned and ran.

Fenton Hardy's head throbbed and his stomach lurched as he opened his eyes.

His face was inches from a streaked stone wall, but he was alive!

His last memory was of gasping for breath as armored figures stood over him, their weapons hissing. Then everything went black.

Fenton Hardy had not expected to be opening his eyes again. Even a cramped cell with salt-stained stone walls beat the alternative.

Fenton lurched up from the chilly stone floor and tottered to the wooden door. It was old, old wood, almost petrified. Fenton peered through a small barred window set high in the door.

His view took in a hallway made of the same streaked stone that lined his cell. A dim bulb hanging from the hall ceiling on a sagging electrical wire gave some light.

Fenton pushed on the door. It gave slightly. Then he heard a metallic rattle, and the door wouldn't budge. Old door, new lock, he thought. Sounds like a cheap padlock.

He fingered the inside of the door. Yes. He could feel splintered wood where new bolts to hold the lock hasp had been screwed in.

Smiling grimly, Fenton went to work. That hasp-and-lock setup might serve well to protect a storeroom, but it wouldn't keep a determined person *inside*.

Fenton had only two tools—a key chain and a pocketknife—but he had plenty of time. At the cost of numerous scratches, a torn fingernail, and a broken knife blade, he loosened the bolts. The hasp swung free, and a good kick opened the door.

Now Fenton was out. The question remained, however, where was he?

The dark, dank corridor had no windows. Fenton found a stairway that went up for five steps before it was blocked by a brick wall. Maybe this wasn't a dungeon. It appeared to be an old cellar.

Fenton kept looking for a way up. All he found was an archway chopped into a wall, opening into a long, winding tunnel. Tracks running down the middle of the passage suggested it might be an abandoned stretch of subway or railway line. Fenton found another opening, leading to a natural cavern with rocky walls.

Nowhere that Fenton wandered, however, did he find a way out of the maze. He did discover something else, though.

While trying to remove the grating from a ventilation riser on the wall, Fenton heard echoing voices rising from a level farther down.

"You pushed your authority too far, Upton, trying to grab Reisenbach like that."

Fenton Hardy froze. He recognized that voice. It belonged to Professor Drake, the man who had hired him to find the Reisenbach papers.

Loosening the screws with his pocketknife, Fenton quietly removed the grating and set it aside. He peered down the duct and saw a pair of figures through a grating on the level below. One man wore combat armor and a very worried expression. "Sir," he said, his voice urgent, "believe me, I never—"

"You never *think,* Upton." The second man said. "Fenton Hardy was working for me—or rather for kindly old Professor Drake."

Fenton stared as the air around the cold-voiced man suddenly shimmered. The man's tall, distinguished form became wiry and bent. His thick gray hair disappeared, replaced by a high, bald forehead. The grim hawk face became mild and rosy-cheeked, with nearsighted blue eyes peering over his glasses. Now the face matched the voice. He *was* Professor Drake!

The professor's mild face was twisted in scorn. "Somehow, Hardy's sons found Reisenbach," Drake said. "There's only one way Reisenbach could be alive today. He had to make a jump *forward* through time. I'm sure you know the machine we acquired from Swift Enterprises travels only to the past. We hoped to rectify that defect with Reisenbach's papers."

So, Professor Drake's purpose had been as phony as his appearance, Fenton thought. Drake knew all about Reisenbach's time machine.

The glacially calm Drake kept talking. "Our problems would have been solved if Reisenbach were on hand to assist me in developing the machine. And since Fenton Hardy was working for me, he would surely have reported finding Reisenbach."

"I—I didn't trust Hardy." Nervous words tumbled from Upton. "Why should we depend on an outsider? Our own people have what it takes—"

"I needed an investigator, not a spy, a thief, or a killer," Drake said, cutting him off. "Your people—and you yourself—interfered where no interference was necessary. You exceeded your authority by bugging the house, when I already had a tap on the phone. Then you jumped the gun by launching a full-scale attack." Drake's voice became more menacing. "Still worse, you *failed*. You didn't deliver Ernst Reisenbach."

"We didn't expect resistance," Upton said.

"When Hardy started shooting, it threw us off. Somehow Hardy's sons and Reisenbach got away."

"You let a pair of boys and an old man elude you. Now precious research time will be lost as we negotiate with a pair of teenagers." Drake made the last word sound like a curse.

"It wasn't my fault!" Upton's voice now held a pleading note. "We didn't—"

"You'd have eagerly seized all the credit if you'd succeeded." Drake's expression went from cold to frozen. "You are equally to blame if you fail. And I'm sure you know that when you work for the Black Dragon, failure is not tolerated."

Fenton stared as Upton raised steel-armored arms against the slight-looking academic. To Fenton's amazement, *Upton* was the one who looked terrified.

"Please! No!" he babbled as Professor Drake pointed at him.

His words were drowned out by a terrible sizzling sound as a blinding flash of light leapt from Drake's outstretched hand to strike Upton. Upton's scream echoed up the ventilation shaft. Fenton Hardy quickly retreated from the grating and the burning stench that rose up the shaft.

The Black Dragon, Fenton mused as he crept through new corridors, searching for a way out. I've heard that name before.

Yes. The name was like a code word among law-enforcement types, representing a shadowy criminal genius. Supposedly he worked behind legitimate business fronts, but the Black Dragon broke any laws that got in his way. When some operation or other got busted by the law, only underlings were arrested. The Black Dragon's soldiers didn't even know what their boss looked like. Police always got conflicting descriptions.

After seeing the Dragon's incredible shape-changing act, Fenton Hardy could understand why. I'm up against a superscientist who can change his appearance and throw lightning bolts from his fingers, Fenton told himself. The sooner I get out of here, the better.

Then the hooting of alarms filled the corridors. Fenton hurled himself around a corner as he heard footsteps clattering down the hall ahead of him. He realized that his captors had discovered that he'd escaped. He had to find a way out.

Fenton looked along the corridor he'd ducked into. There was no hoped-for elevator. Right then he would have taken some rickety stairs or even a rope ladder leading to the surface.

There was only an open door. Fenton sprinted for it as the footsteps came closer.

"Hey!" a voice yelled as he almost reached the doorway.

Fenton snatched a glance over his shoulder without slacking his pace. Great. An armed guard was glaring at him.

"Freeze or I shoot!" the guard threatened.

Instead of obeying, Fenton dashed through the doorway. He skidded to a stop. He was in a huge steel-lined room, and he could see no way out.

Whirling to face the entrance, Fenton saw the guard charging forward. He also saw a huge steel door. Flinging himself against the heavy weight, he swung it shut.

A gunshot rang out, the bullet ricocheting off the metal door with a nerve-shattering *spang!*

Fenton slammed the door shut, then shoved in a steel bolt with a solid *clunk*.

"I've seen bank vaults with less security," Fenton muttered. He could barely hear the guard on the other side of the door.

Of course, Fenton realized, his triumph would be short-lived. The guard would report his position and get reinforcements. For the Black Dragon's technology, cracking that door would be about as tough as opening a can of tuna.

Fenton started searching the dimly lit room for some sort of weapon. Looks like a laboratory, he thought. Maybe I'll find a death ray.

The shadowy edges of the room were taken up with a collection of high-tech components Fenton didn't recognize. But in the center, in the best light, was a compact mechanical setup, a three-foot-wide metal circle with a column rising up from the center to waist height.

Fenton glanced at the controls set in the top of the column. They were simple: power on and off, and a digital setting with the word *year* under it.

"Well, I'll be dipped," Fenton burst out.

"This must be the time machine the Black Dragon spoke about!"

At the same instant, a pinpoint on the heavy door began to glow with heat. Then a bolt of brilliant red light cut right through the metal, carving the steel as if it were cheese.

They'll be in here in a minute, Fenton thought in despair. My time's run out.

Then he looked down at the controls in front of him. Or has it?

A jab of his finger powered the machine up. He quickly set the digital year display.

The steel door fell inward, and heavily armed men poured in. Fenton felt an unpleasant twisting sensation in his gut.

Then the men seemed to disappear in a wash of purple radiance.

5

Hours before Fenton's escape, Joe Hardy stood with his back pressed to the outer rear wall of the family garage. Night had fallen as he, Frank, and their father had entertained Ernst Reisenbach. But Joe feared darkness was no protection from the intruders who had just invaded the house.

Without any conscious orders from his brain, his hands clenched into fists, although he knew fists would be useless against these high-tech thugs. They were armored like the Galactic Storm Troopers from one of his favorite science-fiction flicks.

Joe hated to run away, but he had no choice. He and Frank had to get Professor Reisenbach to safety.

He glanced at the professor, who was crouching beside him. Then, ready to pull back at the first sign of an armored figure, Joe sneaked a glance around the corner of the garage. The area seemed clear.

The soft pad of running footsteps came toward them. Joe turned to see his brother, Frank, running from the cellar door, alone.

"They've got Dad." Frank's whisper was flat as he joined them. Joe took one step toward the cellar before Frank grabbed his arm. "We can't help. All we can do is get out of here."

Frank glanced at the backyard fence. "The question is, which way do we go?"

"I say we go out the front," Joe whispered. "I don't see any guards, and we have a chance of reaching the van. We'll need wheels to get away from these characters."

Behind them, they heard shouting from the cellar. Frank nodded. "Okay. Let's go."

Joe breathed a sigh of relief. His earlier glance around the front had proved correct. The bad guys were so sure of catching us in the house, they didn't bother posting guards, he thought.

There was, however, a large panel truck parked by the curb of the Hardy home.

"That must be how they delivered the attack force," Joe said.

"Right. And the driver will see us if we try to open the garage door," Frank pointed out.

"He won't be able to stop us if we move fast

enough," Joe said. "I'll open the door. You and the prof go for the van. Have your keys ready."

As Frank dug out his keys, Joe was running for the front of the garage. He threw the door up, and Frank and Reisenbach dashed past. Seconds later they were in the van, and Joe heard the welcome sound of the engine revving up. He ran for the passenger-side door, which remained open. The van was rolling even as he jumped aboard.

"Let's move it!" Joe yelled as he buckled in and slammed the door.

Their split-second movements had caught the driver of the truck off guard. They were down the driveway and into the street before he could move the truck to block them.

"Now to get out of here," Frank said grimly as he jockeyed the wheel.

Shouts rose behind them as the attack force stormed onto the front lawn. Leading the charge was the character in the gleaming armored suit. Watching the man bound incredible distances, Joe realized that the metal rods on the outside of the armor must be boosting his regular muscles.

The mechanical assist enabled the man to catch up with the van as it sped down the road. Reisenbach yelled as the attacker leapt. Metal-augmented hands clamped onto the roof of the van.

Joe rooted desperately for some sort of weapon. "Don't bother," Frank said, stony-faced. "I'll take care of him."

A quick jerk on the steering wheel sent the van into a wild swerve. Frank didn't even glance at the threatening figure clinging to the side of the van. His eyes were directed straight ahead.

Their attacker must have seen what Frank was looking at so steadily because he gave out a wild yell.

They were headed for one of the huge old elm trees lining the street. Frank obviously intended to sideswipe the tree and scrape off their unwelcome passenger. He bucked the van even closer to the elm, pouring on the gas.

Joe's eyes went from the tree ahead to the attacker's face, now covered with sweat. "It all comes down to how good you think your armor is," Joe said tightly.

In the end, it turned out that the man had less steel in his backbone than on his suit. An instant before impact, he let go of his holds, tumbling off. Frank kept the van fishtailing onward, missing the tree and roaring down the road.

The panel truck was now rolling in pursuit, but Joe wasn't worried. Their engine was his domain, and he knew the van could make anything in its class look like it was standing still.

Anything except nondescript panel trucks, it seemed.

"It is right on our tail," Professor Reisenbach said nervously, staring into the rearview mirror.

"What did those guys do," Joe wondered, "put a jet engine in that clunker?"

Whatever the bad guys had under the hood of

the panel truck, it was sufficient to keep them right behind the Hardys as they swooped along the nighttime streets of Bayport.

Joe glared back at the truck thundering along mere yards behind them. "These guys are so busy chasing us, I bet we could sucker them right up to police headquarters."

"Those guys also have Dad," Frank reminded him. "Aside from that, I'm not sure the local cops have enough firepower to handle them."

Joe's face went numb. "Right," he muttered. "I forgot about that."

So Frank bypassed downtown Bayport, taking the van to the town's outskirts, barreling down River Road.

"Don't you think you're making it too easy for them, heading into the middle of nowhere like this?" Joe asked his brother. The road was now bordered by thick woods on both sides.

"We'll see how easy it is," Frank said between his teeth, jockeying the van back and forth across the two-lane road, blocking the truck's attempts to pass.

Frustrated, the truck driver sped up, ramming the van in the rear.

"Yeah," Frank gritted. "You can try that *now*. Let's see how you handle *this*."

He whipped the wheel around, sending the van into a screeching turn that had them tottering on two wheels.

The smaller, more agile vehicle stayed upright,

swerving into an opening between trees. It's the mouth of a dirt path, Joe realized.

Larger, heavier, and trapped by its own momentum, the truck kept plowing along the paved road. By the time its headlights appeared in the branch-arched opening behind them, the fugitives in the van had managed to open considerable breathing space.

On the other hand, they couldn't plunge along at top speed on the forest track. Dirt and pine needles spun beneath their tires as Frank jounced them along as fast as he dared.

"They are way behind us, but they still have us in sight," Reisenbach reported from the vantage point he'd taken in the rear of the van.

"I was afraid of that," Frank said.

Joe couldn't get over how calm his brother seemed. The guys in that truck had attacked them, kidnapped their father, and were now chasing them relentlessly. But to hear Frank, you'd think he was deciding his next move at chess, Joe thought.

"This is the place," Frank said suddenly. "Get ready for a *real* bumpy ride."

He extinguished the headlights, and darkness flooded the van. There was no moon, and the starlight couldn't pierce the branches overhead. Frank appeared to be driving by touch—a nerve-wracking process from Joe's point of view. He could hear branches scratching against the side of the van.

"That was a fork in the trail back there,"

Frank reported in the darkness. "We just took the path less traveled. With luck, that truck won't be able to force itself through the undergrowth."

Frank seemed to be right. The glow of the truck's headlights faded behind them.

"We've lost 'em!" Joe said with a grin.

"We lost the truck," Frank corrected him. "They may have people tracking us on foot. Now we've got to make sure we leave them in the dust."

Frank took the van on a weaving course that Joe recognized as an old hiking path through the woods. "We'll catch up with River Road just ahead," Joe said.

"Right," Frank agreed. "Then we can leave those guys lost in the woods while we find a new patch of forest to hide in."

They returned to the hard-top road, Frank turned the lights on, and they sped out of town.

The next morning Joe awoke groggy from lack of sleep. He'd taken the first watch the night before, sitting awake behind the wheel, ready to send them running at the first sign that their pursuers had caught up.

No armored attackers had appeared, and Joe had gotten a chance to rest—until now.

"Whuzzat?" he mumbled as an arm shook him into alertness. Then the events of the last couple of days crashed into his consciousness.

Joe blinked sleep away and rose in a half-crouch. "Trouble?"

"No," Frank reassured him. "Just time to move on. We let you rest as long as we could." He grinned. "You also missed about a million questions from Professor Reisenbach about ourselves, Dad, and who would send those spacemen to knock over our house."

"We'd all like to know the answer to that last one." Joe pulled himself out the rear doors of the van to find the first pale light of dawn filtering through the tree branches. His stomach gave a hollow rumble as he stretched himself.

"I'm starved," Joe said. "Which raises a new question. Where do we get breakfast while we run for our lives?"

"Anyplace we want," Frank replied. "As soon as we change the appearance of the van."

"Right. The bad guys must have an all-points bulletin out on it by now," Joe said.

"The future must be a very dangerous place, if you need to be this prepared for trouble," Professor Reisenbach said. He watched in amazement as the boys buffed away scratches, added racing stripes with a roll of tape, then dug out new side panels from inside the van.

"Do we want to be the meat market or the TV repair?" Joe asked.

"Let's go with the TV repair," Frank said with a grin at Reisenbach. "Since we have an electronics genius aboard."

"Don't laugh," Reisenbach told them. "I kept

half of the Manhattan Project's equipment running back in '44.''

Panels with the words *Super TV Repair* were magnetically attached to the sides of the van. Then the boys added some decals to the front hood and rear doors, and the van was transformed from a funmobile to a business truck.

"I think my jacket will fit the professor." Frank removed something from under the floor panels of the van. It was a slate blue jacket, the kind repairpeople wore, with the words *Super TV Repair* embroidered across the back.

Frank also handed over a baseball cap with the same embroidery. "This will help change your looks," he said to Reisenbach. "Joe and I can pass as your assistants." He stared critically at the van. "Okay, so much for disguises. Let's get rolling. You drive, Joe."

Joe got them two exits farther down the interstate before finally pulling off at a roadside diner.

"This will be my first normal meal in this era," Reisenbach said. "I don't count what we got on the plane or from that microwave."

While they attacked plates of ham, eggs, and hotcakes, Frank paged through the local paper. "No mention of anything odd happening last night. Either the papers didn't get the story before press time, or the news hasn't gotten out yet."

"Maybe we should be glad," Joe said quietly.

"They'd probably splash our pictures around, which I wouldn't particularly want."

They rose to pay their tab. As they reached the front counter, Reisenbach grabbed Joe's arm. "Buy a copy of that paper, too," he said, pointing.

Joe glanced over to see the garish cover of a national news tabloid, *Truth Weekly*. Two-inch-tall red letters ran across the top: "Technocriminals?" Beneath the headline was a picture of two people, a man and his son.

"You sure you want that rag?" he asked dubiously.

"I recognize the man on the cover," Reisenbach said, his voice hollow. All his good humor was gone.

Shrugging, Joe added the paper to their bill. As they drove off, Reisenbach read the lead article aloud. " 'If you believe the press releases of Swift Enterprises, Tom Swift and his son, Tom junior, are scientific geniuses, improving humanity's knowledge and quality of life. The truth, though, is that they are the masterminds of a criminal empire more powerful than most national governments.

" 'If you need proof, consider these questions, which Swift representatives refuse to answer:

" 'Who is responsible for the sabotage that destroyed the Lake Carlopa plant of UNITECH, one of Swift's major high-tech rivals?

" 'What dangerous experiments have resulted in

the complete destruction of two laboratory buildings at the Central Hills, California, complex of Swift Enterprises?

" 'What is the true story behind the supposedly accidental sinking of a research submarine while Swift vessels were conveniently in the same area?

" 'How did it happen that the Takashima space shuttle, the first nongovernmental manned space project, was destroyed on the far side of the moon—while Tom Swift, Jr., happened to be aboard NASA's *Moonstalker* shuttle?' "

The speculation continued, implicating Swift Enterprises and its owner in all sorts of illegal and dangerous activities.

"Tom Swift, Sr.—wasn't he the guy on 'Up Front and in Person' last week?" Joe asked.

"He certainly was," Frank said. "The interviewer asked about his maverick style of inventing, but none of this stuff ever came out. What's your interest in all of this, Professor?"

Ernst Reisenbach sat with the paper crumpled in his hands, an unhappy frown on his face. "He was a student of mine, a brilliant one. Last night I was reminded of a paper he wrote: 'Biofeedback as a Means of Exoskeleton Control.' "

At the boys' blank looks, he pointed to the dent in the van's roof. "Exoskeletons are powered armor, like that man wore last night. I take it this is not everyday technology."

"I've never seen it before," Joe said.

"So, we were attacked by criminals with high-technology equipment, including equipment that Tom Swift wrote about years ago.'' Reisenbach rattled the newspaper, a gleam of excitement in his eyes. ''This paper accuses the Swifts of being technocriminals. It comes together, does it not?''

''You realize that your case relies a lot on a newspaper that regularly reports UFO landings,'' Frank said. ''But at least we have a direction to go in.''

''We do?'' Joe asked.

Frank nodded. ''Cross-country, to California. According to the article, that's where the Swifts live. If Tom Swift's people have kidnapped Dad for some reason, we'll need a bargaining chip.''

Frank spread out the paper, pointing to the picture of Tom Swift, Jr.

''How about Mr. Swift's son?''

6

Well, we've got a target now," Joe Hardy said as he drove along the interstate. "But reaching it is also going to mean a week of cross-country driving. Can we afford that?"

Frank frowned, thinking. "We could probably afford the money—I don't know about the time."

"What do you mean?" Professor Reisenbach asked a little nervously.

"Whether or not we believe that newspaper story, the Swifts operate on a national basis— maybe even an international one," Frank pointed out. "If they're after us, they'll have lots of people out looking."

"And until we catch Tom Swift, Jr., we have no real protection against whatever Swift Enterprises throws against us," Joe finished.

"So what can we do?" an even more worried Reisenbach asked.

"We play hopscotch," Frank said decisively.

The other two looked at him as if he'd gone out of his mind.

"Let me explain. If we want to move quickly, that means taking planes. To do that, we'll have to use our credit card."

"People your age have credit cards?" Professor Reisenbach was undergoing more future shock.

"It's a corporate card from our father's detective agency. We use it on business." Frank looked grim. "I'd say rescuing Dad was business. Important business."

He went back to his plan. "The problem with using the card is that every transaction goes into a computer. That will make it easier for the Swift people to track us down."

"So they may be waiting for us at the airport," Joe said. "We'd save lots of travel time, but drop ourselves right into the bad guys' laps."

Frank nodded. "Suppose, though, we alternated flying with driving, zigzagging our way west, traveling to and from out-of-the-way airports. The bad guys couldn't be sure where we were really heading. And we'd be landing in places where they'd have problems concentrating their people."

"Hopscotching across the country," Joe said. "Now I get it."

"Do we have to do it like this?" Reisenbach asked. "Is there no way to go to the police?"

"How would you expect the police to react to our story?" Frank shook his head. "I have a hard enough time believing it myself. And then, too, they've got Dad."

A hard hand seemed to be squeezing Frank's heart. He'd seen his father overwhelmed by the armored attackers, right before he'd escaped from the basement. He didn't even know for sure that Fenton Hardy had survived.

Frank pushed the thought aside. "We're up against an enemy with lots of money and technology up the wazoo. The bad guys are sure to be scanning airline reservation computers. This is a way to keep a step ahead of them."

He dug into the equipment section of the van, coming up with a laptop computer with a modem attachment. "Find us a pay phone," Frank said to Joe. "We've got some research to do."

While Professor Reisenbach stared in amazement, Frank used the phone line to tap into the airline schedules. Then, with the help of a road map, he compared flights, destinations, times, and distances. "I think our best bet is Wilkes-Barre, Pennsylvania," he announced. "We'll leave the van in their long-term parking lot and grab a plane to Decatur, Georgia. That should put them off our tail."

For the next three days they embarked on hops that took them southeast, northwest, then southwest. Their fourth destination was Twin Falls, Idaho. There, in a motel outside of town, their luck ran out.

It was just a bit after midnight when the motel room door came crashing in. Frank, Joe, and Professor Reisenbach jumped from their beds to find two men standing in the doorway. One was tall, broad, and nasty-looking, a typical rent-a-thug. Frank recognized the other man as Professor Drake, the skinny academic who had hired Fenton Hardy.

"Good idea, Frank, making us wear our clothes to bed," Joe said. "I hate greeting company while I'm undressed."

Drake gave them a thin smile. "You led us quite a chase," he said. "I had to get involved personally, ordering a sweep of all motels within a two-hundred-mile radius of your last landing. But it appears my idea has paid off." Drake smiled at the older man beside the Hardys. "How are you, Professor Reisenbach? I had no idea when I started looking for your papers that I would meet you again."

"Meet me again?" Reisenbach said in a puzzled voice. "I've never seen you before in my life."

"Perhaps not in this guise," Drake said easily, "but I assure you—"

Before Drake could finish, Joe Hardy launched an attack on the big thug. The burly man had time for a brief surprised expression as he dug under his jacket for a gun. Joe was on top of him before the goon could draw the gun out.

Joe smashed his fist in a solar-plexus punch that folded the big man in two. He clouted the thug at the base of his skull, and the man went down.

"I hate to interrupt your little reunion, but we'll be leaving now," Joe told Drake.

The wiry Drake moved to block the door.

Joe took a menacing step toward him. "Don't make me get rough."

Frank was opening his mouth to tell his brother to take it easy when, abruptly, Joe went flying back into the room.

Joe landed full-length on one of the beds, where he lay, shaking his head. "For a little guy, he packs quite a punch."

"That wasn't a punch," Frank said, moving off to one side. He'd heard a soft crackling noise when Drake had touched Joe. Instead of facing Drake directly, Frank edged over to a pole lamp that stood near the door.

Sweeping his foot in a high kick, he toppled the lamp onto the professor. A blinding flash and the sizzle of electricity followed.

"Just as I thought," Frank said, blinking multicolored stars from his eyes. "Drake was protected by some sort of electrical charge, but I seem to have shorted it out."

As his vision cleared, Frank moved to check Drake. But the professor had disappeared. In the doorway now stood a vaguely human-shaped metallic form. It leaned lopsidedly against the door frame, sparks still jumping from its interior circuitry. Both of its glass lens "eyes" had been shattered.

"A robot!" Professor Reisenbach breathed. "Obviously it was covered by a projected three-dimensional image. What else is this era's technology capable of?"

The blinded robot's head swiveled jerkily, centering on the sound of Reisenbach's voice. "You disrupted my holographic shell." Drake's voice was now tinny and staticky. "But you won't leave. I have more people on the way."

The robot tried to move, stumbled, and clattered to the floor.

Joe was off the bed now, shaking his head. "Let's get out of here before Tinhead realizes he's not blocking the door."

"Oh, I'm already aware that this robot's movement systems have failed." Drake's voice came through a little more clearly. "I've decided on other means of dealing with you."

Frank heard the clicking of relays in the sudden silence.

"Out!" he yelled. "Now!"

They were halfway to the car when the robot exploded. The front of the flimsy motel unit blew out, its wooden frame going up in flames.

Joe hesitated, staring at the blaze. "What about the strong-arm guy Drake brought along?"

"We can't save him," Frank said, dragging

his brother back to their rented car. "He'll have to be one more thing the Swifts pay for."

A day later Frank and Joe were trekking across the mountainous backcountry of Central Hills, California. To a casual observer, they would look like hikers, except for the high-quality binoculars both boys carried.

"Are you sure it was a good idea leaving Professor Reisenbach behind in the car?" Joe asked.

"The idea is to stay as mobile as possible in case the Swift people catch up with us again," Frank snapped. "And I think Reisenbach would be more mobile in the car than running around these hills."

He stopped for a second, rubbing a hand over his tired brown eyes. "I didn't mean to snap like that, Joe. All this running and hiding is getting to me."

"Not to mention the nonstop drive from Idaho to southern California," Joe agreed with a shrug. He unfolded a map from his back pocket. "But our trip's almost over. According to this, Swift Enterprises is just beyond that next ridge."

They struggled up a rocky hillside, carefully avoiding any of the marked paths. At last they found themselves overlooking a green valley, with a huge fenced-in complex taking up most of the valley floor.

Frank and Joe lay facedown on a rocky ledge. Each of them aimed his binoculars. "That big structure in the center must be the administration building," Frank said, scanning across the complex. "But they've got at least five other major laboratories—and is that a rocket-launching gantry over on the right?"

"Forget that," Joe said, concentrating his gaze on the front gate and the grounds themselves. "The place is crawling with guards. They've got four armed people at the gate, stopping anyone who wants to come inside. Besides that, they have people patrolling that fence with guard dogs. There are even guys with minibazookas standing around in the open spaces."

Joe took his eyes away from the binoculars to look at Frank. "I've seen secret government setups that didn't have this much security. *Something* is going on in there."

Frank nodded. "Something dirty. The question is, how do we get in to find out what's going on?"

"With those one-man missile launchers, I think even an attack helicopter would have a hard time getting in there," Joe said glumly.

"Hmm," Frank said, narrowing his eyes in thought. "We'll just have to wait for somebody to come out."

Tom Swift sat tensely behind the wheel of his van, waiting for the guard to wave him on. He was glad that Harlan Ames wasn't there. The Swift Enterprises security chief would pop his cork if he saw Tom going out alone. But with the heightened security to protect against attacks by the Black Dragon, Harlan was all over the complex, inspecting defenses, so he wasn't available to stop Tom. Unless, of course, he'd left orders restricting Tom to the complex.

The guard waved the van on, and Tom relaxed. Harlan had left no orders, but then, he probably figured nobody would be stupid enough to venture out of Fortress Swift alone this evening.

"I'm not being stupid," Tom told himself as he drove off into the darkening hills. "I've got a test to run. If my idea is right, we'll have a shot at recovering the time trigger the Black Dragon stole. But to run the test, I can't be near any particle sources. That means getting away from any machines that might fog things up."

Besides, he tried to convince himself, going out quietly would get the job done more quickly, with no time wasted asking for permission. A fast in-and-out job like this had to be less noticeable than an expedition crawling with security people for the Black Dragon's spies to see.

Tom scanned the hills around him. No, nobody was up there. He was just being paranoid. Well, he wasn't going too far from home. The detector array he had set up for the tachyon experiment was just over the next ridge.

Overlooking the detectors was a bald hilltop with a jutting rock ledge. He'd be hidden from the road, and the barren area should be perfect for the experiment he had in mind.

After parking in a dry creek bed, Tom unloaded the van. He'd built a stripped-down time trigger, just the most basic components and a very small power source. He didn't need to fling anything *too* far back into the past. For this experiment he just needed to create a time-warp field and see if his particle detectors registered anything.

Even moving his minimal machine left Tom sweaty as he dragged its components up the slope to the ledge. Finally he had everything in place. The time trigger was hooked up and powered. His detectors were ready.

Tom placed a metal bead in the center of the time trigger. He didn't need a large object, just something to test whether the time-warp field caused a detectible stream of particles, which could be used to track the machine's location.

Tom triggered the time warp. The familiar twisting feeling of wrongness passed through him, and the bead disappeared in a glint of purple light.

Smiling despite the field-induced nausea, Tom turned to the computer hooked up to the particle detectors. If there were any readings—

Just then he heard a slide of gravel from above.

Tom turned to find two guys—one burly and blond, the other dark, lean, and mean—rushing down on him.

Before Tom could even brace himself, he was tackled!

7

Stupid, stupid, stupid! Tom thought as he was slammed to the ground. You deserve this for giving the Black Dragon's goons such an easy shot at you.

He twisted out of the blond attacker's hold and sprang to his feet. This one is the bigger of the two, he thought. Got to take him out first.

The burly young man was on his feet almost as quickly as Tom. As the guy came forward, Tom feinted a punch.

When the guy moved to block it, Tom unleashed his leg in a devastating blow to the midsection. He didn't expect me to know kickboxing, Tom thought with grim triumph.

The blond guy collapsed, gulping for air.

"Joe!" the second attacker cried, taking a

step toward his companion. Then he turned, crouching as he advanced on Tom.

Tom threw a punch to push his opponent's head back, then snapped his foot out at the dark-haired guy's knee. To his astonishment, his blow was deflected by his opponent's forearm. The impact spun Tom halfway around, and the dark-haired guy's foot snaked out to kick Tom behind the left knee.

Although Tom managed to dodge the blow, he landed in an awkward position. His opponent moved immediately to capitalize on his advantage. A fist flew at Tom's face, while the guy's left hand, fingers outstretched, swept at Tom's stomach like a sword.

Tom blocked the punch, then spun to avoid the second attack. He used his spinning momentum to launch a high roundhouse kick for the side of the guy's head.

The kick never landed.

Instead, Tom felt his ankle grasped, and then he was flying, to land with a bone-bruising thud close to the edge of the rocky ledge.

Tom had landed facedown. Now he flung himself around, trying to face his attacker as he scrabbled backward. It wasn't easy. The view seemed to swim in front of his eyes, and the roaring in his head made it difficult to concentrate. He tried to push himself up—

And his elbow went off the ledge.

As he fell back, Tom knew he was helpless.

One push or kick, and he'd go over completely, to land on the hard rock far below.

Instead, the dark-haired attacker grabbed Tom's ankle and pulled him to safety. "We need you in one piece, Swift. At least for the time being," he said in a hard voice. "I've got lots of questions, and you're going to answer them."

"I'm answering no questions," Tom panted, glaring at the guys. At least the world was back in focus again. "Your boss stole that machine. Do you really expect me to help him?"

Confusion made the dark-haired guy's grim look waver. "Our boss? What are you talking about?"

The blond came up, walking half-bent with a hand on his stomach. "Hey, snake-breath, I don't know what kind of garbage you're trying to feed us, but it won't work. We stole *nothing* from you. *You* sent that high-tech goon squad to attack our house and kidnap our father. You remember? Fenton Hardy? We're his sons, Joe and Frank."

His words ran out as he saw the blank look on Tom's face.

"High-tech goon squad?" Tom repeated.

"The guys were dressed in body armor. One even had some sort of exoskeleton that made him superstrong." Frank looked closely at Tom, then said to Joe, "Either this guy is a terrific actor, or he's never heard of this. Maybe only the father is behind the criminal goings-on."

"My father is no crook," Tom said. "But

there is a man who uses science for crime. He stole some prototype equipment from us. I thought you two were working for him, on a low-tech kidnap attempt. But now I— Professor Reisenbach!"

Tom stared beyond his two captors to the thin figure carefully making its way down from the hilltop. The fringe of white hair, the tall, angular form—Tom recognized him immediately from pictures his father had shown him. But this man looked almost exactly like the Reisenbach who had retired from Princeton almost thirty years earlier!

"Yes, I'm Ernst Reisenbach," the professor said, staring at the equipment Tom had set up. "I see you are working on my time-travel experiments."

Frank and Joe Hardy yelled as Tom suddenly leapt to his feet, rushing the scientist. They both piled onto Tom, forcing him down into the dirt, but not before Tom had put a hand over Reisenbach's face.

"What do you think you're doing?" Frank raged. "Just when I was starting to believe you."

"That man has to be a phony," Tom insisted. "The real Reisenbach disappeared thirty years ago. He'd be over ninety today." Tom looked confused. "I touched him because I was sure that wasn't his real appearance, that it had to be a hologram. But it wasn't."

At the word *hologram,* Joe, Frank, and the

professor all stared at Tom. "What do you know about people wearing holograms?" Joe demanded.

"It's a favorite trick of the man who stole our equipment. He hides his identity behind hologram images."

"And maybe sometimes he hides robots under those images, too?" Frank asked.

Now it was Tom's turn to look grim. "So you *have* had a brush with Xavier Mace." He suddenly turned to the older man. "Are you all right?"

Ernst Reisenbach had gone pale, drawing back from Tom as if confronted by a deadly snake.

"Mace!" Reisenbach turned the name into a hiss. "There was an Xavier Mace at Princeton. A brilliant student, but I found him lurking around my private laboratory, where I was engaged in the studies that resulted in this." He gestured to the time trigger. "One day I found the lock on the laboratory door had been tampered with. I decided to lay a trap—and caught Xavier Mace trying to enter my lab."

"What happened?" Frank asked.

"He denied trying to break in, saying he'd only been knocking on the door because he wanted to see me. The university officials found it very embarrassing. In the end, Mace was forced to leave our science program."

"Dad said he had been at school with Mace," Tom said. "But he's never mentioned if they graduated together."

"Wait a second," Joe said, turning to Reisenbach. "You mean you had this guy kicked out of school because he wanted a peek inside your lab? Isn't that a bit much?"

"I assure you, vanity had nothing to do with my decision," Reisenbach said. "I had no intention of announcing my research. Just the opposite. I had promised—sworn to myself—that no one would find out the secrets of time travel until the world was ready."

Watching the three boys staring in silence, Reisenbach shook his head. "You must understand. I knew what could happen when the results of pure science were turned into weapons of destruction. I was one of the scientists who worked to develop the atomic bomb. Less than twenty years later I saw governments threatening one another with atomic weapons. In 1962 we nearly had a nuclear war over the Soviets' establishing missile bases in Cuba. The devices I had helped invent came horribly close to destroying the world. I could never let that happen again."

Frank glanced at Joe. "To him, the Cuban missile crisis was almost yesterday. For us, it's ancient history. None of us was even alive then."

Tom stared hard at Reisenbach. "What are you guys talking about? That was a good thirty years ago."

"There are ways to hop over thirty years," Reisenbach said. He ran a hand over the components of the time trigger. "I am amazed at how compact you have made my apparatus. Miniaturization technology has certainly progressed since 1965.''

Tom's mouth hung open for a second. Then he managed to say, "You—you mean to say you've created a machine that goes *forward* in time? All we've been able to construct is a machine that goes into the past."

"Ah," Reisenbach said. "I believe I know which papers fell into your hands, then. They only represented earlier stages of my work." He turned to the other equipment Tom had set up. "But what is this? It seems to have no connection to my apparatus."

"It has a *very* important connection," Tom said. "I'm hoping to create a device to detect when time machines make the dimensional shift out of the normal universe. The warping effect must result in the creation of a stream of subatomic particles. My equipment should detect those particle streams."

Joe Hardy looked at his brother. "Did you understand that?"

Frank nodded. "I think so. Professor Reisenbach told us that his machine warps out of the four dimensions we know. Up on top of the hill we felt a stomach-twisting sensation when this machine was running. If it put stress on us up there, imagine what happens to atoms near the dimension-warping field. When atoms are put under stress, they emit particles."

Reisenbach and Tom continued to talk in high-order scientific terms for a while longer. "An ingenious idea," Reisenbach said. "And judging by the readings on your equipment, it seems to have worked. But what is the practical purpose of all this?"

"We need to track down a time trigger," Tom said. "One was stolen by the Black Dragon—that's what Xavier Mace calls himself." He turned to the Hardys. "I still don't know why you came after me, but I need your help. I've seen Mace pervert scientific discoveries into weapons of terror. Who knows what he'll do with a time machine?"

"How do we know that you and your dad are the good guys?" Joe challenged him. "What about that newspaper story that calls you technocriminals?"

"In that rag, *Truth Weekly?*" Tom said in disgust. "Don't take my word for it. Check the fine print and see who publishes it."

Frowning, Joe went off to where the Hardys had parked their rental car. A few minutes later he was back, a numb expression on his face as he held out the paper. "It was on the next-to-last page. Published by Dragon Enterprises."

Frank, Joe, and the professor glanced at one another. "Maybe we picked the wrong bad guys in this fight," Joe finally said.

"We certainly need more information," Frank agreed.

They helped Tom disassemble his stripped-down time trigger and loaded it into the van.

Then they got into their own car and followed Tom to the Swift Enterprises complex.

Harlan Ames was waiting at the front gate when they arrived. "What was the big idea of going out alone?" Ames demanded, his face going red under his leathery tan. "We're supposed to be under full security, and you pull a fool stunt like that. Something's happened, and your father has been searching all over for you."

He glanced at the rental car. "Who are those people?"

"They're here to help," Tom said. "I'd better take them straight to Dad."

Tom whisked them straight to the administration building and up the elevator to his father's top-floor office. Mr. Swift sat frowning behind his desk. "I hope you have—"

His voice froze as he stared at Professor Reisenbach, standing behind Tom with the Hardys.

"Professor! Sir!" Mr. Swift was out from behind his desk, hurrying over to shake hands with Reisenbach. "How could you— Oh. You figured out how to come *forward*, too."

Reisenbach nodded and smiled, looking out the window and around the grounds of the Swift complex. "I congratulate you on how far you've come since your student days. I, too, have traveled far, as you surmised.

"I expected this to be a glorious day for me," the professor continued. Then his face turned serious. "Unfortunately, things did not work out that way. These two young men"—he nodded at

Joe and Frank—"narrowly saved me from being kidnapped by a gang of mercenaries. Their father, however, was not so lucky."

Frank spat out the details, his voice low and tight. "At first we thought that you were involved," he told Mr. Swift, "but Tom set us straight."

The professor said, "Yes. Your son also mentioned the name of another former student. Tell me about Xavier Mace."

Tom senior's face went grim. "I expect my son has told you that Mace succeeded in stealing our updated model of your time machine."

Reisenbach nodded, and Tom's father breathed a long sigh.

"Now he's decided to use it, and the government has turned to me for help. Earlier this afternoon a metal box suddenly appeared from nowhere on the President's desk in the Oval Office. It simply materialized in a glow of purple light."

"The guy knows how to make an impression," Joe Hardy whispered to his brother.

"Inside the box was a videotape. I've been sent a copy, via jet fighter. Watch." Mr. Swift tapped a button. Immediately the wall opposite the desk began to glow as a floor-to-ceiling image appeared.

It was a man's face, framed by well-cut dark hair going gray, with steady gray eyes and slightly chubby cheeks that seemed chubbier as the man smiled. The face looked like a Hollywood version of the Perfect Father or Best Friend.

Tom Swift recognized the face immediately as one of the many masks of the Black Dragon, the one he'd worn when threatening to kill Tom back in the old Swift laboratories near Lake Carlopa, New York.

The image on the wall continued to smile. "Mr. President," Mace said in a pleasant voice. "As I'm sure you'll agree by the way this tape has appeared on your desk, I have developed an entirely new delivery system, for messages—"

Mace's smile disappeared. "Or weapons. I assure you, sir, that no amount of missile research or Star Wars technology can protect against it. My delivery system is a time machine. Yes, such machines do exist. If you don't believe me, check with that eminent scientist Tom Swift."

For a second a sneer passed over Mace's face. Then he went on, all business. "My proposal is simple. You are now the leader of the only superpower on earth. Henceforth you will confer with me on all policy matters, and I will have the final say. The world need never know. There will simply be another telephone on your desk. An additional hot line, shall we say. I would warn you not to attempt tracing that line, although with your primitive technology, you would find it impossible." Mace's eyes went flat and ugly for a moment.

"You have one week to consider my proposal. If you accept, merely arrange a press conference and use the words 'A wise leader takes advisement from all quarters.' " Xavier Mace smiled. "I will then arrange for regular communication."

Then the smile faded, and the face looking out from the wall was hard and unyielding. "If after a week you have not agreed, I shall have to give a more potent demonstration of my abilities. A more public demonstration, too."

Mace leaned forward, his eyes icy cold. "Somewhere in America, a city will be destroyed—completely and utterly."

Professor Reisenbach stared at the screen in horror. "With the device he stole, Mace has the technological capability to do it, you know." The professor turned to Mr. Swift. "Have you attempted to send back anything so it materializes in an already existing solid object?"

Tom's father nodded. "We blasted a boulder to bits by moving a small chunk of metal."

Reisenbach shuddered. "I did much the same, back in 1962. When two objects attempt to coexist in the same space and time, they destroy each other, in a tremendous outpouring of energy. Mace has apparently grasped the concept as well."

His eyes roamed around the group. "Imagine attempting that coexistence experiment with a car, a truck, or an office building in, say, downtown Manhattan.''

Frank and Joe Hardy gasped, imagining destruction on a citywide or even larger scale. "He's brought a whole new meaning to the words *time bomb*," Frank said.

Tom, Jr., however, raised a scientific objection. "How could you send back that much mass? Dad and I figured that expanding the time field requires an incredible amount of energy."

"But all Mace has to do is send that mass back a second—or even a fraction of a second—to achieve the explosive effect." Reisenbach shook his head. "Believe me, it *is* theoretically possible. I'll show you the math on it."

The professor frowned at the now-blank screen. "But does he realize the dangers of such a large explosion? Dimensional integrity is very fragile, a fact that is not very evident from our view of the universe. My experiments—"

He stopped, looking at the blank expressions on Tom, Mr. Swift, and the Hardys. "I see I have much to teach you."

Reisenbach spent the rest of the day giving a crash course on the theories and dangers of time travel. "There are some things too dangerous even to attempt experiments on," he said. "One is attempting to time-travel within one's lifetime. The paradox of meeting oneself would be literally self-destructive. The fabric of time is very delicate. It could react catastrophically to mishandling, for instance, to too much warping."

"But, Professor," Frank said, "didn't you take the risk of traveling in your own lifetime?"

To the astonishment of all, the professor blushed and grinned sheepishly. "Yes, I did." He shrugged. "It was foolish of me. However, I did not expect to still be alive by now. And I thought that if I had lived into my nineties, I would most probably be in some old-age home—far away from my cabin in the woods and in no danger of physically confronting my time-traveling self."

Tom digested this and nodded slowly. "A calculated risk, then," he said. "But what did you mean by 'too much warping'?"

"You cannot operate too many time machines in one place," Reisenbach said. "The universe as we know it could not stand the strain."

Even the Swift supper table became an impromptu classroom. Tom's mother had arranged a large meal as soon as she learned of the extra houseguests. Besides Reisenbach, Tom's father had invited the Hardy brothers to stay with his family.

Ernst Reisenbach's eyes lit up in recognition as he arrived for dinner. "Good heavens! I know you. Mary—let me think for a moment—Mary Nestor, is it not?"

"That's right, Professor Reisenbach," Tom's mother said, shaking hands. "Although it's been Mary Swift for a while now."

"I seem to remember that you went out with another one of my students," Reisenbach said. His face suddenly changed. "Oh! It was—"

"That was a long time ago," Mrs. Swift said firmly.

Tom glanced at his father. He had heard some odd stories of his parents' youth. At one point, it seemed, his mother had been romantically involved with Xavier Mace. Apparently Professor Reisenbach remembered that, too.

"Things change over the years," Mr. Swift said. "But I'm sure Mary and I are glad to see you and have you here."

Mrs. Swift nodded, smiling.

A shy smile crept onto Reisenbach's face. "Teachers can only dream of what their students might accomplish in their prime. I am fortunate indeed to see your work, your lovely wife, your son—oh, and this must be your daughter."

Sandra Swift entered the dining room and was introduced. Tom couldn't help noticing that she held on to Joe's hand a little longer than necessary and gave him a big smile. "So you tackled my brother, hmm? I'm sorry I missed that."

"Well, he didn't miss me," Joe said, going into a graphic description of the fight.

Frank Hardy rolled his eyes as Sandra hung on Joe's every word. "I suppose there had to be a teenage girl involved somewhere in all this," he groaned.

"You make it sound as if that always happens," Tom said.

"With Joe, it usually does," Frank responded with a shrug.

As they sat down for supper, Tom noticed that Sandra arranged for Joe to sit beside her at one end of the table. They seemed to draw apart, talking quietly and ignoring the rest of the table.

"It was working on the atomic bomb that turned me to the study of time," Reisenbach said. "The Manhattan Project represented the future of science—research conducted by many hands, controlled by governments. The kind of science I knew—a single mind probing the unknown and turning the knowledge it found to useful application—that seemed over."

Reisenbach smiled. "So I explored a field far from practical application. Or so I thought."

"Your accomplishment was truly incredible," Mr. Swift told the professor. "Today's best theoretical physicists are only beginning to develop concepts you've already put to use."

A shadow passed over Reisenbach's face. "Yes. That rather surprises me."

Frank blinked in puzzlement. "You expected other scientists to develop time machines, too?"

The professor shook his head. "I expected to arrive in a future where my efforts were known." He waved a hand. "Not a time machine in every garage, but that scientists at least would know of my work and perhaps even be expecting me."

"I see what you mean," Tom said. "With a

time machine, you could return to 1965 and arrange the way you'd be received in the future.''

Reisenbach nodded. "But apparently I didn't do that. It's as if I never went back to my own time. I hope we don't discover some unanticipated danger in time travel."

"What sort of danger?" Tom asked.

Reisenbach shook his head. "I've mentioned the fragile fabric of time, and the danger of warp damage. Fifty time machines functioning in the same dimension might cause a convulsion of the space-time continuum." He took a sip of water. "What if we discovered that one time machine operating in the same space for fifty trips could cause the same disaster?"

"I guess then science-fiction writers couldn't use time-travel paradoxes," Frank said, trying to lighten the mood. "No more stories where you go back in time to kill your grandfather before he gets married and has your father. Of course, by killing grandpa, you can't exist. But in order for you to kill him, he must exist. But if he exists, so do you. But if you travel back and kill him. . . ." He grinned. "That always drove me crazy."

Reisenbach chuckled. "Let me drive you a little crazier. If, while going to kill your grandfather, you stopped fifty years before his day and carved your name in a stone wall, then killed your grandfather, will that carving exist or not?"

Frank shook his head. "I was having a hard

enough time with the paradox I suggested. What do you think, Tom?"

Tom frowned in thought. "Quantum physicists would answer yes and no. But I'll say the carving *does* exist, because it predates the point where the possibilities diverge."

"That is my analysis," Reisenbach said, smiling. "There are two futures, which branch off from, well, let's call it the tree trunk of the past. In one future, you exist, in the other, you do not. But the past—the trunk that existed *before* the branching point—will always be marked by the you that *does* exist."

"All this what-if and maybe stuff makes me dizzy," Frank said. "I'm going to make like my brother and concentrate on something else."

"Don't pick on me," Joe said, glancing up from his conversation. "I'm just making friends here. I was telling Sandra about that machine Tom was testing."

"Well, my theory tests out, in spite of interruptions from some people who will remain nameless," Tom said with a grin. "The particle-detector array picked up some distinct meson streams when I caused the time warp. That means I can calibrate a device to detect time machines in operation."

"So maybe the government can track the Black Dragon by homing in on wherever he's building this time bomb," Frank suggested. "He'll have to test the thing to make sure he can back up his threats."

Tom nodded. "The problem is, these detectors will be pretty expensive to produce. The main contact points are made of iridium."

"Iridium? That stuff is rarer than platinum," Frank said. "Can't the contacts be made from some other metal?"

"Iridium gives the best detection range," Tom replied. "Even so, the detector works in an area only about five miles in diameter."

Frank looked concerned. "With a range like that, you'd need a good half-dozen gizmos just to cover Los Angeles." He shrugged. "At least the government will be picking up the tab."

The next morning Tom and Frank were in Mr. Swift's office. Tom's father frowned as he spoke into the telephone. "But how could that happen? When were they last checked?"

Mr. Swift took a deep breath as he listened. "No, I suppose there's nothing we can do about it now. What about the available market? What? Bought up? How can that be?"

He hung up the phone and turned to the boys. "I faxed your plans for the time-warp detector to the government last night," Mr. Swift said, pointing to Tom's prototype. It sat on his desk, its indicator lights blinking.

"We've got a major problem. Somehow the government's main supply of iridium has been contaminated."

"Contaminated?" Tom repeated. "How?"

"Somehow the metals storage vault got filled

with radioactive dust," Mr. Swift said. "The iridium is now too dangerous to handle."

"Vaults like that are protected like Fort Knox," Frank said. "In fact, they're probably *in* Fort Knox. So how could someone walk in there to irradiate the iridium?"

"You couldn't *walk* in with a load of radioactive waste," Tom said, "but someone could warp it in. Someone who wouldn't want the government making time-warp detectors."

"How could the Black Dragon know about your plans?" Frank asked.

"Maybe he was following a similar course of research," Tom said glumly. "You know, great minds running on the same tracks."

He turned to his father. "I guess this means the government has to buy the iridium it needs."

"Which won't be easy," Mr. Swift said. "The metals markets have gone wild. Somebody is trying to corner the world's supply of iridium."

"I wonder who?" Tom's face was as grim as his father's.

"We'll just have to hope that we can either get hold of an alternative supply or find some sort of substitute."

Tom just shook his head.

Mr. Swift looked over at Frank. "And where is your brother?"

Frank looked a little embarrassed. "Sandra offered Joe a tour of the complex. He wanted to see where Professor Reisenbach was working."

"Nothing much to see," Mr. Swift said. "We

set the professor up in the supercollider building. The place is built like a fortress and partly underground, and it's out of the way.''

"Good for security," Frank said.

That brought a smile to Mr. Swift's face. "Oddly enough, Harlan Ames said the same thing.''

"Harlan is the gentleman who was so happy to see us at the gate," Tom explained a bit sheepishly. "He's usually in a better mood. But lately it's been a constant headache for him, trying to keep this place secure.''

"That can't be easy, with eight miles of perimeter fences to patrol," Frank said.

"Harlan's a good man, and he and his people do their best," Mr. Swift said.

Tom, however, was distracted, staring at his detection apparatus.

"Dad," he said suddenly, "are we doing any experiments with the time machines today?''

"No," Mr. Swift said. "We still haven't incorporated the new design input from Professor Reisenbach.''

"Then Harlan—and we—have a new security problem." Tom was staring at his detector. Its lights were flashing urgently, and a screen on the machine was pulsing with information.

"According to this, there's a time warp taking place, right here in the administration building!''

9

Tom Swift, Sr., snatched up the phone on his desk. "Get me Harlan Ames—now!" he barked into the receiver.

He glanced over at his son. "Tom, can that detector of yours pinpoint where the warp is taking place?"

Tom read the glowing screen, looking puzzled. "The reading seems to be right here—no! It's directly *below* us, one or two floors down."

Mr. Swift relayed the location to his security chief, then turned to the boys. "A small army of Harlan's people, plus some technicians, are on the way." He glanced at the boys. "Do you want to get out of here? I intend to stay put."

Frank and Tom both gave longing glances to the office door, but they stayed where they were.

"I get the feeling I'd just be underfoot outside," Frank said with a shrug.

"I think somebody should be watching in case the Black Dragon has any more special deliveries." Tom patted his detector. "And since this is the only working detector, it looks like I'm elected."

"Fine." Mr. Swift picked up the phone and said, "Instituting security precautions, Level Three." Then he pushed a series of buttons on his desk console.

The light coming through the windows suddenly dimmed, and there were muffled metallic noises from the doorway.

Tom took pity on Frank's puzzled look. "Those thumps were carbon-steel bolts shooting through the door frame and into the door. The whole office is armored."

He gestured toward the windows. "Dad raised the reflective shields. From the outside they look like mirrors, though, as you notice, we can see through. Snipers can't get a clear shot at us, and even laser blasts would be reflected off."

Frank's eyebrows rose. "I'm impressed," he said.

The phone sounded, and Mr. Swift put it on the external speaker.

"We found the package." Harlan Ames sounded slightly out of breath. "It's a bomb, about the same size as the test module you sent back on the island. The tech people have disarmed it, and they assure me it's a conventional explosive.''

He made an uncomplimentary noise. ''You'd think a villain like Xavier Mace would at least have sent a nuke.''

Tom's detector suddenly lit up like a Christmas tree. Tom looked at the screen on the machine, and his lips went tight. ''He didn't need a nuke to do this job, Harlan,'' Tom said bitterly. ''That bomb was only a diversion. I'm getting warp readings—lots of them—over by the supercollider. Somehow Mace knew it was the most secure building in the complex—the perfect place to keep someone safe. He doesn't want to blow us up. He's trying to kidnap Professor Reisenbach.''

''The supercollider? That's where Joe and Sandra were going!'' Frank Hardy darted for the office door, then skidded to a halt, turning back to Mr. Swift. ''Please—I've got to go!''

''You and me both,'' Tom said, joining Frank.

Mr. Swift nodded, punching keys on the desk. Seconds later they heard the deep vibration of the heavy bolts coming free.

Tom led the way to the elevator, and he and Frank descended a floor, where they found Harlan Ames already organizing his people for a counterstrike.

''Slow down the intruders any way you can!'' Ames shouted into a walkie-talkie. ''We don't want them getting out.''

He turned to Tom. ''A bunch of the Black

Dragon's robots popped out of thin air, all around the supercollider. Some of them went to secure the building; others cut a hole in the south fence, where the Dragon had a bunch of men waiting. We're trying to pin down the reinforcements and close off the fence again."

"We've got a problem," Tom said. "Sandra and Joe may be at the supercollider."

Harlan Ames's face went pale. "Let's get over there and find out. I hope they haven't encountered any unexpected guests."

In the entrance tunnel of the supercollider building, Joe Hardy knelt over the prone body of a robot, working frantically to pry loose one of its partially torn metal arms.

Sandra Swift stared down at the round metal body with its tanklike treads and bulbous head. "How did you know that hitting it with the fire extinguisher would knock it down like that?"

"I didn't," Joe grunted, finally tearing the arm off. Beneath him, the robot stirred, trying to push itself upright with its other, more spindly arm.

Sandra grabbed the fire extinguisher and whipped it down on the robot's domed head.

"Not there," Joe said, whacking the robot in the midsection. "No room for brains up there. They have to be hidden in the body."

Joe and Sandra had left Professor Reisenbach in the computer room right outside the supercollider chamber, deep in the bowels of the building. He was so enthralled by the technology he was studying, he hadn't even noticed when they left.

Sandra had taken Joe up five levels to the building's ground floor. They were just about to leave the huge partly underground complex when a weird stomach-churning feeling passed through them.

Then the robot they had just disabled had appeared inside the doors in a shimmer of purple light. Although it was a shorter, squatter version of the machine Joe had faced at the motel in Idaho, he figured it had to come from the Black Dragon, warped in on the stolen time trigger. Joe had snatched the first heavy object he could find and knocked the robot flat.

"What was that thing doing here?" Sandra stood poised over the now-still machine, extinguisher at the ready.

"I think it was trying to open the door." Joe glanced from the slender manipulator arm, still attached to the robot, to the control panel that operated the heavy steel doors of the building. "Somehow I'm not quite as eager to go out."

Suddenly Joe snapped his fingers and his eyes went wide. "The professor! Sandra, he's still down there—what should we do?"

"Leave him where he is. He's safer than we are."

A heavy clang reverberated outside the metal doors.

"I think you've got an idea there," Joe said.

"At least whatever's outside can't get in." A louder clang prompted him to add, "Can it?"

"Things could be worse," Sandra said, trying to sound calm. "We're protected here, with a good thick door between us and whatever's going on outside."

Then they heard the hum of tread motors coming down the hall behind them. Joe turned to see another robot rolling to the attack. "Things have just gotten worse," he told Sandra. "Get down!"

This robot had a heavy arm like the one Joe had just disabled. But there was something small in its manipulator hand—something connected to the body of the robot with a thick cable.

Joe knocked Sandra down as the robot raised its left arm at her. A brilliant red beam leapt toward her.

"A laser!" Sandra gasped as the beam flashed over their heads, cutting a gash in the steel doors.

"And we've got nowhere to run," Joe muttered. They were trapped, lying flat at the head of the corridor. The robot blocked the way back, and the sealed door was behind them. Even trying to reach for the door controls would expose them to laser fire.

"What are we supposed to do?" Sandra asked as she huddled on the floor beside him.

"I was hoping you'd have an idea," Joe admitted.

"Well, I'm not the true scientific genius of the family," Sandra told him.

"But you are prettier," Joe said with a grin.

The robot came onward toward the door. At least it had stopped targeting them with its laser.

In fact, Joe realized, it was paying no attention to them at all. As long as he and Sandra hugged the ground, the robot seemed to ignore them.

He decided to test his theory. "Stay put," he said to Sandra, and rose in a low leap to land behind the body of the downed robot.

The other machine whirled around so the sensors in its "head" faced Joe and the laser-tipped hand rose.

Luckily, Joe was already behind the downed metal body when the robot fired. Flooring tile sizzled as the laser scorched an arc where Joe had been an instant before.

"Sandra, keep very still," Joe said. "This bucket of bolts shoots only if we move."

"Are you sure?" Sandra asked.

"Watch." Joe shifted the arm of the downed robot so it swung in the air. The other robot stopped in its progress toward the door controls and fired a laser blast that sliced the manipulator off the slender arm.

As soon as the movement stopped, the attack robot turned away, rolling on to the control panel. It began pressing the control buttons with the tip of the laser.

"We've got one chance," Joe said. He jumped

up, swinging the severed robot arm with all his might.

It smashed into the other robot's hand, shattering the laser weapon. "Can't shoot us now!" Joe snarled.

The robot pivoted, swinging with its other arm. Joe went flying. As he landed, he heard a low rumbling. The door was going up!

A figure bounded past him, yelling like a banshee. It was Sandra Swift, swinging the trusty fire extinguisher over her head. The big metal container hit the robot in the chest, and it toppled back.

"I see Harlan and my brother coming!" Sandra cried. "Let's get out of here!"

Frank Hardy followed Tom Swift, Harlan Ames, and an assault force of security people as they piled out of the administration building. Charging across the open lawns, they spread out in a skirmish line as they passed between two large buildings.

The entrance to the supercollider rose like a small white bunker ahead of them. A mixed group of robots and black-clad human assault troops stood in front of the door. Some were trying to get in. Others attempted to lay down covering fire on the Swift security people, who poured bullets and pale bluish rays into their opponents.

"They're hung up at the door," Harlan Ames

said with grim satisfaction. "We've got 'em now."

With the new reinforcements, the Swift people began moving in. Frank noticed that robots struck by the rays staggered and stopped firing their lasers.

"What is that robot death ray?" Frank asked.

"It's more like a robot stunner—something I whipped up for the next time we dealt with the Black Dragon's mechanical goons," Tom said. "It knocks out their electronic brains."

Without their armored escort, the black-clad assault team lost heart. Weapons began to fall and hands went into the air.

At that moment the steel doors to the supercollider began to rumble upward. Security men swung their weapons to cover the entrance, and several attackers dove to get their own weapons.

"Hold your fire!" Tom yelled to his people. "That's my sister!"

Sure enough, Sandra Swift was leaping from the opening. She took a quick look around, then dove for cover behind a wrecked robot.

"Tom!" Sandra screamed. "We're okay. See if you can get to the professor—he's down near the supercollider chamber!" From his vantage point Frank watched Joe lurch into the open, a metal pole in his hand.

Tom and Harlan charged forward to meet them, the rest of the skirmish line following in a flying wedge. Frank followed. It was only when the remaining intruders started shooting that he realized neither he nor Tom had any weapons.

As that thought crossed Frank's mind, one of the security team went down, wounded in the arm. Tom knelt, made sure the man was okay, then picked up the robot stunner the wounded man had dropped.

A moment later a man carrying what looked like a computer keyboard dropped with a cry. Frank stopped. "Need help?"

"Laser burn," the security trooper said through tight lips. "I'll be okay." He gestured toward the board he carried. "Remote door controls."

"What do we need that for?" Frank asked. "The doors are open now."

"What if we need 'em closed?" the man groaned.

Frank picked up the keyboard and followed the charging security force

Joe had been forced back into the entrance by sniper fire from the few remaining attackers. Sandra Swift kept a low profile behind her cover. Black-clad attackers began retreating into the doorway. Swift security people tried to head them off with bullets, but with Sandra and Joe in the fire zone, they were handicapped in their shooting.

Even so, the rescue squad had almost reached the stairs to the supercollider when something huge and metallic appeared in the corridor behind Joe Hardy.

It was a robot, more human in form than the other metallic attackers. It towered a good three feet over Joe, and something large and sinister gleamed in its right hand.

"Joe, get out of there!" Frank yelled. He fumbled with the control box he carried. Maybe he could get the door between Joe and that thing.

"Behind you!" Tom cried.

Joe whirled, bringing his metal club up. But whatever the robot had came swinging down.

"Got to try—" Tom said through gritted teeth. He aimed the robot stunner, playing its beam along the robot's arm.

The huge metal warrior lurched, its arm freezing. Joe stumbled back out of the doorway as the behemoth tried to swat at him.

"Work, you stupid box," Frank muttered, tapping yet another sequence into the control board. The doors rumbled down, catching against the big robot's arm. For a second it struggled, trying to hold up the doors.

Then a glowing image surrounded the huge robot. Frank recognized the face on the nine-foot-tall hologram. It was Xavier Mace, as he'd seen him on the tape threatening the President. "Don't think you've won!" Mace roared.

The figure suddenly crumpled as the doors knocked the robot down. At the same instant, the people on the battlefield reeled as a horrible wrenching feeling went through them. Tom knew the sensation well. It signaled a time machine in operation. Judging from the intensity of the feeling, it meant lots of time machines operating simultaneously. The floor erupted with a violent explosion. A column of blinding purple light burst from the floors below, near the center of the underground supercollider. Sheets of bluish lightning pulsed around the central lance of flame, sometimes streaking off to strike buildings and people. Frank saw one of the black-clad attackers hit and incinerated.

Then he realized that all the robots on the battlefield were disappearing in shimmers of purple light.

"What's going on?" Harlan Ames yelled over a sudden, shrieking gale. "Why is Mace pulling his machines out?"

"He didn't pull them out. He pulled them in—into the supercollider." The earth suddenly shuddered, hurling them all off their feet. Tom staggered over to where Joe was helping Sandra up. "Get out of here! Remember what Professor Reisenbach told us about too many warp fields coming together?"'

"The universe would react catastrophically," Frank shot back. He grabbed Sandra's free arm, and the four of them ran from the doomed building.

The pulsing column of light was expanding. Security people and the intruders they'd been fighting moments before now all raced away from the supercollider complex.

Tom kept pulling Frank, Joe, and Sandra toward the shelter of one of the lab buildings the attack party had passed on the way to the battle. The ground seemed to ripple under their feet, as if the earth were a wild animal trying to throw them off.

A deafening roar flung them face-first onto the grassy lawn. The air around them seemed to glow purple, then went black. Sandra gasped. "What's going on back there?"

"Laws of nature were broken, and anyone too close is being punished for it," Tom said. "Punished with certain death."

Sandra pushed herself up. "But there are all sorts of technicians down near the supercollider—and Professor Reisenbach!"

"Not anymore," Tom said tightly.

Frank shuddered. "Just last night we were talking about how the paradoxes of time travel could be dangerous. Now one of those paradoxes has killed him."

Tom nodded. "And now we know why he never went back to 1965."

10

This place looks like a war zone, Tom thought, gazing down at the Swift Enterprises complex from his father's office. The lab buildings all showed cracked windows or other damage from the erupting earth. As for the supercollider, only a blackened hole remained where the structure had been.

Two days had passed since the disaster, days filled with frantic activity. Tom and his father had worked to turn the suggestions and designs Professor Reisenbach had given them into a time machine that could reach the future as well as the past. Researchers labored to refine Tom's time-warp detector so it used less iridium. At the same time technicians manufactured detectors with whatever iridium they could get their hands on. Repair crews struggled with the worst damage from the Black Dragon's attack.

And Harlan Ames and the Hardys worked to beef up security around the complex. Swift Enterprises was beginning to look like an embattled fortress, which Tom witnessed firsthand when Frank, Joe, and a work crew came into the office.

"What's going on?" Tom asked, glancing up from the computer he'd set up to supplement his father's office machine.

"We're installing a booby trap for any robots that try to warp into this room," Frank Hardy said as he entered accompanied by his brother and a small army of technicians. The workers installed detection gear and an automated version of Tom's robotic stunner in a corner of the room.

"You know that round robot brain that floats around here?" Frank asked.

"You mean Orb?" Tom said.

Frank nodded. "Joe asked how it seemed to fly, and your people said it was something called maglev."

"Magnetic levitation," Tom said. "We installed strips of superconductive material in the walls. Orb sets up a magnetic field that lets him fly along those tracks."

"When Joe heard that, he asked if those tracks couldn't throw a magnetic field strong enough to hold any robot helpless in the middle of the room. If the detector catches a robot warping in, it triggers the magnetic strips. The magnetic field makes the metal robot float in midair, helpless, and the robot stunner knocks it out.''

Tom's eyebrows rose. ''That is a downright fiendish infiltration defense.''

''Joe's got a pretty nasty imagination when he puts his mind to it.''

Tom gave the younger Hardy a big smile. ''All I can say is, go for it, Joe!''

Joe Hardy didn't return the smile. ''I just wish it hadn't taken that disaster to put the idea in my head.''

Mr. Swift looked up from his desk computer. ''We're fighting a war, Joe. I don't think any of us truly realized that until Mace tried his invasion stunt.''

Joe still looked haunted. ''It sure is a war—if you judge by the casualties. Everybody who was in the supercollider building died in that time-warp mess. Sandra and I had been talking to those people just a couple of minutes before.'' He took a deep breath. ''We were talking to Professor Reisenbach. You know, while we were on the run, I really came to like the old guy.''

''Joe,'' Frank said quietly, ''you saved Sandra.''

''You should see the way she looks at you when she thinks you're not watching,'' Tom added, smothering a grin.

Joe's mood didn't lighten. ''Yeah,'' he said, ''I saved Sandra—this time.'' He headed quickly for the door. "Let's check the hallway. We're almost done in here."

Tom silently watched Joe disappear. Then he turned to Frank. "Is he okay?"

Frank was staring out the door, sadness in his dark eyes. "Joe feels guilty whenever somebody he likes dies and he survives. Joe lost a girlfriend when terrorists rigged a bomb to our car. By sheer bad luck, Iola was the one who triggered it. There was nothing Joe could do. He still blames himself, though."

Frank turned back to Tom. "Right now he wants about fifteen minutes in a small room with Xavier Mace."

"Joe and a few thousand other people," Tom's father said. "Mace robbed the world of a brilliant mind when he killed Ernst Reisenbach."

Mr. Swift's face was grim. "Mace had to know about the dangers of bringing too many warp fields together. Most of the robots out there were inoperative, their brain circuits knocked out by Tom's stunner ray. They were moved by remote control, by an order from Mace."

"But why?" Frank asked

"Why indeed?" Mr. Swift said. "It wasn't to reinforce the raiders inside the supercollider. The robots outside were already out of action."

Mr. Swift's voice was harsh. "Mace did it to create a warp paradox. He wanted to cause that cataclysm. Mace knew his forces were losing. They couldn't kidnap Reisenbach, so Mace decided to eliminate him. Mace would have happily killed hundreds, even thousands, to get one man.''

Tom realized there were tears in his father's eyes. *I never knew how much this teacher meant to Dad,* he thought.

"Ernst Reisenbach achieved the greatest breakthrough in practical science since atomic power,'' Tom senior said tightly. "And that maniac Xavier Mace killed him for it, so he could rule the world.''

He looked at the boys. "That's why we have to beat the Black Dragon.''

"It's too bad we can't actually go out and fight him,'' Frank said. He shook his head. "Listen to me—I sound like a bad imitation of Joe. But this whole defensive thing is pretty hard to take.''

"We don't even know where he is, much less where he's going to strike,'' Tom said. "The government has been checking all of Mace's supposedly legitimate fronts, like the UNITECH plant in Lake Carlopa. And our people are turning out detectors as fast as possible, but there are a lot of cities to cover. We've got only six detectors for the entire East Coast, and most of them are in Washington.''

"If only we had some clue to tell us where the Black Dragon is,'' Frank said. "Something that would give us a chance to take the fight to him.''

Tom glanced over at the older Hardy brother.

"You've got your own bone to pick with Xavier Mace," he said. "He's holding your father."

Frank nodded grimly. "I'm surprised he hasn't used Dad as a hostage, to force Joe and me to work as his spies."

Tom looked at Frank and nodded. He'd been about to mention the possibility that Frank's father might no longer be alive, but he didn't want to add to the pressure and frustration so clearly evident in Frank's face.

"Maybe Mace has a spy in here already," Tom said instead. Ever since the attack, Tom had felt a gnawing doubt. He was convinced that the object of the attack had been the professor. How had the Black Dragon found out exactly where Ernst Reisenbach was working, allowing him to warp in his robots with such pinpoint accuracy? How had Mace discovered their sudden need for iridium? He had asked Harlan Ames those questions, but they'd found no spies.

"Mace hasn't approached *you*, has he?" Tom asked.

"I keep expecting to see one of his holograms glow into existence in front of my face, giving his terms," Frank admitted. "But no, Mace hasn't talked to us. That leads me to think that he doesn't have a lever to use."

"But your father—"

"—may be dead," Frank finished for Tom in a quiet, hard voice. "I saw him go down, and then I had to run. I don't know what happened next." He sighed. "Losing Dad is something we've always had to consider. Just recently, on a big case, we thought he'd been killed. That time it turned out we were wrong. This time—"

Though his face was etched with torment, Frank only shrugged. "Who knows?"

"But you figure that Mace not threatening you with killing your dad is a bad sign," Tom said, finally giving voice to his own suspicions.

"I think so," Frank said. "And I suspect Joe is already convinced." He shook his head. "Unless or until we get to the bottom of this, we won't know for sure."

The workers had finished installing the office booby trap and headed off to work in the hall outside.

As Frank went to follow them, the phone on Mr. Swift's desk rang. Tom's father answered, listened for a moment, then called Frank back. "It's Harlan Ames at the front gate. There's someone there to see you and your brother."

Frank Hardy frowned in puzzlement. "Nobody knows we're here except the government. Even Mom and Aunt Gertrude don't know where we are, just as we don't know where the government agents are hiding them." The Hardys had used Mr. Swift's contacts and some of their own to arrange government protection for their family after discovering the scale of the Black Dragon's plot.

Frank's eyes sharpened. "Maybe we're about to

get the squeeze from Mr. Mace after all. In that case, I'd like you to see what's going on."

Tom's father nodded and got back on the phone. "Harlan, conduct the visitor to my office after you've searched him thoroughly."

Tom was already out the door, returning shortly with Joe Hardy.

It was some time before the visitor finally entered Mr. Swift's office. When he did, he turned out to be a thin, pale man whose mousy brown hair was styled in a conservative cut. He wore an even more conservatively styled gray pinstripe suit, somewhat rumpled from the search Harlan Ames had put the man through, a process that had also ruffled the visitor's feelings.

His watery blue eyes glared at Mr. Swift from behind round steel-framed glasses. "I have never been so insulted in my entire life," he huffed. "Your security guards treated me as if I were some common criminal. That search was most offensive. Then, as I was brought to this building, I saw people digging what appeared to be trenches and gun emplacements."

The visitor leaned across Mr. Swift's desk, raising his voice. "I demand to see Mr. Frank Hardy and Mr. Joe Hardy."

Tom watched his father repress a smile as he spoke. "I apologize for the somewhat odd situation, Mr., ah—"

"Dalton Barnes." The visitor reached into his suit jacket, took out a leather card case, and withdrew a business card, which he handed over. "I am a vice-president of Dumont, Cranston, and Clarkson, a private New York banking firm."

From his tone of voice, Tom thought, he means a *very* private banking firm.

Barnes continued to speak. "Some years ago an envelope was placed in our vault with orders for it to be opened on a certain date. That date was three days ago. We found another sealed envelope inside, with orders to deliver it to a certain address in Bayport." Barnes paused for a moment, looking at them.

"Inquiries showed that a Frank and Joe Hardy do indeed live at that address. When I attempted to deliver the letter, however, I found myself intercepted by government agents. They seemed to think I was bringing a ransom demand. In the end I was told that I could find the gentlemen I was seeking here." Barnes drew himself up very stiffly. "Now, if you please, I would like to meet Frank and Joe Hardy."

"We're right here," Frank said from his position beside the desk. "I'm Frank Hardy, and this is my brother, Joe. Now, what's this about a letter?"

Dalton Barnes's composure cracked completely as he gawked at the two teenage boys. "This is impossible," he said. "The men I'm looking for would have to be old enough to be your grandfathers. The letter I referred to was placed in trust at our bank in 1932."

"Hey," Joe said, "it's a shame we only got

left a letter. Think how much interest even a couple of hundred bucks would have made if it had been deposited back then.''

While Barnes gave Joe a frosty look, Frank reached for his wallet and presented some ID. Then he nudged his brother to do the same. "Mr. Barnes, Joe and I are the only Frank and Joe Hardy who have ever lived at Twenty-three Elm Street in Bayport."

Barnes still hesitated, glancing at Mr. Swift and Tom.

"Anything you need to say you can say in front of these people," Joe said impatiently.

"According to my instructions, you will be able to answer the following question," Barnes finally said. "When I say the words *the chief,* what comes to your mind?"

Joe turned to Frank, Frank turned to Joe, and they both grinned. "Ezra Collig," they said in unison.

Jaw sagging, Barnes handed over the envelope. "I was told to give you the entire package. Now, please sign here, and I'll be on my way."

He left hurriedly, escorted by Harlan Ames's officers, while Joe and Frank were still examining the outer envelope. "It's addressed to Dumont and Cranston. Apparently Clarkson hadn't come on board yet." Joe laughed.

Frank, however, was more interested in the upper right corner of the envelope. "That's a three-cent stamp," he said. "It's postmarked

New York City. I can't read the month, but the year is definitely 1932."

He glanced around. "Who back then would know that Ezra Collig would become chief of the Bayport police?"

They all examined the yellowed envelope. "It's addressed to us—typewritten," Joe said.

He tore open the other envelope, the one that Dalton Barnes had delivered, and his eyes went wide. "I don't believe this!" he gasped.

The message delivered to them across more than sixty years consisted of one typewritten line: "Frank and Joe, Pick up the May 1932 issue of *Unlikely Tales*."

The signature at the bottom was Fenton Hardy's.

11

Okay, I'll bite. What is *Unlikely Tales?*" Joe Hardy asked.

"Obviously, something that was around in 1932," Tom said, turning to his father.

"Don't look at me," Mr. Swift said. "That was before my time."

Frank frowned in thought, studying the other envelope. "You know, I seem to remember that Dad conducted an investigation a long time ago for Dumont, Cranston, and Clarkson."

"So he'd know that bank was still around today," Tom said.

"But how could Dad wind up in 1932?" Joe asked.

"We know the Black Dragon has a time machine. Maybe we'll get some answers when we get hold of *Unlikely Tales,*" Frank replied.

"Which brings us back to my first question," Joe said. "What is *Unlikely Tales?*"

"I think I know where to check," Tom said, heading for his father's computer. "We know it's some kind of publication, because we're referred to an exact issue. And judging from the title, I'd say it was a fiction magazine—either science fiction or fantasy."

He sorted through various computer databases. "It's not a magazine published today. We're obviously dealing with something in the out-of-print listings. Ah! Here it is."

A brief paragraph came up on the screen, which he read aloud. " '*Unlikely Tales* was a pulp science-fiction magazine, one of many that flourished back in the thirties. It ceased publishing due to the paper shortage during World War Two.' "

"So this magazine hasn't been around for ages," Joe said. "I suspect we may be hunting a collector's item here."

Joe was proven right. Visits to numerous specialty magazine shops only got them regretful shakes of the head from owners. After all the dead ends, they were finally rescued the next morning by a very red-faced Harlan Ames.

"Found it up in my attic," he said gruffly, handing over a wrapped package. "My dad was a real fan of those old pulp books when he was a kid. Just on a hunch, I decided to check. This was tucked away between a bunch of *Thrilling*

Wonder Stories and something called *Astounding Tales of Space and Time.*"

"They sure knew how to name magazines back then," Joe said, laughing. "But why did they call them pulps?"

"You'll find out when you open that package," Harlan said. "Be careful. Pulp paper was the cheapest kind available. The older it gets, the more brittle it becomes. If you treat this too roughly, all you'll end up with is a pile of paper dust."

"We hear you," Frank said, carefully taking the package and putting it on Mr. Swift's desk. Undoing the wrappings, he revealed a magazine about seven by ten inches.

The slightly tattered back cover was made of shiny paper and featured a full-color ad telling of the wonderful health benefits from smoking cigarettes whose tobacco had been treated with ultraviolet light.

" 'Protects your throat against impurities,' " Tom read. "This *must* be science fiction."

Frank gently turned the magazine over so they could see the front cover. Joe began laughing at the gaudy picture.

"This is supposed to be science fiction? That guy looks like he's dressed for a gladiator movie!"

The brawny young man on the cover wore a short skirtlike garment and a shiny metal helmet with a spike sticking out the top. The rest was all muscles.

"And the girl must be pretty uncomfortable in that brass bikini," Joe added. Indeed, the young woman clinging to the hero's arm did seem to be wearing a bathing suit made of solid metal.

"That was the way they drew covers for these magazines," Mr. Swift said, chuckling. "Back then this was pretty hot stuff."

"So this is what the future looked like," Tom said. "I don't know which is funnier, the gun the hero is holding or the robot threatening them." To his eyes, the weapon in the hero's hand resembled a collection of oddly shaped light bulbs, while the robot looked like an old-fashioned furnace with claws.

They stopped laughing as they read the fine print. The cover story was a tale called "War Through Time."

The author was Fenton Hardy.

Tom dashed off to make several copies of the story. Everyone began reading as the pages came out of the copier, eager to see what message Fenton Hardy had sent from the past.

" 'Aha, Con Riley thought, a gleam of triumph in his steely blue eyes. The guards were not as thorough as they believed. A short-wave key still remains concealed in my garments.' " Joe Hardy looked up from the manuscript he was reading aloud. "Does anybody know what a 'short-wave key' is supposed to be?"

"I'd guess it's thirties high-tech. The hero uses it to shake the locks apart and escape a 'dungeon whose walls crept with fetid slime.' "

Frank shook his head. "Who'd have guessed that Dad of all people could write like this?"

"I guess he kept it to himself," Joe said, grinning. "Not too many people want detective reports crawling with fetid slime."

"Even so," Mr. Swift said, finishing his copy, "there's a lot of real information crammed between the hokier parts of the story."

"Like the regular rocket-ship service from the moon?" Tom said with a grin.

"No, but his scientist in the story—Reisenstein—is obviously Professor Reisenbach. The villain is called the Black Dragon, and Mr. Hardy described his plans as best he could."

Joe nodded. "The part where kindly old Professor Drake disappears as the Black Dragon turns off his 'bent-light illusion'—that's a hologram."

"I've seen Xavier Mace completely change his face and body that way," Tom said. "The fact is, no one knows what he really looks like. In this story, he turns out to be the usual silly pulp villain—cruel, wolfish face, hawk nose, slit, soulless eyes." Tom shuddered. "But the bit where he disintegrates the guy in 'space-armor' with a superelectric bolt from his hands—well, I've seen the Dragon use energy bolts."

Frank looked a little sick. "You mean, Dad may really have seen that?"

Tom nodded. "I think it's for real. And obviously, the part about stealing a one-way time machine and hiding in the 'present' of 1932 has actually happened." He shrugged. "Too bad he couldn't have told us more about where the Black Dragon's hideout is or what city he plans to blow up."

"It's amazing enough that Fenton Hardy could get any message to us," said Mr. Swift. "He's stranded in the past until we know that our new round-trip machine works." His expression softened a little as he looked at the boys. "This time around we're not talking about a time trigger that flings something into the past, but a full-scale time machine. We're in the middle of the unmanned tests now."

Frank's head came up. "Really? How do you devise a test that proves something has really gone into the future?"

"We used a superaccurate clock, popped it forward a few hours, but it registered the passage of only a few millionths of a second," Tom said. He glanced at the wall clock. "In fact, the first test animal to make a round trip is due to warp in over at the physics lab."

They left the administration tower, stepping onto the same lawn they'd stormed across a couple of days before. The physics lab was one of the buildings they'd charged past, a big, solid structure.

Entering the test lab, they were greeted by a young man named Walton, the head technician. "We're expecting the machine in just seconds now."

A small army of technicians stood poised

around one of the lab tables. The air over the table suddenly glowed purple, and Tom and the others felt the unpleasant twisting sensation that always accompanied the use of a time machine. When it passed, there was a small capsule on the table. Walton and his techs swarmed around the bench, monitoring it for radiation, opening the capsule, and removing its occupant.

The "pilot" was a mouse. Tom watched as it got more physical tests than a returning astronaut.

Walton turned to Mr. Swift. "No indications of any ill effects, sir." He paused for a second. "The machine performs as Professor Reisenbach said it would."

"Great," Tom said.

Frank turned at the tone in Tom's voice. "Are you okay?" he asked. "I thought you'd be more excited about making this whole thing work."

"Yeah, we're a step ahead of the Black Dragon in the time-machine race. But he's still threatening the President to make him a silent partner in our government. And we haven't been able to find the time-warp bomb he's using to back up his threats. An entire city somewhere is going to be destroyed, and what can we do?"

"You did develop a warp detector," Frank pointed out. "With enough of them, we'll home in on the Black Dragon's base."

"But we don't have enough of them! Xavier Mace has either contaminated or bought up all the world's available iridium." Tom shook his head. "Every substitute I come up with leaves a detector with a range of about a square block."

"You'll come up with something," Joe said.

"If only we knew of a place where we could get lots of iridium, really cheap," Tom complained.

An odd look came over his face.

"I must be an idiot!" he exclaimed. "It's been staring me in the face all this time."

"You've figured out a substitute component for your detector?" Joe asked.

Tom shook his head. "I've figured out where to get all the iridium we need and not pay a cent for it."

Now Tom's father joined the conversation. "And where is all this cheap iridium?"

"Not where, Dad. When." Tom smiled at his father. "It's available for the taking—sixty-five million years ago."

12

The Hardys and Mr. Swift stood silent after Tom's brainstorm. From the looks on their faces, Tom judged their reaction was along the lines of, "Have you gone out of your mind?"

"Listen to me a minute before you think I'm completely crazy," he said. "I didn't pick the figure sixty-five million years out of a hat. That's when geologists and paleontologists date the end of the Cretaceous period and the death of the dinosaurs."

"I don't get the connection between dinosaurs and iridium," Joe said.

"You will," Tom responded. "In the geologic strata that mark the end of the age of dinosaurs, there's one layer that's abnormally rich in iridium."

"Wait a second," Frank Hardy said, his brow furrowed in thought. "I've read something about this. Some scientists have a theory that the dinosaurs became extinct because a giant asteroid crashed into the earth. Iridium is rare on earth but found in many asteroids. Dust from the impact—which included a lot of iridium particles—created an enormous cloud that circled the globe. The whole world was dark for years, the temperature plunged, the dinosaurs died out, and a thin layer of iridium was spread all over the earth's surface."

"Dust clouds making the earth go cold?" Joe scoffed. "That sounds like something you would read in *Unlikely Tales*."

"Not so unlikely," Frank said. "Whenever there's a major volcanic eruption, ash in the air spreads all over the planet. It reflects sunlight away from the earth's surface, and the average temperature for that year is lower than normal."

"And in volcanic zones, ash and debris in the air make it dark in the daytime, often for up to a week," Tom said. "Compared to what this killer asteroid is supposed to have done, an erupting volcano would be like a flea belching."

"Searching for this asteroid, if indeed there was one, is a clever solution to our iridium problem," Mr. Swift said. Judging from the expression on his father's face, however, Tom expected to hear a major "but."

Mr. Swift didn't let him down. "But I don't think the solution is as simple as going back to the age of the dinosaurs and sweeping up a lot of dust into a giant pan. As I recall, the iridium layer may be startlingly rich by normal standards, but it's hardly a mother lode. The iridium works out to something like a few parts per million in the regular dust and soil."

Tom grinned. "Actually, Dad, I wasn't thinking of pushing a broom to get the iridium. I thought I'd mine for it."

"Then I hate to disappoint you, son," Mr. Swift said, "but the latest theories suggest that this killer asteroid hit the earth somewhere near the Gulf of Mexico."

"I know that, Dad." Tom fought hard to keep a note of impatience out of his voice. "I wasn't expecting to get at the main body of the asteroid. But I'm willing to bet that as it came down through the atmosphere, chunks must have broken off. Big pieces of iridium might even have been blown back into the air by the impact. We're talking about an explosion that would equal thousands of atomic bomb blasts. Scientists think some debris was blown into orbit. I just have to find one fragment that fell to land."

Mr. Swift's eyes went from Tom to the small capsule with its furry passenger, still on the laboratory bench. "We've proven that a self-contained time machine works. But are you willing to be the first human guinea pig?"

Tom looked steadily at his father. "Wouldn't you be willing? Besides, Professor Reisenbach went through time with no ill effects that we could see.''

Mr. Swift shrugged, apparently not wanting to argue over that point. Instead he turned to practical matters. ''The Black Dragon's time limit is running out,'' he said. ''Even if you bring back all the iridium we need, we'll have to go into crash production to make enough detectors to find him before his deadline.''

Tom's father looked from one face to another. ''This will have to be a top-secret operation. I think we all know Xavier Mace well enough to believe he won't stand by his word if he suspects he'll lose. As soon as he thinks we can find him, he'll detonate his bomb and destroy a helpless city.''

They stood in silence for a long moment. Then Mr. Swift turned briskly to Walton and his team of technicians. ''We're going into production on a full-size time machine. You can call on all the facilities that won't be used for detector manufacturing. I want it ready by yesterday.''

Walton grinned. ''It's a shame we can't use the machine ourselves. Then we could do exactly what you're asking for.'' He started snapping instructions to his team, then turned back to Mr. Swift. ''What size time-warp field should we be working on?''

''Something large enough to fit around the TANC,'' Tom said. ''That's what I'll be taking back with me.''

Joe stared. ''You've got your own tank?''

Frank grinned. "Sounds like just the thing for driving on California freeways."

"It's an acronym, T-A-N-C," Tom said, spelling out the letters. "The initials stand for Transformable Ambulatory Nuclear-powered Craft. TANC is about the size of a monster truck and can transform itself into a jet-plane configuration. It runs on nuclear power." Tom grinned. "And it *is* built as tough as a tank."

"I see," Joe said, a little stunned. "It's not a tank. It's an atom-powered four-by-four that can sprout wings and fly."

"Sounds impressive," Frank said. "What about a crew? I may not be handy with the technical stuff, but I can help with the mining end of the operation."

"Hold on there, big brother," Joe Hardy protested. "You're not going and leaving me behind."

Tom looked embarrassed. "I'm afraid I'm leaving you both behind," he said. "This will be the longest time-jump we've ever attempted, on a machine that we really can't test. Too much could go wrong. We might calculate the wrong spatial coordinates and materialize inside a mountain. Although the power demands seem constant, we've never time-traveled on this scale before. What happens if we get stranded?"

"What happens if everything goes fine, but we get stepped on by a brontosaurus?" Joe asked.

"They've already died out by the era we're aiming for," Tom said.

"Who cares?" Joe responded. "Anything could happen. I'm still volunteering."

"That goes double," Frank said. "We want to do *something* to nail the Black Dragon, and it looks like this is the only way we can be useful."

"Guys, I appreciate what you're saying," Tom began. "But it wouldn't be fair—"

"I think Tom is saying that he has a better understanding of the dangers of this time jump," Mr. Swift said. "Dangers that even I hadn't taken into consideration."

"Maybe you'll feel better when I tell you who I am taking along," Tom said.

"Oh, we're not good enough to come along," Joe said hotly. "But somebody else is."

Tom shook his head. "I think that when you see him, you'll agree that Rob isn't just 'somebody.' " He picked up a phone and punched a code onto the keypad. "Rob," he said into the receiver, "get over to Lab Three in the physics building right away."

Both Frank and Joe Hardy stared in awed silence when Tom's gleaming robot assistant arrived a few moments later. "What's up, Tom?" Rob asked. "With me here, there's nobody to protect your lab."

"I take it that this robot is on our side, not the Black Dragon's," Frank said, taking in the large, human-shaped machine. "He looks a lot less, um—*clunky* is the word I'm looking for, I guess."

Rob's sensor eyes glowed. "Thanks. You must be Frank Hardy."

"Right," Frank said, a little surprised. "How did you know?"

"Oh, information gets around among us machines," Rob told him.

Joe was still taking in Rob's heavy metal arms and legs. "It's a lucky thing you didn't have him along when we first met you," he told Tom. "He'd have turned us into two little piles of chopped meat."

"If I'd known I would wind up playing tackle football without the ball, I *would* have brought him," Tom replied with a laugh. "Actually, Rob was with our technical staff, being fitted with special equipment. Before this whole crisis developed, he was going to be the test pilot for our time machine."

"It's safer than using a real person. All that's necessary is to make the driver's seat bigger," Rob said. "And to keep my hands free I have a lot of gizmos built in—like this camcorder."

Rob turned to face them, and a small lens extended from the center of his chest. "Everybody say 'Cheese!' "

Frank couldn't take his eyes off the robot. "I'm amazed that he seems to have so much personality. He even cracks jokes!"

"Not like the Black Dragon's mechanical flunkies," Joe said.

"It's all in the programming," Rob assured

them. "I'm just lucky that Tom is a great programmer."

"At any rate, I guess Rob is the best copilot you could ask for," Frank had to admit.

"Especially for any heavy work," Joe added.

Even as Tom and his father had developed what they now called Reisenbach units, the Swift complex's manufacturing facilities had been tooling up to build them. Within hours, the first time-warp modules were off the production lines.

Tom supervised as technicians installed the units under the fenders of the TANC vehicle. Rather than projecting the dimension-warping field inward to envelop an object, the new time machine projected its field outward, enveloping itself—and whatever it was attached to—in the field that twisted out of the four-D universe.

Based on appearances, the TANC was just a big, bright red pickup truck with a camper built onto its rear body, standing about twice as tall as Tom himself. As it stood in the middle of its mechanized hangar, it looked ready for a trip to the tall timber. Instead, Tom's parents, Sandra, and the Hardys were seeing Tom off on a trip beyond the dawn of history.

"I've plotted us to emerge in a section of Mexico we know was dry land at the time," Tom said. "It's near the estimated location of the asteroid impact. We'll set up a base camp and use small time-traveling drones to zero in on the date when the asteroid fell. Once we know that, we'll switch to jet-craft mode, take off, make a short time hop, and view the actual impact."

He shrugged. "Then it's a case of tracking a chunk and getting the iridium."

"I'm sure you don't need us to tell you to be careful," Mr. Swift said.

"Good luck, Tom," Sandra put in.

"And *do* be careful, Tom," his mother said.

"I still wish you had room for another passenger," Frank said with a grin.

"Yeah, but I don't think you'd enjoy riding on Rob's lap," Joe added. "Come back safe, Tom."

Tom boarded the TANC and got behind the controls. Rob was already strapped in beside him.

Outside, the spectators had cleared a large space around the TANC.

"Here we go," Tom said, activating the newly installed time-unit controls. His target date and spatial coordinates had already been fed in. All that remained was to power the unit up and hit the Go button.

The cab of the truck-shaped vehicle hummed with power. Again Tom felt a prickling sensation as the hairs on the back of his neck rose in the almost electric atmosphere.

He stabbed a finger at the button.

Outside the windshield, the universe disappeared in a mad swirl of blinding purple light.

13

The terrible stomach-twisting sensation that accompanied time jumps hit Tom, but in much worse form. It was as if giant hands had grabbed the whole universe around him and were trying to reshape it.

Of course, Tom knew that it was his viewpoint being twisted as the time machine reoriented itself among dimensional planes. But his knowledge did little to help the primitive, gut-level feeling that he was being twisted apart. The sensation was incredibly disgusting and seemed to last forever.

Then, abruptly, Tom's world returned to normal as the time machine completed its shift out of the three-dimensional universe. He glanced at the mission clock on the control panel. The whole process had taken only milliseconds.

Tom turned to Rob. "How'd you come through, big guy?"

"There was a momentary distortion of sensory input," Rob said. "I suspect it would be worse for organic life-forms than for mechanical types like me."

"You said it," Tom agreed fervently. "The test mice we sent couldn't tell us about it. And unfortunately, Professor Reisenbach never mentioned that the start of every time jump would wring you out like a damp wash towel."

He rested a hand over his stomach. "I'm glad I didn't have a big meal before we took off."

Tom quickly went down a checklist, examining each indicator on the TANC's control board, making sure the vehicle was in complete operating order. Then he leaned back in his seat, staring out the front windshield.

He didn't quite know what he expected to see. They had twisted out of the three-dimensional universe he knew, so there should be no familiar shapes outside of the warp field. But something familiar was out there—the same purplish glow that seemed to flash at the beginning of time jumps. It was as if the TANC were parked in the midst of a featureless purple fog so heavy that Tom couldn't even make out the ground.

Wait a minute, Tom thought. It's not exactly featureless. There are ripples in the fog, patterns of some kind. He tried to follow them with his eyes, to make some sort of sense out of them, but they came and went too quickly for him to get a clear glimpse. Somehow, though, they gave the impression of tremendous speed, as if he were roaring down a roadway at a few hundred miles an hour while trying to read road signs.

Tom's eyes began to ache, his head pounded, and his stomach threatened to revolt. "Rob," Tom said, "do your electronic eyes register anything out there?"

For several long moments Rob sat silently, his photocell eyes glowing. At last he spoke up. "I sense something—a suggestion of coherent forms in the indistinctness that seems to surround us. But the glimpses are too fleeting. All I receive is a sensation of great velocity."

"Well, we're moving back down the stream of time at a pretty fast clip. The technicians were talking in terms of moving three hours in a microsecond." Tom did some quick figuring on his pocket calculator. "That means we're going back a day every eight millionths of a second. Even so, going back sixty-five million years will take more than two days."

"Fifty-two hours and—" Rob cut off as Tom glared at him. "Yes? Oh, sorry, Tom. You already know that."

"Does looking at the purple light show out there have any ill effects on you?" Tom asked.

Rob looked out the window again. "No."

"Well, if I keep watching it, I think I'm going to get carsick. Or is that time-machine sick? I think I'll change the TANC to space-travel mode. That covers the windows and opens a bathroom, which I think I'll need sometime in the next two days."

Tom activated the control panel marked Transform and tapped a few buttons. A deep-seated humming filled the TANC as an airtight seal slid across the windows. Although he couldn't see the process, Tom knew that the van's boxy form was turning into a sleek bullet shape.

Noise also came from the interior section behind them as a table, chair, and bed unfolded. A kitchen area appeared too, with a microwave oven and a compact freezer holding frozen foods and liquids. Tom spent most of the travel time in the crew quarters, going over a thick pile of paper containing data recorded by instruments at Swift Enterprises during the disaster that killed Dr. Reisenbach.

"I guess if the universe had to go berserk, the best place it could happen would be in the middle of a science complex," he said with a grin.

Tom looked considerably more serious when he rejoined Rob in the control cabin for touchdown.

"Everything all right?" Rob asked.

"Frankly, no." Tom transformed the TANC back to truck mode with jerky jabs at the controls. "Professor Reisenbach once suggested that the fabric of time was fragile. He didn't know *how* fragile. The readings we picked up when those time-traveling robots converged are downright scary. They show that even a single time jump can put dangerous strains on the space-time continuum. Rob, we're on a riskier trip than we imagined."

The mission clock beeped a warning. Seconds later Tom felt the wrenching, twisting sensation as he emerged back into the three-dimensional universe. Then the TANC dropped straight down for about a foot.

They rode out the jolt, and Tom cleared the windshield. The TANC had landed on a low hill covered with coarse grass. Not many flowers, Tom noted, taking in the vista. Then he remembered. Flowering plants had come into existence only in the last half of the Cretaceous period.

In the distance was a wooded area. Only at his second glance did Tom realize that he couldn't identify any of the individual trees. He could see giant ferns, plants that looked like palm and pine trees, and something that looked like a swamp horsetail, only it was the size of a tree.

"No dinosaurs dancing past," Tom reported to Rob, glancing over the terrain. He opened the door. "Let's start sending out the drones."

Rob unloaded twenty football-size metal containers. They were shielded camcorders, outfitted with Reisenbach time-travel units.

"The problem with prehistory is that we have no record of when the killer asteroid came down," Tom said. "So we'll send these little guys off to scout out this location in ten-year intervals over the next two centuries."

"How will we know when they've found anything?"

"Rob, one look will tell us whether that asteroid hit." Tom winced at the twisting sensation of the first drone launch. "And for safety's sake, don't send off all those drones from one place. Remember what happened to Reisenbach. The combined warp effect might blow you up."

Rob stood very still. "Right, Tom."

The drones soon returned, and Tom quickly checked the camcorder viewers. He turned to Rob, holding out one of the drones. "Take a look here."

Rob raised the camera to one of his gleaming photocell eyes. "I can hardly see anything. It's very dark. Was this taken at night?"

"According to the readout, this is high noon a hundred and fifty years from now. It looks like night because of those clouds. They're debris from the asteroid impact."

Tom started resetting the controls on the drones. "Well, now that we know what year the asteroid fell, we still have to pinpoint the exact day."

It took three more passes with the drones to give Tom a firm date for the impact and a good idea of the hour. "Now we load up and make a short time hop to the fateful day," he told Rob.

He took one of the drones and taped a message for his family and friends, now tens of millions of years in the future. Tom sent the machine on its epic journey forward through time. Then he helped Rob load the rest of the drones back aboard the TANC, strapped in, and powered up the time machine. Decades flew by in the wink of an eye. The only drawback was that there was hardly any time to recuperate between the wrench of leaving and the twist of arriving.

After taking a few moments to recover—and to make sure no dinosaurs were blocking his takeoff lanes—Tom hit the Transform controls. "Okay," he said, "let's get this show into the air."

The cab shook slightly as parts of the vehicle around them began to change shape. The boxy lines of the TANC's truck form converted to a sleek, aerodynamic shape for flying. Wings unfolded, the monster-size road wheels sank into their wells and were covered up. Hydraulics extended other wheels as landing gear.

There was a brief jolt as the transmission disconnected and the engines were rerouted to turbine thrusters. While the wings stabilized, Tom and Rob went through the preflight checklist.

"We're ready," Rob reported, his big metal fingers dancing at incredible speed over a console. "Sensors indicate that we have to make a seventy-nine-degree turn to face into the wind. There is sufficient open land for takeoff."

Tom operated the thruster controls. The high

whine of the engines filled the cab. Smoothly the TANC swung around.

"You're on the mark," Rob said.

Tom eased the engines down. "Here comes the takeoff."

He pushed the throttles forward, and the TANC began rolling. It was a bumpy ride. After all, this wasn't a paved airport runway. But the TANC had been built to take punishment.

Tom pulled back on the stick, still goosing the throttle. The turbine whine became a scream, then a roar, and the TANC's ride suddenly became smooth as silk. They had taken to the air.

The line of trees was still ahead of them, and Tom pulled the now-sleek form of the TANC into a steep ascent. The wind of their passage shook the fronds on the fern trees as they passed. Tom concentrated on achieving lots of altitude. He wanted to be above the range of any flying creatures. No sense in taking the risk of getting clipped by a pterodactyl.

When they were high enough, Tom turned to Rob. "Let's set the autopilot for a course to the Caribbean Sea. I want all radar and far-sensing systems on highest gain. We don't want to be caught in the asteroid's way or in the shock waves as it comes down."

Below them rolled an untouched landscape. This was North America, millions of years before the first humans walked the earth. Tom felt an odd pang of loneliness at the vista. Usually when he looked down from an airplane, even in fairly empty country, Tom could spot some sign of human habitation. It might be a house, tilled fields, or even a single straight ribbon of a road stretching across an otherwise desolate expanse.

Here there was nothing. Tom saw rivers and grassland, forests, and the occasional glimpse of a huge animal moving across the ground far below.

Then they were over water. The Caribbean was a much larger sea in this era. It opened not only onto the Atlantic, but also the Pacific Ocean, as well as the shallow sea that split North America into two land masses.

An insistent beeping from the autopilot announced that they had arrived at the computed location. It was a stretch of shallow water only a hundred meters deep. Tom knew that what was now sea bottom would become the Yucatán peninsula, and near the future town of Chicxulub geologists would find a circular impact scar more than a hundred miles wide.

Tom was adjusting the TANC's course to circle the target zone when Rob suddenly spoke up. "Long-distance trackers locking onto something."

Those sensors had been built to detect hostile intercontinental ballistic missiles. Now, however, they traced the path of the deadliest projectile earth may ever have experienced.

Tom gripped the TANC's joystick. "Are we in the way?"

"No. No course deviation required," Rob said. "It's huge. And it's coming in fast."

Tom went to activate his own screen, then brought his hand back. He didn't have to use the radar. Now he saw the asteroid with his own eyes.

It was a shiny point high in the sky, coming closer with terrifying speed. As it came deeper into the atmosphere, friction with the air caused the six-mile-long mass of the space invader to burn until it outshone the sun.

"Cockpit screens!" Tom cried sharply, and Rob activated the control that darkened the view from the cabin. Even so, they could follow the burning mass of light on its downward plunge.

Tom fought the steering controls as the plane was buffeted with massive air turbulence from the heat and speed of the asteroid. "Keep tracking, and bring the time-warp equipment on-line."

Tom's hair bristled as the electrical charge of the readied time machine filled the cab.

"Tracking!" Rob called. "A large piece has broken off from the central mass of the asteroid. Plotting its course—it lands in what will become eastern Tennessee."

The TANC was fighting winds that would make a hurricane look tame, and the killer asteroid hadn't even hit the water yet.

"We're out of here," Tom said, stabbing a finger at the time trigger.

As he spoke, the asteroid impacted. The blinding flash cut through the cockpit as if the shielding didn't exist.

"I hope there's purple light out there as well," Tom said fervently, unable to see. "If we're still here when the shock wave arrives—"

His words were cut off by the wrenching sensation of time warp.

14

Frank Hardy stared at the screen as the asteroid smashed into the earth's crust. A mushroom cloud rose from the impact site, reaching high into the stratosphere. Then the viewpoint shifted, pulling back so far that the earth was just a small globe on the screen.

An inky blot over the Caribbean Sea disfigured the globe. In seconds, plumes of blackness spread across the planet. But they didn't hide the sudden change of the shorelines of Europe, western Africa, and the huge island that Frank knew would later be eastern North America.

Those must be the tidal waves hitting, Frank thought. He shuddered at the idea of what that would have been like. Walls of water miles high must have slammed into the shorelines. Meanwhile, the black stain covered more and more of the earth, until finally the planet became a featureless black ball.

Joe Hardy stuck his head into the computer lab.

"You should check out these machines," Frank said in deep admiration. "Tom ran a simulation program to show what probably happened when that asteroid hit. Real serious stuff."

"I thought you might be more interested in real life," Joe said. "Mr. Swift called to say that Tom sent a time drone back with a message."

When they reached Mr. Swift's office, the whole Swift family was gathered by his desk. "Sit down, boys," he said, his hand over a button on his desk console. "The tape's already in the VCR."

He pressed the button, and Tom's face sprang into larger-than-life existence on the office wall.

"This thing should appear in the physics lab a couple of hours after I left. Well, I've arrived safely in the Cretaceous. I spent the trip here looking over the data from the disaster at the supercollider. Dad, there's bad news in those readings." He reported his findings.

"Anyway," Tom concluded, "we've managed to pinpoint the date and place of the asteroid crash. Next we take off to check it out, to see if any chunks fly off and where they go. We'll give you the whole story when we get back."

Tom grinned. "You may be interested to know that the scientists are right. There was a dust cloud, and it darkened the earth for months on end." The tape ended, and the wall dissolved in a mass of television snow.

"Months without sunlight," Tom's father muttered. "That would have been enough to kill off the plants the dinosaurs lived on in addition to the other effects. At impact the fireball boiled off enough water to create a greenhouse effect, raising temperatures. And then there was the acid rain."

Joe looked baffled. "Acid rain? Like the stuff created from factory smoke?"

Mr. Swift nodded. "But back then the 'factory' was a white-hot asteroid fusing air molecules into nitrogen oxides. When they mixed with water vapor, you got rain like battery acid."

"Dark, cold, heat, and acid," Frank said. "No wonder the dinosaurs died off."

"Well, Tom will tell us all about it when he returns," Sandra said.

"Yes, all we can do is wait." Frank noticed Mrs. Swift still staring at the screen. She's worrying about Tom, he thought.

"There is something I can do, though," Mr. Swift said. "I'm going to look into the lab reports from the destruction of the supercollider. Until we've reached some conclusions, all production and testing of Reisenbach units is suspended."

Harlan Ames called the Hardys later that afternoon. "Got an FBI agent on the line," he said. "The man wants to thank you boys."

Baffled, Frank put the call on the Swift home speakerphone so Joe could hear as well.

A new voice came over the line. "Frank and Joe Hardy?"

"We're here," Joe said.

"This is Agent Carey of the FBI," said the man on the phone. "I understand we have you to thank for catching a very elusive thief."

"That's more than we're understanding right now," Frank said. "Who is this thief?"

"His name is Howard Zeman. He's gone around the country for years, it seems, stealing rare material from university libraries."

Frank remembered the warning he'd issued to the library association. "They caught him stealing papers written by Ernst Reisenbach?"

"Not exactly," Agent Carey said. "He was after something else, but the librarian at the University of California's San Damian campus remembered the warning and your description. She let him into the secure storage area, locked the door, and called the police. They found him stashing away two rare books and a bunch of old magazines, and arrested him."

Frank turned to Joe. "This Zeman guy must be working for the Black Dragon," he said in an undertone. "Maybe he even knows where Mace is."

Speaking louder for the benefit of the phone, Frank said, "We'd like to talk to Mr. Zeman. He may be involved in some thefts touching on current research here at Swift Enterprises."

"That's very irregular," Carey objected.

"Can you hold for a moment? I'd like to alert someone else about this." Frank got Mr. Swift on the intercom and explained the situation.

"Government agents are out beating the bushes for the Black Dragon," Mr. Swift said. "How did they miss this?"

"They're handicapped by the need to keep the Black Dragon's threats secret in order to prevent panic," Frank said. "I think Joe and I might be able to handle the questioning."

"If you two could get Ernst Reisenbach across the country with Xavier Mace snapping at your heels, I'm sure you can handle the interrogation," Mr. Swift said. "Let me get on the phone."

Thanks to Mr. Swift's intervention, the Hardys set off for the San Damian jail with a borrowed car and FBI authorization. When they walked into his cell, Howard Zeman gave them a blank look.

Frank had to admit that Zeman was one of the most ordinary-looking people he'd ever seen. He was somewhere between thirty and forty. His slightly round face with its snub nose was absolutely forgettable, his drab hair not exactly brown, not exactly black. The Hardys had known a secret agent with the same air of ordinariness. He was actually a dangerous operative. Frank reminded himself not to be fooled by appearances.

Zeman squinted his muddy brown eyes. "You don't look like cops," he said in a flat voice.

"We're not," Frank said. "We just want to talk to you about some of the papers you've taken. Papers written by Ernst Reisenbach."

"What papers?" Zeman said, acting as if he'd never heard Reisenbach's name.

"I guess you haven't heard yet," Joe said. "The FBI executed a search warrant on your house in Nebraska. They found it crammed with rare books from the fifteenth and very early sixteenth centuries, dating to the beginning of mechanical printing. What do they call those?"

"Incunabula." Zeman supplied the word, then stopped, his face twisting in annoyance.

"That's right, incunabula." Joe smiled. "Funny you would know such a specialized word. But then, I suppose you learned a lot in those university libraries you visited. Those souvenirs you took from universities all over the country are marked and identifiable. You're going away for a long time, Zeman. Make things easier for yourself. Tell us where the Reisenbach papers went. We know they weren't in your house."

Zeman shrugged, shrinking in upon himself. "You promising me a deal?"

Joe smiled. "I'm promising you nothing but hard time if you don't talk."

"And if I do?"

"I guarantee that we'll intercede on your behalf, for whatever it's worth," said Joe.

Zeman shrugged again, then nodded. "Okay.

It was a private job. This guy hired me. I did it for the easy bucks. It gave me travel money for my real work.''

For a brief second Zeman's face came alive. "I know and understand ancient books like no one on earth. Why should they be locked away from me?"

"That's fine," Frank said, leading them back to the track he wanted to follow. "But tell me more about this guy you did private jobs for."

"I don't know how he found out, but he knew I was an expert at ripping off universities. So I'd remove science papers from libraries for him. It was easy enough, and he paid very well. This Reisenbach job was the largest he ever gave me. I was going all over the country."

"What did the guy look like?" Joe wanted to know.

Zeman shrugged. "Funny thing. He looked like a professor himself. He was skinny, balding, gray hair . . . oh, and he wore those funny half-glasses that you can look over."

"Professor Drake," Joe said, getting excited.

"Alias Xavier Mace," Frank whispered. He turned to Zeman. "How did you get the papers to him? Did you deliver them somewhere?"

"I just dropped them in the mail," Zeman said. "The address was a post office box in Manhattan." He recited the address as Frank wrote it down.

The Hardys thanked him and left.

"A perfect drop," Frank said bitterly as they

left the cells. "A crowded post office in a big city. When the government stakes it out, I bet they catch nobody."

"A dead end," Joe agreed, leading the way down the corridor. "Mace can sure pick 'em. Imagine using a nut who steals rare books as your technospy."

"You wouldn't think Zeman was a nut if he collected baseball cards instead of incunabula," Frank kidded. They were passing the squad room when he suddenly stopped in the doorway. A detective had a couple of books and a pile of old pulp magazines on his desk. He was looking through one of the magazines, and Frank recognized the cover.

He'd know that brass bikini anywhere. The cop was reading the issue of *Unlikely Tales* with their father's story in it.

"Where did you get that?" Frank forced the words through suddenly dry lips.

The detective closed the magazine. "This? It's evidence in the Zeman case. He stole a whole year's worth of these magazines from the Popular Culture Studies research library at the university. Every issue printed in 1932."

Frank and Joe stared at each other, then hurried back to the Swift complex.

"How did Mace know about the magazine?" Joe asked as they drove through the mountains.

"Maybe his agents got wind of our search for copies," Frank said. "At least he doesn't seem to know which issue he needs—yet."

His face set in hard lines. "But he's obviously looking for Dad, and he knows what year. We can't be sure that Zeman was the only one out looking for copies of *Unlikely Tales*."

"We've got to warn Dad!" Joe said.

"We can do better than that," Frank told him. "We're going to go back, pick him up, and bring him to the present."

"How are we going to do that?" Joe demanded. "Tom's father has put all time travel on hold."

"But Swift technicians have already built several two-way time machines," Frank said. "As you'd know if you noticed anything but Sandra Swift. There's a whole warehouse full of tiny new units—small enough for a person to wear, since the field doesn't have to be big enough to cover a truck. But the field thrown by one of those machines will fit around three people with no problem."

"I think the people guarding that warehouse might raise a problem or two," Joe said.

"I don't care about guards or how risky Mr. Swift thinks time travel may be," Frank said. "We might never get another shot at a time machine. Even now, the Black Dragon could have warped somebody back to kill Dad. We've got to get back to 1932—and fast!"

"I've never hot-wired a time machine before," Joe said. "But I guess there's a first for everything."

Frank took them through the front gate of the Swift complex and parked their borrowed company car in the lot to the right of the entrance. Then they started across the grounds, passing the administration building as they headed for the manufacturing works against the eastern perimeter.

No one paid attention as they strolled past the long, low-slung manufacturing building. Workers and technicians swarmed around pallets of incoming electrical materials. "Components for the time-warp detectors," Frank whispered.

Farther along the building front, the activity ceased. Frank stopped to tie his shoe. "This is the shop where they worked on the time machines. The next bay is storage space."

"And I guess that's where they're keeping the machines. There's a guard standing outside."

"Then we'll have to get him out of the way." As Frank rose to his feet, he scooped up a small rock from the ground. They walked on till the guard wasn't looking at them. Then Frank whipped around, hurling the stone at a second-story window above the guard's head.

The security man whirled at the sound of impact, took one look at the spiderweb of cracks in the window, and whipped out his gun. At the same time, Frank yanked Joe down onto the ground. As the guard came over, Frank yelled, "It was a guy with a gun! He was dressed in black, standing on top of that hill over there." Frank pointed at a rise fronting the warehouse. "He must have ducked down the far slope."

Gun at the ready, the guard started climbing the hill, speaking into his walkie-talkie.

Frank got up, leading Joe into the warehouse. "Harlan Ames is going to be real mad at that guy if we get away with this."

Inside, he opened a box, removing one of the time-travel units. "Looks simple enough," he said.

The time machine looked like a life vest made of silvery metallic material, with boxy panels containing power cells and warp components. There was also a pocket that held the control module.

Frank shrugged into the rig, sealed the front, and took the control in his hand.

"Looks like the remote from a fancy VCR," Joe joked as his brother began punching buttons.

"Let's just hope we don't get cable TV," Frank said. "Okay, it's powering up." He felt a prickling sensation as if electricity were filling the air. "Get over here."

As Joe went to join his brother, the warehouse door opened with a screech.

Great, Frank thought. We're caught red-handed.

15

For Tom Swift and Rob the robot, the universe seemed to contort as they warped into the time stream for an instant, then out again. The trip took about three one-thousandths of a second.

"Through the wringer again," Tom said shakily after they'd made the transition back to the three dimensions they knew.

The TANC was still on autopilot, circling the site of the asteroid impact. According to the console readouts, that spectacular event was now a year in the past. The readings said it was spring and midday, but beyond the cockpit it was pitch-black. The TANC shuddered to make headway against strong winds.

"Set a course for the location where the asteroid fragment crashed down," Tom told Rob. "The sooner we finish with this era, the better."

Below them the ocean tossed in angry, towering waves. The TANC had to fight its way through several storm fronts before it finally reached land.

Again the view of the ground below was vastly changed from what Tom had seen on his journey to the impact site. The landscape seemed blighted. Trees were dying, and even from the air Tom could spot giant carcasses that had been picked clean.

He was quickly able to spot the path of the chunk that had broken loose from the asteroid. The heat blast of the white-hot meteor's passage had scorched the land below. A vast track of burnt-out forest and grasslands pointed straight as an arrow across the plains.

Whatever animals had been on the blasted land must have died immediately in flames. But as Tom dropped the TANC lower to scout around, he found many desperate creatures trying to cross the blackened area. A herd of triceratops, no more than skin and bone, stumbled along, looking like gigantic rhinos except for their three-spiked head armor. Tom knew these were plant eaters. From the looks of them, they hadn't found any plants to eat in a long time.

Another figure burst from the cover of some trees. Tom recognized the newcomer immediately as *Tyrannosaurus rex*, the biggest meat eater that ever walked the earth. The monster carnivore did not look as skinny as the plant eaters, Tom noticed.

Sure, he thought, there must be lots of dead and dying animals for him to feed on—for now.

The tyrannosaur was stalking a triceratops that was lagging behind the herd. Tom had watched this scene in countless old movies, but it was different to see it in the flesh. For one thing, the real beasts moved much faster than the Hollywood special-effects monsters.

The triceratops spotted the predator, turned around, and charged. Charred trees crumbled from the vibrations of huge, pounding footsteps. The tyrannosaur leapt nimbly aside, tearing at its prey's sides with foot-long fangs.

Staggering away, the gaunt plant eater tried to aim its three horns at the oncoming predator. But the tyrannosaur slammed into the other beast's flanks, its serrated teeth slashing and slashing again. The triceratops went down, and the meat eater began to feast.

Tom turned away, shuddering.

"I think that's the impact crater ahead," Rob suddenly reported.

Now Tom could make out the shape of a huge pockmark in the ground. Burnt trees lay on the ground, radiating from the round shape like the sunbeams little kids draw, which fan out from the central circle of the sun.

They must have been knocked down by the shock waves when the meteor hit, Tom thought. He remembered the deadly dazzle of the parent asteroid. This chunk must have been glowing like the sun, too.

"I just hope there's enough iridium left after the crash to make this worthwhile," Tom said as he brought the TANC in for a landing inside the crater.

Raw stone walls surrounded them, turned glassy in places by the heat of the meteor's impact.

Tom looked around. "This was not the place to be standing when that chunk of rock came down."

He opened the door, shivering slightly as a chill wind blew at him. An odd, sharp tang filled the air. "Let's get to work," Tom said to Rob.

Together they unloaded the testing and digging apparatus from the rear of the TANC. Their first move was to set up a circle of floodlights to illuminate the center of the crater floor. "Now we can see what we're doing," Tom said.

Next they erected Tom's new core driller in the circle of lights. This machine was like an oil drilling test rig except that its cylindrical drill bit wouldn't go down as far.

When the drill core came back up, they would have a layer-by-layer view of the crater floor, down to forty feet below.

"Somewhere in there we ought to hit iridium," Tom said as he screwed lengths of tubing together to make the drill tripod. "The closer to the surface, the better I'll like it."

"I'm with you on that, Tom," Rob said as he raised one of the finished tripod legs and clamped it in place. "Too much digging gets my finish all scratched and dusty."

"Let's hope that will be the worst of it." Tom glanced around the bare crater floor at the rocky crags of the walls around them. "Although, to tell the truth, I don't see any dinosaurs venturing in here to disturb our work."

Even as he said that, Tom detected a flicker of motion in the darkness beyond their circle of light. The glaring floodlights on their poles made the outer darkness even more impenetrable.

Still, Tom was certain he'd seen something move.

"Do you need my help to finish setting this thing up?" he asked Rob.

The robot surveyed the remaining work. "I can handle it myself. It will take slightly longer, though."

"Take all the time you want," Tom said, heading back to the TANC. After climbing into the cab, he sorted among personal effects until he emerged wearing a heavier jacket and carrying what looked like a short-barreled shotgun.

Rob's gleaming eyes took in the weapon Tom carried. From shoulder stock to muzzle it was only two feet long, although the barrel of the gun was much wider than normal—about an inch and a quarter.

"Going hunting?" Rob asked.

"I hope not," Tom said. "I saw something move out on the crater floor, and I don't intend to check empty-handed." He gestured toward the short-barreled weapon he carried. "This is an update of something Dad invented. Back then he called it his electric rifle."

"I remember reading about that," Rob said. "Does yours shoot lightning bolts, too?"

"No, I powered it down. This baby just gives a nasty electric shock to anything I fire it at. I figure that should be enough to discourage even a large dinosaur."

Tom glanced once more into the nearly impenetrable murk beyond the lights. "At least I hope so."

Rob turned to stare in the direction Tom was looking, his photocell eyes gleaming. "I don't detect anything nearby."

"Hey, I'm not sure we have anything to worry about here," Tom said. "I can't imagine any big dinosaurs going rock-climbing on the crater walls. But maybe something smaller was already down here and noticed our lights. I figure it ought to be checked out."

With his gun at the ready, Tom stepped to the edge of the floodlit circle. "And, Rob?"

"Yes, Tom?"

"If you hear me scream for help, come running."

"Got it." Rob went back to work on the core driller.

Tom wished he could be as matter-of-fact as he stepped out into the darkness.

He was being paranoid, he knew. Logic told him there couldn't be a thirty-foot-tall, hungry specimen of *T. rex* standing in the shadows, ready to devour him.

For one thing, Tom told himself, the light would reflect off its eyes or fangs. Somehow, though, he wasn't exactly comforted by the thought as he set off across the crater floor.

Before he'd left on the search, Tom had debated whether to carry a flashlight. He had finally decided the light would call too much attention to himself, so he would have to rely on the dim natural illumination coming from the deeply clouded sky. That meant that the farther he got from the work site, the more the darkness would close in on him.

After working in those bright lights, I'm effectively blind, he thought. I'll have to wait a few seconds for my night vision to kick in.

He closed his eyes for a second to speed the process. The image of the huge tyrannosaur teeth tearing into the flesh of the triceratops ran through his mind.

Tom opened his eyes.

He was finally getting used to the gloom when he heard a rattling noise to his left.

Peering hard into the darkness, he stepped quietly in that direction, his weapon gripped tightly in one hand.

Another noise came, this time from straight ahead. Tom walked stealthily, his running shoes not making a sound. The muzzle of the shock rifle was pointed toward the sound. What had the noise been? A clawed foot scratching across rubble?

Tom squinted, willing his eyes to pierce the murky shadows. He decided to circle to the left and try to outflank whatever was ahead.

This time the rattling came from his right. With luck, he'd be able to get behind the unseen intruder and catch it in profile against the wall of lights in the center of the crater.

Holding his breath, Tom moved crabwise in a large circle. Soon he'd be at the crater wall, with hard rock behind him and a clear view of the noise maker silhouetted in the lights.

Tom grinned in triumph. Yes, the rattling was definitely off to his left now. He'd circled behind whatever creature might be wandering in the darkness.

Then a voice to his right said, "Drop the shotgun, Swift. I've got you right in my sights."

16

Joe Hardy watched his brother, Frank, desperately go for the control button that would warp them out of the warehouse. Then he grabbed Frank's wrist, stopping him. Joe had just recognized the figure standing in the doorway.

"Wh-what are you doing here?" he stammered to Sandra Swift.

"That's just what I was going to ask you," Sandra said angrily. "I looked out the window of my father's office and saw you two come back. But instead of heading for the administration building, you went skulking off to the manufacturing plants. I came to see what was going on, and I find you stealing one of the time machines." She pointed at the silvery vest Frank was wearing. "The big question now is, why?"

"We're doing it for Dad," Joe said. "You probably heard that the police picked up the guy who was stealing Reisenbach's papers. We learned that he also stole a year's worth of *Unlikely Tales*—from 1932."

Sandra went pale as this information sank in. "How did the Black Dragon find out about that?"

"We don't know," Frank said. "All we know is that our father is in terrible danger. Xavier Mace could be sending assassins back right now."

"So we decided to go back and get Dad before they get a shot at him," Joe said.

Sandra frowned. "But my father stopped all time travel research."

"Right, Sandra. And by the time we persuade your father to ease up on that, the Black Dragon might have an army combing 1932." Joe turned pleading eyes to her. "We figured we'd just go."

Sandra Swift licked her lips, torn between conflicting feelings. Outside the warehouse, they heard the pounding of running feet—lots of them—coming toward them.

Joe watched Sandra's face tighten, as if she'd made up her mind. Stepping out of the warehouse, she pointed toward a distant building. "He went around that corner!" she yelled.

The footsteps drummed off, and Sandra turned back to the Hardys, giving them a lopsided smile. "Well, don't just stand there," she said. "Get going."

Joe joined Frank, and the world disappeared in a rush of purple light.

When the glow died away an instant later, they were in a dim, totally enclosed room.

Joe staggered a little at his first exposure to time travel, his hand on his stomach. "Remind me to tell the Swifts they ought to put a supply of barf bags on that thing."

He quickly surveyed their dim surroundings. "Where are we, anyway?"

"We're in a little-known corner of Grand Central Station, in Manhattan," Frank said. "Remember the case where we tracked down that crime baron hiding out under the station? This is one of the secret rooms we were led to by those homeless people who helped us."

Frank grinned. "Oh, and the time is mid-May 1932."

"That's why I didn't recognize the place," said Joe. "There isn't sixty years of dust on the floor." He gave his brother a puzzled look. "Why did you send us here?"

"Two reasons," Frank said. "One, it's a little more private than popping out of thin air in the middle of Times Square. And two, it's close to the offices of Lane and Jones, the publishers of *Unlikely Tales.*"

"Then let's head over there, get Dad's address, and get out of here." Joe moved to the door.

"After we find a safe place to leave this

gizmo," Frank said, slipping the time machine from his back. He led the way up to the station concourse.

High-vaulted, polished stone walls echoed with the announcements of train arrivals and departures. The floor below hummed with the passage of thousands of people hurrying to or from their trains. Almost all the men wore hats or caps, and even the shabbiest had a suit jacket on. The women wore a variety of light print dresses and close-fitting hats.

"Now I know what they mean by the saying 'As crowded as Grand Central,' " Joe muttered as they made their way through the throng. As they passed the shops, he stared in disbelief at the prices on the hand-lettered signs. "That soda fountain advertises an ice cream sundae for a dime!" he burst out. "And look over there—a bottomless cup of coffee for five cents."

Frank laughed. "You sound just like Professor Reisenbach, only in reverse. This is 1932, remember? Things are a lot cheaper."

"At these prices we could buy up half the city with our pocket change," Joe said, visions of wealth dancing before his eyes. "Think about it. Maybe we could buy some Babe Ruth baseball cards. Maybe the first issue of *Superman.*"

"Or maybe you could go to jail for counterfeiting," Frank said, quickly pouring cold water on his brother's greedy daydreams. "Don't you think people will get a little suspicious when they notice the money you're using to pay for those treasures is dated fifty years in the future?"

"And how are you going to fool the person you're going to leave that with?" Joe asked, pointing at the time machine in Frank's arms.

"I don't have to fool a person, just a machine." Frank stepped up to a bank of automatic lockers, put the backpack-shaped machine inside, closed the door, put a nickel in the slot, and withdrew a key from the lock. "Okay?"

"Okay," Joe said, feeling a little silly. "Let's hope the rest of our visit here goes as smoothly."

But when they finally reached the editorial offices of *Unlikely Tales,* three blocks away, they found a serious roadblock. "I'm afraid it's against our policy to give out authors' addresses," a stern-looking young woman said. The sign on her desk said Assistant to the Editor.

"It's very important for us to talk with Mr. Hardy," Joe said, desperately improvising. "You see, we're only in town for a limited time."

He glanced at Frank, hoping he'd have an idea. His brother only shrugged as the woman shook her head.

"I'm sorry, boys, but those are our rules. If you want to get in touch with Mr. Hardy, you can always write to our Letters page. Perhaps he'll write you back."

She softened a little at their distressed faces.

"Fenton Hardy is turning out to be a very popular author—and on just one story, too. I had another man in asking about him earlier today."

The woman's lips thinned. "He was a very rough type and got quite nasty when I explained why I couldn't give him the address he wanted. I was quite glad he missed me when he tried again."

"He tried again?" Joe asked.

"The man must have come back while I was out to lunch," the editor's assistant said. "He was coming out the door when I returned with my sandwich."

The Hardys exchanged horrified glances.

A rough customer asking for Dad's address, Joe thought. That has Black Dragon written all over it!

"Uh, how long ago did this happen?" he asked, trying to keep his voice level.

The young woman glanced at a wall clock. "I'd say it was a good hour ago."

Joe's mind raced. They *needed* that address. He had to come up with some way for them to get it. "Well, there was another reason why we came to the offices of this wonderful magazine." He flashed his widest smile at the young woman. Please let her buy this, he prayed. "We also hoped to buy some back issues, to complete our collection."

"We get many requests like that." The young woman smiled and rose from behind her desk. "Follow me, and I'll show you what we have."

Joe followed the assistant down the hall to a storage closet, frantically waving behind his back for Frank to stay.

If I can keep her distracted for just a few minutes, Frank will have a shot at the files.

Joe returned with the woman soon, pasting a disappointed look on his face as he walked back down the corridor. Frank was sitting quietly in the chair by the assistant's desk.

"Gee, Frank," Joe said, "I didn't realize this keen magazine goes right back to 1928. We don't have enough money to buy all the issues we need."

"Gosh, that's disappointing," Frank joined right in. "Maybe we can mail in a list with a money order. We could even put in a letter to Mr. Hardy."

"That would be swell," Joe said. "Thanks a lot, miss."

"You're welcome, boys," the young lady said.

They kept sappy smiles on their faces until they were out the door. Then they became all business. "I've got Dad's address," Frank said. "It's 505 West Twenty-seventh Street."

"That other guy has a good hour's start on us." Joe looked plainly worried. "How fast can we get down there, if we can't use any of our money?"

"Do you want to risk another time jump?" Frank asked.

Joe shook his head.

"Then if you've got a nickel, we can take the subway," Frank said. "That's all it costs, but I only have one nickel on me."

Joe rattled his pockets for a moment. "Got one. Let's go."

They found the Forty-second Street subway station surprisingly clean. "You get a lot for five cents," Joe muttered as they dashed down several flights of stairs.

Waiting on the subway platform was agony. At last, the crosstown train came in. They rode it to the Times Square stop. On arrival, Joe led a wild charge up steep stairways and down dim hallways until they reached the platform for the West Side local.

A train was just pulling in as they reached the top of the steps. Joe dove for the doors, battling them until Frank managed to squeze in.

"Only two stops," Joe said, plopping down a little breathless on a stuffed wicker train seat.

"Then we face a stiff walk," Frank said. "That house number must be right by the Hudson River."

They were the first ones off the train at Twenty-eighth Street. Dashing up the stairs, Frank and Joe emerged into a quiet residential neighborhood. Brownstone buildings spread on all sides, lining each block with their rows of high stoops with cast-iron stair railings.

The boys took a moment to get their bearings, then headed south on Seventh Avenue for a block, making a right onto Twenty-seventh

Street. Now they were heading west, eating up the sidewalk with big strides.

In the present this part of town had fallen into neglect. A lot of the old housing this far west had even been abandoned. The 1932 version, however, was extremely lively. Curtains fluttered in every window, and older people leaned out the windows, just taking in the scene.

Joe saw one woman watering flowers in a box set outside her window. Each block had a swirl of small children playing games on the sidewalk or a stoop.

"It should be the next block," Frank said. "We'd better be ready—"

His words were cut off by the sound of gunshots. Joe's blood went cold, and he broke into a headlong run.

Joe had heard a lot of guns as he and Frank worked on cases. Often they were fired at him. He could even identify some guns by the noise they made, but the gunshots he was hearing couldn't exist in 1932—and not for another twenty years.

That snarling, deadly rattle of rapid fire came from an Uzi submachine gun. The only way it could exist here and now was if one of the Black Dragon's agents was firing on Joe's father!

17

Sixty-five million years earlier, in the cloud-shrouded Cretaceous, Tom Swift searched the deep gloom. Was that a deeper shadow over there? "Another human voice was the last thing I expected to hear," he said, playing for time.

"It will be the *last* thing you hear, if you don't drop that piece." The gruff voice came out of the gloom.

Tom looked down at the weapon in his hands. Instead of high-tech protection, he held something a little less useful than a baseball bat. Even if the guy out there was in range, Tom wasn't sure where to aim.

He let the gun clatter to the rocky floor.

"Now kick it away from you," the unseen watcher ordered.

Again Tom did as he was told.

"Now we can talk." Tom saw a deeper section of shadow move. Yes. That's where the man had been covering him. "Call me Steve. I know who you are, Tom Swift."

"So, Steve. I know what I'm doing here. But what brings you back this many million years?" Tom worked hard to keep his voice mild and even.

"Me, I'm hired muscle. A little leg-breaking here, a few broken heads there. Then I hit the big time, working for the Black Dragon himself. In my line of work, you can't do much better than that."

"When I saw you, I kind of guessed who you were working for," Tom said. "Mace stole a working model of a time machine from my father and me."

"Yeah. One of the boss's robotic factories has been turning out copies like hotcakes," Steve said. "He used them to send me and a bunch of other guys back here to dinosaurland. Seems he had some kind of bug planted on one of your people and knew you were coming. Problem was, he didn't know *when* you were coming. So he went for what he called maximum coverage. A whole mess of us were sent back, covering each continent with a radar set and some other equipment."

"Nice work if you can get it," Tom said.

"Not exactly. I guess the boss should have waited until after you had worked out all the bugs." Steve's voice went flat and dangerous. "The go-back button on my time machine don't work. And you know what, Tom? I don't think it was a factory error. See, I had a deal with a couple of buddies of mine. We figured we could get together every once in a while and play cards. I mean, we got time machines, right? We can be right back at our radar screens a second after we left."

"Sounds good," Tom agreed. "But you found a problem."

"I was supposed to host our first game. I'm also the one closest to our real time. I arrived with equipment for a decent camp and a year's supply of comic books and food. So I set myself up on a nice quiet hilltop—not in this burnt-out stuff—and I wait. It's five months now, and none of my pals have shown up yet." Steve's voice went furious. "When I try to go up the line, the stupid machine sits there like a lump of—" He cut off his words with an audible snap of teeth.

His voice was calmer when he spoke again, deadly calm. "But I figured I caught the brass ring when my radar showed something flying this way. I hopped in my ATV and tracked you all the way. You wouldn't be coming here if *you* couldn't catch the express back to hot showers and civilization."

There was a disturbing note in the gunman's voice. "I'll tell ya, I was beginning to get a little crazy. I was even thinking of loading up all my ammo and going dinosaur hunting. Maybe I'd shoot the one that people came from.''

Tom chose not to point out that humans didn't evolve from dinosaurs. He was doing some fast thinking. "Well, if you need a lift back . . ."

"I don't think the boss would be too happy with me if I just tamely let you give me a ride. He'd probably make things pretty unhealthy for me when we got back—especially if you came back with all that iridium.''

Steve's voice got speculative. "On the other hand, if I had a time machine that could go anywhere, I could be a bigger guy than even the Black Dragon.''

He laughed. "Who knows? Maybe those bone diggers millions of years from now will really freak out. They'll ask, 'How did a human skeleton get in with all these dino bones?' ''

That was what Tom had been afraid of hearing. The thug named Steve intended to kill him for his time machine.

Tom glanced back toward the center of the crater. Rob had already set up the core sampler. Now the drill started. With that much noise Rob wouldn't hear a yell for help. He might not even hear a gunshot.

They were near the wall of the impact crater, which rose steep and smooth up to the dark sky. Tom decided to make his move.

Instead of going for the electric rifle, Tom dove for a group of boulders, which he could make out as a scatter of darker shadows in the stormy twilight.

The heavy crack of Steve's rifle going off roared over the distant rumble of the drill. Somewhere on the rocky wall behind him, Tom heard the impact and ricochet of a high-caliber bullet.

As Tom dodged from boulder to boulder, he heard the *click-clack* of a rifle bolt being worked.

What kind of gun is he carrying? Tom wondered. He had expected a storm of machine-gun fire rather than that single loud blast.

"You know, Swift, this isn't going to work," Steve called as he advanced on the boulders. "The Black Dragon sent me ready for everything. I've got an elephant gun for blowing away dinosaurs or anything else. I also have some neat light-intensification goggles. As soon as you're out from behind those rocks, I gotcha."

Keep talking, big mouth, Tom thought as he wormed his way toward a crevice he'd noticed in the inner wall. As long as I know where you are, I know where I don't want to be.

Tom was in luck. The huge crack in the wall provided him with a way to climb twenty feet above the crater floor.

With any luck I've lost him, Tom thought. If not, maybe I can get the drop on him.

He was making his way along a steeply rising ledge when he hit a patch of loose stones, which went rattling down.

Steve was immediately in the crack, firing his rifle upward. The blast was even worse in the confined space. It also sent a storm of pebbles and cracked rock tumbling.

Tom fought against the falling debris, scrabbling higher until he could get off the ledge and take refuge in another seam in the rock. *Can't let him get a clear shot at me,* he thought.

As if in answer to a prayer, it began to rain, a cold, driving downpour that was more like sleet than a summer shower. It certainly cut Steve's visibility. Unfortunately, it also made the rocks slippery.

Tom drove himself on to the crest of the crater wall. Steve raced in pursuit, stopping his climb for an occasional shot.

Tom reached the top of the crater, then started down the outer slope. He thought the climb was bad enough, but the descent was even worse. Tom got caught in a mud slide, which sent him tumbling down the rugged incline. He was battered and bruised by the time he reached the ground below.

Big mistake, Swift, Tom thought as he stared out at the desolation before him. *All that's out here is miles of flattened, burnt-out tree trunks. Your only hope is to circle back and climb up the slope again.*

Spatters of icy rain struck Tom's face. Behind him came the roar of Steve's rifle—or was that a baby cannon? Rock shattered, and Tom ducked for cover.

Rob should have heard at least one of those

shots over the noise of the drill, Tom thought. Where is he?

He couldn't hang around waiting to be rescued, though. Tom dove among the downed trees. He was scraped, battered, and now covered with mud mixed with black ashes. He felt horrible, but at least the crud gave him a little camouflage as he played hide-and-seek for his life.

Tom darted between and under blackened tree limbs. Steve's gun boomed again. Tom rolled over a trunk and found a huge open space facing him.

Once, perhaps, it had been a rolling meadow. Now, with the grass scorched off and not growing back in the midday darkness, it was just a large, muddy expanse. In the distance a herd of tired *Parasaurolophus* trudged along, their heads with long bony crests drooping.

They hadn't even turned at the thunderous blast of Steve's gun. But then, what was a touch of thunder and lightning in this suddenly darkened world they didn't understand.

Tom edged along the mucky plain, trying to slip back between the tree trunks. He froze when he heard a soft chuckle off to his left.

"Outsmarted yourself this time, didn't you, Tom?" Steve's voice was grimly satisfied. "No place to hide out on that mud flat, and I can see you good and clear, backed up against that tree trunk. Hey, you led me a good chase. But it's over now."

Tom could barely make out the killer's form. Steve stood beside another fallen tree, heavy rifle raised to one shoulder.

Shutting his eyes, Tom tensed every muscle for an impossible maneuver, although he knew he could never leap over the trunk behind him before he was hit by a bullet.

Then his eyes flew open as a bone-chilling scream burst from Steve's lips.

A big shape, about Steve's height, seemed to be wrestling with the killer. Could it be Rob? No, Tom decided, the attacker was too short. As Steve fell, Tom got a better look. The attacker was a dinosaur, maybe five feet tall with a long snout. Two three-fingered hands were clamped to Steve's shoulders.

Then the dinosaur bounded up, bringing back its left leg. Tom saw a scaly foot, almost like a bird's, but human size. Then he saw the huge, sickle-shaped talon rising up from the middle toe.

The foot—and its horrifying claw—came down, slashing Steve from his chest to his hips. Then the right foot came down, followed by another slash from the left. The dinosaur seemed to be performing a horrible dance over Steve's body, slashing the now lifeless form to pieces.

Bile burned at the back of Tom's throat. He recognized the creature. It was a deinonychus, a meat eater whose name was Greek for "horrible claw."

Well, it sure lives up to its name, Tom

thought, turning away. I guess I'm lucky. Scientists think that those things hunted in packs.

It was then that he caught the glow of reptilian eyes on him. The deinonychus wasn't alone after all.

And the other carnivore was racing along a downed tree, straight for Tom.

18

As he and Joe ran toward the sound of the gunshots along the suddenly empty street, Frank Hardy heard one full-bodied *bang!* against the snarl of Uzi fire.

At least Dad's alive and fighting back, Frank thought. His feet pounded on the pavement as he tried to get a little more speed out of his legs. They were only a block away from the fight.

From what he knew about guns, the Uzi threw about ten bullets a second, versus one from a 1930s pistol. That rate of fire left Fenton Hardy in deadly danger, but it also gave Frank and Joe a window of opportunity. The largest clip for an Uzi held forty rounds. Continuous fire would leave the gun empty after four seconds.

The boys reached the block that held 505 West

179

Twenty-seventh Street, and Frank took in the situation. Fenton Hardy was trapped on the stoop of the building, crouched behind a low brownstone wall. His ambusher stood across the street, sheltered behind a huge black Packard sedan.

The gunman was a tall, burly character, dressed in a thirties-style double-breasted suit and a wide-brimmed fedora hat.

He looked as if he should be shooting a tommy gun, not the high-tech little bundle of death he was firing. Hot brass cartridges showered from the man's Uzi as he sprayed bullets around Fenton Hardy's hiding place.

The boys' father didn't dare expose himself to return even a single shot.

Frank scanned the rest of the block. At least the neighbors had had the good sense to get off the street when the shooting began.

"If this clown keeps Dad's head down like that, he'll be able to outflank him," Joe said breathlessly. "There's not much cover behind that stoop wall. If Dad can't see where the bullets are coming from, that guy can move to an angle where he can get a clear shot at him."

Joe went to charge forward, but Frank yanked him back, dragging him behind the cover of a stoop on the gunman's side of the street.

"Rushing straight at him will just get us blown away," Frank said.

"But—" Joe protested.

"Just wait a second or two," Frank told him confidently.

His assurance was justified. The rapid rate of fire abruptly stopped. The gunner yanked the clip out and turned it upside down. He had a fresh clip taped to the bottom of the empty one.

In the instant before the man shoved the reload home, Frank darted out from behind his cover. "Now!" he yelled.

The man gaped for a second, slammed the clip into place, and frantically worked the bolt on the Uzi. Frank was still a step and a half away from him as the thug aimed his gun. Desperately, Frank hurled himself into the air.

"Hey, you!" a voice roared from across the street. It was Fenton Hardy, standing up on the stoop, aiming a heavy pistol two-handed at the gunman.

The hired gun whirled, trying to bring his Uzi to bear on Fenton, and Frank slammed into him. They hit the sidewalk together. The gunman clawed at Frank, keeping a hand free to point his weapon at his attacker's head. Now Joe entered the fight, landing a dropkick on the goon's gun hand.

With a wild cry, the gunman watched his Uzi skitter away and fall down a storm drain. He surged up, trying to escape. Frank lunged forward, getting a grip on the gunman's neck. The guy flopped wildly as Frank pressed. Quickly, the thug's struggles became weaker.

"He's out," Joe said.

"And we have to get out of here." Fenton Hardy was across the street now. "No time for talking. If we don't leave quickly, we'll have a lot of explaining to do with this era's police." Fenton ran to the corner, hailing a passing taxicab. Joe looked down at the unconscious gunman. "What do we do with him?"

"Take him along." Frank picked the man up, Joe helped, and they headed for the taxi. "I'm afraid our friend was celebrating too much," Frank said to the driver. "If we don't hurry, he won't catch his train at Grand Central."

In minutes they were back at Grand Central Station. Frank led the way to the lockers and retrieved the time-travel device while Fenton and Joe carried their "under-the-weather friend" with his arms over their shoulders.

Next they headed for the isolated storeroom where the boys had first appeared in 1932. "I didn't get a chance to say how glad I am to see you two," Fenton Hardy said.

"We're just glad to see you alive," Frank responded.

"I suspected that the Black Dragon might bring his 'War Through Time' back to 1932," Fenton said, "so I invested the earnings from my first story in a good gun."

"Your *first* story?" Joe said.

Fenton nodded. "The editor at *Unlikely Tales* bought three others. He really likes my writing. According to him, I have a real knack for describing machines of the future. 'Battle of the

Microwaves' will be the next story to appear. He even wants me to start writing for a new magazine—*Prof Wilder*. It's about this guy who goes around having superscience adventures with his five best friends."

"Sounds pretty ridiculous," Frank said.

Joe only shrugged. "So do some of the things *we* get up to," he said.

A low groan interrupted their conversation. "Looks like our new friend is back among the living," Fenton said. He knelt by the gunman, who lay flat on his back, looking up woozily at them.

"I guess we don't have to ask who sent you after me," Fenton said to the man.

"The big boss was really freaking out," the disarmed thug said, staring at the muzzle of Fenton's gun. "He had this old magazine in his hands—so old, it was falling apart. And he was ripping all the pages, yelling his head off. 'So my face is "seamed and raddled from every vice," is it?' You know, stuff like that, as if he were quoting something."

A huge grin split Fenton Hardy's face. "That was from my story. So the Black Dragon didn't like it, eh? Good."

"The Dragon was so angry he sent me back to 1932 to waste you," the gunman said.

"You got my address from the magazine and then you staked out my rooming house, waiting for me to come out so you could blast me," Fenton said.

The thug gave a sheepish shrug and winced. "Oh, my head!" He looked up at the faces surrounding him and began to sweat. "Hey, I was doing my job!"

"And not doing it very well," Fenton snapped. "Once you found out where I lived, you should have hopped into your time machine and gone back a few months. As soon as the magazine hit the stands, I knew people would have someplace to ask for me. So I was ready for you."

"Wha-what are you going to do to me?" The goon was really sweating now.

"You're going to tell us everything you know about your boss and where he's hiding out," Fenton told him. "Just keep talking. If you don't, we'll dump you in some other time zone, even worse than this one. This is the Depression, when people starved. But there are worse times. How'd you like to be stranded with nothing in your pockets in the middle of a plague year?"

"You wouldn't do that," the man said.

"After you tried to kill my father?" Frank asked. "What do you think?"

The man's face was greasy with sweat. "I—I guess I got no choice. Look, I can tell you where the boss is hanging out. He's got something big he's working on—something that only robots are building. I mean, he's got one of the big tunnels blocked off, locked up like it was a bank vault."

"Where is this tunnel?" Fenton pressed.

"What are the return coordinates for your time machine?"

The thug hung his head and reeled off a set of numbers. The Black Dragon's lair, it turned out, was in downtown New York City.

Xavier Mace had taken over a series of abandoned skyscraper subcellars. But there was more—Mace's probing had discovered a stretch of railroad tunnel that hadn't been used since the Civil War. He'd even broken into the lowest levels of a fort dating back two hundred years. Aboveground, thousands of tourists visited the fort. They never suspected that forty feet below them a scientific genius was launching twisted plans to take over the world.

After hearing about the Black Dragon's fortress and the terrible engine of destruction Mace was building there, Fenton started asking lots of questions. When he was finished with their unwilling informant, he turned to the boys.

"The only ways into the underground complex are through the cellars of buildings that Mace owns. Those entrances are heavily defended and loaded with alarms and detectors."

Fenton shook his head. "Even if we warned the government and they sent an army to storm the place, Mace would have more than enough time to trigger this superbomb of his."

"So what can we do?" Joe asked.

Frank stared down at the silvery time-travel rig in his hands. "We could warp in, knock out the bomb, and leave the Black Dragon with egg on his face when he pushes the button.''

The Hardys looked at one another as Frank went on. "A small party of infiltrators could do the job. Why not us? We know that Mace has spies everywhere, even in Swift Enterprises. But he won't know about us. I say we move immediately, as soon as we're back in the present, and catch him with his pants down."

Fenton and Joe finally agreed. The attack through time would take place as soon as they were back in their own era, with just one stop to drop off their captive.

A tightly packed group winked into existence in a wash of purple brilliance. The four people were in the same abandoned room in Grand Central Station, but more than six decades had passed. The room was dirtier, dingier, and didn't smell very good. A tattered mattress leaned up against one wall.

"Maybe we should have stayed back in 1932," Joe said, looking around.

"Mmmph!" their captive hummed through the gag in his mouth. Before leaving the thirties, the Hardys had taken the precaution of binding the failed gunman with their belts and his tie.

Now the man reeled, his ankles bound together. The Hardys moved the mattress to the floor and laid him down on it.

"Yrrr kmph lrrv mmph!" their captive mumbled.

"I think he's saying we can't leave him here," Frank said.

"Look on the bright side," Joe told the man. "If we get through this, we'll be back to pick you up. If not, well, you'll get loose sooner or later."

Fenton and Joe gathered back around Frank as he carefully set the coordinates on the time machine. They were moving only a second or two into the future, and the location in space wasn't too far away. Fenton took out his pistol. "We'll be striking hard and fast, so I hope we won't need this." He cocked the revolver. "But it's best to be ready."

They vanished in a rush of purple light, to reappear a moment later in a huge, steel-lined room. Waves of nausea flooded through them, but they had no time to take notice.

Fenton shook his head. "This is the room I stole the time machine from!"

Against one wall and filling half the room was a large, high-tech construction, Frank saw. He recognized parts of the giant mechanism—they were huge versions of components from Tom Swift's time machine. "This is it," he whispered. "Now all we have to do is find a way to disable it."

"All I need is a fire ax, or maybe a sledgehammer," Joe said.

They had taken three steps toward the machine when a horde of robots and armed men poured through the open steel door.

Behind them walked the familiar form of Professor Drake. "All the Hardys, in a Swift time machine." He smiled at Joe Hardy. "Planting a bug on you that evening in Idaho was the wisest thing I ever did."

"A bug? On me?" Joe sputtered. "What are you talking about? You never—"

"When my robot scout flung you back on the bed, it also fired a filament microphone into the soft flesh of your neck," Mace interrupted. "The mike is as fine as a hair—you never even felt it. But my people heard everything you heard, Joe. You were my ears in Swift Enterprises. And when you appeared in here, your mike activated several of my security systems."

Mace walked over to the huge time-warp generator. "That warning was quite—if you'll forgive the expression—timely. With your sudden appearance, I now see that my plans are compromised. I can also probably expect a large number of federal agents trying to get in. If I merely try to escape, there will be an enormous manhunt. My course is clear."

The Black Dragon strode over to a console and activated it. A huge electrical charge filled the air. "The President will regret his failure to comply with my reasonable request. This machine is powerful enough to warp five square blocks of downtown Manhattan back several milliseconds. When the buildings try to occupy the same space filled by their past selves, there will be quite an explosion."

"It might be powerful enough to destroy the world," Frank said. "If you were listening through the bug on Joe, you know Professor Reisenbach's warning about the fragility of space-time."

Mace dismissed Frank's words with an airy wave of his hand. "I've taken that into account. This world has shown no appreciation of my genius. Why not erase it and spend my energies reshaping the twentieth century?"

He pointed off to the side. "Mr. Hardy, I'm sure you recognize these."

"Time machines," Fenton said.

"They're all set for 1900. My guards and I, along with one million dollars' worth of gold, will set off in a moment. With my knowledge, I expect to rule the world in ten years. As for this era—"

Mace's finger stabbed down on a console button. A warning hooted, and a computer voice echoed through the room.

"Warning! Primary time trigger has been engaged. Full discharge in ten seconds . . . nine seconds . . . eight seconds . . ."

19

For a long second, Tom Swift could only stare in horror as the carnivore raced lightly down the length of the fallen tree trunk. It was one thing to look at pictures of the deinonychus in books on dinosaurs. It was something else to watch one coming at you, Tom thought. Those big teeth, that huge claw on each foot—

The feet! Every reconstruction of the deinonychus Tom had ever seen gave this killer dinosaur feet like a bird—like a pigeon or a chicken. Maybe it could move as fast as a roadrunner on solid ground, but those feet would be just about useless for running through mud!

Tom moved from where he was standing, at the edge of the mud flat, and started slogging through inches of sticky mud. Of course, he realized, my own feet aren't built too well for mud walking. Please, he prayed, don't let that creature have webbed feet.

Struggling through the sticky mud, he glanced back over his shoulder. The deinonychus had stopped running and was still braced on the top of the log. It was going to jump! Tom had a horrible picture of those hooked claws whipping down.

Then, with a surprised squawk, the dinosaur toppled backward off the log. A second later the deinonychus came back into view, bounding up from behind the fallen tree, slashing with its great claws. There was a sound like fingernails running down the largest blackboard Tom had ever imagined. Then he saw who was fighting with the dinosaur.

It was Rob.

There was a puzzlement in the deinonychus's eyes as it continued to attack its new prey. The dinosaur's small upper arms rested on Rob's shoulders, and its muscular legs pumped, slashing again and again with its killer claws. Tom knew that should have been enough to rip open the belly of even the most heavily armored Cretaceous creature.

But the deinonychus had never encountered metal before. Its blows rang and screeched off Rob's gleaming armor plate.

The robot suddenly pivoted, ducked down, then extended his arms. The deinonychus kicked and arched its back, but Rob had managed to lift it off the ground and over his head, as if he were bench-pressing the dinosaur.

"Come over here, Tom," the robot called as the deinonychus's tail lashed against him.

As Tom climbed over the log, Rob hurled the deinonychus far out into the mud flats. "I think it will be a while before *that* creature goes hunting again," Rob said.

"That thing was about to jump me," Tom said. "How did you stop it?"

"I saw what it was about to do, grabbed its tail, and pulled." Rob led the way through the maze of fallen trees. "By the way, we hit pay dirt on the first test hole. There's a large concentration of iridium about twenty feet down."

Tom suddenly stopped, climbing up on some of the fallen timber. "Wait a second! Steve! There was a guy with a gun. He chased me, and another deinonychus got him."

"I heard the gunshots when I stopped the drill," Rob said. "I also saw the man and the other dinosaur." Rob paused for a second. "Believe me, Tom, there's nothing we can do."

Shuddering, Tom began the long, slippery climb back into the impact crater.

For the better part of the next day, Tom and Rob smashed rock, dug down, and mined iridium. Though the weather was chilly, Tom was sweating. Little trickles of moisture cut channels through the ashy, muddy grime on his face.

But he was smiling. They'd done it. The

TANC was loaded with enough iridium to build all the time-warp detectors they'd need. They could cover every square foot of every city in the United States. "You can run, Black Dragon," Tom muttered to himself, "but now you can't hide."

Tom and Rob finished the job of buttoning up the TANC. Before they had even started loading the iridium, Tom had transformed the vehicle back into its truck shape. Now he and Rob sat in the cab, activating the Reisenbach unit. The prickly electrical charge was in the air as Tom punched the Go button. "Home, Rob," he said.

Despite the stomach-wrenching warp effect, Tom was falling asleep even as the purple radiance enveloped them.

For almost the entire journey toward the future, Tom slept, exhausted by nonstop effort. He was rudely awakened by the clamor of an alarm. This wasn't the polite beeping of the mission clock, letting them know that they were almost in their target time zone. No, it was a raucous noise, coming from the time-warp detector Tom had ordered built into his traveling time machine.

"There's some sort of disturbance in our present," Tom said to Rob, looking at the detector's console. "It's a major disturbance—the readings are off the scale."

As he worked the controls, checking the detector's screen to pinpoint where the enormous warp could be, his face went pale. "I know of only one thing that might cause this kind of distortion. Mace must have triggered his bomb.''

Tom felt even sicker when the screen revealed where the warp was centered. "New York City.''

He turned to the control console. "I'm changing our spatial coordinates," he said to Rob. "Maybe I can home in on the center of this disturbance and stop Mace from doing something very foolish.''

Tom grew more and more uneasy as he watched the controls. "I suspect the Black Dragon doesn't know what he's gotten hold of this time.''

"You mean, he's got a deinonychus by the tail?'' Rob said.

"That's putting it mildly," Tom replied. "The effects of his warp became detectable when we entered 1989.''

He gave Rob a worried glance. "I think the universe isn't going to like what he's trying to do. I know what happened to Professor Reisenbach when he got caught in the backlash from bending the laws of physics too far. And I'm afraid that explosion will look like a popgun going off compared to what Mace has planned.''

Tom's unease grew as they got closer to the center of the disturbance. The Black Dragon's warp field was having effects far beyond the explosive one he'd intended. It was twisting and straining the higher dimensions that made time travel possible. Shock waves in the time stream made the TANC bounce and shudder as badly as it had in the air turbulence during the asteroid impact. The machinery was bucking and twisting as if it were a live animal.

Even worse was the internal wrenching, that torturous feeling that accompanied the transition into time travel. It hit Tom intermittently, as if the time machine were phasing in and out of its dimensional alignment. Tom gulped, trying to keep down the contents of his rebellious stomach.

He had another worry. Every time the TANC gave a lurch, the purple fog outside suddenly became clear, the abstract patterns turning into recognizable shapes. At one point, the fog suddenly coalesced into the Manhattan skyline, all in purplish blue, with a black sky and an incredible thunderstorm going on. The tall skyscrapers seemed to be tilting inward, as if they were being sucked toward a single place downtown in the Wall Street area. Then the twisty feeling intensified, and the vision dissolved.

A little while later Tom seemed to be looking down at a distorted landscape. This time he was getting an aerial view. The perspective was all wrong, and the purplish buildings seemed to shudder. One building fell apart in a display of horrific fireworks as enormous lightning bolts struck it repeatedly. Everything went out of focus, and the purple haze became featureless again.

"We're a year away from the time we're aiming for, and twice now we've almost fallen back into the normal dimensions," Rob said.

" 'Fall' is right," Tom agreed with a shudder. "That first glimpse of the city would put us somewhere in New York Harbor. The second time, we were about fifteen hundred feet off the ground. If we'd actually fallen out of the warp, we'd have dropped like a stone."

He looked helplessly at the console displays. "We can only hope that we'll land where we're aiming for."

But the images outside their windshield—and that tearing, wrenching sensation—came more and more often. It was as if they were at a disco with strobe lights. *Twist!* They got a glance of tourists at a fort. *Twist!* They seemed to be in the cellar of a building. *Twist!* Suddenly they were in a huge room, where purple light glared so brilliantly, it became white.

Tom clung to the control console, searching for something—anything—that was solid. Another shift, another wrench. Tom looked at the indicators. "We've arrived," he croaked.

Outside the windshield, the world had gone mad. They were in the gigantic room they'd last seen, but it seemed to be throbbing out of phase with itself. Everywhere Tom looked he saw a glaring purple radiance. His hair prickled and his skin crawled in the grip of utterly incomprehensible forces.

There were people and robots in the room, seeming to run at random. In some areas people were dashing around at unnaturally high speed, like figures in a film being projected too fast. In others people were moving as slowly as molasses on a cold day.

"Mace's time field is causing horrendous distortions," Tom said. "We've got to stop it!"

He threw open the door of the TANC, which had materialized in an unoccupied corner. The twisting sensation became worse. "Everything's going out of phase!" he yelled.

Behind the confused figures, ghostlike doubles had appeared.

"It's the people's past selves!" Tom said. "They're beginning to come into phase."

With every instant, the doubles became clearer, more solid. "What happens when they touch?" Rob asked.

"When everything in here tries to occupy its former space, the bomb officially goes off," Tom said. "And we're all dead."

He broke into a run, heading toward a large, glowing installation. Tom forced himself not to look back. He didn't want to see if there was a twin stumbling after him.

Tom saw a trio of figures ahead of him—actually six figures, since the trio had twins. He recognized Frank and Joe Hardy. And ahead of them, running for a line of time machines, he recognized the man they'd described as Professor Drake—one of the many forms of Xavier Mace.

"Mace!" Tom yelled over the swirling chaos.

"You've got to stop this thing. It won't just blow up New York. You're straining the whole space-time continuum."

The Black Dragon only laughed wildly. "What do I care?" Xavier Mace roared, still laughing. "I'm out of here!"

An older man who looked very much like Frank Hardy raised a pistol in both hands, aiming it at Mace.

One of the guards noticed and fired his pistol. The bullet must have passed through a space-time distortion, because it moved unnaturally fast. The armed man with the Hardys was hit and went down. One glance told that his wound was mortal.

"Daaaaaaaaaad!" Frank Hardy went berserk. He tore off in a run after the Black Dragon. Tom never knew if it was just his concentration or if time actually was running more slowly in that part of the room. Frank seemed to be moving in slow motion as he went to confront Mace.

The Black Dragon turned, raised his hands, and a blinding flash of energy flew toward Frank. He was hurled back, stumbling in dreamlike slowness as he disintegrated before their eyes.

Joe Hardy was running, too. He saw what happened to his brother. Then he popped into a normal area, sprinted to catch up to the Black Dragon, and threw himself in a flying tackle as Mace again raised his hands.

The Dragon had almost reached his time machine. Then he was hurled screaming to the floor. He thrashed, taking in the chaos around him. "Let go!" Mace shrieked. "Got to get away! My future awaits me in the past!"

His face like stone, Joe Hardy held him down. "Get out of here, Swift," he called. "Find some way, somewhere, to stop this!"

The center of the room, where Joe and Mace were struggling on the floor, began to swirl in a vortex of unimaginable energy. Machines, robots, and howling guards were pulled into it.

Tom Swift flung himself backward, trying to reach the TANC. He sidestepped a ghostly figure of himself that was still moving forward and stumbled to the cab, where a strong metal arm reached out and lifted him in.

"Activate the Reisenbach unit!" Tom gasped. "We have to get out of here before that vortex touches us."

Rob started up their time machine as Tom fumbled the door shut. "Ready," the robot said.

Tom stabbed the Go button. The purple radiance around them intensified.

Then complete chaos hurled them around.

20

The TANC seemed to hurtle sideways, and for Tom the usual twisting feeling became more of a crushing sensation. It was as if a giant were trying to crumple their vehicle like an empty soda can.

Outside the window, figures seemed to be running backward, in slow motion. "We're going back in time, but we haven't made the full dimensional transition," Tom said to Rob, fighting a tearing sensation in his chest. "It's destroying us!"

The figures outside began to alternate, first moving forward, then moving back. "The distortion is catching up with us," Tom gasped. "It's spreading like a storm—a time storm."

His eyes ran over the control readouts. The

coordinates! They were still set for the moment they'd appeared in the huge room. That moment had been in the future when they'd set out to track the strange distortion. Now it was their past. But if they arrived, they'd be coexisting with themselves. And Tom knew that was sure death.

He raised a wavering hand and realized he couldn't reprogram a new destination. He didn't have the strength.

"Rob!" he gasped. "Set new coordinates."

Where should they go? He remembered Joe Hardy's last words. "Find some way, somewhere, to stop this."

All of a sudden, he knew exactly where to go. He gave Rob the necessary orders and sank weakly in his seat.

The TANC lurched. Everything inside seemed to give off an insistent thrumming noise. Tom caught the smell of overheated metal.

Then came the twisting sensation of full emergence from the three-dimensional universe. After the torture he'd been through, caught on the edges of the time storm, it was a relief to pull through to normal time travel.

Tom took a deep breath and glanced over at Rob. "We're out of the storm. Let's just hope we can outrun it."

Escape wasn't easy. The time storm grew by fits and jumps. Sometimes they felt totally normal; other times they saw the purple mist outside their windshields coagulate into terrifying scenes.

Tom saw people torn and distorted by the horrendous forces the Black Dragon had unleashed. With a silent scream, a woman went from adulthood to infancy, obviously aware of what was going on but unable to stop it. He saw a man sheared in half as a vortex of energy sprang up beside him. And everywhere people coalesced with their past selves to become hellish explosions of blinding energy.

Unable to watch any more, Tom rested his head on the control panel. At last the trip clock beeped. Tom didn't know if they had minutes or seconds as they materialized beside a cabin in Ontario, Canada. The date was November 9, 1965. The time was late afternoon.

"Come with me!" Tom said to Rob, leaping from the TANC's cab and running for the cabin. He pounded on the wooden door until someone finally answered.

It was Ernst Reisenbach.

"Professor Reisenbach," Tom said, gasping for breath. "My name is Tom Swift. I'm the son of the man you taught at Princeton. You've got to listen to me. I know you're about to do the final test on your time machine. You can't. If you go ahead with your research, you're handing a terrible weapon to a madman of the future. He'll use it to try to destroy a city, but instead he'll destroy the world—maybe even the universe."

Tom stared into Reisenbach's eyes, and his

heart sank. The man was staring at him as if he were out of his mind. Tom glanced down at himself. His clothes were torn and muddy from his deadly chase sixty-five million years earlier. His hands and face were probably still dirty from that experience, too. His hair was on end, he was gasping, and his face was probably green from too much time-twisting. How could he convince this man?

"I *am* from the future!" Tom frantically insisted. "You've got to believe me!"

Reisenbach leapt back, fear in his face.

He probably thinks I escaped from a mental institution. He's afraid I'll turn homicidal next.

"Please," Tom begged. "How can I convince you?"

Professor Reisenbach was staring over Tom's shoulder. He wet his lips, then pointed. "I—I think you have already," the scientist said.

Tom turned and saw the seven-foot-tall figure of Rob standing behind him. The robot's metal skin was no longer shining in all spots, and he had a series of scratches running down the front of his body, thanks to the claws of the deinonychus. But he was definitely a working robot, not a hoax or a leftover Halloween costume.

Then Tom noticed something else. There was a small protuberance from the center of Rob's chest. It was the lens of the robot's built-in camcorder!

"Rob!" Tom exclaimed. "Were you taping what went on in that big room?"

"I sure was," Rob said. "Thought you'd want me to do it."

"Then come in here. We've got something to show the professor."

Reisenbach staggered back as Tom and his robot stepped into the cabin. "Incredible," the scientist breathed, still staring at Rob. "A walking, talking, thinking machine. How far in the future do you come from?"

"That's not important right now," Tom said, looking around the living room. "Rob, that television. Can you hook your camcorder up to it?"

The robot looked at the TV set. "I can do it."

"Then hurry."

While Rob improvised a connection to the portable television, Tom gave Ernst Reisenbach a quick rundown on what the discovery of his papers years from now would cause.

"So I was successful," the older man said, his eyes shining. "I actually made it to the future, explored it—"

"You also died there," Tom cut in. "Killed by a man who misused your discovery. His name was Xavier Mace."

"Mace!" Reisenbach looked very troubled. "What did he do?"

"He attempted to use your time field as a gigantic bomb," Tom explained. "Instead, he distorted the fabric of the universe so much, I think he tore time loose. It's springing back and forth on itself in a titanic storm. We can show you. Rob? Are you ready?"

"Ready." The robot turned on the television and a low humming came from his chest.

Snow crawled across the screen, then a very clear black-and-white picture appeared on the TV.

Ernst Reisenbach sat silently, watching the horror, the terror of the people, the destruction caused by the time storm.

Tom pointed as the ghosts appeared behind the figures. "You can see the dangerous paradox developing here. The past aspect of this person is being brought into phase with the present. When they try to occupy the same space simultaneously, the result will be catastrophic. Even this much strain on the space-time continuum is causing terrible distortions. You can see that time is obviously running at very different rates in various sections of the room."

Reisenbach went pale as he watched the vortex of destruction forming, engulfing Joe Hardy and Xavier Mace, and sucking the other people in the room into its greedy maw.

"It's breaking down space, destroying everything up and down the time line," Tom said. "Mace didn't know what he was dealing with. He thought he could escape by going into the past. Instead this destruction is raging back toward us right now." He glanced at his watch. "To tell you the truth, I don't know how much longer we have."

"And it's all because of me," Reisenbach said numbly. "Because of my experiments." He began to pace up and down. "When I was younger, I took part in the research that built the atomic bomb. That destroyed two cities and left the world locked in a balance of terror. This time around I swore I would be more careful with my findings.''

Reisenbach gave a short, ironic laugh. ''Instead I have destroyed the world.''

''It doesn't have to be,'' Tom said quickly. ''I came back to see if we can't change the future.''

''How?'' Reisenbach demanded.

''It's a lot to ask of a scientist, I know,'' Tom said. ''You'd have to suppress your results. On the other hand, nobody knows what you were researching.''

Reisenbach frowned in thought. ''What good is credit for a discovery if it destroys the world? I'll have to track down all my papers, anything that might have mentioned my research.'' He looked up, hope in his eyes. ''But it can be done.''

He headed for the kitchen. ''I'll go downstairs and destroy the machine right now.''

Tom grabbed Reisenbach's arm. ''You can't do it that way. That machine has to function, just once. You see, when you operated your time machine, you caused a power drain that blacked out most of the East Coast.''

Reisenbach blinked, bemused. ''I did?''

''Trust me,'' Tom said, ''you did. And that historical event still has to happen.'' He grinned. ''For one thing, there were a lot of babies born because of that blackout.''

"So what are you suggesting?" Reisenbach asked.

"I've given it some thought," Tom said. "My suggestion is that you load all your time research into the time machine. Then set it to go a few minutes into the future, and set the spatial coordinates for as high up in the atmosphere as you can go over the ocean. The machine and the papers will fall as a meteor and burn up. And that will be the end of it."

Reisenbach nodded. "A good plan." He hesitated. "You realize, however, that by doing this, you yourself will cease to exist? The future where you went time-traveling will not occur. Therefore, you cannot be."

Tom shrugged. "Balanced against saving the world, it's a small price. Besides, theory suggests that I'll still exist in the future, in some *alternate* time line. Let's do it."

Together Tom and Reisenbach gathered up all the papers in the cabin, went down to the basement, and placed them in the time machine. With Rob's help they did all the necessary calculations, and Reisenbach set the coordinates on his apparatus.

"We're ready," he said, warming up the machine. Electricity filled the air.

Reisenbach touched a button. Purple radiance filled the room. Abruptly all the lights went out.

And with a brief inrush of imploding air, Tom Swift and Rob the robot disappeared.

21

"Particle detectors ready, Rob?" Tom Swift asked his robot assistant. "We have cosmic rays incoming in less than fifteen seconds."

"You're sure cosmic rays will land right here?" Rob's metal face couldn't show puzzlement, but the seven-foot-tall robot did stare at Tom.

"When our newest satellite is right overhead, a powerful electromagnet snaps on, powerful enough to deflect any passing cosmic rays," Tom told him. "As the rays hit the atmosphere, they—and the particles caused by their collision with air molecules—will land right here."

The young, blond inventor gestured at the array of particle detectors that were spread along the ridge they stood on. Sixty metal cylinders, each five feet wide and five feet high, were scattered in seemingly random patterns. Inside each of the big metal cans was a telescope mirror and a set of phototubes sensitive enough to catch the faintest glimmer of Čerenkov radiation given off by slowing subatomic particles.

Rob's glowing eyes gazed into the evening desert sky. "Why did we power all this up so far in advance of the particle stream?"

"I want to catch some particles coming *ahead* of the rush," Tom explained.

"But cosmic rays move at the speed of light."

"Tachyons are particles that move even faster," Tom said. "They'll show up twenty milliseconds before anything else."

"If they exist," Rob pointed out.

"In theory they do," Tom said. "Now we'll see if the universe is a democracy or a dictatorship."

"You've lost me, Tom," Rob said.

Tom's lean face lit up with a grin, and his blue eyes twinkled. "Either everything that's possible is *allowed* to happen—or everything possible *must* happen."

He glanced at his watch. "We'll know in a second. Ready?"

"I've patched myself into the detector links," Rob said.

They stood silently as Rob read the data flying along the computer linkup. "I've picked up several particle anomalies in advance of the air shower created by the cosmic ray collisions."

The robot was silent for a moment. "It's as if the tachyons arrived *before* those collisions. Does that mean they traveled through time?"

Tom shrugged. "We all travel through time, Rob. What makes tachyons interesting is that they move in the opposite direction from us." His eyes lit up. "And now we've managed to catch them doing it."

The gleaming robot suddenly interrupted. "You've got a phone call."

Tom stared. "What?"

"It's a new improvement I was trying out, building your portable phone into my circuits. Just talk. My sensors will pick up."

A second later, Tom Swift, Sr.'s voice came through Rob's speakers. "Tom, are you there?"

"What's up, Dad?" Tom asked.

"I'd like you to come to my office. A rather interesting package has arrived."

"We're on our way." Tom and Rob walked down the side of the ridge to the van parked on the road below. They drove through the hills until they arrived at a valley sheltering a gleaming complex of buildings. The structures, clean and crisply designed, looked as brand-new as the rock around them seemed ages old.

This was the home of Swift Enterprises, the best invention Tom's father had ever created. Without this high-tech base, Tom's own inventions, like Rob the robot, would never have been possible.

As he pulled up by the administration tower,

in the center of the complex, Tom wondered what the package was that his father wanted to talk to him about. Well, he'd find out soon enough—after a quick elevator ride to Tom Swift, Sr.'s top-floor office.

Tom found his father at his desk. Mr. Swift took the wrapping from a flat box and handed it over. "What do you make of this?"

"It was sent by an S. Reisenbach." Tom frowned. "That's the name of the teacher you mentioned last night on that TV interview."

Tom's father nodded. "Ernst Reisenbach was one of the most brilliant scientists of this century and one of the fathers of nuclear physics. During World War Two, he helped build the first atom bomb. Then Reisenbach was at Princton for the next twenty years, teaching the next generation of scientists—including me."

Mr. Swift smiled. "He showed me that inventing wasn't just tinkering with your hands but with your mind. He turned the theories of physics into reality. When I told the TV interviewer that Reisenbach made me what I am today, I really meant it." He removed a letter from on top of the faded, dusty box in front of him.

" 'Dear Mr. Swift,' " he read aloud. " 'I listened with pride when you mentioned my great-uncle on "Up Front and in Person." We found this box, marked E. Reisenbach, while cleaning out the attic. My husband and I wondered what to do with it until we saw you on TV. We decided that Uncle Ernst would have liked you to have his work.' "

Mr. Swift looked almost embarrassed as he fiddled with the string on the box. "I'm almost afraid to open this. It could be anything from laundry lists to notes for—for almost anything. Reisenbach never explained why, but he stopped publishing papers in the midfifties."

"Whatever's in there has to be old science by now," Tom said with a grin. "I mean, you may find a design for color television."

Mr. Swift opened the box to reveal a pile of slightly yellowed papers covered with tight handwriting. As he read, he frowned.

"What is it, Dad?" Tom asked.

"It's a rough draft for a paper on time paradoxes," Tom's father said. "It's the old story of someone building a time machine, then going back and shooting his grandfather before the grandfather had any children."

"Oh. You mean, would the time traveler exist or not?" Tom said. "Seems to me I've heard that one before."

"Reisenbach adds a further twist. His hypothetical time traveler goes back fifty years before his grandfather's time and carves his initials in the tree. Would the traveler be there or not?"

Tom frowned. "The traveler would be there, even in the alternate future where the time traveler doesn't exist, because the one who *did* exist carved them before the point of decision."

Mr. Swift nodded. "That's essentially what Reisenbach says here."

He went on reading through the other papers in the box, then put them down.

"What's the matter, Dad?" Tom asked. "You seem disappointed."

"I guess I am," Mr. Swift admitted. "All the rest of the stuff here is copies of letters about the responsibility of scientists. They were all written between the end of 1965 and June 1966, when Professor Reisenbach passed away."

He picked up a letter. "It's all pretty much like this. 'My dear Otto,' " Mr. Hardy read aloud. " 'Here is a hypothetical situation, a thought experiment in morals, if you will. You have made the discovery of your life—a discovery that would rank you with Einstein. But a message comes from the future, saying that your discovery, misused, will absolutely and surely destroy the world. What do you do?

" 'For myself, I come to this conclusion. There is no such thing as pure science. People will always sully our creations. In the case of sure doom, we should destroy our work before we allow others to destroy the world. Better to live in obscurity than to destroy the future.' "

Mr. Swift shook his head. "I was expecting to read about physics, not metaphysics and philosophy." He put the letter back in the box and closed it.

At the same moment, the intercom buzzed. "Mr. Swift, a Mr. Fenton Hardy to see you."

"Send him in," Tom's father said, turning toward the door.

A slim, dark-haired man with flecks of gray in his hair stepped in. Behind him came two teenage boys carrying a box. "Mr. Swift, I'm Fenton Hardy," the man said. "These are my sons. The dark-haired one, Frank, is the elder. Joe, the blond one, is the younger."

Tom's father nodded. "Mr. Hardy, boys, this is my son, Tom."

Tom smiled a greeting to the tall, slim older Hardy and his stockier brother. "Nice to meet you," he said with a smile.

Mr. Swift was shaking hands with Fenton Hardy. "What can I do for you?" he asked.

"I'm a private detective, hired by Dr. Antonio DiGanda, the famous paleontologist."

"Someone steal his fossils?" Mr. Swift asked with a smile.

Fenton Hardy shook his head. "He thinks he's the victim of a hoax and has hired me to prove it. Apparently Dr. DiGanda made a wonderful discovery—a set of fossilized footprints from a herd of *Parasaurolophus*. The dinosaurs walked across a mud flat that soon afterward turned to rock."

"And he thinks these footprints are fakes?" Tom asked.

"No, the doctor is sure they're genuine. The problem is that nearby he also found this."

Fenton Hardy turned to his sons, who put the box on Mr. Swift's desk. He opened it and removed a foot-square chunk of rock. Running diagonally across the stone was a human footprint.

"This was found in the same stratum, buried under twenty feet. It should date back sixty-five million years."

"I didn't think dinosaurs wore shoes," Tom said.

"Especially expensive running shoes that only came out this year," Fenton Hardy said. "I checked the pattern of the sole—it's a SuperSole All-sports. It's unmistakable."

"We'll be happy to give you any scientific help in determining the authenticity of the—Tom! What are you doing?" Mr. Swift demanded.

Almost in a trance, Tom had taken the stone block, placed it on the floor, and placed his foot in the print.

"Sorry, Dad," he apologized. "I just had to try it. I bought this pair of SuperSoles yesterday."

Tom shook his head. "Weird—it fits my foot exactly."

Then he laughed. "But you'd think I'd remember if I had been chased by dinosaurs."

Frank, Joe, and the others laughed, too.

"You'd think so," Joe said. "You'd think so."

Be sure not to miss
Tom Swift's next adventure:

Tom is putting the finishing touches on an astounding new device—a Total Reality Generator. A powerful computer interfaces with the human mind, re-creating the true-to-life conditions of space flight. But an untested program has been inserted into the system, and it's about to propel Tom into an uncharted fantasy world from which he may never return!

The program is based on Galaxy Masters, a role-playing game at Tom's school. But as the images and icons touch his nerves and surge into his mind, the game turns frighteningly authentic. Suddenly he is drawn into battle with the most powerfully sinister forces of the imagination—locked in a life-and-death struggle with the master of evil, Dedstorm . . . in Tom Swift #10, *Mind Games*.

THE PENGUIN
AMERICAN LIBRARY

EDITOR: JOHN SEELYE

THE CALL OF THE WILD, WHITE FANG, AND OTHER STORIES

Born in 1935, Andrew Sinclair took his doctorate at Harvard University and Cambridge University and became a noted social historian and novelist. He has written major works on Prohibition and feminism in the United States and biographies of John Ford and J. P. Morgan. Sinclair spent more than two years working through all the family papers to write his definitive biography of Jack London, *Jack* (1977). His television version of London's *Martin Eden* is now in worldwide release. Andrew Sinclair is married and has two sons.

Born in Atlanta, Georgia, in 1923, James Dickey earned his B.A. and M.A. degrees from Vanderbilt University, graduating magna cum laude, Phi Beta Kappa. He began devoting his full time to poetry at the age of thirty-eight. A Guggenheim Fellow, he was twice appointed Poetry Consultant to the Library of Congress. In addition to his many volumes of poetry, he is the author of the novel *Deliverance*.

THE CALL OF THE WILD, WHITE FANG,

and
Other Stories

Jack London

Edited by ANDREW SINCLAIR

Introduction by JAMES DICKEY

PENGUIN BOOKS

Penguin Books Ltd, Harmondsworth,
Middlesex, England
Penguin Books, 40 West 23rd Street,
New York, New York 10010, U.S.A.
Penguin Books Australia Ltd, Ringwood,
Victoria, Australia
Penguin Books Canada Limited, 2801 John Street,
Markham, Ontario, Canada L3R 1B4
Penguin Books (N.Z.) Ltd, 182–190 Wairau Road,
Auckland 10, New Zealand

"Bâtard" first published in *The Faith of Men and Other Stories* by
the Macmillan Company 1904
The Call of the Wild first published by the Macmillan Company 1903
"Love of Life" first published in *Love of Life and Other Stories* by
the Macmillan Company 1907
White Fang first published by the Macmillan Company 1906
Published together in The Penguin American Library 1981
Reprinted 1982, 1983

LIBRARY OF CONGRESS CATALOGING IN PUBLICATION DATA
London, Jack, 1876–1916.
The call of the wild, White fang, and other stories.
(The Penguin American library)
CONTENTS: Bâtard.—The call of the wild.—
Love of life—White fang.—
A note on Jack London's life and works.
I. Sinclair, Andrew.   II. Title.
III. Series: Penguin American library.
PS3523.O46A6 1980   813'.52   80-19658
ISBN 0 14 039.001 4

Printed in the United States of America by
George Banta Co., Inc., Harrisonburg, Virginia
Set in CRT Caslon

Contents

Introduction

"Primeval" is a word often used to describe Jack London's work, his attitude toward existence, and his own life. From the beginning of the intensive self-education he undertook early in his adolescence through the end of his life at the age of forty, he prided himself on his "animality," and identified with his chosen totem beast, the wolf. His gullible friend, the California poet George Sterling, called him Wolf, he referred to his wife as Mate-Woman, named his ill-fated mansion in the Sonoma Valley Wolf House, and created his most memorable human character, Wolf Larsen, in *The Sea Wolf*. Larsen exemplifies all of the characteristics London admired most: courage, resourcefulness, ruthlessness, and above all, a strength of will that he partly bases on that of Milton's Satan in *Paradise Lost*. Larsen's favorite lines from Milton are "To reign is worth ambition, though in hell:/Better to reign in hell than serve in heaven," a sentiment with which London certainly concurred.

This attitude toward the *figure* of the wolf—a kind of Presence, an image, a symbolic and very personal representation of a mythologized human being—is pervasive throughout all of London's Arctic tales and is implied in many of his other fictions. The reader should willingly give himself over to this interpretation of the wolf, and conjure the animal up in the guise of the mysterious, shadowy, and dangerous figment that London imagines it to be. We should encounter the Londonian wolf as we would a spirit symbolic of the deepest forest, the most extremely high and forbidding mountain range, the most desolate snowfield: in short, as the ultimate wild creature, supreme in savagery, mystery, and beauty.

The mythic wolf that London "found" in his single winter spent in the Canadian North during the Klondike Gold Rush of 1897–98 and imbued with strangeness and ferocity bears in fact little resemblance to any true wolf ever observed. In studies by biologist Adolph Murie and researchers like L. David Mech and Boyce Rensberger, the wolf emerges as a shy and likable animal with a strong aversion to fighting. There is no evidence that any wild wolf has ever killed a human being in North America. As Rensberger notes, "It has a rather playful, friendly nature among its fellows. Research findings to date show wolves to exhibit many of the behavioral patterns that should find favor among the more sentimentally inclined animal lovers."

And yet London's wolf is very much a part of the consciousness of many people, and as the wolf's habitat continues to shrink under the pressure of oil pipelines and other industrial encroachments, its mystery and its savage spirituality increase, now that vulnerability has been added. We need London's mythical wolf almost as much as we need the wildernesses of the world, for without such ghost-animals from the depths of the human subconscious we are alone with ourselves.

That Jack London, the Klondike, the wolf, and the dog should have come together in exactly the circumstances that the gold-fever afforded seems not so much a merely fortunate conjunction of events but a situation tinged strongly with elements of predestination, of fate. Born in poverty only a little above the truly abject, London displayed almost from the beginning such a will to dominate as might have been envied by Satan himself, or for that matter, by Milton. His early years were spent as a boy criminal, specializing in the piracy of oyster beds in San Francisco Bay, as a tramp on the roads and railroads of the United States and Canada, and as a laborer—or what he called a work-beast—in various menial and humiliating jobs, which fixed his mind irrevocably in favor of the exploited working classes and against any and all forms of capitalism, at least in theory.

During his later travels and his battles for survival in the economic wilderness, he came quickly to the belief that knowledge is indeed power. In his case, knowledge was more than the simple and too-abstract word "power" implied; it was muscle, blood, teeth, and stamina; it gave the force and direction that the will must take. When he landed in the Yukon in 1897, he had already read, with virtually superhuman voraciousness, hundreds of books and articles, principally in the fields of sociology, biology, and philosophy. He was alive with ideas and a search for ultimate meaning that amounted to an obsessively personal quest, and shared with the pre-Socratic philosophers—Thales, who assumed that water is the basic substance; Anaximenes, who believed the same thing of air; Anaximander, with his space or "boundlessness"; and Heraclitus, with process and fire—a belief that the great All is single and can be known. As he moved farther into the winter wilderness of the northern latitudes, he came increasingly to the conclusion that the "white silence" of the North is the indifferently triumphant demonstration of the All, the arena where the knowable Secret could most unequivocally be apprehended and, as the conditions demanded, lived. The snowfields, mountains, forests, and enormous frozen lakes were to London only the strictest, most spectacular, and unarguable symbols of the universal abyss, the eternal mystery at the heart of nothingness, or the eternal nothingness at the heart of mystery, as Herman Melville saw it in *Moby Dick.*

> Is it that by its [whiteness's] indefiniteness it shadows forth the heartless voids and immensities of the universe, and thus stabs us from behind with the thought of annihilation, when beholding the white depths of the milky way? Or is it that as in essence whiteness is not so much a color as the visible absence of color, and at the same time the concrete of all colors; is it for these reasons that there is such a dumb blankness, full of meaning, in a wide landscape of snows—a colorless, all-color of atheism from which we shrink?

London's whiteness, though its similarities of meaning are strikingly close to Melville's, has also some basic differences.

> A vast silence reigned over the land. The land itself was a desolation, lifeless, without movement, so lone and cold that the spirit of it was not even that of sadness. There was a hint in it of laughter, but of a laughter more terrible than any sadness—a laughter that was mirthless as the smile of the Sphinx, a laughter cold as the frost and partaking of the grimness of infallibility. It was the masterful and incommunicable wisdom of eternity laughing at the futility of life and the effort of life. It was the Wild, the savage, frozen-hearted Northland Wild.

London's scattered but deeply *felt* reading had so imbued him with Darwinian principles that he looked on the landscape of the Yukon as a kind of metaphysical arena in which natural selection and the survival of the fittest were enacted unendingly, illustrating (though to no perceiver but the casual) the "Law." The North is a background that determines character and action, bringing out in men certain qualities from the psychic depths of the race of all living beings. London does not attempt, as Melville does, to strike through the "mask." The "mask" in London's tales is more the classic masl of the actor, the mask that each participant feels rising to his face from the setting of the drama, the frozen features that *rerum natura* has always reserved for it.

As George Orwell has remarked, London's instincts "lay toward acceptance of a 'natural aristocracy' of strength, beauty and talent." Few writers have dwelt with such fixation on superlatives: "the strongest," "the biggest," "the handsomest," "the most cunning," "the fiercest," "the most ruthless." One cannot read these stories without agreeing with Orwell that "there is something in London [that] takes a kind of pleasure in the whole cruel process. It is not so much an approval of the harshness of nature, as a mystical belief that nature *is* like that. 'Nature red in tooth and claw.' Perhaps fierceness is the price of survival. The young slay the old, the strong slay the weak, by an inexorable law." London insists, as Melville does not, that there is a morality inherent in the twin drives of animal evolution; brute survival and the desire of the species to reproduce itself are not primary but exclusive motivations.

In this savage theater of extremes, this vast stage of indifference, where "the slightest whisper seemed sacrilege," London felt himself to be a man speaking out of the void of cosmic neutrality and even to it and for it, wearing, really, no mask but his half-frozen face, from which issued in steam and ice the truth of existence: the way things are.

The actors are men and dogs.

Down the frozen waterway toiled a string of wolfish dogs. Their bristly fur was rimed with frost. Their breath froze in the air as it left their mouths, spouting forth in spumes of vapor that settled upon the hair of their bodies and formed into crystals of frost. Leather harness was on the dogs. . .

In advance of the dogs, on wide snowshoes, toiled a man. At the rear of the sled toiled a second man. On the sled, in the box, lay a third man whose toil was over—a man whom the Wild had conquered and beaten down until he would never move nor struggle again. It is not the way of the Wild to like movement.

In the Arctic and particularly in the Gold Rush Arctic, the dog was of paramount importance. Men could not cover the great distances involved, much less carry their food and equipment, on foot. There were as yet no machines, not even railroads. Horses would have bogged down hopelessly in the snow and could not have lived off the food, such as fish, that the environment supplied. The solution to the finding and mining of gold was the dog, because of its physical qualifications, its adaptability, and even its kinship to other creatures occupying the "natural" scheme of things in which it was to function.

London's anthropomorphizing of animals is well known, and the instances in which he overindulges this tendency are frequent and sometimes absurd. He was no Rilke or Lawrence, seemingly able to project his own human point of observation into another entity, either living or inorganic, and *become* the contemplated Other. He could not and certainly would not have wanted to know, as Aldous Huxley said Lawrence did, "by personal experience, what it was like to be a tree or a daisy or a breaking wave or even the mysterious moon itself. He could get inside the skin of an animal and could tell you in the most convincing detail how it felt and how, dimly, inhumanly, it thought." London had no wish to negate himself in favor of becoming an animal; the London dog or wolf is presented not as itself but as London feels that *he* would feel if he were embodied in the form of a dog or a wolf. The self-dramatizing Nietzschean is always very much present. In the canine battle scenes, for example, London analyzes with an almost absurd and quite human confidence the various "tactics" employed by the participants.

> But Buck possessed a quality that made for greatness— imagination. He fought by instinct, but he could fight by head as well. He rushed, as though attempting the old shoulder trick, but at the last instant swept low to the snow and in. His teeth closed on Spitz's left fore leg. There was a crunch of breaking bone, and the white dog faced him on three legs. Thrice he tried to knock him over, then repeated the trick and broke the right fore leg.

Anyone who has ever seen dogs fighting knows that such subtleties as "the old shoulder trick" do not occur; if the affair is not merely one of a good deal of threatening noise, then one dog just goes for the other in any way possible. When London describes what dogs *do* rather than what they "think"—how they *look* when listening, how they appear when in repose, how they pace when restless or hungry—he is very good. When he makes a primitive philosopher of the dog in the same sense in which the author is himself a primitive philosopher, the result is less convincing. One believes of Bâtard that in five years "he heard but one kind word, received but one soft stroke of a hand, and then he did not know what manner of things they were." It is quite conceivable that a dog that had never received such treatment would not know how to respond. On the other hand, Buck's mystique of racial fulfillment, his metaphysical musculature, are so plainly impossible that one is tempted to forgo passages like:

> He was sounding the deeps of his nature, and of the parts of his nature that were deeper than he, going back into the womb of Time. He was mastered by the sheer surging of life, the tidal wave of being, the perfect joy of each

separate muscle, joint, and sinew in that it was everything that was not death, that it was aglow and rampant, expressing itself in movement, flying exultantly under the stars and over the face of dead matter that did not move.

Likewise, White Fang's encounter with the Californian electric streetcars "that were to him colossal screaming lynxes" is not the product of a first-rate imagination. London merely knew that, since White Fang had lived in the Arctic and lynxes also lived there, and since lynxes sometimes make noises and streetcars also make them, he could feel justified in combining these items in a figure of speech the reader would be inclined to take as reasonable because neither reader nor lynx nor London nor streetcars could prove it was not. A moment's reflection, however, should disclose how farfetched the image is; the dog would simply have been bothered by the utter *unfamiliarity* of the machine, would simply have apprehended it as a large noisemaking *something,* though assuredly no lynx.

White Fang was conceived as a "complete antithesis and companion piece to *The Call of the Wild.*" London averred that "I'm going to reverse the process. Instead of the devolution or decivilization of a dog, I'm going to give the evolution, the civilization of a dog—development of domesticity, faithfulness, love, morality, and all the amenities and virtues." Yet, why is *White Fang*—more than twice as long as *The Call of the Wild* and a good deal more virtue-bent in the human sense of intention, a story in which the animal protagonist ends not as the leader of a pack of wild wolves but crooning his "love-growl" amidst a chorus of city women rubbing his ears and calling him the Blessed Wolf—why is it so markedly inferior to the story of reversion? Largely, I think, because the events depicted in *The Call of the Wild* are closer to what one *wants* to see happen: because we desire the basic, the "natural," the *"what is"* to win and not the world of streetcars and sentimentalism that we have made. Thus, in a sense, if we accede to London's narrative we also are approving of God and his white, mocking malevolence, his "Law" maintaining sway over all the irrelevances and over-subtleties of mechanized life. We like the author for putting the perspective in this way, and especially in a way as forthright, inexorable, exciting, and involving as he commands.

The key to London's effectiveness is to be found in his complete absorption in the world he evokes. The author is *in* and committed to his creations to a degree very nearly unparalleled in the composition of fiction. The resulting go-for-broke, event-intoxicated, head-long wild-Irish prose-fury completely overrides a great many stylistic lapses and crudities that would ordinarily cause readers to smile. As Orwell notes, "the texture of the writing is poor, the phrases are worn and obvious, and the dialogue is erratic."

True, but it is nonetheless also true that London has at his best the ability to involve the reader in his story so thoroughly that nothing matters but *what* happens; in this sense he is basic indeed. His primary concern is action, with no pause to allow the savoring of verbal nuances or subtleties of insight. "La vérité, c'est dans la nuance," said Flaubert. London would have left that notion behind in the dog blood crystallizing on the ice floe, the eddying plume of a miner's frozen breath. His style is in presenting what *is,* and that only. As a writer London is at his most compelling in "presentational immediacy"; the more the passage relates to the nerves and feelings of the body, the more effective it is.

As he turned to go on, he spat speculatively. There was a sharp, explosive crackle that startled him. He spat again. And again, in the air, before it could fall to the snow, the spittle crackled. He knew that at fifty below spittle

crackled on the snow, but this spittle had crackled in the
air.

He is an artist of violent action, exemplifying what
the American poet Allen Tate meant when he said: "I
think of my poems as commentaries on those human
situations from which there is no escape." Once caught
in London's swirling, desperate, life-and-death violence, the reader has no escape either, for it is a vision
of exceptional and crucial vitality. London's most char-
acteristic tales have the graphic power of the best cin-
ema, and I for one hope that the film medium has not
exhausted such possibilities as the latest adaptations
assayed seem to encourage. Be that as it may, the
quintessential Jack London is in the on-rushing com-
pulsiveness of his northern stories. Few men have
more convincingly examined the connection between
the creative powers of the individual writer and the unconscious drive to breed and to survive, found in the
natural world.

—James Dickey

A Note on the Text

The text of this edition follows the texts of the first book editions of "Bâtard," published in *The Faith of Men and Other Stories* by the Macmillan Company in April 1904; of *The Call of the Wild,* published by the Macmillan Company in July 1903; of "Love of Life," published in *Love of Life and Other Stories* by the Macmillan Company in September 1907; and of *White Fang,* published by the Macmillan Company in September 1906. Jack London tended not to revise what he had first written for magazine publication, but he relied a great deal on the typing and editing of his second wife, Charmian Kittredge London, and on George Brett, his editor at the Macmillan Company. Brett actually bought *The Call of the Wild* outright for two thousand dollars because Jack London wanted to buy an old sloop for sailing. The editor recognized its potential and supervised it through the press. It made London's international reputation, as Brett promised that it would.

Very few corrections have been made in this edition, and only when London's use of archaisms or inversion makes the text unintelligible to the modern reader. Similarly, there have been very few changes in spelling or punctuation, for London was a master at the rhythms and halts of his prose style. As the discriminating H. L. Mencken wrote of him, "No other popular writer of his time did any better writing than you will find in *The Call of the Wild.* . . . Here, indeed, are all the elements of sound fiction: clear thinking, a sense of character, the dramatic instinct, and, above all, the adept putting together of words—words charming and slyly significant, words arranged, in a French phrase, for the respiration and the ear."

The Call of the Wild,
White Fang,
and Other Stories

BÂTARD

Bâtard was a devil. This was recognized throughout the Northland. "Hell's Spawn" he was called by many men, but his master, Black Leclère, chose for him the shameful name "Bâtard." Now Black Leclère was also a devil, and the twain were well matched. There is a saying that when two devils come together, hell is to pay. This is to be expected, and this certainly was to be expected when Bâtard and Black Leclère came together. The first time they met, Bâtard was a part-grown puppy, lean and hungry, with bitter eyes; and they met with a snap and snarl, and wicked looks, for Leclère's upper lip had a wolfish way of lifting and showing the white, cruel teeth. And it lifted then, and his eyes glinted viciously, as he reached for Bâtard and dragged him out from the squirming litter. It was certain that they divined each other, for on the instant Bâtard had buried his puppy fangs in Leclère's hand, and Leclère, thumb and finger, was coolly choking his young life out of him.

"Sacredam," the Frenchman said softly, flirting the quick blood from his bitten hand and gazing down on the little puppy choking and gasping in the snow.

Leclère turned to John Hamlin, storekeeper of the Sixty Mile Post. "Dat fo' w'at Ah lak heem. 'Ow moch, eh, you, M'sieu'? 'Ow moch? Ah buy heem, now; Ah buy heem queek."

21

And because he hated him with an exceeding bitter hate, Leclère bought Bâtard and gave him his shameful name. And for five years the twain adventured across the Northland, from St. Michael's and the Yukon delta to the head-reaches of the Pelly and even so far as the Peace River, Athabasca, and the Great Slave. And they acquired a reputation for uncompromising wickedness, the like of which never before attached itself to man and dog.

Bâtard did not know his father,—hence his name, —but, as John Hamlin knew, his father was a great gray timber wolf. But the mother of Bâtard, as he dimly remembered her, was snarling, bickering, obscene, husky, full-fronted and heavy-chested, with a malign eye, a cat-like grip on life, and a genius for trickery and evil. There was neither faith nor trust in her. Her treachery alone could be relied upon, and her wild-wood amours attested her general depravity. Much of evil and much of strength were there in these, Bâtard's progenitors, and, bone and flesh of their bone and flesh, he had inherited it all. And then came Black Leclère, to lay his heavy hand on the bit of pulsating puppy life, to press and prod and mould till it became a big bristling beast, acute in knavery, overspilling with hate, sinister, malignant, diabolical. With a proper master Bâtard might have made an ordinary, fairly efficient sled-dog. He never got the chance: Leclère but confirmed him in his congenital iniquity.

The history of Bâtard and Leclère is a history of war—of five cruel, relentless years, of which their first meeting is fit summary. To begin with, it was Leclère's fault, for he hated with understanding and intelligence, while the long-legged, ungainly puppy hated only blindly, instinctively, without reason or method. At first there were no refinements of cruelty (these were to come later), but simple beatings and crude brutalities. In one of these Bâtard had an ear injured. He never regained control of the riven muscles, and ever after the ear drooped limply down to keep keen the memory of his tormentor. And he never forgot.

His puppyhood was a period of foolish rebellion. He was always worsted, but he fought back because it was his nature to fight back. And he was unconquerable. Yelping shrilly from the pain of lash and club, he none the less contrived always to throw in the defiant snarl, the bitter vindictive menace of his soul which fetched without fail more blows and beatings. But his was his mother's tenacious grip on life. Nothing could kill him. He flourished under misfortune, grew fat with famine, and out of his terrible struggle for life developed a preternatural intelligence. His were the stealth and cunning of the husky, his mother, and the fierceness and valor of the wolf, his father.

Possibly it was because of his father that he never wailed. His puppy yelps passed with his lanky legs, so that he became grim and taciturn, quick to strike, slow to warn. He answered curse with snarl, and blow with snap, grinning the while his implacable hatred; but never again, under the extremest agony, did Leclère bring from him the cry of fear nor of pain. This unconquerableness but fanned Leclère's wrath and stirred him to greater deviltries.

Did Leclère give Bâtard half a fish and to his mates whole ones, Bâtard went forth to rob other dogs of their fish. Also he robbed caches and expressed himself in a thousand rogueries, till he became a terror to all dogs and masters of dogs. Did Leclère beat Bâtard and fondle Babette,—Babette who was not half the worker he was,—why Bâtard threw her down in the snow and broke her hind leg in his heavy jaws, so that Leclère was forced to shoot her. Likewise, in bloody battles, Bâtard mastered all his team-mates, set them the law of trail and forage, and made them live to the law he set.

In five years he heard but one kind word, received

but one soft stroke of a hand, and then he did not know
what manner of things they were. He leaped like the
untamed thing he was, and his jaws were together in a
flash. It was the missionary at Sunrise, a newcomer in
the country, who spoke the kind word and gave the
soft stroke of the hand. And for six months after, he
wrote no letters home to the States, and the surgeon at
McQuestion travelled two hundred miles on the ice to
save him from blood-poisoning.

Men and dogs looked askance at Bâtard when he
drifted into their camps and posts. The men greeted
him with feet threateningly lifted for the kick, the dogs
with bristling manes and bared fangs. Once a man did
kick Bâtard, and Bâtard, with quick wolf snap, closed
his jaws like a steel trap on the man's calf and crunched
down to the bone. Whereat the man was determined to
have his life, only Black Leclère, with ominous eyes
and naked hunting-knife, stepped in between. The killing of Bâtard—ah, *sacredam, that* was a pleasure
Leclère reserved for himself. Some day it would happen, or else—bah! who was to know? Anyway, the
problem would be solved.

For they had become problems to each other. The
very breath each drew was a challenge and a menace to
the other. Their hate bound them together as love
could never bind. Leclère was bent on the coming of
the day when Bâtard should wilt in spirit and cringe
and whimper at his feet. And Bâtard—Leclère knew
what was in Bâtard's mind, and more than once had
read it in Bâtard's eyes. And so clearly had he read
that, when Bâtard was at his back, he made it a point to
glance often over his shoulder.

Men marvelled when Leclère refused large money
for the dog. "Some day you will kill him and be out his
price," said John Hamlin once, when Bâtard lay panting in the snow where Leclère had kicked him, and no
one knew whether his ribs were broken, and no one
dared look to see.

"Dat," said Leclère, dryly, "dat is my biz'ness, *M'sieu'*."

And the men marvelled that Bâtard did not run away. They did not understand. But Leclère understood. He was a man who lived much in the open, beyond the sound of human tongue, and he had learned the voices of wind and storm, the sigh of night, the whisper of dawn, the clash of day. In a dim way he could hear the green things growing, the running of the sap, the bursting of the bud. And he knew the subtle speech of the things that moved, of the rabbit in the snare, the moody raven beating the air with hollow wing, the baldface shuffling under the moon, the wolf like a gray shadow gliding betwixt the twilight and the dark. And to him Bâtard spoke clear and direct. Full well he understood why Bâtard did not run away, and he looked more often over his shoulder.

When in anger, Bâtard was not nice to look upon, and more than once he had leapt for Leclère's throat, to be stretched quivering and senseless in the snow, by the butt of the ever ready dogwhip. And so Bâtard learned to bide his time. When he reached his full strength and prime of youth, he thought the time had come. He was broad-chested, powerfully-muscled, of far more than ordinary size, and his neck from head to shoulders was a mass of bristling hair—to all appearances a full-blooded wolf. Leclère was lying asleep in his furs when Bâtard deemed the time to be ripe. He crept upon him stealthily, head low to earth and lone ear laid back, with a feline softness of tread. Bâtard breathed gently, very gently, and not till he was close at hand did he raise his head. He paused for a moment and looked at the bronzed full throat, naked and knotty, and swelling to a deep steady pulse. The slaver dripped down his fangs and slid off his tongue at the sight, and in that moment he remembered his drooping ear, his uncounted blows and prodigious wrongs, and without a sound sprang on the sleeping man.

Leclère awoke to the pang of the fangs in his throat, and, perfect animal that he was, he awoke clear-headed and with full comprehension. He closed on Bâtard's windpipe with both his hands, and rolled out of his furs to get his weight uppermost. But the thousands of Bâtard's ancestors had clung at the throats of unnumbered moose and caribou and dragged them down, and the wisdom of those ancestors was his. When Leclère's weight came on top of him, he drove his hind legs upward and in, and clawed down chest and abdomen, ripping and tearing through skin and muscle. And when he felt the man's body wince above him and lift, he worried and shook at the man's throat. His team-mates closed around in a snarling circle, and Bâtard, with failing breath and fading sense, knew that their jaws were hungry for him. But that did not matter—it was the man, the man above him, and he ripped and clawed, and shook and worried, to the last ounce of his strength. But Leclère choked him with both his hands, till Bâtard's chest heaved and writhed for the air denied, and his eyes glazed and set, and his jaws slowly loosened, and his tongue protruded black and swollen.

"Eh? *Bon,* you devil!" Leclère gurgled, mouth and throat clogged with his own blood, as he shoved the dizzy dog from him.

And then Leclère cursed the other dogs off as they fell upon Bâtard. They drew back into a wider circle, squatting alertly on their haunches and licking their chops, the hair on every neck bristling and erect.

Bâtard recovered quickly, and at sound of Leclère's voice, tottered to his feet and swayed weakly back and forth.

"A-h-ah! You beeg devil!" Leclère spluttered, "Ah fix you; Ah fix you plentee, by *Gar!*"

Bâtard, the air biting into his exhausted lungs like wine, flashed full into the man's face, his jaws missing and coming together with a metallic clip. They rolled over and over on the snow, Leclère striking madly with his fists. Then they separated, face to face, and circled back and forth before each other. Leclère could have drawn his knife. His rifle was at his feet. But the beast in him was up and raging. He would do the thing with his hands—and his teeth. Bâtard sprang in, but Leclère knocked him over with a blow of the fist, fell upon him, and buried his teeth to the bone in the dog's shoulder.

It was a primordial setting and a primordial scene, such as might have been in the savage youth of the world. An open space in a dark forest, a ring of grinning wolf-dogs, and in the centre two beasts, locked in combat, snapping and snarling, raging madly about, panting, sobbing, cursing, straining, wild with passion, in a fury of murder, ripping and tearing and clawing in elemental brutishness.

But Leclère caught Bâtard behind the ear with a blow from his fist, knocking him over, and, for the instant, stunning him. Then Leclère leaped upon him with his feet, and sprang up and down, striving to grind him into the earth. Both Bâtard's hind legs were broken ere Leclère ceased that he might catch breath.

"A-a-ah! A-a-ah!" he screamed, incapable of speech, shaking his fist, through sheer impotence of throat and larynx.

But Bâtard was indomitable. He lay there in a helpless welter, his lip feebly lifting and writhing to the snarl he had not the strength to utter. Leclère kicked him, and the tired jaws closed on the ankle, but could not break the skin.

Then Leclère picked up the whip and proceeded almost to cut him to pieces, at each stroke of the lash crying: "Dis taim Ah break you! Eh? By *Gar!* Ah break you!"

In the end, exhausted, fainting from loss of blood, he crumpled up and fell by his victim, and when the wolf-dogs closed in to take their vengeance, with his last consciousness dragged his body on top of Bâtard to shield him from their fangs.

This occurred not far from Sunrise, and the missionary, opening the door to Leclère a few hours later, was surprised to note the absence of Bâtard from the team. Nor did his surprise lessen when Leclère threw back the robes from the sled, gathered Bâtard into his arms, and staggered across the threshold. It happened that the surgeon of McQuestion, who was something of a gadabout, was up on a gossip, and between them they proceeded to repair Leclère.

"Merci, non," said he. *"Do you fix firs' de dog. To die? Non.* Eet is not good. Becos' heem Ah mus' yet break. Dat fo' w'at he mus' not die."

The surgeon called it a marvel, the missionary a miracle, that Leclère pulled through at all; and so weakened was he, that in the spring the fever got him, and he went on his back again. Bâtard had been in even worse plight, but his grip on life prevailed, and the bones of his hind legs knit, and his organs righted themselves, during the several weeks he lay strapped to the floor. And by the time Leclère, finally convalescent, sallow and shaky, took the sun by the cabin door, Bâtard had reasserted his supremacy among his kind, and brought not only his own team-mates but the missionary's dogs into subjection.

He moved never a muscle, nor twitched a hair, when, for the first time, Leclère tottered out on the missionary's arm, and sank down slowly and with infinite caution on the three-legged stool.

"Bon!" he said. *"Bon!* De good sun!" And he stretched out his wasted hands and washed them in the warmth.

Then his gaze fell on the dog, and the old light blazed back in his eyes. He touched the missionary lightly on the arm. *"Mon père,* dat is one beeg devil, dat Bâtard. You will bring me one pistol, so, dat Ah drink de sun in peace."

And thenceforth for many days he sat in the sun before the cabin door. He never dozed, and the pistol lay always across his knees. Bâtard had a way, the first thing each day, of looking for the weapon in its wonted place. At sight of it he would lift his lip faintly in token that he understood, and Leclère would lift his own lip in an answering grin. One day the missionary took note of the trick.

"Bless me!" he said. "I really believe the brute comprehends."

Leclère laughed softly. "Look you, *mon père*. Dat w'at Ah now spik, to dat does he lissen."

As if in confirmation, Bâtard just perceptibly wriggled his lone ear up to catch the sound.

"Ah say 'keel.'"

Bâtard growled deep in his throat, the hair bristled along his neck, and every muscle went tense and expectant.

"Ah lift de gun, so, like dat." And suiting action to word, he sighted the pistol at Bâtard.

Bâtard, with a single leap, sideways, landed around the corner of the cabin out of sight.

"Bless me!" he repeated at intervals.

Leclère grinned proudly.

"But why does he not run away?"

The Frenchman's shoulders went up in the racial shrug that means all things from total ignorance to infinite understanding.

"Then why do you not kill him?"

Again the shoulders went up.

"*Mon père,*" he said after a pause, "de taim is not yet. He is one beeg devil. Some taim Ah break heem, so, an' so, all to leetle bits. Hey? Some taim. *Bon!*"

A day came when Leclère gathered his dogs together and floated down in a bateau to Forty Mile, and so on to the Porcupine, where he took a commission from the P. C. Company, and went exploring for the better part of a year. After that he poled up the Koyokuk to deserted Arctic City, and later came drifting back, from camp to camp, along the Yukon. And during the long months Bâtard was well lessoned. He learned many tortures, and, notably, the torture of hunger, the torture of thirst, the torture of fire, and, worst of all, the torture of music.

Like the rest of his kind, he did not enjoy music. It gave him exquisite anguish, racking him nerve by nerve, and ripping apart every fibre of his being. It made him howl, long and wolf-like, as when the wolves bay the stars on frosty nights. He could not help howling. It was his one weakness in the contest with Leclère, and it was his shame. Leclère, on the other hand, passionately loved music—as passionately as he loved strong drink. And when his soul clamored for expression, it usually uttered itself in one or the other of the two ways, and more usually in both ways. And when he had drunk, his brain a-lilt with unsung song and the devil in him aroused and rampant, his soul found its supreme utterance in torturing Bâtard.

"Now we will haf a leetle museek," he would say. "Eh? W'at you t'ink, Bâtard?"

It was only an old and battered harmonica, tenderly treasured and patiently repaired; but it was the best that money could buy, and out of its silver reeds he drew weird vagrant airs that men had never heard before. Then Bâtard, dumb of throat, with teeth tight clenched, would back away, inch by inch, to the farthest cabin corner. And Leclère, playing, playing, a stout club tucked under his arm, followed the animal up, inch by inch, step by step, till there was no further retreat.

At first Bâtard would crowd himself into the smallest possible space, grovelling close to the floor; but as the music came nearer and nearer, he was forced to uprear, his back jammed into the logs, his fore legs fanning the air as though to beat off the rippling waves of sound.

He still kept his teeth together, but severe muscular contractions attacked his body, strange twitchings and jerkings, till he was all a-quiver and writhing in silent torment. As he lost control, his jaws spasmodically wrenched apart, and deep throaty vibrations issued forth, too low in the register of sound for human ear to catch. And then, nostrils distended, eyes dilated, hair bristling in helpless rage, arose the long wolf howl. It came with a slurring rush upward, swelling to a great heart-breaking burst of sound, and dying away in sadly cadenced woe—then the next rush upward, octave upon octave; the bursting heart; and the infinite sorrow and misery, fainting, fading, falling, and dying slowly away.

It was fit for hell. And Leclère, with fiendish ken, seemed to divine each particular nerve and heartstring, and with long wails and tremblings and sobbing minors to make it yield up its last shred of grief. It was frightful, and for twenty-four hours after, Bâtard was nervous and unstrung, starting at common sounds, tripping over his own shadow, but, withal, vicious and masterful with his team-mates. Nor did he show signs of a breaking spirit. Rather did he grow more grim and taciturn, biding his time with an inscrutable patience that began to puzzle and weigh upon Leclère. The dog would lie in the firelight, motionless, for hours, gazing straight before him at Leclère, and hating him with his bitter eyes.

Often the man felt that he had bucked against the very essence of life—the unconquerable essence that swept the hawk down out of the sky like a feathered thunderbolt, that drove the great gray goose across the zones, that hurled the spawning salmon through two thousand miles of boiling Yukon flood. At such times he felt impelled to express his own unconquerable essence; and with strong drink, wild music, and Bâtard, he indulged in vast orgies, wherein he pitted his puny strength in the face of things, and challenged all that was, and had been, and was yet to be.

"Dere is somet'ing dere," he affirmed, when the rhythmed vagaries of his mind touched the secret chords of Bâtard's being and brought forth the long lugubrious howl. "Ah pool eet out wid bot' my han's, so, an' so. Ha! Ha! Eet is fonee! Eet is ver' fonee! De priest chant, de womans pray, de mans swear, de leetle bird go *peep-peep*, Bâtard, heem go *yow-yow*—an' eet is all de ver' same t'ing. Ha! Ha!"

Father Gautier, a worthy priest, once reproved him with instances of concrete perdition. He never reproved him again.

"Eet may be so, *mon père*," he made answer. "An' Ah t'ink Ah go troo hell a-snappin', lak de hemlock troo de fire. Eh, *mon père?*"

But all bad things come to an end as well as good, and so with Black Leclère. On the summer low water, in a poling boat, he left McDougall for Sunrise. He left McDougall in company with Timothy Brown, and arrived at Sunrise by himself. Further, it was known that they had quarrelled just previous to pulling out; for the *Lizzie,* a wheezy ten-ton sternwheeler, twenty-four hours behind, beat Leclère in by three days. And when he did get in, it was with a clean-drilled bullet-hole through his shoulder muscle, and a tale of ambush and murder.

A strike had been made at Sunrise, and things had changed considerably. With the infusion of several hundred gold-seekers, a deal of whiskey, and half a dozen equipped gamblers, the missionary had seen the page of his years of labor with the Indians wiped clean. When the squaws became preoccupied with cooking beans and keeping the fire going for the wifeless miners, and the bucks with swapping their warm furs for black bottles and broken timepieces, he took to his bed, said "bless me" several times, and departed to his final accounting in a rough-hewn, oblong box. Whereupon the gamblers moved their roulette and faro tables into the mission house, and the click of chips and clink of glasses went up from dawn till dark and to dawn again.

Now Timothy Brown was well beloved among these adventurers of the North. The one thing against him was his quick temper and ready fist,—a little thing, for which his kind heart and forgiving hand more than atoned. On the other hand, there was nothing to atone for Black Leclère. He was "black," as more than one remembered deed bore witness, while he was as well hated as the other was beloved. So the men of Sunrise put an antiseptic dressing on his shoulder and hauled him before Judge Lynch.

It was a simple affair. He had quarrelled with Timothy Brown at McDougall. With Timothy Brown he had left McDougall. Without Timothy Brown he had arrived at Sunrise. Considered in the light of his evilness, the unanimous conclusion was that he had killed Timothy Brown. On the other hand, Leclère acknowledged their facts, but challenged their conclusion, and gave his own explanation. Twenty miles out of Sunrise he and Timothy Brown were poling the boat along the rocky shore. From that shore two rifle-shots rang out. Timothy Brown pitched out of the boat and went down bubbling red, and that was the last of Timothy Brown. He, Leclère, pitched into the bottom of the boat with a stinging shoulder. He lay very quiet, peeping at the shore. After a time two Indians stuck up their heads and came out to the water's edge, carrying between them a birch-bark canoe. As they launched it, Leclère let fly. He potted one, who went over the side after the manner of Timothy Brown. The other dropped into the bottom of the canoe, and then canoe and poling boat went down the stream in a drifting battle. After that they hung up on a split current, and the canoe passed on one side of an island, the poling boat on the other. That was the last of the canoe, and he came on into Sunrise. Yes, from the way the Indian in the canoe jumped, he was sure he had potted him. That was all.

This explanation was not deemed adequate. They gave him ten hours' grace while the *Lizzie* steamed down to investigate. Ten hours later she came wheezing back to Sunrise. There had been nothing to investigate. No evidence had been found to back up his statements. They told him to make his will, for he possessed a fifty-thousand-dollar Sunrise claim, and they were a law-abiding as well as a law-giving breed.

Leclère shrugged his shoulders. "Bot one t'ing," he said, "a leetle, w'at you call, favor—a leetle favor, dat is eet. I gif my feefty t'ousan' dollair to de church. I gif my husky dog, Bâtard, to de devil. De leetle favor? Firs' you hang heem, an' den you hang me. Eet is good, eh?"

Good it was, they agreed, that Hell's Spawn should break trail for his master across the last divide, and the court was adjourned down to the river bank, where a big spruce tree stood by itself. Slackwater Charley put a hangman's knot in the end of a hauling-line, and the noose was slipped over Leclère's head and pulled tight around his neck. His hands were tied behind his back, and he was assisted to the top of a cracker box. Then the running end of the line was passed over an overhanging branch, drawn taut, and made fast. To kick the box out from under would leave him dancing on the air.

"Now for the dog," said Webster Shaw, sometime mining engineer. "You'll have to rope him, Slackwater."

Leclère grinned. Slackwater took a chew of tobacco, rove a running noose, and proceeded leisurely to coil a few turns in his hand. He paused once or twice to brush particularly offensive mosquitoes from off his face. Everybody was brushing mosquitoes, except Leclère, about whose head a small cloud was visible. Even Bâtard, lying full-stretched on the ground, with his fore paws rubbed the pests away from eyes and mouth.

But while Slackwater waited for Bâtard to lift his head, a faint call came from the quiet air, and a man was seen running across the flat from Sunrise. It was the storekeeper.

"C-call 'er off, boys," he panted, as he came in among them. "Little Sandy and Bernadotte's jes' got in," he explained with returning breath. "Landed down below an' come up by the short cut. Got the Beaver with 'm. Picked 'm up in his canoe, stuck in a back channel, with a couple of bullet holes in 'm. Other buck was Klok-Kutz, the one that knocked spots out of his squaw and dusted."

"Eh? W'at Ah say? Eh?" Leclère cried exultantly. "Dat de one fo' sure! Ah know. Ah spik true."

"The thing to do is to teach these damned Siwashes a little manners," spoke Webster Shaw. "They're getting fat and sassy, and we'll have to bring them down a peg. Round in all the bucks and string up the Beaver for an object lesson. That's the programme. Come on and let's see what he's got to say for himself."

"Heh, M'sieu'!" Leclère called, as the crowd began to melt away through the twilight in the direction of Sunrise. "Ah lak ver' moch to see de fon."

"Oh, we'll turn you loose when we come back," Webster Shaw shouted over his shoulder. "In the meantime meditate on your sins and the ways of Providence. It will do you good, so be grateful."

As is the way with men who are accustomed to great hazards, whose nerves are healthy and trained in patience, so it was with Leclère, who settled himself to the long wait—which is to say that he reconciled his mind to it. There was no settling of the body, for the taut rope forced him to stand rigidly erect. The least relaxation of the leg muscles pressed the rough-fibred noose into his neck, while the upright position caused him much pain in his wounded shoulder. He projected his under lip and expelled his breath upward along his face to blow the mosquitoes away from his eyes. But the situation had its compensation. To be snatched from the maw of death was well worth a little bodily suffering, only it was unfortunate that he should miss the hanging of the Beaver.

And so he mused, till his eyes chanced to fall upon Bâtard, head between fore paws and stretched on the ground asleep. And then Leclère ceased to muse. He studied the animal closely, striving to sense if the sleep were real or feigned. Bâtard's sides were heaving regularly, but Leclère felt that the breath came and went a shade too quickly; also he felt that there was a vigilance or alertness to every hair that belied unshackling sleep. He would have given his Sunrise claim to be assured that the dog was not awake, and once, when one of his joints cracked, he looked quickly and guiltily at Bâtard to see if he roused. He did not rouse then, but a few minutes later he got up slowly and lazily, stretched, and looked carefully about him.

"*Sacredam,*" said Leclère under his breath.

Assured that no one was in sight or hearing, Bâtard sat down, curled his upper lip almost into a smile, looked up at Leclère, and licked his chops.

"Ah see my feenish," the man said, and laughed sardonically aloud.

Bâtard came nearer, the useless ear wabbling, the good ear cocked forward with devilish comprehension. He thrust his head on one side quizzically, and advanced with mincing, playful steps. He rubbed his body gently against the box till it shook and shook again. Leclère teetered carefully to maintain his equilibrium.

"Bâtard," he said calmly, "look out. Ah keel you."

Bâtard snarled at the word and shook the box with greater force. Then he upreared, and with his fore paws threw his weight against it higher up. Leclère kicked out with one foot, but the rope bit into his neck and checked so abruptly as nearly to overbalance him.

"Hi, ya! *Chook! Mush-on!*" he screamed.

Bâtard retreated, for twenty feet or so, with a fiendish levity in his bearing that Leclère could not mistake. He remembered the dog often breaking the scum of ice on the water hole, by lifting up and throwing his weight upon it; and, remembering, he understood what he now had in mind. Bâtard faced about and paused. He showed his white teeth in a grin, which Leclère answered; and then hurled his body through the air, in full charge, straight for the box.

Fifteen minutes later, Slackwater Charley and Webster Shaw, returning, caught a glimpse of a ghostly pendulum swinging back and forth in the dim light. As they hurriedly drew in closer, they made out the man's inert body, and a live thing that clung to it, and shook and worried, and gave to it the swaying motion.

"Hi, ya! *Chook!* you Spawn of Hell!" yelled Webster Shaw.

But Bâtard glared at him, and snarled threateningly, without loosing his jaws.

Slackwater Charley got out his revolver, but his hand was shaking, as with a chill, and he fumbled.

"Here, you take it," he said, passing the weapon over.

Webster Shaw laughed shortly, drew a sight between the gleaming eyes, and pressed the trigger. Bâtard's body twitched with the shock, threshed the ground spasmodically for a moment, and went suddenly limp. But his teeth still held fast locked.

THE CALL OF
THE WILD

Contents

CHAPTER I

Into the Primitive

"Old longings nomadic leap,
     Chafing at custom's chain;
Again from its brumal sleep
     Wakens the ferine strain."

Buck did not read the newspapers, or he would have known that trouble was brewing, not alone for himself, but for every tide-water dog, strong of muscle and with warm, long hair, from Puget Sound to San Diego. Because men, groping in the Arctic darkness, had found a yellow metal, and because steamship and transportation companies were booming the find, thousands of men were rushing into the Northland. These men wanted dogs, and the dogs they wanted were heavy dogs, with strong muscles by which to toil, and furry coats to protect them from the frost.

Buck lived at a big house in the sun-kissed Santa Clara Valley. Judge Miller's place, it was called. It stood back from the road, half hidden among the trees, through which glimpses could be caught of the wide cool veranda that ran around its four sides. The house was approached by gravelled driveways which wound about through wide-spreading lawns and under the interlacing boughs of tall poplars. At the rear things were on even a more spacious scale than at the front. There were great stables, where a dozen grooms and boys held forth, rows of vine-clad servants' cottages, an endless and orderly array of outhouses, long grape arbors, green pastures, orchards, and berry patches. Then there was the pumping plant for the artesian well, and the big cement tank where Judge Miller's boys took their morning plunge and kept cool in the hot afternoon.

And over this great demesne Buck ruled. Here he was born, and here he had lived the four years of his life. It was true, there were other dogs. There could not but be other dogs on so vast a place, but they did not count. They came and went, resided in the populous kennels, or lived obscurely in the recesses of the house after the fashion of Toots, the Japanese pug, or Ysabel, the Mexican hairless,—strange creatures that rarely put nose out of doors or set foot to ground. On the other hand, there were the fox terriers, a score of them at least, who yelped fearful promises at Toots and Ysabel looking out of the windows at them and protected by a legion of housemaids armed with brooms and mops.

But Buck was neither house-dog nor kennel-dog. The whole realm was his. He plunged into the swimming tank or went hunting with the Judge's sons; he escorted Mollie and Alice, the Judge's daughters, on long twilight or early morning rambles; on wintry nights he lay at the Judge's feet before the roaring library fire; he carried the Judge's grandsons on his back, or rolled them in the grass, and guarded their footsteps through wild adventures down to the fountain in the stable yard, and even beyond, where the paddocks were, and the berry patches. Among the terriers he stalked imperiously, and Toots and Ysabel he utterly ignored, for he was king,—king over all creeping, crawling, flying things of Judge Miller's place, humans included.

His father, Elmo, a huge St. Bernard, had been the Judge's inseparable companion, and Buck bid fair to follow in the way of his father. He was not so large,—he weighed only one hundred and forty pounds,—for his mother, Shep, had been a Scotch shepherd dog. Nevertheless, one hundred and forty pounds, to which was added the dignity that comes of good living and universal respect, enabled him to carry himself in right royal fashion. During the four years since his puppy-hood he had lived the life of a sated aristocrat; he had a fine pride in himself, was even a trifle egotistical, as country gentlemen sometimes become because of their insular situation. But he had saved himself by not becoming a mere pampered house-dog. Hunting and kindred outdoor delights had kept down the fat and hardened his muscles; and to him, as to the cold-tubbing races, the love of water had been a tonic and a health preserver.

And this was the manner of dog Buck was in the fall of 1897, when the Klondike strike dragged men from all the world into the frozen North. But Buck did not read the newspapers, and he did not know that Manuel, one of the gardener's helpers, was an undesirable acquaintance. Manuel had one besetting sin. He loved to play Chinese lottery. Also, in his gambling, he had one besetting weakness—faith in a system; and this made his damnation certain. For to play a system requires money, while the wages of a gardener's helper do not lap over the needs of a wife and numerous progeny.

The Judge was at a meeting of the Raisin Growers' Association, and the boys were busy organizing an athletic club, on the memorable night of Manuel's treachery. No one saw him and Buck go off through the orchard on what Buck imagined was merely a stroll. And with the exception of a solitary man, no one saw them arrive at the little flag station known as College Park. This man talked with Manuel, and money chinked between them.

"You might wrap up the goods before you deliver 'm," the stranger said gruffly, and Manuel doubled a piece of stout rope around Buck's neck under the collar.

"Twist it, an' you'll choke 'm plentee," said Manuel, and the stranger grunted a ready affirmative.

Buck had accepted the rope with quiet dignity. To

be sure, it was an unwonted performance: but he had learned to trust in men he knew, and to give them credit for a wisdom that outreached his own. But when the ends of the rope were placed in the stranger's hands, he growled menacingly. He had merely intimated his displeasure, in his pride believing that to intimate was to command. But to his surprise the rope tightened around his neck, shutting off his breath. In quick rage he sprang at the man, who met him halfway, grappled him close by the throat, and with a deft twist threw him over on his back. Then the rope tightened mercilessly, while Buck struggled in a fury, his tongue lolling out of his mouth and his great chest panting futilely. Never in all his life had he been so vilely treated, and never in all his life had he been so angry. But his strength ebbed, his eyes glazed, and he knew nothing when the train was flagged and the two men threw him into the baggage car.

The next he knew, he was dimly aware that his tongue was hurting and that he was being jolted along in some kind of a conveyance. The hoarse shriek of a locomotive whistling a crossing told him where he was. He had travelled too often with the Judge not to know the sensation of riding in a baggage car. He opened his eyes, and into them came the unbridled anger of a kidnapped king. The man sprang for his throat, but Buck was too quick for him. His jaws closed on the hand, nor did they relax till his senses were choked out of him once more.

"Yep, has fits," the man said, hiding his mangled hand from the baggageman, who had been attracted by the sounds of struggle. "I'm takin' 'm up for the boss to 'Frisco. A crack dog-doctor there thinks that he can cure 'm."

Concerning that night's ride, the man spoke most eloquently for himself, in a little shed back of a saloon on the San Francisco waterfront.

"All I get is fifty for it," he grumbled; "an' I wouldn't do it over for a thousand, cold cash."

His hand was wrapped in a bloody handkerchief, and the right trouser leg was ripped from knee to ankle.

"How much did the other mug get?" the saloon-keeper demanded.

"A hundred," was the reply. "Wouldn't take a sou less, so help me."

"That makes a hundred and fifty," the saloon-keeper calculated; "and he's worth it, or I'm a square-head."

The kidnapper undid the bloody wrappings and looked at his lacerated hand. "If I don't get the hydrophoby—"

"It'll be because you was born to hang," laughed the saloon-keeper. "Here, lend me a hand before you pull your freight," he added.

Dazed, suffering intolerable pain from throat and tongue, with the life half throttled out of him, Buck attempted to face his tormentors. But he was thrown down and choked repeatedly, till they succeeded in filing the heavy brass collar from off his neck. Then the rope was removed, and he was flung into a cagelike crate.

There he lay for the remainder of the weary night, nursing his wrath and wounded pride. He could not understand what it all meant. What did they want with him, these strange men? Why were they keeping him pent up in this narrow crate? He did not know why, but he felt oppressed by the vague sense of impending calamity. Several times during the night he sprang to his feet when the shed door rattled open, expecting to see the Judge, or the boys at least. But each time it was the bulging face of the saloon-keeper that peered in at him by the sickly light of a tallow candle. And each time the joyful bark that trembled in Buck's throat was twisted into a savage growl.

But the saloon-keeper let him alone, and in the morning four men entered and picked up the crate. More tormentors, Buck decided, for they were evil-looking creatures, ragged and unkempt; and he stormed and raged at them through the bars. They only laughed and poked sticks at him, which he promptly assailed with his teeth till he realized that that was what they wanted. Whereupon he lay down sullenly and allowed the crate to be lifted into a wagon. Then he, and the crate in which he was imprisoned, began a passage through many hands. Clerks in the express office took charge of him; he was carted about in another wagon; a truck carried him, with an assortment of boxes and parcels, upon a ferry steamer; he was trucked off the steamer into a great railway depot, and finally he was deposited in an express car.

For two days and nights this express car was dragged along at the tail of shrieking locomotives; and for two days and nights Buck neither ate nor drank. In his anger he had met the first advances of the express messengers with growls, and they had retaliated by teasing him. When he flung himself against the bars, quivering and frothing, they laughed at him and taunted him. They growled and barked like detestable dogs, mewed, and flapped their arms and crowed. It was all very silly, he knew, but therefore the more outrage to his dignity, and his anger waxed and waxed. He did not mind the hunger so much, but the lack of water caused him severe suffering and fanned his wrath to fever-pitch. For that matter, high-strung and finely sensitive, the ill treatment had flung him into a fever, which was fed by the inflammation of his parched and swollen throat and tongue.

He was glad for one thing: the rope was off his neck. That had given them an unfair advantage; but now that it was off, he would show them. They would never get another rope around his neck. Upon that he was resolved. For two days and nights he neither ate nor drank, and during those two days and nights of torment, he accumulated a fund of wrath that boded ill for whoever first fell foul of him. His eyes turned bloodshot, and he was metamorphosed into a raging fiend. So changed was he that the Judge himself would not have recognized him; and the express messengers breathed with relief when they bundled him off the train at Seattle.

Four men gingerly carried the crate from the wagon into a small, high-walled back yard. A stout man, with a red sweater that sagged generously at the neck, came out and signed the book for the driver. That was the man, Buck divined, the next tormentor, and he hurled himself savagely against the bars. The man smiled grimly, and brought a hatchet and a club.

"You ain't going to take him out now?" the driver asked.

"Sure," the man replied, driving the hatchet into the crate for a pry.

There was an instantaneous scattering of the four men who had carried it in, and from safe perches on top the wall they prepared to watch the performance.

Buck rushed at the splintering wood, sinking his teeth into it, surging and wrestling with it. Wherever the hatchet fell on the outside, he was there on the inside, snarling and growling, as furiously anxious to get out as the man in the red sweater was calmly intent on getting him out.

"Now, you red-eyed devil," he said, when he had made an opening sufficient for the passage of Buck's body. At the same time he dropped the hatchet and shifted the club to his right hand.

And Buck was truly a red-eyed devil, as he drew himself together for the spring, hair bristling, mouth foaming, a mad glitter in his bloodshot eyes. Straight at the man he launched his one hundred and forty pounds of fury, surcharged with the pent passion of two days and nights. In mid air, just as his jaws were about to close on the man, he received a shock that checked his body and brought his teeth together with an agonizing clip. He whirled over, fetching the ground on his back and side. He had never been struck by a club in his life, and did not understand. With a snarl that was part bark and more scream he was again on his feet and launched into the air. And again the shock came and he was brought crushingly to the ground. This time he was aware that it was the club, but his madness knew no caution. A dozen times he charged, and as often the club broke the charge and smashed him down.

After a particularly fierce blow he crawled to his feet, too dazed to rush. He staggered limply about, the blood flowing from nose and mouth and ears, his beautiful coat sprayed and flecked with bloody slaver. Then the man advanced and deliberately dealt him a frightful blow on the nose. All the pain he had endured was as nothing compared with the exquisite agony of this. With a roar that was almost lionlike in its ferocity, he again hurled himself at the man. But the man, shifting the club from right to left, coolly caught him by the under jaw, at the same time wrenching downward and backward. Buck described a complete circle in the air, and half of another, then crashed to the ground on his head and chest.

For the last time he rushed. The man struck the shrewd blow he had purposely withheld for so long, and Buck crumpled up and went down, knocked utterly senseless.

"He's no slouch at dog-breakin', that's wot I say," one of the men on the wall cried enthusiastically.

"Druther break cayuses any day, and twice on Sundays," was the reply of the driver, as he climbed on the wagon and started the horses.

Buck's senses came back to him, but not his strength. He lay where he had fallen, and from there he watched the man in the red sweater.

" 'Answers to the name of Buck,' " the man soliloquized, quoting from the saloon-keeper's letter which had announced the consignment of the crate and contents. "Well, Buck, my boy," he went on in a genial voice, "we've had our little ruction, and the best thing we can do is to let it go at that. You've learned your place, and I know mine. Be a good dog and all 'll go well and the goose hang high. Be a bad dog, and I'll whale the stuffin' outa you. Understand?"

As he spoke he fearlessly patted the head he had so mercilessly pounded, and though Buck's hair involuntarily bristled at touch of the hand, he endured it without protest. When the man brought him water he drank eagerly, and later bolted a generous meal of raw meat, chunk by chunk, from the man's hand.

He was beaten (he knew that); but he was not broken. He saw, once for all, that he stood no chance against a man with a club. He had learned the lesson, and in all his after life he never forgot it. That club was a revelation. It was his introduction to the reign of primitive law, and he met the introduction halfway. The facts of life took on a fiercer aspect; and while he faced that aspect uncowed, he faced it with all the latent cunning of his nature aroused. As the days went by, other dogs came, in crates and at the ends of ropes, some docilely, and some raging and roaring as he had come; and, one and all, he watched them pass under the dominion of the man in the red sweater. Again and again, as he looked at each brutal performance, the lesson was driven home to Buck: a man with a club was a lawgiver, a master to be obeyed, though not necessarily conciliated. Of this last Buck was never guilty, though he did see beaten dogs that fawned upon the man, and wagged their tails, and licked his hand. Also he saw one dog, that would neither conciliate nor obey, finally killed in the struggle for mastery.

Now and again men came, strangers, who talked excitedly, wheedlingly, and in all kinds of fashions to the man in the red sweater. And at such times that money passed between them the strangers took one or more of the dogs away with them. Buck wondered where they went, for they never came back; but the fear of the future was strong upon him, and he was glad each time when he was not selected.

Yet his time came, in the end, in the form of a little weazened man who spat broken English and many strange and uncouth exclamations which Buck could not understand.

"Sacredam!" he cried, when his eyes lit upon Buck. "Dat one dam bully dog! Eh? How moch?"

"Three hundred, and a present at that," was the prompt reply of the man in the red sweater. "And seein' it's government money, you ain't got no kick coming, eh, Perrault?"

Perrault grinned. Considering that the price of dogs had been boomed skyward by the unwonted demand, it was not an unfair sum for so fine an animal. The Canadian Government would be no loser, nor would its despatches travel the slower. Perrault knew dogs, and when he looked at Buck he knew that he was one in a thousand— "One in ten t'ousand," he commented mentally.

Buck saw money pass between them, and was not surprised when Curly, a good-natured Newfoundland, and he were led away by the little weazened man. That was the last he saw of the man in the red sweater, and as Curly and he looked at receding Seattle from the deck of the *Narwhal,* it was the last he saw of the warm Southland. Curly and he were taken below by Perrault and turned over to a black-faced giant called François. Perrault was a French-Canadian, and swarthy; but François was a French-Canadian half-breed, and twice as swarthy. They were a new kind of men to Buck (of which he was destined to see many more), and while he developed no affection for them, he none the less grew honestly to respect them. He speedily learned that Perrault and François were fair men, calm and impartial in administering justice, and too wise in the way of dogs to be fooled by dogs.

In the 'tween-decks of the *Narwhal*, Buck and Curly joined two other dogs. One of them was a big, snow-white fellow from Spitzbergen who had been brought away by a whaling captain, and who had later accompanied a Geological Survey into the Barrens. He was friendly, in a treacherous sort of way, smiling into one's face the while he meditated some underhand trick, as, for instance, when he stole from Buck's food at the first meal. As Buck sprang to punish him, the lash of François's whip sang through the air, reaching the culprit first; and nothing remained to Buck but to recover the bone. That was fair of François, he decided, and the half-breed began his rise in Buck's estimation.

The other dog made no advances, nor received any; also, he did not attempt to steal from the newcomers. He was a gloomy, morose fellow, and he showed Curly plainly that all he desired was to be left alone, and further, that there would be trouble if he were not left alone. "Dave" he was called, and he ate and slept, or yawned between times, and took interest in nothing, not even when the *Narwhal* crossed Queen Charlotte Sound and rolled and pitched and bucked like a thing possessed. When Buck and Curly grew excited, half wild with fear, he raised his head as though annoyed, favored them with an incurious glance, yawned, and went to sleep again.

Day and night the ship throbbed to the tireless pulse of the propeller, and though one day was very like another, it was apparent to Buck that the weather was steadily growing colder. At last, one morning, the propeller was quiet, and the *Narwhal* was pervaded with an atmosphere of excitement. He felt it, as did the other dogs, and knew that a change was at hand. François leashed them and brought them on deck. At the first step upon the cold surface, Buck's feet sank into a white mushy something very like mud. He sprang back with a snort. More of this white stuff was falling through the air. He shook himself, but more of it fell upon him. He sniffed it curiously, then licked some up on his tongue. It bit like fire, and the next instant was gone. This puzzled him. He tried it again, with the same result. The onlookers laughed uproariously, and he felt ashamed, he knew not why, for it was his first snow.

CHAPTER II

The Law of
Club and Fang

B uck's first day on the Dyea beach was like a nightmare. Every hour was filled with shock and surprise. He had been suddenly jerked from the heart of
civilization and flung into the heart of things primordial. No lazy, sun-kissed life was this, with nothing to
do but loaf and be bored. Here was neither peace, nor
rest, nor a moment's safety. All was confusion and action, and every moment life and limb were in peril.
There was imperative need to be constantly alert; for
these dogs and men were not town dogs and men.
They were savages, all of them, who knew no law but
the law of club and fang.

He had never seen dogs fight as these wolfish creatures fought, and his first experience taught him an
unforgetable lesson. It is true, it was a vicarious experience, else he would not have lived to profit by it. Curly
was the victim. They were camped near the log store,
where she, in her friendly way, made advances to a
husky dog the size of a full-grown wolf, though not
half so large as she. There was no warning, only a leap
in like a flash, a metallic clip of teeth, a leap out equally
swift, and Curly's face was ripped open from eye to
jaw.

It was the wolf manner of fighting, to strike and leap
away; but there was more to it than this. Thirty or

forty huskies ran to the spot and surrounded the combatants in an intent and silent circle. Buck did not comprehend that silent intentness, nor the eager way with which they were licking their chops. Curly rushed her antagonist, who struck again and leaped aside. He met her next rush with his chest, in a peculiar fashion that tumbled her off her feet. She never regained them. This was what the onlooking huskies had waited for. They closed in upon her, snarling and yelping, and she was buried, screaming with agony, beneath the bristling mass of bodies.

So sudden was it, and so unexpected, that Buck was taken aback. He saw Spitz run out his scarlet tongue in a way he had of laughing; and he saw François, swinging an axe, spring into the mess of dogs. Three men with clubs were helping him to scatter them. It did not take long. Two minutes from the time Curly went down, the last of her assailants were clubbed off. But she lay there limp and lifeless in the bloody, trampled snow, almost literally torn to pieces, the swart halfbreed standing over her and cursing horribly. The scene often came back to Buck to trouble him in his sleep. So that was the way. No fair play. Once down, that was the end of you. Well, he would see to it that he never went down. Spitz ran out his tongue and laughed again, and from that moment Buck hated him with a bitter and deathless hatred.

Before he had recovered from the shock caused by the tragic passing of Curly, he received another shock. François fastened upon him an arrangement of straps and buckles. It was a harness, such as he had seen the grooms put on the horses at home. And as he had seen horses work, so he was set to work, hauling François on a sled to the forest that fringed the valley, and returning with a load of firewood. Though his dignity was sorely hurt by thus being made a draught animal, he was too wise to rebel. He buckled down with a will and did his best, though it was all new and strange. François was stern, demanding instant obedience, and by virtue of his whip receiving instant obedience; while Dave, who was an experienced wheeler, nipped Buck's hind quarters whenever he was in error. Spitz was the leader, likewise experienced, and while he could not always get at Buck, he growled sharp reproof now and again, or cunningly threw his weight in the traces to jerk Buck into the way he should go. Buck learned easily, and under the combined tuition of his two mates and François made remarkable progress. Ere they returned to camp he knew enough to stop at "ho," to go ahead at "mush," to swing wide on the bends, and to keep clear of the wheeler when the loaded sled shot downhill at their heels.

"T'ree vair' good dogs," François told Perrault. "Dat Buck, heem pool lak hell. I tich heem queek as anyt'ing."

By afternoon, Perrault, who was in a hurry to be on the trail with his despatches, returned with two more dogs. "Billee" and "Joe" he called them, two brothers, and true huskies both. Sons of the one mother though they were, they were as different as day and night. Billee's one fault was his excessive good nature, while Joe was the very opposite, sour and introspective, with a perpetual snarl and a malignant eye. Buck received them in comradely fashion, Dave ignored them, while Spitz proceeded to thrash first one and then the other. Billee wagged his tail appeasingly, turned to run when he saw that appeasement was of no avail, and cried (still appeasingly) when Spitz's sharp teeth scored his flank. But no matter how Spitz circled, Joe whirled around on his heels to face him, mane bristling, ears laid back, lips writhing and snarling, jaws clipping together as fast as he could snap, and eyes diabolically gleaming—the incarnation of belligerent fear. So terrible was his appearance that Spitz was forced to forego disciplining him, but to cover his own discomfiture he turned upon the inoffensive and wailing Billee and drove him to the confines of the camp.

By evening Perrault secured another dog, an old husky, long and lean and gaunt, with a battle-scarred face and a single eye, which flashed a warning of prowess that commanded respect. He was called Sol-leks, which means the Angry One. Like Dave, he asked nothing, gave nothing, expected nothing; and when he marched slowly and deliberately into their midst, even Spitz left him alone. He had one peculiarity which Buck was unlucky enough to discover. He did not like to be approached on his blind side. Of this offence Buck was unwittingly guilty, and the first knowledge he had of his indiscretion was when Sol-leks whirled upon him and slashed his shoulder to the bone for three inches up and down. Forever after Buck avoided his blind side, and to the last of their comradeship had no more trouble. His only apparent ambition, like Dave's, was to be left alone; though, as Buck was afterward to learn, each of them possessed one other and even more vital ambition.

That night Buck faced the great problem of sleeping. The tent, illumined by a candle, glowed warmly in the midst of the white plain; and when he, as a matter of course, entered it, both Perrault and François bombarded him with curses and cooking utensils, till he recovered from his consternation and fled ignominiously into the outer cold. A chill wind was blowing that nipped him sharply and bit with especial venom into his wounded shoulder. He lay down on the snow and attempted to sleep, but the frost soon drove him shivering to his feet. Miserable and disconsolate, he wandered about among the many tents, only to find that one place was as cold as another. Here and there savage dogs rushed upon him, but he bristled his neck-hair and snarled (for he was learning fast), and they let him go his way unmolested.

Finally an idea came to him. He would return and see how his own team-mates were making out. To his astonishment, they had disappeared. Again he wandered about through the great camp, looking for them, and again he returned. Were they in the tent? No, that could not be, else he would not have been driven out. Then where could they possibly be? With drooping tail and shivering body, very forlorn indeed, he aimlessly circled the tent. Suddenly the snow gave way beneath his forelegs and he sank down. Something wriggled under his feet. He sprang back, bristling and snarling, fearful of the unseen and unknown. But a friendly little yelp reassured him, and he went back to investigate. A whiff of warm air ascended to his nostrils, and there, curled up under the snow in a snug ball, lay Billee. He whined placatingly, squirmed and wriggled to show his good will and intentions, and even ventured, as a bribe for peace, to lick Buck's face with his warm wet tongue.

Another lesson. So that was the way they did it, eh? Buck confidently selected a spot, and with much fuss and waste effort proceeded to dig a hole for himself. In a trice the heat from his body filled the confined space and he was asleep. The day had been long and arduous, and he slept soundly and comfortably, though he growled and barked and wrestled with bad dreams.

Nor did he open his eyes till roused by the noises of the waking camp. At first he did not know where he was. It had snowed during the night and he was completely buried. The snow walls pressed him on every side, and a great surge of fear swept through him—the fear of the wild thing for the trap. It was a token that he was harking back through his own life to the lives of his forebears; for he was a civilized dog, an unduly civilized dog, and of his own experience knew no trap and so could not of himself fear it. The muscles of his whole body contracted spasmodically and instinctively, the hair on his neck and shoulders stood on end, and

with a ferocious snarl he bounded straight up into the
blinding day, the snow flying about him in a flashing
cloud. Ere he landed on his feet, he saw the white camp
spread out before him and knew where he was and remembered all that had passed from the time he went
for a stroll with Manuel to the hole he had dug for
himself the night before.

A shout from François hailed his appearance. "Wot
I say?" the dog-driver cried to Perrault. "Dat Buck for
sure learn queek as anyt'ing."

Perrault nodded gravely. As courier for the Canadian Government, bearing important despatches, he
was anxious to secure the best dogs, and he was particularly gladdened by the possession of Buck.

Three more huskies were added to the team inside
an hour, making a total of nine, and before another
quarter of an hour had passed they were in harness and
swinging up the trail toward the Dyea Cañon. Buck
was glad to be gone, and though the work was hard he
found he did not particularly despise it. He was surprised at the eagerness which animated the whole team
and which was communicated to him; but still more
surprising was the change wrought in Dave and Sol-
leks. They were new dogs, utterly transformed by the
harness. All passiveness and unconcern had dropped
from them. They were alert and active, anxious that
the work should go well, and fiercely irritable with
whatever, by delay or confusion, retarded that work.
The toil of the traces seemed the supreme expression
of their being, and all that they lived for and the only
thing in which they took delight.

Dave was wheeler or sled dog, pulling in front of
him was Buck, then came Sol-leks; the rest of the team
was strung out ahead, single file, to the leader, which
position was filled by Spitz.

Buck had been purposely placed between Dave and
Sol-leks so that he might receive instruction. Apt

scholar that he was, they were equally apt teachers, never allowing him to linger long in error, and enforcing their teaching with their sharp teeth. Dave was fair and very wise. He never nipped Buck without cause, and he never failed to nip him when he stood in need of it. As François's whip backed him up, Buck found it to be cheaper to mend his ways than to retaliate. Once, during a brief halt, when he got tangled in the traces and delayed the start, both Dave and Sol-leks flew at him and administered a sound trouncing. The resulting tangle was even worse, but Buck took good care to keep the traces clear thereafter; and ere the day was done, so well had he mastered his work, his mates about ceased nagging him. François's whip snapped less frequently, and Perrault even honored Buck by lifting up his feet and carefully examining them.

It was a hard day's run, up the Cañon, through Sheep Camp, past the Scales and the timberline, across glaciers and snowdrifts hundreds of feet deep, and over the great Chilcoot Divide, which stands between the salt water and the fresh and guards forbiddingly the sad and lonely North. They made good time down the chain of lakes which fills the craters of extinct volcanoes, and late that night pulled into the huge camp at the head of Lake Bennett, where thousands of goldseekers were building boats against the break-up of the ice in the spring. Buck made his hole in the snow and slept the sleep of the exhausted just, but all too early was routed out in the cold darkness and harnessed with his mates to the sled.

That day they made forty miles, the trail being packed; but the next day, and for many days to follow, they broke their own trail, worked harder, and made poorer time. As a rule, Perrault travelled ahead of the team, packing the snow with webbed shoes to make it easier for them. François, guiding the sled at the gee-pole, sometimes exchanged places with him, but not often. Perrault was in a hurry, and he prided himself on his knowledge of ice, which knowledge was indispensable, for the fall ice was very thin, and where there was swift water, there was no ice at all.

Day after day, for days unending, Buck toiled in the traces. Always, they broke camp in the dark, and the first gray of dawn found them hitting the trail with fresh miles reeled off behind them. And always they pitched camp after dark, eating their bit of fish, and crawling to sleep into the snow. Buck was ravenous. The pound and a half of sun-dried salmon, which was his ration for each day, seemed to go nowhere. He never had enough, and suffered from perpetual hunger pangs. Yet the other dogs, because they weighed less and were born to the life, received a pound only of the fish and managed to keep in good condition.

He swiftly lost the fastidiousness which had characterized his old life. A dainty eater, he found that his mates, finishing first, robbed him of his unfinished ration. There was no defending it. While he was fighting off two or three, it was disappearing down the throats of the others. To remedy this, he ate as fast as they; and, so greatly did hunger compel him, he was not above taking what did not belong to him. He watched and learned. When he saw Pike, one of the new dogs, a clever malingerer and thief, slyly steal a slice of bacon when Perrault's back was turned, he duplicated the performance the following day, getting away with the whole chunk. A great uproar was raised, but he was unsuspected; while Dub, an awkward blunderer who was always getting caught, was punished for Buck's misdeed.

This first theft marked Buck as fit to survive in the hostile Northland environment. It marked his adaptability, his capacity to adjust himself to changing conditions, the lack of which would have meant swift and terrible death. It marked, further, the decay or going to pieces of his moral nature, a vain thing and a handicap in the ruthless struggle for existence. It was all well enough in the Southland, under the law of love and fellowship, to respect private property and personal feelings; but in the Northland, under the law of club and fang, whoso took such things into account was a fool, and in so far as he observed them he would fail to prosper.

Not that Buck reasoned it out. He was fit, that was all, and unconsciously he accommodated himself to the new mode of life. All his days, no matter what the odds, he had never run from a fight. But the club of the man in the red sweater had beaten into him a more fundamental and primitive code. Civilized, he could have died for a moral consideration, say the defence of Judge Miller's riding-whip; but the completeness of his decivilization was now evidenced by his ability to flee from the defence of a moral consideration and so save his hide. He did not steal for joy of it, but because of the clamor of his stomach. He did not rob openly, but stole secretly and cunningly, out of respect for club and fang. In short, the things he did were done because it was easier to do them than not to do them.

His development (or retrogression) was rapid. His muscles became hard as iron, and he grew callous to all ordinary pain. He achieved an internal as well as external economy. He could eat anything, no matter how loathsome or indigestible, and, once eaten, the juices of his stomach extracted the last least particle of nutriment; and his blood carried it to the farthest reaches of his body, building it into the toughest and stoutest of tissues. Sight and scent became remarkably keen, while his hearing developed such acuteness that in his sleep he heard the faintest sound and knew whether it heralded peace or peril. He learned to bite the ice out with his teeth when it collected between his toes; and when he was thirsty and there was a thick scum of ice over the water hole, he would break it by rearing and striking it with stiff fore legs. His most conspicuous trait was an ability to scent the wind and forecast it a night in advance. No matter how breathless the air when he dug his nest by tree or bank, the wind that later blew inevitably found him to leeward, sheltered and snug.

And not only did he learn by experience, but instincts long dead became alive again. The domesticated generations fell from him. In vague ways he remembered back to the youth of the breed, to the time the wild dogs ranged in packs through the primeval forest and killed their meat as they ran it down. It was no task for him to learn to fight with cut and slash and the quick wolf snap. In this manner had fought forgotten ancestors. They quickened the old life within him, and the old tricks which they had stamped into the heredity of the breed were his tricks. They came to him without effort or discovery, as though they had been his always. And when, on the still cold nights, he pointed his nose at a star and howled long and wolflike, it was his ancestors, dead and dust, pointing nose at star and howling down through the centuries and through him. And his cadences were their cadences, the cadences which voiced their woe and what to them was the meaning of the stillness, and the cold, and dark.

Thus, as token of what a puppet thing life is, the ancient song surged through him and he came into his own again; and he came because men had found a yellow metal in the North, and because Manuel was a gardener's helper whose wages did not lap over the needs of his wife and divers small copies of himself.

CHAPTER III

The Dominant
Primordial Beast

The dominant primordial beast was strong in Buck, and under the fierce conditions of trail life it grew and grew. Yet it was a secret growth. His newborn cunning gave him poise and control. He was too busy adjusting himself to the new life to feel at ease, and not only did he not pick fights, but he avoided them whenever possible. A certain deliberateness characterized his attitude. He was not prone to rashness and precipitate action; and in the bitter hatred between him and Spitz he betrayed no impatience, shunned all offensive acts.

On the other hand, possibly because he divined in Buck a dangerous rival, Spitz never lost an opportunity of showing his teeth. He even went out of his way to bully Buck, striving constantly to start the fight which could end only in the death of one or the other. Early in the trip this might have taken place had it not been for an unwonted accident. At the end of this day they made a bleak and miserable camp on the shore of Lake Le Barge. Driving snow, a wind that cut like a white-hot knife, and darkness had forced them to grope for a camping place. They could hardly have fared worse. At their backs rose a perpendicular wall of rock, and Perrault and François were compelled to make their fire and spread their sleeping robes on the ice of the lake itself. The tent they had discarded at Dyea in order to travel light. A few sticks of driftwood furnished them with a fire that thawed down through the ice and left them to eat supper in the dark.

Close in under the sheltering rock Buck made his nest. So snug and warm was it that he was loath to leave it when François distributed the fish which he had first thawed over the fire. But when Buck finished his ration and returned, he found his nest occupied. A warning snarl told him that the trespasser was Spitz. Till now Buck had avoided trouble with his enemy, but this was too much. The beast in him roared. He sprang upon Spitz with a fury which surprised them both, and Spitz particularly, for his whole experience with Buck had gone to teach him that his rival was an unusually timid dog, who managed to hold his own only because of his great weight and size.

François was surprised, too, when they shot out in a tangle from the disrupted nest and he divined the cause of the trouble. "A-a-ah!" he cried to Buck. "Gif it to heem, by Gar! Gif it to heem, the dirty t'eef!"

Spitz was equally willing. He was crying with sheer rage and eagerness as he circled back and forth for a chance to spring in. Buck was no less eager, and no less cautious, as he likewise circled back and forth for the advantage. But it was then that the unexpected happened, the thing which projected their struggle for supremacy far into the future, past many a weary mile of trail and toil.

An oath from Perrault, the resounding impact of a club upon a bony frame, and a shrill yelp of pain, heralded the breaking forth of pandemonium. The camp was suddenly discovered to be alive with skulking furry forms—starving huskies, four or five score of them, who had scented the camp from some Indian village. They had crept in while Buck and Spitz were fighting, and when the two men sprang among them with stout clubs they showed their teeth and fought back. They were crazed by the smell of the food. Perrault found one with head buried in the grub-box. His club landed heavily on the gaunt ribs, and the grub-box was capsized on the ground. On the instant a score of the famished brutes were scrambling for the bread and bacon. The clubs fell upon them unheeded. They yelped and howled under the rain of blows, but struggled none the less madly till the last crumb had been devoured.

In the meantime the astonished team-dogs had burst out of their nests only to be set upon by the fierce invaders. Never had Buck seen such dogs. It seemed as though their bones would burst through their skins. They were mere skeletons, draped loosely in draggled hides, with blazing eyes and slavered fangs. But the hunger-madness made them terrifying, irresistible. There was no opposing them. The team-dogs were swept back against the cliff at the first onset. Buck was beset by three huskies, and in a trice his head and shoulders were ripped and slashed. The din was frightful. Billee was crying as usual. Dave and Sol-leks, dripping blood from a score of wounds, were fighting bravely side by side. Joe was snapping like a demon. Once, his teeth closed on the foreleg of a husky, and he crunched down through the bone. Pike, the malingerer, leaped upon the crippled animal, breaking its neck with a quick flash of teeth and a jerk. Buck got a frothing adversary by the throat, and was sprayed with blood when his teeth sank through the jugular. The warm taste of it in his mouth goaded him to greater fierceness. He flung himself upon another, and at the same time felt teeth sink into his own throat. It was Spitz, treacherously attacking from the side.

Perrault and François, having cleaned out their part of the camp, hurried to save their sled-dogs. The wild wave of famished beasts rolled back before them, and

Buck shook himself free. But it was only for a moment. The two men were compelled to run back to save the grub; upon which the huskies returned to the attack on the team. Billee, terrified into bravery, sprang through the savage circle and fled away over the ice. Pike and Dub followed on his heels, with the rest of the team behind. As Buck drew himself together to spring after them, out of the tail of his eye he saw Spitz rush upon him with the evident intention of overthrowing him. Once off his feet and under that mass of huskies, there was no hope for him. But he braced himself to the shock of Spitz's charge, then joined the flight out on the lake.

Later, the nine team-dogs gathered together and sought shelter in the forest. Though unpursued, they were in a sorry plight. There was not one who was not wounded in four or five places, while some were wounded grievously. Dub was badly injured in a hind leg; Dolly, the last husky added to the team at Dyea, had a badly torn throat; Joe had lost an eye; while Billee, the good-natured, with an ear chewed and rent to ribbons, cried and whimpered throughout the night. At daybreak they limped warily back to camp, to find the marauders gone and the two men in bad tempers. Fully half their grub supply was gone. The huskies had chewed through the sled lashings and canvas coverings. In fact, nothing, no matter how remotely eatable, had escaped them. They had eaten a pair of Perrault's moose-hide moccasins, chunks out of the leather traces, and even two feet of lash from the end of François's whip. He broke from a mournful contemplation of it to look over his wounded dogs.

"Ah, my frien's," he said softly, "mebbe it mek you mad dog, dose many bites. Mebbe all mad dog, sacre-dam! Wot you t'ink, eh, Perrault?"

The courier shook his head dubiously. With four hundred miles of trail still between him and Dawson, he could ill afford to have madness break out among his dogs. Two hours of cursing and exertion got the harnesses into shape, and the wound-stiffened team was under way, struggling painfully over the hardest part of the trail they had yet encountered, and for that matter, the hardest between them and Dawson.

The Thirty Mile River was wide open. Its wild water defied the frost, and it was in the eddies only and in the quiet places that the ice held at all. Six days of exhausting toil were required to cover those thirty terrible miles. And terrible they were, for every foot of them was accomplished at the risk of life to dog and man. A dozen times, Perrault, nosing the way, broke through the ice bridges, being saved by the long pole he carried, which he so held that it fell each time across the hole made by his body. But a cold snap was on, the thermometer registering fifty below zero, and each time he broke through he was compelled for very life to build a fire and dry his garments.

Nothing daunted him. It was because nothing daunted him that he had been chosen for government courier. He took all manner of risks, resolutely thrusting his little weazened face into the frost and struggling on from dim dawn to dark. He skirted the frowning shores on rim ice that bent and crackled under foot and upon which they dared not halt. Once, the sled broke through, with Dave and Buck, and they were half-frozen and all but drowned by the time they were dragged out. The usual fire was necessary to save them. They were coated solidly with ice, and the two men kept them on the run around the fire, sweating and thawing, so close that they were singed by the flames.

At another time Spitz went through, dragging the whole team after him up to Buck, who strained backward with all his strength, his fore paws on the slippery edge and the ice quivering and snapping all around.

But behind him was Dave, likewise straining backward, and behind the sled was François, pulling till his tendons cracked.

Again, the rim ice broke away before and behind, and there was no escape except up the cliff. Perrault scaled it by a miracle, while François prayed for just that miracle; and with every thong and sled lashing and the last bit of harness rove into a long rope, the dogs were hoisted, one by one, to the cliff crest. François came up last, after the sled and load. Then came the search for a place to descend, which descent was ultimately made by the aid of the rope, and night found them back on the river with a quarter of a mile to the day's credit.

By the time they made the Hootalinqua and good ice, Buck was played out. The rest of the dogs were in like condition; but Perrault, to make up lost time, pushed them late and early. The first day they covered thirty-five miles to the Big Salmon; the next day thirty-five more to the Little Salmon; the third day forty miles, which brought them well up toward the Five Fingers.

Buck's feet were not so compact and hard as the feet of the huskies. His had softened during the many generations since the day his last wild ancestor was tamed by a cave-dweller or river man. All day long he limped in agony, and camp once made, lay down like a dead dog. Hungry as he was, he would not move to receive his ration of fish, which François had to bring to him. Also, the dog-driver rubbed Buck's feet for half an hour each night after supper, and sacrificed the tops of his own moccasins to make four moccasins for Buck. This was a great relief, and Buck caused even the weazened face of Perrault to twist itself into a grin one morning, when François forgot the moccasins and Buck lay on his back, his four feet waving appealingly in the air, and refused to budge without them. Later his feet grew hard to the trail, and the worn-out footgear was thrown away.

At the Pelly one morning, as they were harnessing up, Dolly, who had never been conspicuous for anything, went suddenly mad. She announced her condition by a long, heartbreaking wolf howl that sent every dog bristling with fear, then sprang straight for Buck. He had never seen a dog go mad, nor did he have any reason to fear madness; yet he knew that here was horror, and fled away from it in a panic. Straight away he raced, with Dolly, panting and frothing, one leap behind; nor could she gain on him, so great was his terror, nor could he leave her, so great was her madness. He plunged through the wooded breast of the island, flew down to the lower end, crossed a back channel filled with rough ice to another island, gained a third island, curved back to the main river, and in desperation started to cross it. And all the time, though he did not look, he could hear her snarling just one leap behind. François called to him a quarter of a mile away and he doubled back, still one leap ahead, gasping painfully for air and putting all his faith in that François would save him. The dog-driver held the axe poised in his hand, and as Buck shot past him the axe crashed down upon mad Dolly's head.

Buck staggered over against the sled, exhausted, sobbing for breath, helpless. This was Spitz's opportunity. He sprang upon Buck, and twice his teeth sank into his unresisting foe and ripped and tore the flesh to the bone. Then François's lash descended, and Buck had the satisfaction of watching Spitz receive the worst whipping as yet administered to any of the team.

"One devil, dat Spitz," remarked Perrault. "Some dam day heem keel dat Buck."

"Dat Buck two devils," was François's rejoinder. "All de tam I watch dat Buck I know for sure. Lissen: some dam fine day heem get mad lak hell an' den heem chew dat Spitz all up an' spit heem out on de snow. Sure. I know."

From then on it was war between them. Spitz, as lead-dog and acknowledged master of the team, felt his supremacy threatened by this strange Southland dog. And strange Buck was to him, for of the many Southland dogs he had known, not one had shown up worthily in camp and on trail. They were all too soft, dying under the toil, the frost, and starvation. Buck was the exception. He alone endured and prospered, matching the husky in strength, savagery, and cunning. Then he was a masterful dog, and what made him dangerous was the fact that the club of the man in the red sweater had knocked all blind pluck and rashness out of his desire for mastery. He was preëminently cunning, and could bide his time with a patience that was nothing less than primitive.

It was inevitable that the clash for leadership should come. Buck wanted it. He wanted it because it was his nature, because he had been gripped tight by that nameless, incomprehensible pride of the trail and trace—that pride which holds dogs in the toil to the last gasp, which lures them to die joyfully in the harness, and breaks their hearts if they are cut out of the harness. This was the pride of Dave as wheel-dog, of Sol-leks as he pulled with all his strength; the pride that laid hold of them at break of camp, transforming them from sour and sullen brutes into straining, eager, ambitious creatures; the pride that spurred them on all day and dropped them at pitch of camp at night, letting them fall back into gloomy unrest and uncontent. This was the pride that bore up Spitz and made him thrash the sled-dogs who blundered and shirked in the traces or hid away at harness-up time in the morning. Likewise it was this pride that made him fear Buck as a possible lead-dog. And this was Buck's pride, too.

He openly threatened the other's leadership. He

came between him and the shirks he should have punished. And he did it deliberately. One night there was a heavy snowfall, and in the morning Pike, the malingerer, did not appear. He was securely hidden in his nest under a foot of snow. François called him and sought him in vain. Spitz was wild with wrath. He raged through the camp, smelling and digging in every likely place, snarling so frightfully that Pike heard and shivered in his hiding-place.

But when he was at last unearthed, and Spitz flew at him to punish him, Buck flew, with equal rage, in between. So unexpected was it, and so shrewdly managed, that Spitz was hurled backward and off his feet. Pike, who had been trembling abjectly, took heart at this open mutiny, and sprang upon his overthrown leader. Buck, to whom fair play was a forgotten code, likewise sprang upon Spitz. But François, chuckling at the incident while unswerving in the administration of justice, brought his lash down upon Buck with all his might. This failed to drive Buck from his prostrate rival, and the butt of the whip was brought into play. Half-stunned by the blow, Buck was knocked backward and the lash laid upon him again and again, while Spitz soundly punished the many times offending Pike.

In the days that followed, as Dawson grew closer and closer, Buck still continued to interfere between Spitz and the culprits; but he did it craftily, when François was not around. With the covert mutiny of Buck, a general insubordination sprang up and increased. Dave and Sol-leks were unaffected, but the rest of the team went from bad to worse. Things no longer went right. There was continual bickering and jangling. Trouble was always afoot, and at the bottom of it was Buck. He kept François busy, for the dog-driver was in constant apprehension of the life-and-death struggle between the two which he knew must take place sooner or later; and on more than one night the sounds of quarrelling and strife among the other dogs turned him out of his sleeping robe, fearful that Buck and Spitz were at it.

But the opportunity did not present itself, and they pulled into Dawson one dreary afternoon with the great fight still to come. Here were many men, and countless dogs, and Buck found them all at work. It seemed the ordained order of things that dogs should work. All day they swung up and down the main street in long teams, and in the night their jingling bells still went by. They hauled cabin logs and firewood, freighted up to the mines, and did all manner of work that horses did in the Santa Clara Valley. Here and there Buck met Southland dogs, but in the main they were the wild wolf husky breed. Every night, regularly, at nine, at twelve, at three, they lifted a nocturnal song, a weird and eerie chant, in which it was Buck's delight to join.

With the aurora borealis flaming coldly overhead, or the stars leaping in the frost dance, and the land numb and frozen under its pall of snow, this song of the huskies might have been the defiance of life, only it was pitched in minor key, with long-drawn wailings and half-sobs, and was more the pleading of life, the articulate travail of existence. It was an old song, old as the breed itself—one of the first songs of the younger world in a day when songs were sad. It was invested with the woe of unnumbered generations, this plaint by which Buck was so strangely stirred. When he moaned and sobbed, it was with the pain of living that was of old the pain of his wild fathers, and the fear and mystery of the cold and dark that was to them fear and mystery. And that he should be stirred by it marked the completeness with which he harked back through the ages of fire and roof to the raw beginnings of life in the howling ages.

Seven days from the time they pulled into Dawson,

they dropped down the steep bank by the Barracks to the Yukon Trail, and pulled for Dyea and Salt Water. Perrault was carrying despatches if anything more urgent than those he had brought in; also, the travel pride had gripped him, and he purposed to make the record trip of the year. Several things favored him in this. The week's rest had recuperated the dogs and put them in thorough trim. The trail they had broken into the country was packed hard by later journeyers. And further, the police had arranged in two or three places deposits of grub for dog and man, and he was travelling light.

They made Sixty Mile, which is a fifty-mile run, on the first day; and the second day saw them booming up the Yukon well on their way to Pelly. But such splendid running was achieved not without great trouble and vexation on the part of François. The insidious revolt led by Buck had destroyed the solidarity of the team. It no longer was as one dog leaping in the traces. The encouragement Buck gave the rebels led them into all kinds of petty misdemeanors. No more was Spitz a leader greatly to be feared. The old awe departed, and they grew equal to challenging his authority. Pike robbed him of half a fish one night, and gulped it down under the protection of Buck. Another night Dub and Joe fought Spitz and made him forego the punishment they deserved. And even Billee, the good-natured, was less good-natured, and whined not half so placatingly as in former days. Buck never came near Spitz without snarling and bristling menacingly. In fact, his conduct approached that of a bully, and he was given to swaggering up and down before Spitz's very nose.

The breaking down of discipline likewise affected the dogs in their relations with one another. They quarrelled and bickered more than ever among themselves, till at times the camp was a howling bedlam. Dave and Sol-leks alone were unaltered, though they were made irritable by the unending squabbling. François swore strange barbarous oaths, and stamped the snow in futile rage, and tore his hair. His lash was always singing among the dogs, but it was of small avail. Directly his back was turned they were at it again. He backed up Spitz with his whip, while Buck backed up the remainder of the team. François knew he was behind all the trouble, and Buck knew he knew; but Buck was too clever ever again to be caught red-handed. He worked faithfully in the harness, for the toil had become a delight to him; yet it was a greater delight slyly to precipitate a fight amongst his mates and tangle the traces.

At the mouth of the Tahkeena, one night after supper, Dub turned up a snowshoe rabbit, blundered it, and missed. In a second the whole team was in full cry. A hundred yards away was a camp of the Northwest Police, with fifty dogs, huskies all, who joined the chase. The rabbit sped down the river, turned off into a small creek, up the frozen bed of which it held steadily. It ran lightly on the surface of the snow, while the dogs ploughed through by main strength. Buck led the pack, sixty strong, around bend after bend, but he could not gain. He lay down low to the race, whining eagerly, his splendid body flashing forward, leap by leap, in the wan white moonlight. And leap by leap, like some pale frost wraith, the snowshoe rabbit flashed on ahead.

All that stirring of old instincts which at stated periods drives men out from the sounding cities to forest and plain to kill things by chemically propelled leaden pellets, the blood lust, the joy to kill—all this was Buck's, only it was infinitely more intimate. He was ranging at the head of the pack, running the wild thing down, the living meat, to kill with his own teeth and wash his muzzle to the eyes in warm blood.

There is an ecstasy that marks the summit of life,

and beyond which life cannot rise. And such is the paradox of living, this ecstasy comes when one is most alive, and it comes as a complete forgetfulness that one is alive. This ecstasy, this forgetfulness of living, comes to the artist, caught up and out of himself in a sheet of flame; it comes to the soldier, war-mad on a stricken field and refusing quarter; and it came to Buck, leading the pack, sounding the old wolf-cry, straining after the food that was alive and that fled swiftly before him through the moonlight. He was sounding the deeps of his nature, and of the parts of his nature that were deeper than he, going back into the womb of Time. He was mastered by the sheer surging of life, the tidal wave of being, the perfect joy of each separate muscle, joint, and sinew in that it was everything that was not death, that it was aglow and rampant, expressing itself in movement, flying exultantly under the stars and over the face of dead matter that did not move.

But Spitz, cold and calculating even in his supreme moods, left the pack and cut across a narrow neck of land where the creek made a long bend around. Buck did not know of this, and as he rounded the bend, the frost wraith of a rabbit still flitting before him, he saw another and larger frost wraith leap from the over-hanging bank into the immediate path of the rabbit. It was Spitz. The rabbit could not turn, and as the white teeth broke its back in mid air it shrieked as loudly as a stricken man may shriek. At sound of this, the cry of Life plunging down from Life's apex in the grip of Death, the full pack at Buck's heels raised a hell's chorus of delight.

Buck did not cry out. He did not check himself, but drove in upon Spitz, shoulder to shoulder, so hard that he missed the throat. They rolled over and over in the powdery snow. Spitz gained his feet almost as though he had not been overthrown, slashing Buck down the shoulder and leaping clear. Twice his teeth clipped together, like the steel jaws of a trap, as he backed away for better footing, with lean and lifting lips that writhed and snarled.

In a flash Buck knew it. The time had come. It was to the death. As they circled about, snarling, ears laid back, keenly watchful for the advantage, the scene came to Buck with a sense of familiarity. He seemed to remember it all,—the white woods, and earth, and moonlight, and the thrill of battle. Over the whiteness and silence brooded a ghostly calm. There was not the faintest whisper of air—nothing moved, not a leaf quivered, the visible breaths of the dogs rising slowly and lingering in the frosty air. They had made short work of the snowshoe rabbit, these dogs that were ill-tamed wolves; and they were now drawn up in an expectant circle. They, too, were silent, their eyes only gleaming and their breaths drifting slowly upward. To Buck it was nothing new or strange, this scene of old time. It was as though it had always been, the wonted way of things.

Spitz was a practised fighter. From Spitzbergen through the Arctic, and across Canada and the Barrens, he had held his own with all manner of dogs and achieved to mastery over them. Bitter rage was his, but never blind rage. In passion to rend and destroy, he never forgot that his enemy was in like passion to rend and destroy. He never rushed till he was prepared to receive a rush; never attacked till he had first defended that attack.

In vain Buck strove to sink his teeth in the neck of the big white dog. Wherever his fangs struck for the softer flesh, they were countered by the fangs of Spitz. Fang clashed fang, and lips were cut and bleeding, but Buck could not penetrate his enemy's guard. Then he warmed up and enveloped Spitz in a whirlwind of rushes. Time and time again he tried for the snow-white throat, where life bubbled near to the surface, and each time and every time Spitz slashed him and got away. Then Buck took to rushing, as though for the throat, when, suddenly drawing back his head and curving in from the side, he would drive his shoulder at the shoulder of Spitz, as a ram by which to overthrow him. But instead, Buck's shoulder was slashed down each time as Spitz leaped lightly away.

Spitz was untouched, while Buck was streaming with blood and panting hard. The fight was growing desperate. And all the while the silent and wolfish circle waited to finish off whichever dog went down. As Buck grew winded, Spitz took to rushing, and he kept him staggering for footing. Once Buck went over, and the whole circle of sixty dogs started up; but he recovered himself, almost in mid air, and the circle sank down again and waited.

But Buck possessed a quality that made for greatness—imagination. He fought by instinct, but he could fight by head as well. He rushed, as though attempting the old shoulder trick, but at the last instant swept low to the snow and in. His teeth closed on Spitz's left fore leg. There was a crunch of breaking bone, and the white dog faced him on three legs. Thrice he tried to knock him over, then repeated the trick and broke the right fore leg. Despite the pain and helplessness, Spitz struggled madly to keep up. He saw the silent circle, with gleaming eyes, lolling tongues, and silvery breaths drifting upward, closing in upon him as he had seen similar circles close in upon beaten antagonists in the past. Only this time he was the one who was beaten.

There was no hope for him. Buck was inexorable. Mercy was a thing reserved for gentler climes. He manoeuvred for the final rush. The circle had tightened till he could feel the breaths of the huskies on his flanks. He could see them, beyond Spitz and to either side, half crouching for the spring, their eyes fixed upon him. A pause seemed to fall. Every animal was motionless as though turned to stone. Only Spitz quivered and bristled as he staggered back and forth, snarling with horrible menace, as though to frighten off impending death. Then Buck sprang in and out; but while he was in, shoulder had at last squarely met shoulder. The dark circle became a dot on the moonflooded snow as Spitz disappeared from view. Buck stood and looked on, the successful champion, the dominant primordial beast who had made his kill and found it good.

CHAPTER IV

Who Has Won to Mastership

"Eh? Wot I say? I spik true w'en I say dat Buck two devils."

This was François's speech next morning when he discovered Spitz missing and Buck covered with wounds. He drew him to the fire and by its light pointed them out.

"Dat Spitz fight lak hell," said Perrault, as he surveyed the gaping rips and cuts.

"An' dat Buck fight lak two hells," was François's answer. "An' now we make good time. No more Spitz, no more trouble, sure."

While Perrault packed the camp outfit and loaded the sled, the dog-driver proceeded to harness the dogs. Buck trotted up to the place Spitz would have occupied as leader; but François, not noticing him, brought Sol-leks to the coveted position. In his judgment, Sol-leks was the best lead-dog left. Buck sprang upon Sol-leks in a fury, driving him back and standing in his place.

"Eh? eh?" François cried, slapping his thighs gleefully. "Look at dat Buck. Heem keel dat Spitz, heem t'ink to take de job."

"Go 'way, Chook!" he cried, but Buck refused to budge.

He took Buck by the scruff of the neck, and though the dog growled threateningly, dragged him to one side and replaced Sol-leks. The old dog did not like it, and showed plainly that he was afraid of Buck. François was obdurate, but when he turned his back Buck again displaced Sol-leks, who was not at all unwilling to go.

François was angry. "Now, by Gar, I feex you!" he cried, coming back with a heavy club in his hand.

Buck remembered the man in the red sweater, and retreated slowly; nor did he attempt to charge in when Sol-leks was once more brought forward. But he circled just beyond the range of the club, snarling with bitterness and rage; and while he circled he watched the club so as to dodge it if thrown by François, for he was become wise in the way of clubs.

The driver went about his work, and he called to Buck when he was ready to put him in his old place in front of Dave. Buck retreated two or three steps. François followed him up, whereupon he again retreated. After some time of this, François threw down the club, thinking that Buck feared a thrashing. But Buck was in open revolt. He wanted, not to escape a clubbing, but to have the leadership. It was his by right. He had earned it, and he would not be content with less.

Perrault took a hand. Between them they ran him about for the better part of an hour. They threw clubs at him. He dodged. They cursed him, and his fathers and mothers before him, and all his seed to come after him down to the remotest generation, and every hair on his body and drop of blood in his veins; and he answered curse with snarl and kept out of their reach. He did not try to run away, but retreated around and around the camp, advertising plainly that when his desire was met, he would come in and be good.

François sat down and scratched his head. Perrault looked at his watch and swore. Time was flying, and they should have been on the trail an hour gone. François scratched his head again. He shook it and grinned sheepishly at the courier, who shrugged his shoulders in sign that they were beaten. Then François went up to where Sol-leks stood and called to Buck. Buck laughed, as dogs laugh, yet kept his distance. François unfastened Sol-leks's traces and put him back in his old place. The team stood harnessed to the sled in an unbroken line, ready for the trail. There was no place for Buck save at the front. Once more François called, and once more Buck laughed and kept away.

"T'row down de club," Perrault commanded.

François complied, whereupon Buck trotted in, laughing triumphantly, and swung around into position at the head of the team. His traces were fastened, the sled broken out, and with both men running they dashed out on to the river trail.

Highly as the dog-driver had forevalued Buck, with his two devils, he found, while the day was yet young, that he had undervalued. At a bound Buck took up the duties of leadership; and where judgment was required, and quick thinking and quick acting, he showed himself the superior even of Spitz, of whom François had never seen an equal.

But it was in giving the law and making his mates live up to it, that Buck excelled. Dave and Sol-leks did not mind the change in leadership. It was none of their business. Their business was to toil, and toil mightily, in the traces. So long as that were not interfered with, they did not care what happened. Billee, the good-natured, could lead for all they cared, so long as he kept order. The rest of the team, however, had grown unruly during the last days of Spitz, and their surprise was great now that Buck proceeded to lick them into shape.

Pike, who pulled at Buck's heels, and who never put an ounce more of his weight against the breast-band than he was compelled to do, was swiftly and repeatedly shaken for loafing; and ere the first day was done he was pulling more than ever before in his life. The first night in camp, Joe, the sour one, was punished roundly—a thing that Spitz had never succeeded in doing. Buck simply smothered him by virtue of superior weight, and cut him up till he ceased snapping and began to whine for mercy.

The general tone of the team picked up immediately. It recovered its old-time solidarity, and once more the dogs leaped as one dog in the traces. At the Rink Rapids two native huskies, Teek and Koona, were added; and the celerity with which Buck broke them in took away François's breath.

"Nevaire such a dog as dat Buck!" he cried. "No, nevaire! Heem worth one t'ousan' dollair, by Gar! Eh? Wot you say, Perrault?"

And Perrault nodded. He was ahead of the record then, and gaining day by day. The trail was in excellent condition, well packed and hard, and there was no new-fallen snow with which to contend. It was not too cold. The temperature dropped to fifty below zero and remained there the whole trip. The men rode and ran by turn, and the dogs were kept on the jump, with but infrequent stoppages.

The Thirty Mile River was comparatively coated with ice, and they covered in one day going out what had taken them ten days coming in. In one run they made a sixty-mile dash from the foot of Lake Le Barge to the White Horse Rapids. Across Marsh, Tagish, and Bennett (seventy miles of lakes), they flew so fast that the man whose turn it was to run towed behind the sled at the end of a rope. And on the last night of the second week they topped White Pass and dropped down the sea slope with the lights of Skaguay and of the shipping at their feet.

It was a record run. Each day for fourteen days they had averaged forty miles. For three days Perrault and François threw chests up and down the main street of

Skaguay and were deluged with invitations to drink, while the team was the constant centre of a worshipful crowd of dog-busters and mushers. Then three or four western bad men aspired to clean out the town, were riddled like pepperboxes for their pains, and public interest turned to other idols. Next came official orders. François called Buck to him, threw his arms around him, wept over him. And that was the last of François and Perrault. Like other men, they passed out of Buck's life for good.

A Scotch half-breed took charge of him and his mates, and in company with a dozen other dog teams he started back over the weary trail to Dawson. It was no light running now, nor record time, but heavy toil each day, with a heavy load behind; for this was the mail train, carrying word from the world to the men who sought gold under the shadow of the Pole.

Buck did not like it, but he bore up well to the work, taking pride in it after the manner of Dave and Solleks, and seeing that his mates, whether they prided in it or not, did their fair share. It was a monotonous life, operating with machine-like regularity. One day was very like another. At a certain time each morning the cooks turned out, fires were built, and breakfast was eaten. Then, while some broke camp, others harnessed the dogs, and they were under way an hour or so before the darkness fell which gave warning of dawn. At night, camp was made. Some pitched the flies, others cut firewood and pine boughs for the beds, and still others carried water or ice for the cooks. Also, the dogs were fed. To them, this was the one feature of the day, though it was good to loaf around, after the fish was eaten, for an hour or so with the other dogs, of which there were five score and odd. There were fierce fighters among them, but three battles with the fiercest brought Buck to mastery, so that when he bristled and showed his teeth they got out of his way.

Best of all, perhaps, he loved to lie near the fire, hind legs crouched under him, fore-legs stretched out in front, head raised, and eyes blinking dreamily at the flames. Sometimes he thought of Judge Miller's big house in the sun-kissed Santa Clara Valley, and of the cement swimming-tank, and Ysabel, the Mexican hairless, and Toots, the Japanese pug; but oftener he remembered the man in the red sweater, the death of Curly, the great fight with Spitz, and the good things he had eaten or would like to eat. He was not homesick. The Sunland was very dim and distant, and such memories had no power over him. Far more potent were the memories of his heredity that gave things he had never seen before a seeming familiarity; the instincts (which were but the memories of his ancestors become habits) which had lapsed in later days, and still later, in him, quickened and became alive again.

Sometimes as he crouched there, blinking dreamily at the flames, it seemed that the flames were of another fire, and that as he crouched by this other fire he saw another and different man from the half-breed cook before him. This other man was shorter of leg and longer of arm, with muscles that were stringy and knotty rather than rounded and swelling. The hair of this man was long and matted, and his head slanted back under it from the eyes. He uttered strange sounds, and seemed very much afraid of the darkness, into which he peered continually, clutching in his hand, which hung midway between knee and foot, a stick with a heavy stone made fast to the end. He was all but naked, a ragged and fire-scorched skin hanging part way down his back, but on his body there was much hair. In some places, across the chest and shoulders and down the outside of the arms and thighs, it was matted into almost a thick fur. He did not stand erect, but with trunk inclined forward from the hips, on legs that bent at the knees. About his body there was a peculiar springiness, or resiliency, almost catlike, and a quick alertness as of one who lived in perpetual fear of things seen and unseen.

At other times this hairy man squatted by the fire with head between his legs and slept. On such occasions his elbows were on his knees, his hands clasped above his head as though to shed rain by the hairy arms. And beyond that fire, in the circling darkness, Buck could see many gleaming coals, two by two, always two by two, which he knew to be the eyes of great beasts of prey. And he could hear the crashing of their bodies through the undergrowth, and the noises they made in the night. And dreaming there by the Yukon bank, with lazy eyes blinking at the fire, these sounds and sights of another world would make the hair to rise along his back and stand on end across his shoulders and up his neck, till he whimpered low and suppressedly, or growled softly, and the half-breed cook shouted at him, "Hey, you Buck, wake up!" Whereupon the other world would vanish and the real world come into his eyes, and he would get up and yawn and stretch as though he had been asleep.

It was a hard trip, with the mail behind them, and the heavy work wore them down. They were short of weight and in poor condition when they made Dawson, and should have had a ten days' or a week's rest at least. But in two days' time they dropped down the Yukon bank from the Barracks, loaded with letters for the outside. The dogs were tired, the drivers grumbling, and to make matters worse, it snowed every day. This meant a soft trail, greater friction on the runners, and heavier pulling for the dogs; yet the drivers were fair through it all, and did their best for the animals.

Each night the dogs were attended to first. They ate before the drivers ate, and no man sought his sleeping-robe till he had seen to the feet of the dogs he drove. Still, their strength went down. Since the beginning of the winter they had travelled eighteen hundred miles, dragging sleds the whole weary distance; and eighteen hundred miles will tell upon life of the toughest. Buck stood it, keeping his mates up to their work and maintaining discipline, though he too was very tired. Billee cried and whimpered regularly in his sleep each night. Joe was sourer than ever, and Sol-leks was unapproachable, blind side or other side.

But it was Dave who suffered most of all. Something had gone wrong with him. He became more morose and irritable, and when camp was pitched at once made his nest, where his driver fed him. Once out of the harness and down, he did not get on his feet again till harness-up time in the morning. Sometimes, in the traces, when jerked by a sudden stoppage of the sled, or by straining to start it, he would cry out with pain. The driver examined him, but could find nothing. All the drivers became interested in his case. They talked it over at mealtime, and over their last pipes before going to bed, and one night they held a consultation. He was brought from his nest to the fire and was pressed and prodded till he cried out many times. Something was wrong inside, but they could locate no broken bones, could not make it out.

By the time Cassiar Bar was reached, he was so weak that he was falling repeatedly in the traces. The Scotch half-breed called a halt and took him out of the team, making the next dog, Sol-leks, fast to the sled. His intention was to rest Dave, letting him run free behind the sled. Sick as he was, Dave resented being taken out, grunting and growling while the traces were unfastened, and whimpering broken-heartedly when he saw Sol-leks in the position he had held and served so long. For the pride of trace and trail was his, and, sick unto death, he could not bear that another dog should do his work.

When the sled started, he floundered in the soft

snow alongside the beaten trail, attacking Sol-leks with his teeth, rushing against him and trying to thrust him off into the soft snow on the other side, striving to leap inside his traces and get between him and the sled, and all the while whining and yelping and crying with grief and pain. The half-breed tried to drive him away with the whip; but he paid no heed to the stinging lash, and the man had not the heart to strike harder. Dave refused to run quietly on the trail behind the sled, where the going was easy, but continued to flounder alongside in the soft snow, where the going was most difficult, till exhausted. Then he fell, and lay where he fell, howling lugubriously as the long train of sleds churned by.

With the last remnant of his strength he managed to stagger along behind till the train made another stop, when he floundered past the sleds to his own, where he stood alongside Sol-leks. His driver lingered a moment to get a light for his pipe from the man behind. Then he returned and started his dogs. They swung out on the trail with remarkable lack of exertion, turned their heads uneasily, and stopped in surprise. The driver was surprised, too; the sled had not moved. He called his comrades to witness the sight. Dave had bitten through both of Sol-leks's traces, and was standing directly in front of the sled in his proper place.

He pleaded with his eyes to remain there. The driver was perplexed. His comrades talked of how a dog could break its heart through being denied the work that killed it, and recalled instances they had known, where dogs, too old for the toil, or injured, had died because they were cut out of the traces. Also, they held it a mercy, since Dave was to die anyway, that he should die in the traces, heart-easy and content. So he was harnessed in again, and proudly he pulled as of old, though more than once he cried out involuntarily from the bite of his inward hurt. Several times he fell down and was dragged in the traces, and once the sled ran upon him so that he limped thereafter in one of his hind legs.

But he held out till camp was reached, when his driver made a place for him by the fire. Morning found him too weak to travel. At harness-up time he tried to crawl to his driver. By convulsive efforts he got on his feet, staggered, and fell. Then he wormed his way forward slowly toward where the harnesses were being put on his mates. He would advance his fore legs and drag up his body with a sort of hitching movement, when he would advance his fore legs and hitch ahead again for a few more inches. His strength left him, and the last his mates saw of him he lay gasping in the snow and yearning toward them. But they could hear him mournfully howling till they passed out of sight behind a belt of river timber.

Here the train was halted. The Scotch half-breed slowly retraced his steps to the camp they had left. The men ceased talking. A revolver-shot rang out. The man came back hurriedly. The whips snapped, the bells tinkled merrily, the sleds churned along the trail; but Buck knew, and every dog knew, what had taken place behind the belt of river trees.

CHAPTER V

The Toil of Trace
and Trail

Thirty days from the time it left Dawson, the Salt Water Mail, with Buck and his mates at the fore, arrived at Skaguay. They were in a wretched state, worn out and worn down. Buck's one hundred and forty pounds had dwindled to one hundred and fifteen. The rest of his mates, though lighter dogs, had relatively lost more weight than he. Pike, the malingerer, who, in his lifetime of deceit, had often successfully feigned a hurt leg, was now limping in earnest. Sol-leks was limping, and Dub was suffering from a wrenched shoulder-blade.

They were all terribly footsore. No spring or rebound was left in them. Their feet fell heavily on the trail, jarring their bodies and doubling the fatigue of a day's travel. There was nothing the matter with them except that they were dead tired. It was not the dead-tiredness that comes through brief and excessive effort, from which recovery is a matter of hours; but it was the dead-tiredness that comes through the slow and prolonged strength drainage of months of toil. There was no power of recuperation left, no reserve strength to call upon. It had been all used, the last least bit of it. Every muscle, every fibre, every cell, was tired, dead tired. And there was reason for it. In less than five months they had travelled twenty-five hundred miles, during the last eighteen hundred of which they had had but five days' rest. When they arrived at Skaguay they were apparently on their last legs. They could barely keep the traces taut, and on the down grades just managed to keep out of the way of the sled.

"Mush on, poor sore feets," the driver encouraged them as they tottered down the main street of Skaguay. "Dis is de las'. Den we get one long res'. Eh? For sure. One bully long res'."

The drivers confidently expected a long stopover. Themselves, they had covered twelve hundred miles with two days' rest, and in the nature of reason and common justice they deserved an interval of loafing. But so many were the men who had rushed into the Klondike, and so many were the sweethearts, wives, and kin that had not rushed in, that the congested mail was taking on Alpine proportions; also, there were official orders. Fresh batches of Hudson Bay dogs were to take the places of those worthless for the trail. The worthless ones were to be got rid of, and, since dogs count for little against dollars, they were to be sold.

Three days passed, by which time Buck and his mates found how really tired and weak they were. Then, on the morning of the fourth day, two men from the States came along and bought them, harness and all, for a song. The men addressed each other as "Hal" and "Charles." Charles was a middle-aged, lightish-colored man, with weak and watery eyes and a mustache that twisted fiercely and vigorously up, giving the lie to the limply drooping lip it concealed. Hal was a youngster of nineteen or twenty, with a big Colt's revolver and a hunting knife strapped about him on a belt that fairly bristled with cartridges. This belt was the most salient thing about him. It advertised his callowness—a callowness sheer and unutterable. Both men were manifestly out of place, and why such as they should adventure the North is part of the mystery of things that passes understanding.

Buck heard the chaffering, saw the money pass between the man and the Government agent, and knew that the Scotch half-breed and the mail-train drivers were passing out of his life on the heels of Perrault and François and the others who had gone before. When driven with his mates to the new owners' camp, Buck saw a slipshod and slovenly affair, tent half-stretched, dishes unwashed, everything in disorder; also, he saw a woman. "Mercedes" the men called her. She was Charles's wife and Hal's sister—a nice family party.

Buck watched them apprehensively as they proceeded to take down the tent and load the sled. There was a great deal of effort about their manner, but no businesslike method. The tent was rolled into an awkward bundle three times as large as it should have been. The tin dishes were packed away unwashed. Mercedes continually fluttered in the way of her men and kept up an unbroken chattering of remonstrance and advice. When they put a clothes-sack on the front of the sled, she suggested it should go on the back; and when they had it put on the back, and covered it over with a couple of other bundles, she discovered overlooked articles which could abide nowhere else but in that very sack, and they unloaded again.

Three men from a neighboring tent came out and looked on, grinning and winking at one another.

"You've got a right smart load as it is," said one of them; "and it's not me should tell you your business, but I wouldn't tote that tent along if I was you."

"Undreamed of!" cried Mercedes, throwing up her hands in dainty dismay. "However in the world could I manage without a tent?"

"It's springtime, and you won't get any more cold weather," the man replied.

She shook her head decidedly, and Charles and Hal put the last odds and ends on top the mountainous load.

"Think it'll ride?" one of the men asked.

"Why shouldn't it?" Charles demanded rather shortly.

"Oh, that's all right, that's all right," the man hastened meekly to say. "I was just a-wonderin', that is all. It seemed a mite top-heavy."

Charles turned his back and drew the lashings down as well as he could, which was not in the least well.

"An' of course the dogs can hike along all day with that contraption behind them," affirmed a second of the men.

"Certainly," said Hal, with freezing politeness, taking hold of the gee-pole with one hand and swinging his whip from the other. "Mush!" he shouted. "Mush on there!"

The dogs sprang against the breastbands, strained hard for a few moments, then relaxed. They were unable to move the sled.

"The lazy brutes, I'll show them," he cried, preparing to lash out at them with the whip.

But, Mercedes interfered, crying, "Oh, Hal, you mustn't," as she caught hold of the whip and wrenched it from him. "The poor dears! Now you must promise you won't be harsh with them for the rest of the trip, or I won't go a step."

"Precious lot you know about dogs," her brother sneered; "and I wish you'd leave me alone. They're lazy, I tell you, and you've got to whip them to get anything out of them. That's their way. You ask any one. Ask one of those men."

Mercedes looked at them imploringly, untold repugnance at sight of pain written in her pretty face.

"They're weak as water, if you want to know," came the reply from one of the men. "Plum tuckered out, that's what's the matter. They need a rest."

"Rest be blanked," said Hal, with his beardless lips; and Mercedes said, "Oh!" in pain and sorrow at the oath.

But she was a clannish creature, and rushed at once to the defense of her brother. "Never mind that man," she said pointedly. "You're driving our dogs, and you do what you think best with them."

Again Hal's whip fell upon the dogs. They threw themselves against the breast-bands, dug their feet into the packed snow, got down low to it, and put forth all their strength. The sled held as though it were an anchor. After two efforts, they stood still, panting. The whip was whistling savagely, when once more Mercedes interfered. She dropped on her knees before Buck, with tears in her eyes, and put her arms around his neck.

"You poor, poor dears," she cried sympathetically, "why don't you pull hard? Then you wouldn't be whipped." Buck did not like her, but he was feeling too miserable to resist her, taking it as part of the day's miserable work.

One of the onlookers, who had been clenching his teeth to suppress hot speech, now spoke up:—

"It's not that I care a whoop what becomes of you, but for the dogs' sakes I just want to tell you, you can help them a mighty lot by breaking out that sled. The runners are froze fast. Throw your weight against the gee-pole, right and left, and break it out."

A third time the attempt was made, but this time, following the advice, Hal broke out the runners which had been frozen to the snow. The overloaded and unwieldy sled forged ahead, Buck and his mates struggling frantically under the rain of blows. A hundred yards ahead the path turned and sloped steeply into the main street. It would have required an experienced man to keep the top-heavy sled upright, and Hal was not such a man. As they swung on the turn the sled went over, spilling half its load through the loose lashings. The dogs never stopped. The lightened sled bounded on its side behind them. They were angry because of the ill treatment they had received and the unjust load. Buck was raging. He broke into a run, the team following his lead. Hal cried "Whoa! whoa!" but they gave no heed. He tripped and was pulled off his feet. The capsized sled ground over him, and the dogs dashed on up the street, adding to the gayety of Skaguay as they scattered the remainder of the outfit along its chief thoroughfare.

Kind-hearted citizens caught the dogs and gathered up the scattered belongings. Also, they gave advice. Half the load and twice the dogs if they ever expected to reach Dawson, was what was said. Hal and his sister and brother-in-law listened unwillingly, pitched tent, and overhauled the outfit. Canned goods were turned out that made men laugh, for canned goods on the Long Trail is a thing to dream about. "Blankets for a hotel," quoth one of the men who laughed and helped. "Half as many is too much; get rid of them. Throw away that tent, and all those dishes,—who's going to wash them, anyway? Good Lord, do you think you're travelling on a Pullman?"

And so it went, the inexorable elimination of the superfluous. Mercedes cried when her clothes-bags were dumped on the ground and article after article was thrown out. She cried in general, and she cried in particular over each discarded thing. She clasped hands about knees, rocking back and forth broken-heartedly. She averred she would not go an inch, not for a dozen Charleses. She appealed to everybody and to everything, finally wiping her eyes and proceeding to cast out even articles of apparel that were imperative necessaries. And in her zeal, when she had finished with her own, she attacked the belongings of her men and went through them like a tornado.

This accomplished, the outfit, though cut in half, was still a formidable bulk. Charles and Hal went out in the evening and bought six Outside dogs. These, added to the six of the original team, and Teek and Koona, the huskies obtained at the Rink Rapids on the record trip, brought the team up to fourteen. But the Outside dogs, though practically broken in since their landing, did not amount to much. Three were short-haired pointers, one was a Newfoundland, and the other two were mongrels of indeterminate breed. They did not seem to know anything, these newcomers. Buck and his comrades looked upon them with disgust, and though he speedily taught them their places and what not to do, he could not teach them what to do. They did not take kindly to trace and trail. With the exception of the two mongrels, they were bewildered and spirit-broken by the strange savage environment in which they found themselves and by the ill treatment they had received. The two mongrels were without spirit at all; bones were the only things breakable about them.

With the newcomers hopeless and forlorn, and the old team worn out by twenty-five hundred miles of continuous trail, the outlook was anything but bright. The two men, however, were quite cheerful. And they were proud, too. They were doing the thing in style, with fourteen dogs. They had seen other sleds depart over the Pass for Dawson, or come in from Dawson, but never had they seen a sled with so many as four-teen dogs. In the nature of Arctic travel there was a reason why fourteen dogs should not drag one sled, and that was that one sled could not carry the food for fourteen dogs. But Charles and Hal did not know this. They had worked the trip out with a pencil, so much to a dog, so many dogs, so many days, Q.E.D. Mercedes looked over their shoulders and nodded comprehensively, it was all so very simple.

Late next morning Buck led the long team up the street. There was nothing lively about it, no snap or go in him and his fellows. They were starting dead weary. Four times he had covered the distance between Salt Water and Dawson, and the knowledge that, jaded and tired, he was facing the same trail once more, made him bitter. His heart was not in the work, nor was the heart of any dog. The Outsides were timid and frightened, the Insides without confidence in their masters.

Buck felt vaguely that there was no depending upon these two men and the woman. They did not know how to do anything, and as the days went by it became apparent that they could not learn. They were slack in all things, without order or discipline. It took them half the night to pitch a slovenly camp, and half the morning to break that camp and get the sled loaded in fashion so slovenly that for the rest of the day they were occupied in stopping and rearranging the load. Some days they did not make ten miles. On other days they were unable to get started at all. And on no day did they succeed in making more than half the distance used by the men as a basis in their dog-food computation.

It was inevitable that they should go short on dog-food. But they hastened it by overfeeding, bringing the day nearer when underfeeding would commence. The Outside dogs, whose digestions had not been trained by chronic famine to make the most of little, had voracious appetites. And when, in addition to this, the worn-out huskies pulled weakly, Hal decided that the orthodox ration was too small. He doubled it. And to cap it all, when Mercedes, with tears in her pretty eyes and a quaver in her throat, could not cajole him into giving the dogs still more, she stole from the fish sacks and fed them slyly. But it was not food that Buck and the huskies needed, but rest. And though they were making poor time, the heavy load they dragged sapped their strength severely.

Then came the underfeeding. Hal awoke one day to the fact that his dog-food was half gone and the distance only quarter covered; further, that for love or money no additional dog-food was to be obtained. So he cut down even the orthodox ration and tried to increase the day's travel. His sister and brother-in-law seconded him; but they were frustrated by their heavy outfit and their own incompetence. It was a simple matter to give the dogs less food; but it was impossible to make the dogs travel faster, while their own inability to get under way earlier in the morning prevented them from travelling longer hours. Not only did they not know how to work dogs, but they did not know how to work themselves.

The first to go was Dub. Poor blundering thief that he was, always getting caught and punished, he had none the less been a faithful worker. His wrenched shoulder-blade, untreated and unrested, went from bad to worse, till finally Hal shot him with the big Colt's revolver. It is a saying of the country that an Outside dog starves to death on the ration of the husky, so the six Outside dogs under Buck could do no less than die on half the ration of the husky. The Newfoundland went first, followed by the three short-haired pointers, the two mongrels hanging more grittily on to life, but going in the end.

By this time all the amenities and gentlenesses of the Southland had fallen away from the three people. Shorn of its glamour and romance, Arctic travel became to them a reality too harsh for their manhood and womanhood. Mercedes ceased weeping over the dogs, being too occupied with weeping over herself and with quarrelling with her husband and brother. To quarrel was the one thing they were never too weary to do. Their irritability arose out of their misery, increased with it, doubled upon it, outdistanced it. The wonderful patience of the trail which comes to men who toil hard and suffer sore, and remain sweet of speech and kindly, did not come to these two men and the woman. They had no inkling of such a patience. They were stiff and in pain; their muscles ached, their bones ached, their very hearts ached; and because of this they became sharp of speech, and hard words were first on their lips in the morning and last at night.

Charles and Hal wrangled whenever Mercedes gave them a chance. It was the cherished belief of each that he did more than his share of the work, and neither forbore to speak this belief at every opportunity. Sometimes Mercedes sided with her husband, sometimes with her brother. The result was a beautiful and unending family quarrel. Starting from a dispute as to which should chop a few sticks for the fire (a dispute which concerned only Charles and Hal), presently would be lugged in the rest of the family, fathers, mothers, uncles, cousins, people thousands of miles away, and some of them dead. That Hal's views on art, or the sort of society plays his mother's brother wrote, should have anything to do with the chopping of a few sticks of firewood, passes comprehension; nevertheless the quarrel was as likely to tend in that direction as in the direction of Charles's political prejudices. And that Charles's sister's tale-bearing tongue should be relevant to the building of a Yukon fire was apparent only to Mercedes, who disburdened herself of copious opinions upon that topic, and incidentally upon a few other traits unpleasantly peculiar to her husband's family. In the meantime the fire remained unbuilt, the camp half pitched, and the dogs unfed.

Mercedes nursed a special grievance—the grievance of sex. She was pretty and soft, and had been chivalrously treated all her days. But the present treatment by her husband and brother was everything save chivalrous. It was her custom to be helpless. They complained. Upon which impeachment of what to her was her most essential sex-prerogative, she made their lives unendurable. She no longer considered the dogs, and because she was sore and tired, she persisted in riding on the sled. She was pretty and soft, but she weighed one hundred and twenty pounds—a lusty last straw to the load dragged by the weak and starving animals. She rode for days, till they fell in the traces and the sled stood still. Charles and Hal begged her to get off and walk, pleaded with her, entreated, the while she wept and importuned Heaven with a recital of their brutality.

On one occasion they took her off the sled by main strength. They never did it again. She let her legs go limp like a spoiled child, and sat down on the trail. They went on their way, but she did not move. After they had travelled three miles they unloaded the sled, came back for her, and by main strength put her on the sled again.

In the excess of their own misery they were callous to the suffering of their animals. Hal's theory, which he practised on others, was that one must get hardened. He had started out preaching it to his sister and brother-in-law. Failing there, he hammered it into the dogs with a club. At the Five Fingers the dog-food gave out, and a toothless old squaw offered to trade them a few pounds of frozen horse-hide for the Colt's revolver that kept the big hunting-knife company at Hal's hip. A poor substitute for food was this hide, just as it had been stripped from the starved horses of the cattlemen six months back. In its frozen state it was more like strips of galvanized iron, and when a dog wrestled it into his stomach it thawed into thin and innutritious leathery strings and into a mass of short hair, irritating and indigestible.

And through it all Buck staggered along at the head of the team as in a nightmare. He pulled when he could; when he could no longer pull, he fell down and remained down till blows from whip or club drove him to his feet again. All the stiffness and gloss had gone out of his beautiful furry coat. The hair hung down, limp and draggled, or matted with dried blood where

Hal's club had bruised him. His muscles had wasted away to knotty strings, and the flesh pads had disappeared, so that each rib and every bone in his frame were outlined cleanly through the loose hide that was wrinkled in folds of emptiness. It was heartbreaking, only Buck's heart was unbreakable. The man in the red sweater had proved that.

As it was with Buck, so was it with his mates. They were perambulating skeletons. There were seven all together, including him. In their very great misery they had become insensible to the bite of the lash or the bruise of the club. The pain of the beating was dull and distant, just as the things their eyes saw and their ears heard seemed dull and distant. They were not half living, or quarter living. They were simply so many bags of bones in which sparks of life fluttered faintly. When a halt was made, they dropped down in the traces like dead dogs, and the spark dimmed and paled and seemed to go out. And when the club or whip fell upon them, the spark fluttered feebly up, and they tottered to their feet and staggered on.

There came a day when Billee, the good-natured, fell and could not rise. Hal had traded off his revolver, so he took the axe and knocked Billee on the head as he lay in the traces, then cut the carcass out of the harness and dragged it to one side. Buck saw, and his mates saw, and they knew that this thing was very close to them. On the next day Koona went, and but five of them remained: Joe, too far gone to be malignant; Pike, crippled and limping, only half conscious and not conscious enough longer to malinger; Sol-leks, the one-eyed, still faithful to the toil of trace and trail, and mournful in that he had so little strength with which to pull; Teek, who had not travelled so far that winter and who was now beaten more than the others because he was fresher; and Buck, still at the head of the team, but no longer enforcing discipline or striving to enforce it, blind with weakness half the time and keeping the trail by the loom of it and by the dim feel of his feet.

It was beautiful spring weather, but neither dogs nor humans were aware of it. Each day the sun rose earlier and set later. It was dawn by three in the morning, and twilight lingered till nine at night. The whole long day was a blaze of sunshine. The ghostly winter silence had given way to the great spring murmur of awakening life. This murmur arose from all the land, fraught with the joy of living. It came from the things that lived and moved again, things which had been as dead and which had not moved during the long months of frost. The sap was rising in the pines. The willows and aspens were bursting out in young buds. Shrubs and vines were putting on fresh garbs of green. Crickets sang in the nights, and in the days all manner of creeping, crawling things rustled forth into the sun. Partridges and woodpeckers were booming and knocking in the forest. Squirrels were chattering, birds singing, and overhead honked the wild-fowl driving up from the south in cunning wedges that split the air.

From every hill slope came the trickle of running water, the music of unseen fountains. All things were thawing, bending, snapping. The Yukon was straining to break loose the ice that bound it down. It ate away from beneath; the sun ate from above. Air holes formed, fissures sprang and spread apart, while thin sections of ice fell through bodily into the river. And amid all this bursting, rending, throbbing of awakening life, under the blazing sun and through the soft-sighing breezes, like wayfarers to death, staggered the two men, the woman, and the huskies.

With the dogs falling, Mercedes weeping and riding, Hal swearing innocuously, and Charles's eyes wistfully watering, they staggered into John Thornton's camp at the mouth of White River. When they halted, the dogs dropped down as though they had all been struck dead. Mercedes dried her eyes and looked at John Thornton. Charles sat down on a log to rest. He sat down very slowly and painstakingly what of his great stiffness. Hal did the talking. John Thornton was whittling the last touches on an axe-handle he had made from a stick of birch. He whittled and listened, gave monosyllabic replies, and, when it was asked, terse advice. He knew the breed, and he gave his advice in the certainty that it would not be followed.

"They told us up above that the bottom was dropping out of the trail and that the best thing for us to do was to lay over," Hal said in response to Thornton's warning to take no more chances on the rotten ice. "They told us we couldn't make White River, and here we are." This last with a sneering ring of triumph in it.

"And they told you true," John Thornton answered. "The bottom's likely to drop out at any moment. Only fools, with the blind luck of fools, could have made it. I tell you straight, I wouldn't risk my carcass on that ice for all the gold in Alaska."

"That's because you're not a fool, I suppose," said Hal. "All the same, we'll go on to Dawson." He uncoiled his whip. "Get up there, Buck! Hi! Get up there! Mush on!"

Thornton went on whittling. It was idle, he knew, to get between a fool and his folly, while two or three fools more or less would not alter the scheme of things.

But the team did not get up at the command. It had long since passed into the stage where blows were required to rouse it. The whip flashed out, here and there, on its merciless errands. John Thornton compressed his lips. Sol-leks was the first to crawl to his feet. Teek followed. Joe came next, yelping with pain. Pike made painful efforts. Twice he fell over, when half up, and on the third attempt managed to rise. Buck made no effort. He lay quietly where he had fallen. The lash bit into him again and again, but he neither whined nor struggled. Several times Thornton started, as though to speak, but changed his mind. A moisture came into his eyes, and, as the whipping continued, he arose and walked irresolutely up and down.

This was the first time Buck had failed, in itself a sufficient reason to drive Hal into a rage. He exchanged the whip for the customary club. Buck refused to move under the rain of heavier blows which now fell upon him. Like his mates, he was barely able to get up, but, unlike them, he had made up his mind not to get up. He had a vague feeling of impending doom. This had been strong upon him when he pulled in to the bank, and it had not departed from him. What of the thin and rotten ice he had felt under his feet all day, it seemed that he sensed disaster close at hand, out there ahead on the ice where his master was trying to drive him. He refused to stir. So greatly had he suffered, and so far gone was he, that the blows did not hurt much. And as they continued to fall upon him, the spark of life within flickered and went down. It was nearly out. He felt strangely numb. As though from a great distance, he was aware that he was being beaten. The last sensations of pain left him. He no longer felt anything, though very faintly he could hear the impact of the club upon his body. But it was no longer his body, it seemed so far away.

And then, suddenly, without warning, uttering a cry that was inarticulate and more like the cry of an animal, John Thornton sprang upon the man who wielded the club. Hal was hurled backward, as though struck by a falling tree. Mercedes screamed. Charles looked on wistfully, wiped his watery eyes, but did not get up because of his stiffness.

John Thornton stood over Buck, struggling to control himself, too convulsed with rage to speak.

"If you strike that dog again, I'll kill you," he at last managed to say in a choking voice.

"It's my dog," Hal replied, wiping the blood from

his mouth as he came back. "Get out of my way, or I'll fix you. I'm going to Dawson."

Thornton stood between him and Buck, and evinced no intention of getting out of the way. Hal drew his long hunting-knife. Mercedes screamed, cried, laughed, and manifested the chaotic abandonment of hysteria. Thornton rapped Hal's knuckles with the axe-handle, knocking the knife to the ground. He rapped his knuckles again as he tried to pick it up. Then he stooped, picked it up himself, and with two strokes cut Buck's traces.

Hal had no fight left in him. Besides, his hands were full with his sister, or his arms, rather; while Buck was too near dead to be of further use in hauling the sled. A few minutes later they pulled out from the bank and down the river. Buck heard them go and raised his head to see. Pike was leading, Sol-leks was at the wheel, and between were Joe and Teek. They were limping and staggering. Mercedes was riding the loaded sled. Hal guided at the gee-pole, and Charles stumbled along in the rear.

As Buck watched them, Thornton knelt beside him and with rough, kindly hands searched for broken bones. By the time his search had disclosed nothing more than many bruises and a state of terrible starvation, the sled was a quarter of a mile away. Dog and man watched it crawling along over the ice. Suddenly, they saw its back end drop down, as into a rut, and the gee-pole, with Hal clinging to it, jerk into the air. Mercedes's scream came to their ears. They saw Charles turn and make one step to run back, and then a whole section of ice give way and dogs and humans disappear. A yawning hole was all that was to be seen. The bottom had dropped out of the trail.

John Thornton and Buck looked at each other.

"You poor devil," said John Thornton, and Buck licked his hand.

CHAPTER VI

For the Love of a Man

When John Thornton froze his feet in the previous December, his partners had made him comfortable and left him to get well, going on themselves up the river to get out a raft of saw-logs for Dawson. He was still limping slightly at the time he rescued Buck, but with the continued warm weather even the slight limp left him. And here, lying by the river bank through the long spring days, watching the running water, listening lazily to the songs of birds and the hum of nature, Buck slowly won back his strength.

A rest comes very good after one has travelled three thousand miles, and it must be confessed that Buck waxed lazy as his wounds healed, his muscles swelled out, and the flesh came back to cover his bones. For that matter, they were all loafing,—Buck, John Thornton, and Skeet and Nig,—waiting for the raft to come that was to carry them down to Dawson. Skeet was a little Irish setter who early made friends with Buck, who, in a dying condition, was unable to resent her first advances. She had the doctor trait which some dogs possess; and as a mother cat washes her kittens, so she washed and cleansed Buck's wounds. Regularly, each morning after he had finished his breakfast, she performed her self-appointed task, till he came to look for her ministrations as much as he did for Thornton's.

Nig, equally friendly, though less demonstrative, was a huge black dog, half bloodhound and half deerhound, with eyes that laughed and a boundless good nature.

To Buck's surprise these dogs manifested no jealousy toward him. They seemed to share the kindliness and largeness of John Thornton. As Buck grew stronger they enticed him into all sorts of ridiculous games, in which Thornton himself could not forbear to join; and in this fashion Buck romped through his convalescence and into a new existence. Love, genuine passionate love, was his for the first time. This he had never experienced at Judge Miller's down in the sun-kissed Santa Clara Valley. With the Judge's sons, hunting and tramping, it had been a working partnership; with the Judge's grandsons, a sort of pompous guardianship; and with the Judge himself, a stately and dignified friendship. But love that was feverish and burning, that was adoration, that was madness, it had taken John Thornton to arouse.

This man had saved his life, which was something; but, further, he was the ideal master. Other men saw to the welfare of their dogs from a sense of duty and business expediency; he saw to the welfare of his as if they were his own children, because he could not help it. And he saw further. He never forgot a kindly greeting or a cheering word, and to sit down for a long talk with them ("gas" he called it) was as much his delight as theirs. He had a way of taking Buck's head roughly between his hands, and resting his own head upon Buck's, of shaking him back and forth, the while calling him ill names that to Buck were love names. Buck knew no greater joy than that rough embrace and the sound of murmured oaths, and at each jerk back and forth it seemed that his heart would be shaken out of his body so great was its ecstasy. And when, released, he sprang to his feet, his mouth laughing, his eyes eloquent, his throat vibrant with unuttered sound, and in that fashion remained without movement, John Thornton would reverently exclaim, "God! you can all but speak!"

Buck had a trick of love expression that was akin to hurt. He would often seize Thornton's hand in his mouth and close so fiercely that the flesh bore the impress of his teeth for some time afterward. And as Buck understood the oaths to be love words, so the man understood this feigned bite for a caress.

For the most part, however, Buck's love was expressed in adoration. While he went wild with happiness when Thornton touched him or spoke to him, he did not seek these tokens. Unlike Skeet, who was wont to shove her nose under Thornton's hand and nudge and nudge till petted, or Nig, who would stalk up and rest his great head on Thornton's knee, Buck was content to adore at a distance. He would lie by the hour, eager, alert, at Thornton's feet, looking up into his face, dwelling upon it, studying it, following with keenest interest each fleeting expression, every movement or change of feature. Or, as chance might have it, he would lie farther away, to the side or rear, watching the outlines of the man and the occasional movements of his body. And often, such was the communion in which they lived, the strength of Buck's gaze would draw John Thornton's head around, and he would return the gaze, without speech, his heart shining out of his eyes as Buck's heart shone out.

For a long time after his rescue, Buck did not like Thornton to get out of his sight. From the moment he left the tent to when he entered it again, Buck would follow at his heels. His transient masters since he had come into the Northland had bred in him a fear that no master could be permanent. He was afraid that Thornton would pass out of his life as Perrault and François and the Scotch half-breed had passed out. Even in the night, in his dreams, he was haunted by this fear. At such times he would shake off sleep and creep through the chill to the flap of the tent, where he would stand and listen to the sound of his master's breathing.

But in spite of this great love he bore John Thornton, which seemed to bespeak the soft civilizing influence, the strain of the primitive, which the Northland had aroused in him, remained alive and active. Faithfulness and devotion, things born of fire and roof, were his; yet he retained his wildness and wiliness. He was a thing of the wild, come in from the wild to sit by John Thornton's fire, rather than a dog of the soft Southland stamped with the marks of generations of civilization. Because of his very great love, he could not steal from this man, but from any other man, in any other camp, he did not hesitate an instant; while the cunning with which he stole enabled him to escape detection.

His face and body were scored by the teeth of many dogs, and he fought as fiercely as ever and more shrewdly. Skeet and Nig were too good-natured for quarrelling,—besides, they belonged to John Thornton; but the strange dog, no matter what the breed or valor, swiftly acknowledged Buck's supremacy or found himself struggling for life with a terrible antagonist. And Buck was merciless. He had learned well the law of club and fang, and he never forewent an advantage or drew back from a foe he had started on the way to Death. He had lessoned from Spitz, and from the chief fighting dogs of the police and mail, and knew there was no middle course. He must master or be mastered; while to show mercy was a weakness. Mercy did not exist in the primordial life. It was misunderstood for fear, and such misunderstandings made for death. Kill or be killed, eat or be eaten, was the law; and this mandate, down out of the depths of Time, he obeyed.

He was older than the days he had seen and the breaths he had drawn. He linked the past with the present, and the eternity behind him throbbed through him in a mighty rhythm to which he swayed as the tides and seasons swayed. He sat by John Thornton's fire, a broad-breasted dog, white-fanged and long-furred; but behind him were the shades of all manner of dogs, half-wolves and wild wolves, urgent and prompting, tasting the savor of the meat he ate, thirsting for the water he drank, scenting the wind with him, listening with him and telling him the sounds made by the wild life in the forest, dictating his moods, directing his actions, lying down to sleep with him when he lay down, and dreaming with him and beyond him and becoming themselves the stuff of his dreams.

So peremptorily did these shades beckon him, that each day mankind and the claims of mankind slipped farther from him. Deep in the forest a call was sounding, and as often as he heard this call, mysteriously thrilling and luring, he felt compelled to turn his back upon the fire and the beaten earth around it, and to plunge into the forest, and on and on, he knew not where or why; nor did he wonder where or why, the call sounding imperiously, deep in the forest. But as often as he gained the soft unbroken earth and the green shade, the love for John Thornton drew him back to the fire again.

Thornton alone held him. The rest of mankind was as nothing. Chance travellers might praise or pet him; but he was cold under it all, and from a too demonstrative man he would get up and walk away. When Thornton's partners, Hans and Pete, arrived on the long-expected raft, Buck refused to notice them till he learned they were close to Thornton; after that he tolerated them in a passive sort of way, accepting favors from them as though he favored them by accepting. They were of the same large type as Thornton, living close to the earth, thinking simply and seeing clearly; and ere they swung the raft into the big eddy by the saw-mill at Dawson, they understood Buck and his ways, and did not insist upon an intimacy such as obtained with Skeet and Nig.

For Thornton, however, his love seemed to grow and grow. He, alone among men, could put a pack upon Buck's back in the summer travelling. Nothing was too great for Buck to do, when Thornton commanded. One day (they had grub-staked themselves from the proceeds of the raft and left Dawson for the head-waters of the Tanana) the men and dogs were sitting on the crest of a cliff which fell away, straight down, to naked bed-rock three hundred feet below. John Thornton was sitting near the edge, Buck at his shoulder. A thoughtless whim seized Thornton, and he drew the attention of Hans and Pete to the experiment he had in mind. "Jump, Buck!" he commanded, sweeping his arm out and over the chasm. The next instant he was grappling with Buck on the extreme edge, while Hans and Pete were dragging them back into safety.

"It's uncanny," Pete said, after it was over and they had caught their speech.

Thornton shook his head. "No, it is splendid, and it is terrible, too. Do you know, it sometimes makes me afraid."

"I'm not hankering to be the man that lays hands on you while he's around," Pete announced conclusively, nodding his head toward Buck.

"Py Jingo!" was Hans's contribution. "Not mineself either."

It was at Circle City, ere the year was out, that Pete's apprehensions were realized. "Black" Burton, a man evil-tempered and malicious, had been picking a quarrel with a tenderfoot at the bar, when Thornton stepped good-naturedly between. Buck, as was his custom, was lying in a corner, head on paws, watching his master's every action. Burton struck out, without warning, straight from the shoulder. Thornton was sent spinning, and saved himself from falling only by clutching the rail of the bar.

Those who were looking on heard what was neither bark nor yelp, but a something which is best described as a roar, and they saw Buck's body rise up in the air as he left the floor for Burton's throat. The man saved his life by instinctively throwing out his arm, but was hurled backward to the floor with Buck on top of him. Buck loosed his teeth from the flesh of the arm and drove in again for the throat. This time the man succeeded only in partly blocking, and his throat was torn open. Then the crowd was upon Buck, and he was driven off; but while a surgeon checked the bleeding, he prowled up and down, growling furiously, attempting to rush in, and being forced back by an array of hostile clubs. A "miners' meeting," called on the spot, decided that the dog had sufficient provocation, and Buck was discharged. But his reputation was made, and from that day his name spread through every camp in Alaska.

Later on, in the fall of the year, he saved John Thornton's life in quite another fashion. The three partners were lining a long and narrow poling-boat down a bad stretch of rapids on the Forty-Mile Creek. Hans and Pete moved along the bank, snubbing with a thin Manila rope from tree to tree, while Thornton remained in the boat, helping its descent by means of a pole, and shouting directions to the shore. Buck, on the bank, worried and anxious, kept abreast of the boat, his eyes never off his master.

At a particularly bad spot, where a ledge of barely submerged rocks jutted out into the river, Hans cast off the rope, and, while Thornton poled the boat out into the stream, ran down the bank with the end in his hand to snub the boat when it had cleared the ledge. This it did, and was flying down-stream in a current as swift as a mill-race, when Hans checked it with the rope and checked too suddenly. The boat flirted over and snubbed in to the bank bottom up, while Thornton, flung sheer out of it, was carried down-stream toward the worst part of the rapids, a stretch of wild water in which no swimmer could live.

Buck had sprung in on the instant; and at the end of three hundred yards, amid a mad swirl of water, he overhauled Thornton. When he felt him grasp his tail, Buck headed for the bank, swimming with all his splendid strength. But the progress shoreward was slow, the progress down-stream amazingly rapid. From below came the fatal roaring where the wild current went wilder and was rent in shreds and spray by the rocks which thrust through like the teeth of an enormous comb. The suck of the water as it took the beginning of the last steep pitch was frightful, and Thornton knew that the shore was impossible. He scraped furiously over a rock, bruised across a second, and struck a third with crushing force. He clutched its slippery top with both hands, releasing Buck, and above the roar of the churning water shouted: "Go, Buck! Go!"

Buck could not hold his own, and swept on downstream, struggling desperately, but unable to win back. When he heard Thornton's command repeated, he partly reared out of the water, throwing his head high, as though for a last look, then turned obediently toward the bank. He swam powerfully and was dragged ashore by Pete and Hans at the very point where swimming ceased to be possible and destruction began.

They knew that the time a man could cling to a slippery rock in the face of that driving current was a matter of minutes, and they ran as fast as they could up the bank to a point far above where Thornton was hanging on. They attached the line with which they had been snubbing the boat to Buck's neck and shoulders, being

careful that it should neither strangle him nor impede
his swimming, and launched him into the stream. He
struck out boldly, but not straight enough into the
stream. He discovered the mistake too late, when
Thornton was abreast of him and a bare half-dozen
strokes away while he was being carried helplessly past.

Hans promptly snubbed with the rope, as though
Buck were a boat. The rope thus tightening on him in
the sweep of the current, he was jerked under the surface, and under the surface he remained till his body
struck against the bank and he was hauled out. He was
half drowned, and Hans and Pete threw themselves
upon him, pounding the breath into him and the water
out of him. He staggered to his feet and fell down. The
faint sound of Thornton's voice came to them, and
though they could not make out the words of it, they
knew that he was in his extremity. His master's voice
acted on Buck like an electric shock. He sprang to his
feet and ran up the bank ahead of the men to the point
of his previous departure.

Again the rope was attached and he was launched,
and again he struck out, but this time straight into the
stream. He had miscalculated once, but he would not
be guilty of it a second time. Hans paid out the rope,
permitting no slack, while Pete kept it clear of coils.
Buck held on till he was on a line straight above
Thornton; then he turned, and with the speed of an
express train headed down upon him. Thornton saw
him coming, and, as Buck struck him like a battering
ram, with the whole force of the current behind him,
he reached up and closed with both arms around the
shaggy neck. Hans snubbed the rope around the tree,
and Buck and Thornton were jerked under the water.
Strangling, suffocating, sometimes one uppermost and
sometimes the other, dragging over the jagged bottom,
smashing against rocks and snags, they veered in to the
bank.

Thornton came to, belly downward and being violently propelled back and forth across a drift log by Hans and Pete. His first glance was for Buck, over whose limp and apparently lifeless body Nig was setting up a howl, while Skeet was licking the wet face and closed eyes. Thornton was himself bruised and battered, and he went carefully over Buck's body, when he had been brought around, finding three broken ribs.

"That settles it," he announced. "We camp right here." And camp they did, till Buck's ribs knitted and he was able to travel.

That winter, at Dawson, Buck performed another exploit, not so heroic, perhaps, but one that put his name many notches higher on the totem-pole of Alaskan fame. This exploit was particularly gratifying to the three men; for they stood in need of the outfit which it furnished, and were enabled to make a long-desired trip into the virgin East, where miners had not yet appeared. It was brought about by a conversation in the Eldorado Saloon, in which men waxed boastful of their favorite dogs. Buck, because of his record, was the target for these men, and Thornton was driven stoutly to defend him. At the end of half an hour one man stated that his dog could start a sled with five hundred pounds and walk off with it; a second bragged six hundred for his dog; and a third, seven hundred.

"Pooh! pooh!" said John Thornton; "Buck can start a thousand pounds."

"And break it out? and walk off with it for a hundred yards?" demanded Matthewson, a Bonanza King, he of the seven hundred vaunt.

"And break it out, and walk off with it for a hundred yards," John Thornton said coolly.

"Well," Matthewson said, slowly and deliberately, so that all could hear, "I've got a thousand dollars that says he can't. And there it is." So saying, he slammed a sack of gold dust of the size of a bologna sausage down upon the bar.

Nobody spoke. Thornton's bluff, if bluff it was, had been called. He could feel a flush of warm blood creeping up his face. His tongue had tricked him. He did not know whether Buck could start a thousand pounds. Half a ton! The enormousness of it appalled him. He had great faith in Buck's strength and had often thought him capable of starting such a load; but never, as now, had he faced the possibility of it, the eyes of a dozen men fixed upon him, silent and waiting. Further, he had no thousand dollars; nor had Hans or Pete.

"I've got a sled standing outside now, with twenty fifty-pound sacks of flour on it," Matthewson went on with brutal directness; "so don't let that hinder you."

Thornton did not reply. He did not know what to say. He glanced from face to face in the absent way of a man who has lost the power of thought and is seeking somewhere to find the thing that will start it going again. The face of Jim O'Brien, a Mastodon King and old-time comrade, caught his eyes. It was as a cue to him, seeming to rouse him to do what he would never have dreamed of doing.

"Can you lend me a thousand?" he asked, almost in a whisper.

"Sure," answered O'Brien, thumping down a plethoric sack by the side of Matthewson's. "Though it's little faith I'm having, John, that the beast can do the trick."

The Eldorado emptied its occupants into the street to see the test. The tables were deserted, and the dealers and gamekeepers came forth to see the outcome of the wager and to lay odds. Several hundred men, furred and mittened, banked around the sled within easy distance. Matthewson's sled, loaded with a thousand pounds of flour, had been standing for a couple of hours, and in the intense cold (it was sixty below zero) the runners had frozen fast to the hard-packed snow. Men offered odds of two to one that Buck could not budge the sled. A quibble arose concerning the phrase "break out." O'Brien contended it was Thornton's privilege to knock the runners loose, leaving Buck to "break it out" from a dead standstill. Matthewson insisted that the phrase included breaking the runners from the frozen grip of the snow. A majority of the men who had witnessed the making of the bet decided in his favor, whereat the odds went up to three to one against Buck.

There were no takers. Not a man believed him capable of the feat. Thornton had been hurried into the wager, heavy with doubt; and now that he looked at the sled itself, the concrete fact, with the regular team of ten dogs curled up in the snow before it, the more impossible the task appeared. Matthewson waxed jubilant.

"Three to one!" he proclaimed. "I'll lay you another thousand at that figure, Thornton. What d'ye say?"

Thornton's doubt was strong in his face, but his fighting spirit was aroused—the fighting spirit that soars above odds, fails to recognize the impossible, and is deaf to all save the clamor for battle. He called Hans and Pete to him. Their sacks were slim, and with his own the three partners could rake together only two hundred dollars. In the ebb of their fortunes, this sum was their total capital; yet they laid it unhesitatingly against Matthewson's six hundred.

The team of ten dogs was unhitched, and Buck, with his own harness, was put into the sled. He had caught the contagion of the excitement, and he felt that in some way he must do a great thing for John Thornton. Murmurs of admiration at his splendid appearance went up. He was in perfect condition, without an ounce of superfluous flesh, and the one hundred and fifty pounds that he weighed were so many pounds of grit

and virility. His furry coat shone with the sheen of silk.
Down the neck and across the shoulders, his mane, in
repose as it was, half bristled and seemed to lift with
every movement, as though excess of vigor made each
particular hair alive and active. The great breast and
heavy fore legs were no more than in proportion with
the rest of the body, where the muscles showed in tight
rolls underneath the skin. Men felt these muscles and
proclaimed them hard as iron, and the odds went down
to two to one.

"Gad, sir! Gad, sir!" stuttered a member of the latest dynasty, a king of the Skookum Benches. "I offer
you eight hundred for him, sir, before the test, sir;
eight hundred just as he stands."

Thornton shook his head and stepped to Buck's side.

"You must stand off from him," Matthewson protested. "Free play and plenty of room."

The crowd fell silent; only could be heard the voices
of the gamblers vainly offering two to one. Everybody
acknowledged Buck a magnificent animal, but twenty
fifty-pound sacks of flour bulked too large in their eyes
for them to loosen their pouch-strings.

Thornton knelt down by Buck's side. He took his
head in his two hands and rested cheek on cheek. He
did not playfully shake him, as was his wont, or murmur soft love curses; but he whispered in his ear. "As
you love me, Buck. As you love me," was what he
whispered. Buck whined with suppressed eagerness.

The crowd was watching curiously. The affair was
growing mysterious. It seemed like a conjuration. As
Thornton got to his feet, Buck seized his mittened
hand between his jaws, pressing in with his teeth and
releasing slowly, half-reluctantly. It was the answer, in
terms, not of speech, but of love. Thornton stepped
well back.

"Now, Buck," he said.

Buck tightened the traces, then slacked them for a

matter of several inches. It was the way he had learned.

"Gee!" Thornton's voice rang out, sharp in the tense silence.

Buck swung to the right, ending the movement in a plunge that took up the slack and with a sudden jerk arrested his one hundred and fifty pounds. The load quivered, and from under the runners arose a crisp crackling.

"Haw!" Thornton commanded.

Buck duplicated the manoeuvre, this time to the left. The crackling turned into a snapping, the sled pivoting and the runners slipping and grating several inches to the side. The sled was broken out. Men were holding their breaths, intensely unconscious of the fact.

"Now, MUSH!"

Thornton's command cracked out like a pistol-shot. Buck threw himself forward, tightening the traces with a jarring lunge. His whole body was gathered compactly together in the tremendous effort, the muscles writhing and knotting like live things under the silky fur. His great chest was low to the ground, his head forward and down, while his feet were flying like mad, the claws scarring the hard-packed snow in parallel grooves. The sled swayed and trembled, half-started forward. One of his feet slipped, and one man groaned aloud. Then the sled lurched ahead in what appeared a rapid succession of jerks, though it never really came to a dead stop again ... half an inch ... an inch ... two inches. ... The jerks perceptibly diminished; as the sled gained momentum, he caught them up, till it was moving steadily along.

Men gasped and began to breathe again, unaware that for a moment they had ceased to breathe. Thornton was running behind, encouraging Buck with short, cheery words. The distance had been measured off, and as he neared the pile of firewood which marked the end of the hundred yards, a cheer began to grow and grow, which burst into a roar as he passed the firewood and halted at command. Every man was tearing himself loose, even Matthewson. Hats and mittens were flying in the air. Men were shaking hands, it did not matter with whom, and bubbling over in a general incoherent babel.

But Thornton fell on his knees beside Buck. Head was against head, and he was shaking him back and forth. Those who hurried up heard him cursing Buck, and he cursed him long and fervently, and softly and lovingly.

"Gad, sir! Gad, sir!" spluttered the Skookum Bench king. "I'll give you a thousand for him, sir, a thousand, sir—twelve hundred, sir."

Thornton rose to his feet. His eyes were wet. The tears were streaming frankly down his cheeks. "Sir," he said to the Skookum Bench king, "no, sir. You can go to hell, sir. It's the best I can do for you, sir."

Buck seized Thornton's hand in his teeth. Thornton shook him back and forth. As though animated by a common impulse, the onlookers drew back to a respectful distance; nor were they again indiscreet enough to interrupt.

CHAPTER VII

The Sounding of
the Call

When Buck earned sixteen hundred dollars in five minutes for John Thornton, he made it possible for his master to pay off certain debts and to journey with his partners into the East after a fabled lost mine, the history of which was as old as the history of the country. Many men had sought it; few had found it; and more than a few there were who had never returned from the quest. This lost mine was steeped in tragedy and shrouded in mystery. No one knew of the first man. The oldest tradition stopped before it got back to him. From the beginning there had been an ancient and ramshackle cabin. Dying men had sworn to it, and to the mine the site of which it marked, clinching their testimony with nuggets that were unlike any known grade of gold in the Northland.

But no living man had looted this treasure house, and the dead were dead; wherefore John Thornton and Pete and Hans, with Buck and half a dozen other dogs, faced into the East on an unknown trail to achieve where men and dogs as good as themselves had failed. They sledded seventy miles up the Yukon, swung to the left into the Stewart River, passed the Mayo and the McQuestion, and held on until the Stewart itself became a streamlet, threading the upstanding peaks which marked the backbone of the continent.

John Thornton asked little of man or nature. He was unafraid of the wild. With a handful of salt and a rifle he could plunge into the wilderness and fare wherever he pleased and as long as he pleased. Being in no haste, Indian fashion, he hunted his dinner in the course of the day's travel; and if he failed to find it, like the Indian, he kept on travelling, secure in the knowledge that sooner or later he would come to it. So, on this great journey into the East, straight meat was the bill of fare, ammunition and tools principally made up the load on the sled, and the time-card was drawn upon the limitless future.

To Buck it was boundless delight, this hunting, fishing, and indefinite wandering through strange places. For weeks at a time they would hold on steadily, day after day; and for weeks upon end they would camp, here and there, the dogs loafing and the men burning holes through frozen muck and gravel and washing countless pans of dirt by the heat of the fire. Sometimes they went hungry, sometimes they feasted riotously, all according to the abundance of game and the fortune of hunting. Summer arrived, and dogs and men packed on their backs, rafted across blue mountain lakes, and descended or ascended unknown rivers in slender boats whipsawed from the standing forest.

The months came and went, and back and forth they twisted through the uncharted vastness, where no men were and yet where men had been if the Lost Cabin were true. They went across divides in summer blizzards, shivered under the midnight sun on naked mountains between the timber line and the eternal snows, dropped into summer valleys amid swarming gnats and flies, and in the shadows of glaciers picked strawberries and flowers as ripe and fair as any the Southland could boast. In the fall of the year they penetrated a weird lake country, sad and silent, where wildfowl had been, but where then there was no life nor sign of life—only the blowing of chill winds, the forming of ice in sheltered places, and the melancholy rippling of waves on lonely beaches.

And through another winter they wandered on the obliterated trails of men who had gone before. Once, they came upon a path blazed through the forest, an ancient path, and the Lost Cabin seemed very near. But the path began nowhere and ended nowhere, and it remained mystery, as the man who made it and the reason he made it remained mystery. Another time they chanced upon the time-graven wreckage of a hunting lodge, and amid the shreds of rotted blankets John Thornton found a long-barrelled flint-lock. He knew it for a Hudson Bay Company gun of the young days in the Northwest, when such a gun was worth its height in beaver skins packed flat. And that was all— no hint as to the man who in an early day had reared the lodge and left the gun among the blankets.

Spring came on once more, and at the end of all their wandering they found, not the Lost Cabin, but a shallow placer in a broad valley where the gold showed like yellow butter across the bottom of the washing-pan. They sought no farther. Each day they worked earned them thousands of dollars in clean dust and nuggets, and they worked every day. The gold was sacked in moose-hide bags, fifty pounds to the bag, and piled like so much firewood outside the spruce-bough lodge. Like giants they toiled, days flashing on the heels of days like dreams as they heaped the treasure up.

There was nothing for the dogs to do, save the hauling in of meat now and again that Thornton killed, and Buck spent long hours musing by the fire. The vision of the short-legged hairy man came to him more frequently, now that there was little work to be done; and often, blinking by the fire, Buck wandered with him in that other world which he remembered.

The salient thing of this other world seemed fear. When he watched the hairy man sleeping by the fire, head between his knees and hands clasped above, Buck saw that he slept restlessly, with many starts and awakenings, at which times he would peer fearfully into the darkness and fling more wood upon the fire. Did they walk by the beach of a sea, where the hairy man gathered shell-fish and ate them as he gathered, it was with eyes that roved everywhere for hidden danger and with legs prepared to run like the wind at its first appearance. Through the forest they crept noiselessly, Buck at the hairy man's heels; and they were alert and vigilant, the pair of them, ears twitching and moving and nostrils quivering, for the man heard and smelled as keenly as Buck. The hairy man could spring up into the trees and travel ahead as fast as on the ground, swinging by the arms from limb to limb, sometimes a dozen feet apart, letting go and catching, never falling, never missing his grip. In fact, he seemed as much at home among the trees as on the ground; and Buck had memories of nights of vigil spent beneath trees wherein the hairy man roosted, holding on tightly as he slept.

And closely akin to the visions of the hairy man was the call still sounding in the depths of the forest. It filled him with a great unrest and strange desires. It caused him to feel a vague, sweet gladness, and he was aware of wild yearnings and stirrings for he knew not what. Sometimes he pursued the call into the forest, looking for it as though it were a tangible thing, barking softly or defiantly, as the mood might dictate. He would thrust his nose into the cool wood moss, or into the black soil where long grasses grew, and snort with joy at the fat earth smells; or he would crouch for hours, as if in concealment, behind fungus-covered trunks of fallen trees, wide-eyed and wide-eared to all that moved and sounded about him. It might be, lying thus, that he hoped to surprise this call he could not understand. But he did not know why he did these various things. He was impelled to do them, and did not reason about them at all.

Irresistible impulses seized him. He would be lying in camp, dozing lazily in the heat of the day, when suddenly his head would lift and his ears cock up, intent and listening, and he would spring to his feet and dash away, and on and on, for hours, through the forest aisles and across the open spaces where the niggerheads bunched. He loved to run down dry watercourses, and to creep and spy upon the bird life in the woods. For a day at a time he would lie in the underbrush where he could watch the partridges drumming and strutting up and down. But especially he loved to run in the dim twilight of the summer midnights, listening to the subdued and sleepy murmurs of the forest, reading signs and sounds as man may read a book, and seeking for the mysterious something that called—called, waking or sleeping, at all times, for him to come.

One night he sprang from sleep with a start, eager-eyed, nostrils quivering and scenting, his mane bristling in recurrent waves. From the forest came the call (or one note of it, for the call was many noted), distinct and definite as never before—a long-drawn howl, like, yet unlike, any noise made by husky dog. And he knew it, in the old familiar way, as a sound heard before. He sprang through the sleeping camp and in swift silence dashed through the woods. As he drew closer to the cry he went more slowly, with caution in every movement, till he came to an open place among the trees, and looking out saw, erect on haunches, with nose pointed to the sky, a long, lean, timber wolf.

He had made no noise, yet it ceased from its howling and tried to sense his presence. Buck stalked into the open, half crouching, body gathered compactly together, tail straight and stiff, feet falling with unwonted care. Every movement advertised commingled threatening and overture of friendliness. It was the menacing truce that marks the meeting of wild beasts that prey. But the wolf fled at sight of him. He followed, with wild leapings, in a frenzy to overtake. He ran him into a blind channel, in the bed of the creek, where a timber jam barred the way. The wolf whirled about, pivoting on his hind legs after the fashion of Joe and of all cornered husky dogs, snarling and bristling, clipping his teeth together in a continuous and rapid succession of snaps.

Buck did not attack, but circled him about and hedged him in with friendly advances. The wolf was suspicious and afraid; for Buck made three of him in weight, while his head barely reached Buck's shoulder. Watching his chance he darted away, and the chase was resumed. Time and again he was cornered, and the thing repeated, though he was in poor condition or Buck could not so easily have overtaken him. He would run till Buck's head was even with his flank, when he would whirl around at bay, only to dash away again at the first opportunity.

But in the end Buck's pertinacity was rewarded; for the wolf, finding that no harm was intended, finally sniffed noses with him. Then they became friendly, and played about in the nervous, half-coy way with which fierce beasts belie their fierceness. After some time of this the wolf started off at an easy lope in a manner that plainly showed he was going somewhere. He made it clear to Buck that he was to come, and they ran side by side through the sombre twilight, straight up the creek bed, into the gorge from which it issued, and across the bleak divide where it took its rise.

On the opposite slope of the watershed they came down into a level country where were great stretches of forest and many streams, and through these great stretches they ran steadily, hour after hour, the sun rising higher and the day growing warmer. Buck was wildly glad. He knew he was at last answering the call, running by the side of his wood brother toward the place from where the call surely came. Old memories were coming upon him fast, and he was stirring to them as of old he stirred to the realities of which they were the shadows. He had done this thing before, somewhere in that other and dimly remembered world, and he was doing it again, now, running free in the open, the unpacked earth underfoot, the wide sky overhead.

They stopped by a running stream to drink, and, stopping, Buck remembered John Thornton. He sat down. The wolf started on toward the place from where the call surely came, then returned to him, sniffing noses and making actions as though to encourage him. But Buck turned about and started slowly on the back track. For the better part of an hour the wild brother ran by his side, whining softly. Then he sat down, pointed his nose upward and howled. It was a mournful howl, and as Buck held steadily on his way he heard it grow faint and fainter until it was lost in the distance.

John Thornton was eating dinner when Buck dashed into camp and sprang upon him in a frenzy of affection, overturning him, scrambling upon him, licking his face, biting his hand—"playing the general tom-fool," as John Thornton characterized it, the while he shook Buck back and forth and cursed him lovingly.

For two days and nights Buck never left camp, never let Thornton out of his sight. He followed him about at his work, watched him while he ate, saw him into his blankets at night and out of them in the morning. But after two days the call in the forest began to sound more imperiously than ever. Buck's restlessness came back on him, and he was haunted by recollections of the wild brother, and of the smiling land beyond the

divide and the run side by side through the wide forest
stretches. Once again he took to wandering in the
woods, but the wild brother came no more; and though
he listened through long vigils, the mournful howl was
never raised.

He began to sleep out at night, staying away from
camp for days at a time; and once he crossed the divide
at the head of the creek and went down into the land of
timber and streams. There he wandered for a week,
seeking vainly for fresh sign of the wild brother, killing
his meat as he travelled and travelling with the long,
easy lope that seems never to tire. He fished for salmon
in a broad stream that emptied somewhere into the sea,
and by this stream he killed a large black bear, blinded
by the mosquitoes while likewise fishing, and raging
through the forest helpless and terrible. Even so, it was
a hard fight, and it aroused the last latent remnants of
Buck's ferocity. And two days later, when he returned
to his kill and found a dozen wolverenes quarrelling
over the spoil, he scattered them like chaff; and those
that fled left two behind who would quarrel no more.

The blood-longing became stronger than ever before. He was a killer, a thing that preyed, living on the
things that lived, unaided, alone, by virtue of his own
strength and prowess, surviving triumphantly in a hostile environment where only the strong survived. Because of all this he became possessed of a great pride in
himself, which communicated itself like a contagion to
his physical being. It advertised itself in all his movements, was apparent in the play of every muscle, spoke
plainly as speech in the way he carried himself, and
made his glorious furry coat if anything more glorious.
But for the stray brown on his muzzle and above his
eyes, and for the splash of white hair that ran midmost
down his chest, he might well have been mistaken for a
gigantic wolf, larger than the largest of the breed.
From his St. Bernard father he had inherited size and

weight, but it was his shepherd mother who had given shape to that size and weight. His muzzle was the long wolf muzzle, save that it was larger than the muzzle of any wolf; and his head, somewhat broader, was the wolf head on a massive scale.

His cunning was wolf cunning, and wild cunning; his intelligence, shepherd intelligence and St. Bernard intelligence; and all this, plus an experience gained in the fiercest of schools, made him as formidable a creature as any that roamed the wild. A carnivorous animal, living on a straight meat diet, he was in full flower, at the high tide of his life, overspilling with vigor and virility. When Thornton passed a caressing hand along his back, a snapping and crackling followed the hand, each hair discharging its pent magnetism at the contact. Every part, brain and body, nerve tissue and fibre, was keyed to the most exquisite pitch; and between all the parts there was a perfect equilibrium or adjustment. To sights and sounds and events which required action, he responded with lightning-like rapidity. Quickly as a husky dog could leap to defend from attack or to attack, he could leap twice as quickly. He saw the movement, or heard sound, and responded in less time than another dog required to compass the mere seeing or hearing. He perceived and determined and responded in the same instant. In point of fact the three actions of perceiving, determining, and responding were sequential; but so infinitesimal were the intervals of time between them that they appeared simultaneous. His muscles were surcharged with vitality, and snapped into play sharply, like steel springs. Life streamed through him in splendid flood, glad and rampant, until it seemed that it would burst him asunder in sheer ecstasy and pour forth generously over the world.

"Never was there such a dog," said John Thornton one day, as the partners watched Buck marching out of camp.

"When he was made, the mould was broke," said Pete.

"Py jingo! I t'ink so mineself," Hans affirmed.

They saw him marching out of camp, but they did not see the instant and terrible transformation which took place as soon as he was within the secrecy of the forest. He no longer marched. At once he became a thing of the wild, stealing along softly, cat-footed, a passing shadow that appeared and disappeared among the shadows. He knew how to take advantage of every cover, to crawl on his belly like a snake, and like a snake to leap and strike. He could take a ptarmigan from its nest, kill a rabbit as it slept, and snap in mid air the little chipmunks fleeing a second too late for the trees. Fish, in open pools, were not too quick for him; nor were beaver, mending their dams, too wary. He killed to eat, not from wantonness; but he preferred to eat what he killed himself. So a lurking humor ran through his deeds, and it was his delight to steal upon the squirrels, and, when he all but had them, to let them go, chattering in mortal fear to the tree-tops.

As the fall of the year came on, the moose appeared in greater abundance, moving slowly down to meet the winter in the lower and less rigorous valleys. Buck had already dragged down a stray part-grown calf; but he wished strongly for larger and more formidable quarry, and he came upon it one day on the divide at the head of the creek. A band of twenty moose had crossed over from the land of streams and timber, and chief among them was a great bull. He was in a savage temper, and, standing over six feet from the ground, was as formidable an antagonist as ever Buck could desire. Back and forth the bull tossed his great palmated antlers, branching to fourteen points and embracing seven feet within the tips. His small eyes burned with a vicious and bitter light, while he roared with fury at sight of Buck.

From the bull's side, just forward of the flank, protruded a feathered arrow-end, which accounted for his savageness. Guided by that instinct which came from the old hunting days of the primordial world, Buck proceeded to cut the bull out from the herd. It was no slight task. He would bark and dance about in front of the bull, just out of reach of the great antlers and of the terrible splay hoofs which could have stamped his life out with a single blow. Unable to turn his back on the fanged danger and go on, the bull would be driven into paroxysms of rage. At such moments he charged Buck, who retreated craftily, luring him on by a simulated inability to escape. But when he was thus separated from his fellows, two or three of the younger bulls would charge back upon Buck and enable the wounded bull to rejoin the herd.

There is a patience of the wild—dogged, tireless, persistent as life itself—that holds motionless for endless hours the spider in its web, the snake in its coils, the panther in its ambuscade; this patience belongs peculiarly to life when it hunts its living food; and it belonged to Buck as he clung to the flank of the herd, retarding its march, irritating the young bulls, worrying the cows with their half-grown calves, and driving the wounded bull mad with helpless rage. For half a day this continued. Buck multiplied himself, attacking from all sides, enveloping the herd in a whirlwind of menace, cutting out his victim as fast as it could rejoin its mates, wearing out the patience of creatures preyed upon, which is a lesser patience than that of creatures preying.

As the day wore along and the sun dropped to its bed in the northwest (the darkness had come back and the fall nights were six hours long), the young bulls retraced their steps more and more reluctantly to the aid of their beset leader. The down-coming winter was harrying them on to the lower levels, and it seemed they could never shake off this tireless creature that held them back. Besides, it was not the life of the herd, or of the young bulls, that was threatened. The life of only one member was demanded, which was a remoter interest than their lives, and in the end they were content to pay the toll.

As twilight fell the old bull stood with lowered head, watching his mates—the cows he had known, the calves he had fathered, the bulls he had mastered—as they shambled on at a rapid pace through the fading light. He could not follow, for before his nose leaped the merciless fanged terror that would not let him go. Three hundredweight more than half a ton he weighed; he had lived a long, strong life, full of fight and struggle, and at the end he faced death at the teeth of a creature whose head did not reach beyond his great knuckled knees.

From then on, night and day, Buck never left his prey, never gave it a moment's rest, never permitted it to browse the leaves of trees or the shoots of young birch and willow. Nor did he give the wounded bull opportunity to slake his burning thirst in the slender trickling streams they crossed. Often, in desperation, he burst into long stretches of flight. At such times Buck did not attempt to stay him, but loped easily at his heels, satisfied with the way the game was played, lying down when the moose stood still, attacking him fiercely when he strove to eat or drink.

The great head drooped more and more under its tree of horns, and the shambling trot grew weaker and weaker. He took to standing for long periods, with nose to the ground and dejected ears dropped limply; and Buck found more time in which to get water for himself and in which to rest. At such moments, panting with red lolling tongue and with eyes fixed upon the big bull, it appeared to Buck that a change was coming over the face of things. He could feel a new stir in the land. As the moose were coming into the land, other kinds of life were coming in. Forest and stream and air seemed palpitant with their presence. The news of it was borne in upon him, not by sight, or sound, or smell, but by some other and subtler sense. He heard nothing, saw nothing, yet knew that the land was somehow different; that through it strange things were afoot and ranging; and he resolved to investigate after he had finished the business in hand.

At last, at the end of the fourth day, he pulled the great moose down. For a day and a night he remained by the kill, eating and sleeping, turn and turn about. Then, rested, refreshed and strong, he turned his face toward camp and John Thornton. He broke into the long easy lope, and went on, hour after hour, never at loss for the tangled way, heading straight home through strange country with a certitude of direction that put man and his magnetic needle to shame.

As he held on he became more and more conscious of the new stir in the land. There was life abroad in it different from the life which had been there throughout the summer. No longer was this fact borne in upon him in some subtle, mysterious way. The birds talked of it, the squirrels chattered about it, the very breeze whispered of it. Several times he stopped and drew in the fresh morning air in great sniffs, reading a message which made him leap on with greater speed. He was oppressed with a sense of calamity happening, if it were not calamity already happened; and as he crossed the last watershed and dropped down into the valley toward camp, he proceeded with greater caution.

Three miles away he came upon a fresh trail that sent his neck hair rippling and bristling. It led straight toward camp and John Thornton. Buck hurried on, swiftly and stealthily, every nerve straining and tense, alert to the multitudinous details which told a story—all but the end. His nose gave him a varying description of the passage of the life on the heels of which he was travelling. He remarked the pregnant silence of the forest. The bird life had flitted. The squirrels were in hiding. One only he saw,—a sleek gray fellow, flattened against a gray dead limb so that he seemed a part of it, a woody excrescence upon the wood itself.

As Buck slid along with the obscureness of a gliding shadow, his nose was jerked suddenly to the side as though a positive force had gripped and pulled it. He followed the new scent into a thicket and found Nig. He was lying on his side, dead where he had dragged himself, an arrow protruding, head and feathers, from either side of his body.

A hundred yards farther on, Buck came upon one of the sled-dogs Thornton had bought in Dawson. This dog was thrashing about in a death-struggle, directly on the trail, and Buck passed around him without stopping. From the camp came the faint sound of many voices, rising and falling in a sing-song chant. Bellying forward to the edge of the clearing, he found Hans, lying on his face, feathered with arrows like a porcupine. At the same instant Buck peered out where the spruce-bough lodge had been and saw what made his hair leap straight up on his neck and shoulders. A gust of overpowering rage swept over him. He did not know that he growled, but he growled aloud with a terrible ferocity. For the last time in his life he allowed passion to usurp cunning and reason, and it was because of his great love for John Thornton that he lost his head.

The Yeehats were dancing about the wreckage of the spruce-bough lodge when they heard a fearful roaring and saw rushing upon them an animal the like of which they had never seen before. It was Buck, a live hurricane of fury, hurling himself upon them in a frenzy to destroy. He sprang at the foremost man (it was the chief of the Yeehats), ripping the throat wide open till the rent jugular spouted a fountain of blood. He did not pause to worry the victim, but ripped in passing, with the next bound tearing wide the throat of a second man. There was no withstanding him. He plunged about in their very midst, tearing, rending, destroying, in constant and terrific motion which defied the arrows they discharged at him. In fact, so inconceivably rapid were his movements, and so closely were the Indians tangled together, that they shot one another with the arrows; and one young hunter, hurling a spear at Buck in mid air, drove it through the chest of another hunter with such force that the point broke through the skin of the back and stood out beyond. Then a panic seized the Yeehats, and they fled in terror to the woods, proclaiming as they fled the advent of the Evil Spirit.

And truly Buck was the Fiend incarnate, raging at their heels and dragging them down like deer as they raced through the trees. It was a fateful day for the Yeehats. They scattered far and wide over the country, and it was not till a week later that the last of the survivors gathered together in a lower valley and counted their losses. As for Buck, wearying of the pursuit, he returned to the desolated camp. He found Pete where he had been killed in his blankets in the first moment of surprise. Thornton's desperate struggle was fresh-written on the earth, and Buck scented every detail of it down to the edge of a deep pool. By the edge, head and fore feet in the water, lay Skeet, faithful to the last. The pool itself, muddy and discolored from the sluice boxes, effectually hid what it contained, and it contained John Thornton; for Buck followed his trace into the water, from which no trace led away.

All day Buck brooded by the pool or roamed restlessly about the camp. Death, as a cessation of movement, as a passing out and away from the lives of the living, he knew, and he knew John Thornton was dead.

It left a great void in him, somewhat akin to hunger, but a void which ached and ached, and which food could not fill. At times, when he paused to contemplate the carcasses of the Yeehats, he forgot the pain of it; and at such times he was aware of a great pride in himself,—a pride greater than any he had yet experienced. He had killed man, the noblest game of all, and he had killed in the face of the law of club and fang. He sniffed the bodies curiously. They had died so easily. It was harder to kill a husky dog than them. They were no match at all, were it not for their arrows and spears and clubs. Thenceforward he would be unafraid of them except when they bore in their hands their arrows, spears, and clubs.

Night came on, and a full moon rose high over the trees into the sky, lighting the land till it lay bathed in ghostly day. And with the coming of the night, brooding and mourning by the pool, Buck became alive to a stirring of the new life in the forest other than that which the Yeehats had made. He stood up, listening and scenting. From far away drifted a faint, sharp yelp, followed by a chorus of similar sharp yelps. As the moments passed the yelps grew closer and louder. Again Buck knew them as things heard in that other world which persisted in his memory. He walked to the centre of the open space and listened. It was the call, the many-noted call, sounding more luringly and compelling than ever before. And as never before, he was ready to obey. John Thornton was dead. The last tie was broken. Man and the claims of man no longer bound him.

Hunting their living meat, as the Yeehats were hunting it, on the flanks of the migrating moose, the wolf pack had at last crossed over from the land of streams and timber and invaded Buck's valley. Into the clearing where the moonlight streamed, they poured in a silvery flood; and in the center of the clearing stood

Buck, motionless as a statue, waiting their coming. They were awed, so still and large he stood, and a moment's pause fell, till the boldest one leaped straight for him. Like a flash Buck struck, breaking the neck. Then he stood, without movement, as before, the stricken wolf rolling in agony behind him. Three others tried it in sharp succession; and one after the other they drew back, streaming blood from slashed throats or shoulders.

This was sufficient to fling the whole pack forward, pell-mell, crowded together, blocked and confused by its eagerness to pull down the prey. Buck's marvellous quickness and agility stood him in good stead. Pivoting on his hind legs, and snapping and gashing, he was everywhere at once, presenting a front which was apparently unbroken so swiftly did he whirl and guard from side to side. But to prevent them from getting behind him, he was forced back, down past the pool and into the creek bed, till he brought up against a high gravel bank. He worked along to a right angle in the bank which the men had made in the course of mining, and in this angle he came to bay, protected on three sides and with nothing to do but face the front.

And so well did he face it, that at the end of half an hour the wolves drew back discomfited. The tongues of all were out and lolling, the white fangs showing cruelly white in the moonlight. Some were lying down with heads raised and ears pricked forward; others stood on their feet, watching him; and still others were lapping water from the pool. One wolf, long and lean and gray, advanced cautiously, in a friendly manner, and Buck recognized the wild brother with whom he had run for a night and a day. He was whining softly, and, as Buck whined, they touched noses.

Then an old wolf, gaunt and battle-scarred, came forward. Buck writhed his lips into the preliminary of a snarl, but sniffed noses with him. Whereupon the old

wolf sat down, pointed nose at the moon, and broke out
the long wolf howl. The others sat down and howled.
And now the call came to Buck in unmistakable accents. He, too, sat down and howled. This over, he
came out of his angle and the pack crowded around
him, sniffing in half-friendly, half-savage manner. The
leaders lifted the yelp of the pack and sprang away into
the woods. The wolves swung in behind, yelping in
chorus. And Buck ran with them, side by side with the
wild brother, yelping as he ran.

And here may well end the story of Buck. The years
were not many when the Yeehats noted a change in the
breed of timber wolves, for some were seen with
splashes of brown on head and muzzle, and with a rift
of white centring down the chest. But more remarkable than this, the Yeehats tell of a Ghost Dog that
runs at the head of the pack. They are afraid of this
Ghost Dog, for it has cunning greater than they, stealing from their camps in fierce winters, robbing their
traps, slaying their dogs, and defying their bravest
hunters.

Nay, the tale grows worse. Hunters there are who
fail to return to the camp, and hunters there have been
whom their tribesmen found with throats slashed
cruelly open and with wolf prints about them in the
snow greater than the prints of any wolf. Each fall,
when the Yeehats follow the movement of the moose,
there is a certain valley which they never enter. And
women there are who become sad when the word goes
over the fire of how the Evil Spirit came to select that
valley for an abiding-place.

In the summers there is one visitor, however, to that
valley, of which the Yeehats do not know. It is a great,
gloriously coated wolf, like, and yet unlike, all other
wolves. He crosses alone from the smiling timber land
and comes down into an open space among the trees.

Here a yellow stream flows from rotted moose-hide sacks and sinks into the ground, with long grasses growing through it and vegetable mould overrunning it and hiding its yellow from the sun; and here he muses for a time, howling once, long and mournfully, ere he departs.

But he is not always alone. When the long winter nights come on and the wolves follow their meat into the lower valleys, he may be seen running at the head of the pack through the pale moonlight or glimmering borealis, leaping gigantic above his fellows, his great throat a-bellow as he sings a song of the younger world, which is the song of the pack.

LOVE OF LIFE

"This out of all will remain—
 They have lived and have tossed:
So much of the game will be gain,
 Though the gold of the dice has been lost."

They limped painfully down the bank, and once the foremost of the two men staggered among the rough-strewn rocks. They were tired and weak, and their faces had the drawn expression of patience which comes of hardship long endured. They were heavily burdened with blanket packs which were strapped to their shoulders. Head-straps, passing across the forehead, helped support these packs. Each man carried a rifle. They walked in a stooped posture, the shoulders well forward, the head still farther forward, the eyes bent upon the ground.

"I wish we had just about two of them cartridges that's layin' in that cache of ourn," said the second man.

His voice was utterly and drearily expressionless. He spoke without enthusiasm; and the first man, limping into the milky stream that foamed over the rocks, vouchsafed no reply.

The other man followed at his heels. They did not remove their foot-gear, though the water was icy cold—so cold that their ankles ached and their feet

141

went numb. In places the water dashed against their knees, and both men staggered for footing.

The man who followed slipped on a smooth boulder, nearly fell, but recovered himself with a violent effort, at the same time uttering a sharp exclamation of pain. He seemed faint and dizzy and put out his free hand while he reeled, as though seeking support against the air. When he had steadied himself he stepped forward, but reeled again and nearly fell. Then he stood still and looked at the other man, who had never turned his head.

The man stood still for fully a minute, as though debating with himself. Then he called out:

"I say, Bill, I've sprained my ankle."

Bill staggered on through the milky water. He did not look around. The man watched him go, and though his face was expressionless as ever, his eyes were like the eyes of a wounded deer.

The other man limped up the farther bank and continued straight on without looking back. The man in the stream watched him. His lips trembled a little, so that the rough thatch of brown hair which covered them was visibly agitated. His tongue even strayed out to moisten them.

"Bill!" he cried out.

It was the pleading cry of a strong man in distress, but Bill's head did not turn. The man watched him go, limping grotesquely and lurching forward with stammering gait up the slow slope toward the soft sky-line of the low-lying hill. He watched him go till he passed over the crest and disappeared. Then he turned his gaze and slowly took in the circle of the world that remained to him now that Bill was gone.

Near the horizon the sun was smouldering dimly, almost obscured by formless mists and vapors, which gave an impression of mass and density without outline or tangibility. The man pulled out his watch, the while resting his weight on one leg. It was four o'clock, and as the season was near the last of July or first of August,—he did not know the precise date within a week or two,—he knew that the sun roughly marked the northwest. He looked to the south and knew that somewhere beyond those bleak hills lay the Great Bear Lake; also, he knew that in that direction the Arctic Circle cut its forbidding way across the Canadian Barrens. This stream in which he stood was a feeder to the Coppermine River, which in turn flowed north and emptied into Coronation Gulf and the Arctic Ocean. He had never been there, but he had seen it, once, on a Hudson Bay Company chart.

Again his gaze completed the circle of the world about him. It was not a heartening spectacle. Everywhere was soft sky-line. The hills were all low-lying. There were no trees, no shrubs, no grasses—naught but a tremendous and terrible desolation that sent fear swiftly dawning into his eyes.

"Bill!" he whispered, once and twice; "Bill!"

He cowered in the midst of the milky water, as though the vastness were pressing in upon him with overwhelming force, brutally crushing him with its complacent awfulness. He began to shake as with an ague-fit, till the gun fell from his hand with a splash. This served to rouse him. He fought with his fear and pulled himself together, groping in the water and recovering the weapon. He hitched his pack farther over on his left shoulder, so as to take a portion of its weight from off the injured ankle. Then he proceeded, slowly and carefully, wincing with pain, to the bank.

He did not stop. With a desperation that was madness, unmindful of the pain, he hurried up the slope to the crest of the hill over which his comrade had disappeared—more grotesque and comical by far than that limping, jerking comrade. But at the crest he saw a shallow valley, empty of life. He fought with his fear again, overcame it, hitched the pack still farther over on his left shoulder, and lurched on down the slope.

The bottom of the valley was soggy with water, which the thick moss held, spongelike, close to the surface. This water squirted out from under his feet at every step, and each time he lifted a foot the action culminated in a sucking sound as the wet moss reluctantly released its grip. He picked his way from muskeg to muskeg, and followed the other man's footsteps along and across the rocky ledges which thrust like islets through the sea of moss.

Though alone, he was not lost. Farther on he knew he would come to where dead spruce and fir, very small and weazened, bordered the shore of a little lake, the *titchin-nichilie,* in the tongue of the country, the "land of little sticks." And into that lake flowed a small stream, the water of which was not milky. There was rush-grass on that stream—this he remembered well—but no timber, and he would follow it till its first trickle ceased at a divide. He would cross this divide to the first trickle of another stream, flowing to the west, which he would follow until it emptied into the river Dease, and here he would find a cache under an upturned canoe and piled over with many rocks. And in this cache would be ammunition for his empty gun, fish-hooks and lines, a small net—all the utilities for the killing and snaring of food. Also, he would find flour,—not much,—a piece of bacon, and some beans.

Bill would be waiting for him there, and they would paddle away south down the Dease to the Great Bear Lake. And south across the lake they would go, ever south, till they gained the Mackenzie. And south, still south, they would go, while the winter raced vainly after them, and the ice formed in the eddies, and the days grew chill and crisp, south to some warm Hudson Bay Company post, where timber grew tall and generous and there was grub without end.

These were the thoughts of the man as he strove onward. But hard as he strove with his body, he strove equally hard with his mind, trying to think that Bill had not deserted him, that Bill would surely wait for him at the cache. He was compelled to think this thought, or else there would not be any use to strive, and he would have lain down and died. And as the dim ball of the sun sank slowly into the northwest he covered every inch—and many times—of his and Bill's flight south before the downcoming winter. And he conned the grub of the cache and the grub of the Hudson Bay Company post over and over again. He had not eaten for two days; for a far longer time he had not had all he wanted to eat. Often he stooped and picked pale muskeg berries, put them into his mouth, and chewed and swallowed them. A muskeg berry is a bit of seed enclosed in a bit of water. In the mouth the water melts away and the seed chews sharp and bitter. The man knew there was no nourishment in the berries, but he chewed them patiently with a hope greater than knowledge and defying experience.

At nine o'clock he stubbed his toe on a rocky ledge, and from sheer weariness and weakness staggered and fell. He lay for some time, without movement, on his side. Then he slipped out of the pack-straps and clumsily dragged himself into a sitting posture. It was not yet dark, and in the lingering twilight he groped about among the rocks for shreds of dry moss. When he had gathered a heap he built a fire,—a smouldering, smudgy fire,—and put a tin pot of water on to boil.

He unwrapped his pack and the first thing he did was to count his matches. There were sixty-seven. He counted them three times to make sure. He divided them into several portions, wrapping them in oil paper, disposing of one bunch in his empty tobacco pouch, of another bunch in the inside band of his battered hat, of a third bunch under his shirt on the chest. This accom-

plished, a panic came upon him, and he unwrapped
them all and counted them again. There were still
sixty-seven.

He dried his wet foot-gear by the fire. The moccasins were in soggy shreds. The blanket socks were
worn through in places, and his feet were raw and
bleeding. His ankle was throbbing, and he gave it an
examination. It had swollen to the size of his knee. He
tore a long strip from one of his two blankets and
bound the ankle tightly. He tore other strips and bound
them about his feet to serve for both moccasins and
socks. Then he drank the pot of water, steaming hot,
wound his watch, and crawled between his blankets.

He slept like a dead man. The brief darkness around
midnight came and went. The sun arose in the north-
east—at least the day dawned in that quarter, for the
sun was hidden by gray clouds.

At six o'clock he awoke, quietly lying on his back.
He gazed straight up into the gray sky and knew that
he was hungry. As he rolled over on his elbow he was
startled by a loud snort, and saw a bull caribou regarding him with alert curiosity. The animal was not more
than fifty feet away, and instantly into the man's mind
leaped the vision and the savor of a caribou steak sizzling and frying over a fire. Mechanically he reached
for the empty gun, drew a bead, and pulled the trigger.
The bull snorted and leaped away, his hoofs rattling
and clattering as he fled across the ledges.

The man cursed and flung the empty gun from him.
He groaned aloud as he started to drag himself to his
feet. It was a slow and arduous task. His joints were
like rusty hinges. They worked harshly in their
sockets, with much friction, and each bending or un-
bending was accomplished only through a sheer exertion of will. When he finally gained his feet, another
minute or so was consumed in straightening up, so that
he could stand erect as a man should stand.

He crawled up a small knoll and surveyed the prospect. There were no trees, no bushes, nothing but a gray sea of moss scarcely diversified by gray rocks, gray lakelets, and gray streamlets. The sky was gray. There was no sun nor hint of sun. He had no idea of north, and he had forgotten the way he had come to this spot the night before. But he was not lost. He knew that. Soon he would come to the land of the little sticks. He felt that it lay off to the left somewhere, not far—possibly just over the next low hill.

He went back to put his pack into shape for travelling. He assured himself of the existence of his three separate parcels of matches, though he did not stop to count them. But he did linger, debating, over a squat moose-hide sack. It was not large. He could hide it under his two hands. He knew that it weighed fifteen pounds,—as much as all the rest of the pack,—and it worried him. He finally set it to one side and proceeded to roll the pack. He paused to gaze at the squat moose-hide sack. He picked it up hastily with a defiant glance about him, as though the desolation were trying to rob him of it; and when he rose to his feet to stagger on into the day, it was included in the pack on his back.

He bore away to the left, stopping now and again to eat muskeg berries. His ankle had stiffened, his limp was more pronounced, but the pain of it was as nothing compared with the pain of his stomach. The hunger pangs were sharp. They gnawed and gnawed until he could not keep his mind steady on the course he must pursue to gain the land of little sticks. The muskeg berries did not allay this gnawing, while they made his tongue and the roof of his mouth sore with their irritating bite.

He came upon a valley where rock ptarmigan rose on whirring wings from the ledges and muskegs. Ker—ker—ker was the cry they made. He threw stones at them, but could not hit them. He placed his pack on the ground and stalked them as a cat stalks a sparrow. The sharp rocks cut through his pants' legs till his knees left a trail of blood; but the hurt was lost in the hurt of his hunger. He squirmed over the wet moss, saturating his clothes and chilling his body; but he was not aware of it, so great was his fever for food. And always the ptarmigan rose, whirring, before him, till their ker—ker—ker became a mock to him, and he cursed them and cried aloud at them with their own cry.

Once he crawled upon one that must have been asleep. He did not see it till it shot up in his face from its rocky nook. He made a clutch as startled as was the rise of the ptarmigan, and there remained in his hand three tail-feathers. As he watched its flight he hated it, as though it had done him some terrible wrong. Then he returned and shouldered his pack.

As the day wore along he came into valleys or swales where game was more plentiful. A band of caribou passed by, twenty and odd animals, tantalizingly within rifle range. He felt a wild desire to run after them, a certitude that he could run them down. A black fox came toward him, carrying a ptarmigan in his mouth. The man shouted. It was a fearful cry, but the fox, leaping away in fright, did not drop the ptarmigan.

Late in the afternoon he followed a stream, milky with lime, which ran through sparse patches of rush-grass. Grasping these rushes firmly near the root, he pulled up what resembled a young onion-sprout no larger than a shingle-nail. It was tender, and his teeth sank into it with a crunch that promised deliciously of food. But its fibers were tough. It was composed of stringy filaments saturated with water, like the berries, and devoid of nourishment. He threw off his pack and went into the rush-grass on hands and knees, crunching and munching, like some bovine creature.

He was very weary and often wished to rest—to lie

down and sleep; but he was continually driven on—not so much by his desire to gain the land of little sticks as by his hunger. He searched little ponds for frogs and dug up the earth with his nails for worms, though he knew in spite that neither frogs nor worms existed so far north.

He looked into every pool of water vainly, until, as the long twilight came on, he discovered a solitary fish, the size of a minnow, in such a pool. He plunged his arm in up to the shoulder, but it eluded him. He reached for it with both hands and stirred up the milky mud at the bottom. In his excitement he fell in, wetting himself to the waist. Then the water was too muddy to admit of his seeing the fish, and he was compelled to wait until the sediment had settled.

The pursuit was renewed, till the water was again muddied. But he could not wait. He unstrapped the tin bucket and began to bale the pool. He baled wildly at first, splashing himself and flinging the water so short a distance that it ran back into the pool. He worked more carefully, striving to be cool, though his heart was pounding against his chest and his hands were trembling. At the end of half an hour the pool was nearly dry. Not a cupful of water remained. And there was no fish. He found a hidden crevice among the stones through which it had escaped to the adjoining and larger pool—a pool which he could not empty in a night and a day. Had he known of the crevice, he could have closed it with a rock at the beginning and the fish would have been his.

Thus he thought, and crumpled up and sank down upon the wet earth. At first he cried softly to himself, then he cried loudly to the pitiless desolation that ringed him around; and for a long time after he was shaken by great dry sobs.

He built a fire and warmed himself by drinking quarts of hot water, and made camp on a rocky ledge in

the same fashion he had the night before. The last
thing he did was to see that his matches were dry and
to wind his watch. The blankets were wet and clammy.
His ankle pulsed with pain. But he knew only that he
was hungry, and through his restless sleep he dreamed
of feasts and banquets and of food served and spread in
all imaginable ways.

He awoke chilled and sick. There was no sun. The
gray of earth and sky had become deeper, more pro-
found. A raw wind was blowing, and the first flurries of
snow were whitening the hilltops. The air about him
thickened and grew white while he made a fire and
boiled more water. It was wet snow, half rain, and the
flakes were large and soggy. At first they melted as
soon as they came in contact with the earth, but ever
more fell, covering the ground, putting out the fire,
spoiling his supply of moss-fuel.

This was a signal for him to strap on his pack and
stumble onward, he knew not where. He was not concerned with the land of little sticks, nor with Bill and
the cache under the upturned canoe by the river
Dease. He was mastered by the verb "to eat." He was
hunger-mad. He took no heed of the course he pursued, so long as that course led him through the swale
bottoms. He felt his way through the wet snow to the
watery muskeg berries, and went by feel as he pulled
up the rush-grass by the roots. But it was tasteless stuff
and did not satisfy. He found a weed that tasted sour
and he ate all he could find of it, which was not much,
for it was a creeping growth, easily hidden under the
several inches of snow.

He had no fire that night, nor hot water, and
crawled under his blanket to sleep the broken hunger-
sleep. The snow turned into a cold rain. He awakened
many times to feel it falling on his upturned face. Day
came—a gray day and no sun. It had ceased raining.
The keenness of his hunger had departed. Sensibility,
as far as concerned the yearning for food, had been ex-

hausted. There was a dull, heavy ache in his stomach, but it did not bother him so much. He was more rational, and once more he was chiefly interested in the land of little sticks and the cache by the river Dease.

He ripped the remnant of one of his blankets into strips and bound his bleeding feet. Also, he recinched the injured ankle and prepared himself for a day of travel. When he came to his pack, he paused long over the squat moose-hide sack, but in the end it went with him.

The snow had melted under the rain, and only the hilltops showed white. The sun came out, and he succeeded in locating the points of the compass, though he knew now that he was lost. Perhaps, in his previous days' wanderings, he had edged away too far to the left. He now bore off to the right to counteract the possible deviation from his true course.

Though the hunger pangs were no longer so exquisite, he realized that he was weak. He was compelled to pause for frequent rests, when he attacked the muskeg berries and rush-grass patches. His tongue felt dry and large, as though covered with a fine hairy growth, and it tasted bitter in his mouth. His heart gave him a great deal of trouble. When he had travelled a few minutes it would begin a remorseless thump, thump, thump, and then leap up and away in a painful flutter of beats that choked him and made him go faint and dizzy.

In the middle of the day he found two minnows in a large pool. It was impossible to bale it, but he was calmer now and managed to catch them in his tin bucket. They were no longer than his little finger, but he was not particularly hungry. The dull ache in his stomach had been growing duller and fainter. It seemed almost that his stomach was dozing. He ate the fish raw, masticating with painstaking care, for the eating was an act of pure reason. While he had no desire to eat, he knew that he must eat to live.

In the evening he caught three more minnows, eat-

ing two and saving the third for breakfast. The sun had
dried stray shreds of moss, and he was able to warm
himself with hot water. He had not covered more than
ten miles that day; and the next day, travelling whenever his heart permitted him, he covered no more than
five miles. But his stomach did not give him the slightest uneasiness. It had gone to sleep. He was in a
strange country, too, and the caribou were growing
more plentiful, also the wolves. Often their yelps
drifted across the desolation, and once he saw three of
them slinking away before his path.

Another night; and in the morning, being more rational, he untied the leather string that fastened the
squat moose-hide sack. From its open mouth poured a
yellow stream of coarse gold-dust and nuggets. He
roughly divided the gold in halves, caching one half on
a prominent ledge, wrapped in a piece of blanket, and
returning the other half to the sack. He also began to
use strips of the one remaining blanket for his feet. He
still clung to his gun, for there were cartridges in that
cache by the river Dease.

This was a day of fog, and this day hunger awoke in
him again. He was very weak and was afflicted with a
giddiness which at times blinded him. It was no un-
common thing now for him to stumble and fall; and
stumbling once, he fell squarely into a ptarmigan nest.
There were four newly hatched chicks, a day old—little specks of pulsating life no more than a mouthful;
and he ate them ravenously, thrusting them alive into
his mouth and crunching them like egg-shells between
his teeth. The mother ptarmigan beat about him with
great outcry. He used his gun as a club with which to
knock her over, but she dodged out of reach. He threw
stones at her and with one chance shot broke a wing.
Then she fluttered away, running, trailing the broken
wing, with him in pursuit.

The little chicks had no more than whetted his appetite. He hopped and bobbed clumsily along on his injured ankle, throwing stones and screaming hoarsely at times; at other times hopping and bobbing silently along, picking himself up grimly and patiently when he fell, or rubbing his eyes with his hand when the giddiness threatened to overpower him.

The chase led him across swampy ground in the bottom of the valley, and he came upon footprints in the soggy moss. They were not his own—he could see that. They must be Bill's. But he could not stop, for the mother ptarmigan was running on. He would catch her first, then he would return and investigate.

He exhausted the mother ptarmigan; but he exhausted himself. She lay panting on her side. He lay panting on his side, a dozen feet away, unable to crawl to her. And as he recovered she recovered, fluttering out of reach as his hungry hand went out to her. The chase was resumed. Night settled down and she escaped. He stumbled from weakness and pitched head foremost on his face, cutting his cheek, his pack upon his back. He did not move for a long while; then he rolled over on his side, wound his watch, and lay there until morning.

Another day of fog. Half of his last blanket had gone into foot-wrappings. He failed to pick up Bill's trail. It did not matter. His hunger was driving him too compellingly—only—only he wondered if Bill, too, were lost. By midday the irk of his pack became too oppressive. Again he divided the gold, this time merely spilling half of it on the ground. In the afternoon he threw the rest of it away, there remaining to him only the half-blanket, the tin bucket, and the rifle.

An hallucination began to trouble him. He felt confident that one cartridge remained to him. It was in the chamber of the rifle and he had overlooked it. On the other hand, he knew all the time that the chamber was empty. But the hallucination persisted. He fought it off for hours, then threw his rifle open and was confronted with emptiness. The disappointment was as bitter as though he had really expected to find the cartridge.

He plodded on for half an hour, when the hallucination arose again. Again he fought it, and still it persisted, till for very relief he opened his rifle to unconvince himself. At times his mind wandered farther afield, and he plodded on, a mere automaton, strange conceits and whimsicalities gnawing at his brain like worms. But these excursions out of the real were of brief duration, for ever the pangs of the hunger-bite called him back. He was jerked back abruptly once from such an excursion by a sight that caused him nearly to faint. He reeled and swayed, doddering like a drunken man to keep from falling. Before him stood a horse. A horse! He could not believe his eyes. A thick mist was in them, intershot with sparkling points of light. He rubbed his eyes savagely to clear his vision, and beheld, not a horse, but a great brown bear. The animal was studying him with bellicose curiosity.

The man had brought his gun halfway to his shoulder before he realized. He lowered it and drew his hunting-knife from its beaded sheath at his hip. Before him was meat and life. He ran his thumb along the edge of his knife. It was sharp. The point was sharp. He would fling himself upon the bear and kill it. But his heart began its warning thump, thump, thump. Then followed the wild upward leap and tattoo of flutters, the pressing as of an iron band about his forehead, the creeping of the dizziness into his brain.

His desperate courage was evicted by a great surge of fear. In his weakness, what if the animal attacked him? He drew himself up to his most imposing stature, gripping the knife and staring hard at the bear. The bear advanced clumsily a couple of steps, reared up, and gave vent to a tentative growl. If the man ran, he would run after him; but the man did not run. He was animated now with the courage of fear. He, too, growled, savagely, terribly, voicing the fear that is to life germane and that lies twisted about life's deepest roots.

The bear edged away to one side, growling menacingly, himself appalled by this mysterious creature that appeared upright and unafraid. But the man did not move. He stood like a statue till the danger was past, when he yielded to a fit of trembling and sank down into the wet moss.

He pulled himself together and went on, afraid now in a new way. It was not the fear that he should die passively from lack of food, but that he should be destroyed violently before starvation had exhausted the last particle of the endeavor in him that made toward surviving. There were the wolves. Back and forth across the desolation drifted their howls, weaving the very air into a fabric of menace that was so tangible that he found himself, arms in the air, pressing it back from him as it might be the walls of a wind-blown tent.

Now and again the wolves, in packs of two and three, crossed his path. But they sheered clear of him. They were not in sufficient numbers, and besides they were hunting the caribou, which did not battle, while this strange creature that walked erect might scratch and bite.

In the late afternoon he came upon scattered bones where the wolves had made a kill. The débris had been a caribou calf an hour before, squawking and running and very much alive. He contemplated the bones, clean-picked and polished, pink with the cell-life in them which had not yet died. Could it possibly be that he might be that ere the day was done! Such was life, eh? A vain and fleeting thing. It was only life that pained. There was no hurt in death. To die was to sleep. It meant cessation, rest. Then why was he not content to die?

But he did not moralize long. He was squatting in the moss, a bone in his mouth, sucking at the shreds of life that still dyed it faintly pink. The sweet meaty taste, thin and elusive almost as a memory, maddened him. He closed his jaws on the bones and crunched. Sometimes it was the bone that broke, sometimes his teeth. Then he crushed the bones between rocks, pounded them to a pulp, and swallowed them. He pounded his fingers, too, in his haste, and yet found a moment in which to feel surprise at the fact that his fingers did not hurt much when caught under the descending rock.

Came frightful days of snow and rain. He did not know when he made camp, when he broke camp. He travelled in the night as much as in the day. He rested wherever he fell, crawled on whenever the dying life in him flickered up and burned less dimly. He, as a man, no longer strove. It was the life in him, unwilling to die, that drove him on. He did not suffer. His nerves had become blunted, numb, while his mind was filled with weird visions and delicious dreams.

But ever he sucked and chewed on the crushed bones of the caribou calf, the least remnants of which he had gathered up and carried with him. He crossed no more hills or divides, but automatically followed a large stream which flowed through a wide and shallow valley. He did not see this stream nor this valley. He saw nothing save visions. Soul and body walked or crawled side by side, yet apart, so slender was the thread that bound them.

He awoke in his right mind, lying on his back on a rocky ledge. The sun was shining bright and warm. Afar off he heard the squawking of caribou calves. He was aware of vague memories of rain and wind and snow, but whether he had been beaten by the storm for two days or two weeks he did not know.

For some time he lay without movement, the genial

sunshine pouring upon him and saturating his miserable body with its warmth. A fine day, he thought. Perhaps he could manage to locate himself. By a painful effort he rolled over on his side. Below him flowed a wide and sluggish river. Its unfamiliarity puzzled him. Slowly he followed it with his eyes, winding in wide sweeps among the bleak, bare hills, bleaker and barer and lower-lying than any hills he had yet encountered. Slowly, deliberately, without excitement or more than the most casual interest, he followed the course of the strange stream toward the sky-line and saw it emptying into a bright and shining sea. He was still unexcited. Most unusual, he thought, a vision or a mirage—more likely a vision, a trick of his disordered mind. He was confirmed in this by sight of a ship lying at anchor in the midst of the shining sea. He closed his eyes for a while, then opened them. Strange how the vision persisted! Yet not strange. He knew there were no seas or ships in the heart of the barren lands, just as he had known there was no cartridge in the empty rifle.

He heard a snuffle behind him—a half-choking gasp or cough. Very slowly, because of his exceeding weakness and stiffness, he rolled over on his other side. He could see nothing near at hand, but he waited patiently. Again came the snuffle and cough, and outlined between two jagged rocks not a score of feet away he made out the gray head of a wolf. The sharp ears were not pricked so sharply as he had seen them on other wolves; the eyes were bleared and bloodshot, the head seemed to droop limply and forlornly. The animal blinked continually in the sunshine. It seemed sick. As he looked it snuffled and coughed again.

This, at least, was real, he thought, and turned on the other side so that he might see the reality of the world which had been veiled from him before by the vision. But the sea still shone in the distance and the ship was plainly discernible. Was it reality, after all? He closed his eyes for a long while and thought, and then it came to him. He had been making north by east, away from the Dease Divide and into the Coppermine Valley. This wide and sluggish river was the Coppermine. That shining sea was the Arctic Ocean. That ship was a whaler, strayed east, far east, from the mouth of the Mackenzie, and it was lying at anchor in Coronation Gulf. He remembered the Hudson Bay Company chart he had seen long ago, and it was all clear and reasonable to him.

He sat up and turned his attention to immediate affairs. He had worn through the blanket-wrappings, and his feet were shapeless lumps of raw meat. His last blanket was gone. Rifle and knife were both missing. He had lost his hat somewhere, with the bunch of matches in the band, but the matches against his chest were safe and dry inside the tobacco pouch and oil paper. He looked at his watch. It marked eleven o'clock and was still running. Evidently he had kept it wound.

He was calm and collected. Though extremely weak, he had no sensation of pain. He was not hungry. The thought of food was not even pleasant to him, and whatever he did was done by his reason alone. He ripped off his pants' legs to the knees and bound them about his feet. Somehow he had succeeded in retaining the tin bucket. He would have some hot water before he began what he foresaw was to be a terrible journey to the ship.

His movements were slow. He shook as with a palsy. When he started to collect dry moss, he found he could not rise to his feet. He tried again and again, then contented himself with crawling about on hands and knees. Once he crawled near to the sick wolf. The animal dragged itself reluctantly out of his way, licking its chops with a tongue which seemed hardly to have the strength to curl. The man noticed that the tongue was

not the customary healthy red. It was a yellowish
brown and seemed coated with a rough and half-dry
mucus.

After he had drunk a quart of hot water the man
found he was able to stand, and even to walk as well as
a dying man might be supposed to walk. Every minute
or so he was compelled to rest. His steps were feeble
and uncertain, just as the wolf's that trailed him were
feeble and uncertain; and that night, when the shining
sea was blotted out by blackness, he knew he was
nearer to it by no more than four miles.

Throughout the night he heard the cough of the
sick wolf, and now and then the squawking of the caribou calves. There was life all around him, but it was
strong life, very much alive and well, and he knew the
sick wolf clung to the sick man's trail in the hope that
the man would die first. In the morning, on opening his
eyes, he beheld it regarding him with a wistful and
hungry stare. It stood crouched, with tail between its
legs, like a miserable and woe-begone dog. It shivered
in the chill morning wind, and grinned dispiritedly
when the man spoke to it in a voice that achieved no
more than a hoarse whisper.

The sun rose brightly, and all morning the man tottered and fell toward the ship on the shining sea. The
weather was perfect. It was the brief Indian Summer of
the high latitudes. It might last a week. To-morrow or
next day it might be gone.

In the afternoon the man came upon a trail. It was of
another man, who did not walk, but who dragged himself on all fours. The man thought it might be Bill, but
he thought in a dull, uninterested way. He had no curiosity. In fact, sensation and emotion had left him. He
was no longer susceptible to pain. Stomach and nerves
had gone to sleep. Yet the life that was in him drove
him on. He was very weary, but it refused to die. It was
because it refused to die that he still ate muskeg berries

and minnows, drank his hot water, and kept a wary eye on the sick wolf.

He followed the trail of the other man who dragged himself along, and soon came to the end of it—a few fresh-picked bones where the soggy moss was marked by the foot-pads of many wolves. He saw a squat moose-hide sack, mate to his own, which had been torn by sharp teeth. He picked it up, though its weight was almost too much for his feeble fingers. Bill had carried it to the last. Ha! ha! He would have the laugh on Bill. He would survive and carry it to the ship in the shining sea. His mirth was hoarse and ghastly, like a raven's croak, and the sick wolf joined him, howling lugubriously. The man ceased suddenly. How could he have the laugh on Bill if that were Bill; if those bones, so pinky-white and clean, were Bill?

He turned away. Well, Bill had deserted him; but he would not take the gold, nor would he suck Bill's bones. Bill would have, though, had it been the other way around, he mused as he staggered on.

He came to a pool of water. Stooping over in quest of minnows, he jerked his head back as though he had been stung. He had caught sight of his reflected face. So horrible was it that sensibility awoke long enough to be shocked. There were three minnows in the pool, which was too large to drain; and after several ineffectual attempts to catch them in the tin bucket he forbore. He was afraid, because of his great weakness, that he might fall in and drown. It was for this reason that he did not trust himself to the river astride one of the many drift-logs which lined its sand-spits.

That day he decreased the distance between him and the ship by three miles; the next day by two—for he was crawling now as Bill had crawled; and the end of the fifth day found the ship still seven miles away and him unable to make even a mile a day. Still the Indian Summer held on, and he continued to crawl and faint, turn and turn about; and ever the sick wolf coughed and wheezed at his heels. His knees had become raw meat like his feet, and though he padded them with the shirt from his back it was a red track he left behind him on the moss and stones. Once, glancing back, he saw the wolf licking hungrily his bleeding trail, and he saw sharply what his own end might be—unless—unless he could get the wolf. Then began as grim a tragedy of existence as was ever played—a sick man that crawled, a sick wolf that limped, two creatures dragging their dying carcasses across the desolation and hunting each other's lives.

Had it been a well wolf, it would not have mattered so much to the man; but the thought of going to feed the maw of that loathsome and all but dead thing was repugnant to him. He was finicky. His mind had begun to wander again, and to be perplexed by hallucinations, while his lucid intervals grew rarer and shorter.

He was awakened once from a faint by a wheeze close in his ear. The wolf leaped lamely back, losing its footing and falling in its weakness. It was ludicrous, but he was not amused. Nor was he even afraid. He was too far gone for that. But his mind was for the moment clear, and he lay and considered. The ship was no more than four miles away. He could see it quite distinctly when he rubbed the mists out of his eyes, and he could see the white sail of a small boat cutting the water of the shining sea. But he could never crawl those four miles. He knew that, and was very calm in the knowledge. He knew that he could not crawl half a mile. And yet he wanted to live. It was unreasonable that he should die after all he had undergone. Fate asked too much of him. And, dying, he declined to die. It was stark madness, perhaps, but in the very grip of Death he defied Death and refused to die.

He closed his eyes and composed himself with infinite precaution. He steeled himself to keep above the suffocating languor that lapped like a rising tide through all the wells of his being. It was very like a sea, this deadly languor, that rose and rose and drowned his consciousness bit by bit. Sometimes he was all but submerged, swimming through oblivion with a faltering stroke; and again, by some strange alchemy of soul, he would find another shred of will and strike out more strongly.

Without movement he lay on his back, and he could hear, slowly drawing near and nearer, the wheezing intake and output of the sick wolf's breath. It drew closer, ever closer, through an infinitude of time, and he did not move. It was at his ear. The harsh dry tongue grated like sandpaper against his cheek. His hands shot out—or at least he willed them to shoot out. The fingers were curved like talons, but they closed on empty air. Swiftness and certitude require strength, and the man had not this strength.

The patience of the wolf was terrible. The man's patience was no less terrible. For half a day he lay motionless, fighting off unconsciousness and waiting for the thing that was to feed upon him and upon which he wished to feed. Sometimes the languid sea rose over him and he dreamed long dreams; but ever through it all, waking and dreaming, he waited for the wheezing breath and the harsh caress of the tongue.

He did not hear the breath, and he slipped slowly from some dream to the feel of the tongue along his hand. He waited. The fangs pressed softly; the pressure increased; the wolf was exerting its last strength in an effort to sink teeth in the food for which it had waited so long. But the man had waited long, and the lacerated hand closed on the jaw. Slowly, while the wolf struggled feebly and the hand clutched feebly, the other hand crept across to a grip. Five minutes later the whole weight of the man's body was on top of the wolf. The hands had not sufficient strength to choke the wolf, but the face of the man was pressed close to the throat of the wolf and the mouth of the man was full of hair. At the end of half an hour the man was aware of a warm trickle in his throat. It was not pleasant. It was like molten lead being forced into his stomach, and it was forced by his will alone. Later the man rolled over on his back and slept.

There were some members of a scientific expedition on the whale-ship *Bedford*. From the deck they remarked a strange object on the shore. It was moving down the beach toward the water. They were unable to classify it, and, being scientific men, they climbed into the whale-boat alongside and went ashore to see. And they saw something that was alive but which could hardly be called a man. It was blind, unconscious. It squirmed along the ground like some monstrous worm. Most of its efforts were ineffectual, but it was persistent, and it writhed and twisted and went ahead perhaps a score of feet an hour.

Three weeks afterward the man lay in a bunk on the whale-ship *Bedford*, and with tears streaming down his wasted cheeks told who he was and what he had undergone. He also babbled incoherently of his mother, of sunny Southern California, and a home among the orange groves and flowers.

The days were not many after that when he sat at table with the scientific men and ship's officers. He gloated over the spectacle of so much food, watching it anxiously as it went into the mouths of others. With the disappearance of each mouthful an expression of deep regret came into his eyes. He was quite sane, yet he hated those men at mealtime. He was haunted by a fear that the food would not last. He inquired of the cook, the cabin boy, the captain, concerning the food stores. They reassured him countless times; but he could not believe them, and pried cunningly about the lazarette to see with his own eyes.

It was noticed that the man was getting fat. He grew stouter with each day. The scientific men shook their heads and theorized. They limited the man at his meals, but still his girth increased and he swelled prodigiously under his shirt.

The sailors grinned. They knew. And when the scientific men set a watch on the man, they knew too. They saw him slouch for'ard after breakfast, and, like a mendicant, with outstretched palm, accost a sailor. The sailor grinned and passed him a fragment of sea biscuit. He clutched it avariciously, looked at it as a miser looks at gold, and thrust it into his shirt bosom. Similar were the donations from other grinning sailors.

The scientific men were discreet. They let him alone. But they privily examined his bunk. It was lined with hardtack; the mattress was stuffed with hardtack; every nook and cranny was filled with hardtack. Yet he was sane. He was taking precautions against another possible famine—that was all. He would recover from it, the scientific men said; and he did, ere the *Bedford's* anchor rumbled down in San Francisco Bay.

WHITE FANG

Contents

PART FOUR
THE SUPERIOR GODS

PART FIVE
THE TAME

PART ONE: THE WILD

❧

CHAPTER I

The Trail of the Meat

Dark spruce forest frowned on either side the frozen waterway. The trees had been stripped by a recent wind of their white covering of frost, and they seemed to lean toward each other, black and ominous, in the fading light. A vast silence reigned over the land. The land itself was a desolation, lifeless, without movement, so lone and cold that the spirit of it was not even that of sadness. There was a hint in it of laughter, but of a laughter more terrible than any sadness—a laughter that was mirthless as the smile of the Sphinx, a laughter cold as the frost and partaking of the grimness of infallibility. It was the masterful and incommunicable wisdom of eternity laughing at the futility of life and the effort of life. It was the Wild, the savage, frozen-hearted Northland Wild.

But there *was* life, abroad in the land and defiant. Down the frozen waterway toiled a string of wolfish dogs. Their bristly fur was rimed with frost. Their breath froze in the air as it left their mouths, spouting forth in spumes of vapor that settled upon the hair of their bodies and formed into crystals of frost. Leather harness was on the dogs, and leather traces attached them to a sled which dragged along behind. The sled was without runners. It was made of stout birch-bark, and its full surface rested on the snow. The front end

169

of the sled was turned up, like a scroll, in order to force
down and under the bore of soft snow that surged like
a wave before it. On the sled, securely lashed, was a
long and narrow oblong box. There were other things
on the sled—blankets, an axe, and a coffee-pot and
frying-pan; but prominent, occupying most of the
space, was the long and narrow oblong box.

In advance of the dogs, on wide snowshoes, toiled a
man. At the rear of the sled toiled a second man. On
the sled, in the box, lay a third man whose toil was
over,—a man whom the Wild had conquered and
beaten down until he would never move nor struggle
again. It is not the way of the Wild to like movement.
Life is an offence to it, for life is movement; and the
Wild aims always to destroy movement. It freezes the
water to prevent it running to the sea; it drives the sap
out of the trees till they are frozen to their mighty
hearts; and most ferociously and terribly of all does the
Wild harry and crush into submission man—man, who
is the most restless of life, ever in revolt against the
dictum that all movement must in the end come to the
cessation of movement.

But at front and rear, unawed and indomitable,
toiled the two men who were not yet dead. Their
bodies were covered with fur and soft-tanned leather.
Eyelashes and cheeks and lips were so coated with the
crystals from their frozen breath that their faces were
not discernible. This gave them the seeming of ghostly
masques, undertakers in a spectral world at the funeral
of some ghost. But under it all they were men, pene-
trating the land of desolation and mockery and silence,
puny adventurers bent on colossal adventure, pitting
themselves against the might of a world as remote and
alien and pulseless as the abysses of space.

They travelled on without speech, saving their
breath for the work of their bodies. On every side was
the silence, pressing upon them with a tangible pres-

ence. It affected their minds as the many atmospheres of deep water affect the body of the diver. It crushed them with the weight of unending vastness and unalterable decree. It crushed them into the remotest recesses of their own minds, pressing out of them, like juices from the grape, all the false ardors and exaltations and undue self-values of the human soul, until they perceived themselves finite and small, specks and motes, moving with weak cunning and little wisdom amidst the play and interplay of the great blind elements and forces.

An hour went by, and a second hour. The pale light of the short sunless day was beginning to fade, when a faint far cry arose on the still air. It soared upward with a swift rush, till it reached its topmost note, where it persisted, palpitant and tense, and then slowly died away. It might have been a lost soul wailing, had it not been invested with a certain sad fierceness and hungry eagerness. The front man turned his head until his eyes met the eyes of the man behind. And then, across the narrow oblong box, each nodded to the other.

A second cry arose, piercing the silence with needle-like shrillness. Both men located the sound. It was to the rear, somewhere in the snow expanse they had just traversed. A third and answering cry arose, also to the rear and to the left of the second cry.

"They're after us, Bill," said the man at the front.

His voice sounded hoarse and unreal, and he had spoken with apparent effort.

"Meat is scarce," answered his comrade. "I ain't seen a rabbit sign for days."

Thereafter they spoke no more, though their ears were keen for the hunting-cries that continued to rise behind them.

At the fall of darkness they swung the dogs into a cluster of spruce trees on the edge of the waterway and made a camp. The coffin, at the side of the fire, served for seat and table. The wolf-dogs, clustered on the far side of the fire, snarled and bickered among themselves, but evinced no inclination to stray off into the darkness.

"Seems to me, Henry, they're stayin' remarkable close to camp," Bill commented.

Henry, squatting over the fire and settling the pot of coffee with a piece of ice, nodded. Nor did he speak till he had taken his seat on the coffin and begun to eat.

"They know where their hides is safe," he said. "They'd sooner eat grub than be grub. They're pretty wise, them dogs."

Bill shook his head. "Oh, I don't know."

His comrade looked at him curiously. "First time I ever heard you say anythin' about their not bein' wise."

"Henry," said the other, munching with deliberation the beans he was eating, "did you happen to notice the way them dogs kicked up when I was a-feedin' 'em?"

"They did cut up more'n usual," Henry acknowledged.

"How many dogs 've we got, Henry?"

"Six."

"Well, Henry . . ." Bill stopped for a moment, in order that his words might gain greater significance. "As I was sayin', Henry, we've got six dogs. I took six fish out of the bag. I gave one fish to each dog, an', Henry, I was one fish short."

"You counted wrong."

"We've got six dogs," the other reiterated dispassionately. "I took out six fish. One Ear didn't get no fish. I come back to the bag afterward an' got 'm his fish."

"We've only got six dogs," Henry said.

"Henry," Bill went on, "I won't say they was all dogs, but there was seven of 'm that got fish."

Henry stopped eating to glance across the fire and count the dogs.

"There's only six now," he said.

"I saw the other one run off across the snow," Bill announced with cool positiveness. "I saw seven."

His comrade looked at him commiseratingly, and said, "I'll be almighty glad when this trip's over."

"What d'ye mean by that?" Bill demanded.

"I mean that this load of ourn is gettin' on your nerves, an' that you're beginnin' to see things."

"I thought of that," Bill answered gravely. "An' so, when I saw it run off across the snow, I looked in the snow an' saw its tracks. Then I counted the dogs an' there was still six of 'em. The tracks is there in the snow now. D'ye want to look at 'em? I'll show 'm to you."

Henry did not reply, but munched on in silence, until, the meal finished, he topped it with a final cup of coffee. He wiped his mouth with the back of his hand and said:

"Then you're thinkin' as it was—"

A long wailing cry, fiercely sad, from somewhere in the darkness, had interrupted him. He stopped to listen to it; then he finished his sentence with a wave of his hand toward the sound of the cry, "—one of them?"

Bill nodded. "I'd a blame sight sooner think that than anything else. You noticed yourself the row the dogs made."

Cry after cry, and answering cries, were turning the silence into a bedlam. From every side the cries arose, and the dogs betrayed their fear by huddling together and so close to the fire that their hair was scorched by the heat. Bill threw on more wood, before lighting his pipe.

"I'm thinkin' you're down in the mouth some," Henry said.

"Henry . . ." He sucked meditatively at his pipe for

some time before he went on. "Henry, I was a-thinkin' what a blame sight luckier he is than you an' me'll ever be."

He indicated the third person by a downward thrust of the thumb to the box on which they sat.

"You an' me, Henry, when we die, we'll be lucky if we get enough stones over our carcases to keep the dogs off of us."

"But we ain't got people an' money an' all the rest, like him," Henry rejoined. "Long-distance funerals is somethin' you an' me can't exactly afford."

"What gets me, Henry, is what a chap like this, that's a lord or something in his own country, and that's never had to bother about grub nor blankets, why he comes a-buttin' round the God-forsaken ends of the earth—that's what I can't exactly see."

"He might have lived to a ripe old age if he'd stayed to home," Henry agreed.

Bill opened his mouth to speak, but changed his mind. Instead, he pointed toward the wall of darkness that pressed about them from every side. There was no suggestion of form in the utter blackness; only could be seen a pair of eyes gleaming like live coals. Henry indicated with his head a second pair, and a third. A circle of the gleaming eyes had drawn about their camp. Now and again a pair of eyes moved, or disappeared to appear again a moment later.

The unrest of the dogs had been increasing, and they stampeded, in a surge of sudden fear, to the near side of the fire, cringing and crawling about the legs of the men. In the scramble one of the dogs had been overturned on the edge of the fire, and it had yelped with pain and fright as the smell of its singed coat possessed the air. The commotion caused the circle of eyes to shift restlessly for a moment and even to withdraw a bit, but it settled down again as the dogs became quiet.

"Henry, it's a blame misfortune to be out of ammunition."

Bill had finished his pipe and was helping his companion spread the bed of fur and blanket upon the spruce boughs which he had laid over the snow before supper. Henry grunted, and began unlacing his moccasins.

"How many cartridges did you say you had left?" he asked.

"Three," came the answer. "An' I wisht 'twas three hundred. Then I'd show 'em what for, damn 'em!"

He shook his fist angrily at the gleaming eyes, and began securely to prop his moccasins before the fire.

"An' I wisht this cold snap'd break," he went on. "It's ben fifty below for two weeks now. An' I wisht I'd never started on this trip, Henry. I don't like the looks of it. It don't feel right, somehow. An' while I'm wishin', I wisht the trip was over an' done with, an' you an' me a-sittin' by the fire in Fort McGurry just about now an' playin' cribbage—that's what I wisht."

Henry grunted and crawled into bed. As he dozed off he was aroused by his comrade's voice.

"Say, Henry, that other one that come in an' got a fish—why didn't the dogs pitch into it? That's what's botherin' me."

"You're botherin' too much, Bill," came the sleepy reponse. "You was never like this before. You jes' shut up now, an' go to sleep, an' you'll be all hunkydory in the mornin'. Your stomach's sour, that's what's botherin' you."

The men slept, breathing heavily, side by side, under the one covering. The fire died down, and the gleaming eyes drew closer the circle they had flung about the camp. The dogs clustered together in fear, now and again snarling menacingly as a pair of eyes drew close. Once their uproar became so loud that Bill woke up. He got out of bed carefully, so as not to disturb the sleep of his comrade, and threw more wood on the fire. As it began to flame up, the circle of eyes drew farther back. He glanced casually at the huddling dogs.

He rubbed his eyes and looked at them more sharply. Then he crawled back into the blankets.

"Henry," he said. "Oh, Henry."

Henry groaned as he passed from sleep to waking, and demanded, "What's wrong now?"

"Nothin'," came the answer; "only there's seven of 'em again. I just counted."

Henry acknowledged receipt of the information with a grunt that slid into a snore as he drifted back into sleep.

In the morning it was Henry who awoke first and routed his companion out of bed. Daylight was yet three hours away, though it was already six o'clock; and in the darkness Henry went about preparing breakfast, while Bill rolled the blankets and made the sled ready for lashing.

"Say, Henry," he asked suddenly, "how many dogs did you say we had?"

"Six."

"Wrong," Bill proclaimed triumphantly.

"Seven again?" Henry queried.

"No, five; one's gone."

"The hell!" Henry cried in wrath, leaving the cooking to come and count the dogs.

"You're right, Bill," he concluded. "Fatty's gone."

"An' he went like greased lightnin' once he got started. Couldn't 've seen 'm for smoke."

"No chance at all," Henry concluded. "They jes' swallowed 'm alive. I bet he was yelpin' as he went down their throats, damn 'em!"

"He always was a fool dog," said Bill.

"But no fool dog ought to be fool enough to go off an' commit suicide that way." He looked over the remainder of the team with a speculative eye that summed up instantly the salient traits of each animal. "I bet none of the others would do it."

"Couldn't drive 'em away from the fire with a club,"

Bill agreed. "I always did think there was somethin' wrong with Fatty, anyway."

And this was the epitaph of a dead dog on the Northland trail—less scant than the epitaph of many another dog, of many a man.

CHAPTER II

The She-Wolf

B reakfast eaten and the slim camp-outfit lashed to the sled, the men turned their backs on the cheery fire and launched out into the darkness. At once began to rise the cries that were fiercely sad—cries that called through the darkness and cold to one another and answered back. Conversation ceased. Daylight came at nine o'clock. At midday the sky to the south warmed to rose-color, and marked where the bulge of the earth intervened between the meridian sun and the northern world. But the rose-color swiftly faded. The gray light of day that remained lasted until three o'clock, when it, too, faded, and the pall of the Arctic night descended upon the lone and silent land.

As darkness came on, the hunting-cries to right and left and rear drew closer—so close that more than once they sent surges of fear through the toiling dogs, throwing them into short-lived panics.

At the conclusion of one such panic, when he and Henry had got the dogs back in the traces, Bill said:

"I wisht they'd strike game somewheres, an' go away an' leave us alone."

"They do get on the nerves horrible," Henry sympathized.

They spoke no more until camp was made.

Henry was bending over and adding ice to the bubbling pot of beans when he was startled by the sound of a blow, an exclamation from Bill, and a sharp snarling cry of pain among the dogs. He straightened up in time to see a dim form disappearing across the snow into the shelter of the dark. Then he saw Bill, standing amid the dogs, half triumphant, half crest-fallen, in one hand a stout club, in the other the tail and part of the body of a sun-cured salmon.

"It got half of it," he announced; "but I got a whack at it jes' the same. D'ye hear it squeal?"

"What'd it look like?" Henry asked.

"Couldn't see. But it had four legs an' a mouth an' hair an' looked like any dog."

"Must be a tame wolf, I reckon."

"It's damned tame, whatever it is, comin' in here at feedin' time an' gettin' its whack of fish."

That night, when supper was finished and they sat on the oblong box and pulled at their pipes, the circle of gleaming eyes drew in even closer than before.

"I wisht they'd spring up a bunch of moose or somethin', an' go away an' leave us alone," Bill said.

Henry grunted with an intonation that was not all sympathy, and for a quarter of an hour they sat on in silence, Henry staring at the fire, and Bill at the circle of eyes that burned in the darkness just beyond the firelight.

"I wisht we was pullin' into McGurry right now," he began again.

"Shut up your wishin' an' your croakin'," Henry burst out angrily. "Your stomach's sour. That's what's ailin' you. Swallow a spoonful of sody, an' you'll sweeten up wonderful an' be more pleasant company."

In the morning, Henry was aroused by fervid blasphemy that proceeded from the mouth of Bill. Henry propped himself up on an elbow and looked to see his comrade standing among the dogs beside the replenished fire, his arms raised in objurgation, his face distorted with passion.

"Hello!" Henry called. "What's up now?"

"Frog's gone," came the answer.

"No."

"I tell you yes."

Henry leaped out of the blankets and to the dogs. He counted them with care, and then joined his partner in cursing the powers of the Wild that had robbed them of another dog.

"Frog was the strongest dog of the bunch," Bill pronounced finally.

"An' he was no fool dog neither," Henry added.

And so was recorded the second epitaph in two days.

A gloomy breakfast was eaten, and the four remaining dogs were harnessed to the sled. The day was a repetition of the days that had gone before. The men toiled without speech across the face of the frozen world. The silence was unbroken save by the cries of their pursuers, that, unseen, hung upon their rear. With the coming of night in the mid-afternoon, the cries sounded closer as the pursuers drew in according to their custom; and the dogs grew excited and frightened, and were guilty of panics that tangled the traces and further depressed the two men.

"There, that'll fix you fool critters," Bill said with satisfaction that night, standing erect at completion of his task.

Henry left his cooking to come and see. Not only had his partner tied the dogs up, but he had tied them, after the Indian fashion, with sticks. About the neck of each dog he had fastened a leather thong. To this, and so close to the neck that the dog could not get his teeth to it, he had tied a stout stick four or five feet in length. The other end of the stick, in turn, was made fast to a stake in the ground by means of a leather thong. The dog was unable to gnaw through the leather at his own end of the stick. The stick prevented him from getting at the leather that fastened the other end.

Henry nodded his head approvingly.

"It's the only contraption that'll ever hold One Ear," he said. "He can gnaw through leather as clean as a knife an' jes' about half as quick. They all 'll be here in the mornin' hunkydory."

"You jes' bet they will," Bill affirmed. "If one of 'em turns up missin', I'll go without my coffee."

"They jes' know we ain't loaded to kill," Henry remarked at bed-time, indicating the gleaming circle that hemmed them in. "If we could put a couple of shots into 'em, they'd be more respectful. They come closer every night. Get the firelight out of your eyes an' look hard—there! Did you see that one?"

For some time the two men amused themselves with watching the movement of vague forms on the edge of the firelight. By looking closely and steadily at where a pair of eyes burned in the darkness, the form of the animal would slowly take shape. They could even see these forms move at times.

A sound among the dogs attracted the men's attention. One Ear was uttering quick, eager whines, lunging at the length of his stick toward the darkness, and desisting now and again in order to make frantic attacks on the stick with his teeth.

"Look at that, Bill," Henry whispered.

Full into the firelight, with a stealthy, sidelong movement, glided a doglike animal. It moved with commingled mistrust and daring, cautiously observing the men, its attention fixed on the dogs. One Ear strained the full length of the stick toward the intruder and whined with eagerness.

"That fool One Ear don't seem scairt much," Bill said in a low tone.

"It's a she-wolf," Henry whispered back, "an' that accounts for Fatty an' Frog. She's the decoy for the pack. She draws out the dog an' then all the rest pitches in an' eats 'm up."

The fire crackled. A log fell apart with a loud spluttering noise. At the sound of it the strange animal leaped back into the darkness.

"Henry, I'm a-thinkin'," Bill announced.

"Thinkin' what?"

"I'm a-thinkin' that was the one I lambasted with the club."

"Ain't the slightest doubt in the world," was Henry's response.

"An' right here I want to remark," Bill went on, "that that animal's familyarity with campfires is suspicious an' immoral."

"It knows for certain more'n a self-respectin' wolf ought to know," Henry agreed. "A wolf that knows enough to come in with the dogs at feedin' time has had experiences."

"Ol' Villan had a dog once that run away with the wolves," Bill cogitated aloud. "I ought to know. I shot it out of the pack in a moose pasture over on Little Stick. An' Ol' Villan cried like a baby. Hadn't seen it for three years, he said. Ben with the wolves all that time."

"I reckon you've called the turn, Bill. That wolf's a dog, an' it's eaten fish many's the time from the hand of man."

"An' if I get a chance at it, that wolf that's a dog'll be jes' meat," Bill declared. "We can't afford to lose no more animals."

"But you've only got three cartridges," Henry objected.

"I'll wait for a dead sure shot," was the reply.

In the morning Henry renewed the fire and cooked breakfast to the accompaniment of his partner's snoring.

"You was sleepin' jes' too comfortable for anythin'," Henry told him, as he routed him out for breakfast. "I hadn't the heart to rouse you."

Bill began to eat sleepily. He noticed that his cup

was empty and started to reach for the pot. But the pot was beyond arm's length and beside Henry.

"Say, Henry," he chided gently, "ain't you forgot somethin'?"

Henry looked about with great carefulness and shook his head. Bill held up the empty cup.

"You don't get no coffee," Henry announced.

"Ain't run out?" Bill asked anxiously.

"Nope."

"Ain't thinkin' it'll hurt my digestion?"

"Nope."

A flush of angry blood pervaded Bill's face.

"Then it's jes' warm an' anxious I am to be hearin' you explain yourself," he said.

"Spanker's gone," Henry answered.

Without haste, with the air of one resigned to misfortune, Bill turned his head, and from where he sat counted the dogs.

"How'd it happen?" he asked apathetically.

Henry shrugged his shoulders. "Don't know. Unless One Ear gnawed 'm loose. He couldn't a-done it himself, that's sure."

"The darned cuss." Bill spoke gravely and slowly, with no hint of the anger that was raging within. "Jes' because he couldn't chew himself loose, he chews Spanker loose."

"Well, Spanker's troubles is over, anyway; I guess he's digested by this time an' cavortin' over the landscape in the bellies of twenty different wolves," was Henry's epitaph on this, the latest lost dog. "Have some coffee, Bill."

But Bill shook his head.

"Go on," Henry pleaded, elevating the pot.

Bill shoved his cup aside. "I'll be ding-dong-danged if I do. I said I wouldn't if ary dog turned up missin', an' I won't."

"It's darn good coffee," Henry said enticingly.

But Bill was stubborn, and he ate a dry breakfast, washed down with mumbled curses at One Ear for the trick he had played.

"I'll tie 'em up out of reach of each other to-night," Bill said, as they took the trail.

They had travelled little more than a hundred yards, when Henry, who was in front, bent down and picked up something with which his snowshoe had collided. It was dark, and he could not see it, but he recognized it by the touch. He flung it back, so that it struck the sled and bounced along until it fetched up on Bill's snowshoes.

"Mebbe you'll need that in your business," Henry said.

Bill uttered an exclamation. It was all that was left of Spanker—the stick with which he had been tied.

"They ate 'm hide an' all," Bill announced. "The stick's as clean as a whistle. They've ate the leather offen both ends. They're damn hungry, Henry, an' they'll have you an' me guessin' before this trip's over."

Henry laughed defiantly. "I ain't been trailed this way by wolves before, but I've gone through a whole lot worse an' kept my health. Takes more'n a handful of them pesky critters to do for yours truly, Bill, my son."

"I don't know, I don't know," Bill muttered ominously.

"Well, you'll know all right when we pull into McGurry."

"I ain't feelin' special enthusiastic," Bill persisted.

"You're off color, that's what's the matter with you," Henry dogmatized. "What you need is quinine, an' I'm goin' to dose you up stiff as soon as we make McGurry."

Bill grunted his disagreement with the diagnosis, and lapsed into silence. The day was like all the days. Light came at nine o'clock. At twelve o'clock the southern horizon was warmed by the unseen sun; and then began the cold gray of afternoon that would merge, three hours later, into night.

It was just after the sun's futile effort to appear, that Bill slipped the rifle from under the sled-lashings and said:

"You keep right on, Henry, I'm goin' to see what I can see."

"You'd better stick by the sled," his partner protested. "You've only got three cartridges, an' there's no tellin' what might happen."

"Who's croakin' now?" Bill demanded triumphantly.

Henry made no reply, and plodded on alone, though often he cast anxious glances back into the gray solitude where his partner had disappeared. An hour later, taking advantage of the cut-offs around which the sled had to go, Bill arrived.

"They're scattered an' rangin' along wide," he said, "keepin' up with us an' lookin' for game at the same time. You see, they're sure of us, only they know they've got to wait to get us. In the meantime they're willin' to pick up anythin' eatable that comes handy."

"You mean they *think* they're sure of us," Henry objected pointedly.

But Bill ignored him. "I seen some of them. They're pretty thin. They ain't had a bite in weeks, I reckon, outside of Fatty an' Frog an' Spanker; an' there's so many of 'em that that didn't go far. They're remarkable thin. Their ribs is like washboards, an' their stomachs is right up against their backbones. They're pretty desperate, I can tell you. They'll be goin' mad, yet, an' then watch out."

A few minutes later, Henry, who was now travelling behind the sled, emitted a low, warning whistle. Bill turned and looked, then quietly stopped the dogs. To the rear, from around the last bend and plainly into view, on the very trail they had just covered, trotted a furry, slinking form. Its nose was to the trail, and it trotted with a peculiar, sliding, effortless gait. When they halted, it halted, throwing up its head and regarding them steadily with nostrils that twitched as it caught and studied the scent of them.

"It's the she-wolf," Bill whispered.

The dogs had lain down in the snow, and he walked past them to join his partner at the sled. Together they watched the strange animal that had pursued them for days and that had already accomplished the destruction of half their dog-team.

After a searching scrutiny, the animal trotted forward a few steps. This it repeated several times, till it was a short hundred yards away. It paused, head up, close by a clump of spruce trees, and with sight and scent studied the outfit of the watching men. It looked at them in a strangely wistful way, after the manner of a dog; but in its wistfulness there was none of the dog affection. It was a wistfulness bred of hunger, as cruel as its own fangs, as merciless as the frost itself.

It was large for a wolf, its gaunt frame advertising the lines of an animal that was among the largest of its kind.

"Stands pretty close to two feet an' a half at the shoulders," Henry commented. "An' I'll bet it ain't far from five feet long."

"Kind of strange color for a wolf," was Bill's criticism. "I never seen a red wolf before. Looks almost cinnamon to me."

The animal was certainly not cinnamon-colored. Its coat was the true wolf-coat. The dominant color was gray, and yet there was to it a faint reddish hue—a hue that was baffling, that appeared and disappeared, that was more like an illusion of the vision, now gray, distinctly gray, and again giving hints and glints of a vague redness of color not classifiable in terms of ordinary experience.

"Looks for all the world like a big husky sled-dog," Bill said. "I wouldn't be s'prised to see it wag its tail.

"Hello, you husky!" he called. "Come here, you, whatever-your-name-is."

"Ain't a bit scairt of you," Henry laughed.

Bill waved his hand at it threateningly and shouted loudly; but the animal betrayed no fear. The only change in it that they could notice was an accession of alertness. It still regarded them with the merciless wistfulness of hunger. They were meat, and it was hungry; and it would like to go in and eat them if it dared.

"Look here, Henry," Bill said, unconsciously lowering his voice to a whisper because of what he meditated. "We've got three cartridges. But it's a dead shot. Couldn't miss it. It's got away with three of our dogs, an' we oughter put a stop to it. What d'ye say?"

Henry nodded his consent. Bill cautiously slipped the gun from under the sled-lashing. The gun was on the way to his shoulder, but it never got there. For in that instant the she-wolf leaped sidewise from the trail into the clump of spruce trees and disappeared.

The two men looked at each other. Henry whistled long and comprehendingly.

"I might have knowed it," Bill chided himself aloud, as he replaced the gun. "Of course a wolf that knows enough to come in with the dogs at feedin' time, 'd know all about shooting-irons. I tell you right now, Henry, that critter's the cause of all our trouble. We'd have six dogs at the present time, 'stead of three, if it wasn't for her. An' I tell you right now, Henry, I'm goin' to get her. She's too smart to be shot in the open. But I'm goin' to lay for her. I'll bushwhack her as sure as my name is Bill."

"You needn't stray off too far in doin' it," his partner admonished. "If that pack ever starts to jump you, them three cartridges 'd be wuth no more'n three whoops in hell. Them animals is damn hungry, an' once they start in, they'll sure get you, Bill."

They camped early that night. Three dogs could not drag the sled so fast nor for so long hours as could six, and they were showing unmistakable signs of playing out. And the men went early to bed, Bill first seeing to it that the dogs were tied out of gnawing-reach of one another.

But the wolves were growing bolder, and the men were aroused more than once from their sleep. So near did the wolves approach, that the dogs became frantic with terror, and it was necessary to replenish the fire from time to time in order to keep the adventurous marauders at safer distance.

"I've hearn sailors talk of sharks followin' a ship," Bill remarked, as he crawled back into the blankets after one such replenishing of the fire. "Well, them wolves is land sharks. They know their business better'n we do, an' they ain't a-holdin' our trail this way for their health. They're goin' to get us. They're sure goin' to get us, Henry."

"They've half got you a'ready, a-talkin' like that," Henry retorted sharply. "A man's half licked when he says he is. An' you're half eaten from the way you're goin' on about it."

"They've got away with better men than you an' me," Bill answered.

"Oh, shet up your croakin'. You make me all-fired tired."

Henry rolled over angrily on his side, but was surprised that Bill made no similar display of temper. This was not Bill's way, for he was easily angered by sharp words. Henry thought long over it before he went to sleep, and as his eyelids fluttered down and he dozed off, the thought in his mind was: "There's no mistakin' it, Bill's almighty blue. I'll have to cheer him up tomorrow."

CHAPTER III

The Hunger Cry

The day began auspiciously. They had lost no dogs during the night, and they swung out upon the trail and into the silence, the darkness, and the cold with spirits that were fairly light. Bill seemed to have forgotten his forebodings of the previous night, and even waxed facetious with the dogs when, at midday, they overturned the sled on a bad piece of trail.

It was an awkward mix-up. The sled was upside down and jammed between a tree-trunk and a huge rock, and they were forced to unharness the dogs in order to straighten out the tangle. The two men were bent over the sled and trying to right it, when Henry observed One Ear sidling away.

"Here, you, One Ear!" he cried, straightening up and turning around on the dog.

But One Ear broke into a run across the snow, his traces trailing behind him. And there, out in the snow of their back-track, was the she-wolf waiting for him. As he neared her, he became suddenly cautious. He slowed down to an alert and mincing walk and then stopped. He regarded her carefully and dubiously, yet desirefully. She seemed to smile at him, showing her teeth in an ingratiating rather than a menacing way. She moved toward him a few steps, playfully, and then halted. One Ear drew near to her, still alert and cautious, his tail and ears in the air, his head held high.

He tried to sniff noses with her, but she retreated playfully and coyly. Every advance on his part was accompanied by a corresponding retreat on her part. Step by step she was luring him away from the security of his human companionship. Once, as though a warning had in vague ways flitted through his intelligence, he turned his head and looked back at the overturned sled, at his team-mates, and at the two men who were calling to him.

But whatever idea was forming in his mind, was dissipated by the she-wolf, who advanced upon him, sniffed noses with him for a fleeting instant, and then resumed her coy retreat before his renewed advances.

In the meantime, Bill had bethought himself of the rifle. But it was jammed beneath the overturned sled, and by the time Henry had helped him to right the load, One Ear and the she-wolf were too close together and the distance too great to risk a shot.

Too late, One Ear learned his mistake. Before they saw the cause, the two men saw him turn and start to run back toward them. Then, approaching at right angles to the trail and cutting off his retreat, they saw a dozen wolves, lean and gray, bounding across the snow. On the instant, the she-wolf's coyness and playfulness disappeared. With a snarl she sprang upon One Ear. He thrust her off with his shoulder, and, his retreat cut off and still intent on regaining the sled, he altered his course in an attempt to circle around to it. More wolves were appearing every moment and joining in the chase. The she-wolf was one leap behind One Ear and holding her own.

"Where are you goin'?" Henry suddenly demanded, laying his hand on his partner's arm.

Bill shook it off. "I won't stand it," he said. "They ain't a-goin' to get any more of our dogs if I can help it."

Gun in hand, he plunged into the underbrush that lined the side of the trail. His intention was apparent enough. Taking the sled as the centre of the circle that One Ear was making, Bill planned to tap that circle at a point in advance of the pursuit. With his rifle, in the broad daylight, it might be possible for him to awe the wolves and save the dog.

"Say, Bill!" Henry called after him. "Be careful! Don't take no chances!"

Henry sat down on the sled and watched. There was nothing else for him to do. Bill had already gone from sight; but now and again, appearing and disappearing amongst the underbrush and the scattered clumps of spruce, could be seen One Ear. Henry judged his case to be hopeless. The dog was thoroughly alive to its danger, but it was running on the outer circle while the wolf-pack was running on the inner and shorter circle. It was vain to think of One Ear so outdistancing his pursuers as to be able to cut across their circle in advance of them and to regain the sled.

The different lines were rapidly approaching a point. Somewhere out there in the snow, screened from his sight by trees and thickets, Henry knew that the wolf-pack, One Ear, and Bill were coming together. All too quickly, far more quickly than he had expected, it happened. He heard a shot, then two shots in rapid succession, and he knew that Bill's ammunition was gone. Then he heard a great outcry of snarls and yelps. He recognized One Ear's yell of pain and terror, and he heard a wolf-cry that bespoke a stricken animal. And that was all. The snarls ceased. The yelping died away. Silence settled down again over the lonely land.

He sat for a long while upon the sled. There was no need for him to go and see what had happened. He knew it as though it had taken place before his eyes. Once, he roused with a start and hastily got the axe out from underneath the lashings. But for some time longer he sat and brooded, the two remaining dogs crouching and trembling at his feet.

At last he arose in a weary manner, as though all the resilience had gone out of his body, and proceeded to fasten the dogs to the sled. He passed a rope over his shoulder, a man-trace, and pulled with the dogs. He did not go far. At the first hint of darkness he hastened to make a camp, and he saw to it that he had a generous supply of firewood. He fed the dogs, cooked and ate his supper, and made his bed close to the fire.

But he was not destined to enjoy that bed. Before his eyes closed the wolves had drawn too near for safety. It no longer required an effort of the vision to see them. They were all about him and the fire, in a narrow circle, and he could see them plainly in the firelight, lying down, sitting up, crawling forward on their bellies, or slinking back and forth. They even slept. Here and there he could see one curled up in the snow like a dog, taking the sleep that was now denied himself.

He kept the fire brightly blazing, for he knew that it alone intervened between the flesh of his body and their hungry fangs. His two dogs stayed close by him, one on either side, leaning against him for protection, crying and whimpering, and at times snarling desperately when a wolf approached a little closer than usual. At such moments, when his dogs snarled, the whole circle would be agitated, the wolves coming to their feet and pressing tentatively forward, a chorus of snarls and eager yelps rising about him. Then the circle would lie down again, and here and there a wolf would resume its broken nap.

But this circle had a continuous tendency to draw in upon him. Bit by bit, an inch at a time, with here a wolf bellying forward, and there a wolf bellying forward, the circle would narrow until the brutes were almost within springing distance. Then he would seize brands from the fire and hurl them into the pack. A hasty drawing back always resulted, accompanied by angry yelps and frightened snarls when a well-aimed brand struck and scorched a too daring animal.

Morning found the man haggard and worn, wide-eyed from want of sleep. He cooked breakfast in the darkness, and at nine o'clock, when, with the coming of daylight, the wolf-pack drew back, he set about the task he had planned through the long hours of the night. Chopping down young saplings, he made them crossbars of a scaffold by lashing them high up to the trunks of standing trees. Using the sled-lashing for a heaving rope, and with the aid of the dogs, he hoisted the coffin to the top of the scaffold.

"They got Bill, an' they may get me, but they'll sure never get you, young man," he said, addressing the dead body in its tree-sepulchre.

Then he took the trail, the lightened sled bounding along behind the willing dogs; for they, too, knew that safety lay only in the gaining of Fort McGurry. The wolves were now more open in their pursuit, trotting sedately behind and ranging along on either side, their red tongues lolling out, their lean sides showing the undulating ribs with every movement. They were very lean, mere skin-bags stretched over bony frames, with strings for muscles—so lean that Henry found it in his mind to marvel that they still kept their feet and did not collapse forthright in the snow.

He did not dare travel until dark. At midday, not only did the sun warm the southern horizon, but it even thrust its upper rim, pale and golden, above the sky-line. He received it as a sign. The days were growing longer. The sun was returning. But scarcely had the cheer of its light departed, than he went into camp. There were still several hours of gray daylight and sombre twilight, and he utilized them in chopping an enormous supply of firewood.

With night came horror. Not only were the starving

wolves growing bolder, but lack of sleep was telling upon Henry. He dozed despite himself, crouching by the fire, the blankets about his shoulders, the axe between his knees, and on either side a dog pressing close against him. He awoke once and saw in front of him, not a dozen feet away, a big gray wolf, one of the largest of the pack. And even as he looked, the brute deliberately stretched himself after the manner of a lazy dog, yawning full in his face and looking upon him with a possessive eye, as if, in truth, he were merely a delayed meal that was soon to be eaten.

This certitude was shown by the whole pack. Fully a score he could count, staring hungrily at him or calmly sleeping in the snow. They reminded him of children gathered about a spread table and awaiting permission to begin to eat. And he was the food they were to eat! He wondered how and when the meal would begin.

As he piled wood on the fire he discovered an appreciation of his own body which he had never felt before. He watched his moving muscles and was interested in the cunning mechanism of his fingers. By the light of the fire he crooked his fingers slowly and repeatedly, now one at a time, now all together, spreading them wide or making quick gripping movements. He studied the nail-formation, and prodded the finger-tips, now sharply, and again softly, gauging the while the nerve-sensations produced. It fascinated him, and he grew suddenly fond of this subtle flesh of his that worked so beautifully and smoothly and delicately. Then he would cast a glance of fear at the wolf-circle drawn expectantly about him, and like a blow the realization would strike him that this wonderful body of his, this living flesh, was no more than so much meat, a quest of ravenous animals, to be torn and slashed by their hungry fangs, to be sustenance to them as the moose and the rabbit had often been sustenance to him.

He came out of a doze that was half nightmare, to

see the red-hued she-wolf before him. She was not more than half a dozen feet away, sitting in the snow and wistfully regarding him. The two dogs were whimpering and snarling at his feet, but she took no notice of them. She was looking at the man, and for some time he returned her look. There was nothing threatening about her. She looked at him merely with a great wistfulness, but he knew it to be the wistfulness of an equally great hunger. He was the food, and the sight of him excited in her the gustatory sensations. Her mouth opened, the saliva drooled forth, and she licked her chops with the pleasure of anticipation.

A spasm of fear went through him. He reached hastily for a brand to throw at her. But even as he reached, and before his fingers had closed on the missile, she sprang back into safety; and he knew that she was used to having things thrown at her. She had snarled as she sprang away, baring her white fangs to their roots, all her wistfulness vanishing, being replaced by a carnivorous malignity that made him shudder. He glanced at the hand that held the brand, noticing the cunning delicacy of the fingers that gripped it, how they adjusted themselves to all the inequalities of the surface, curling over and under and about the rough wood, and one little finger, too close to the burning portion of the brand, sensitively and automatically writhing . back from the hurtful heat to a cooler gripping-place; and in the same instant he seemed to see a vision of those same sensitive and delicate fingers being crushed and torn by the white teeth of the she-wolf. Never had he been so fond of this body of his as now when his tenure of it was so precarious.

All night, with burning brands, he fought off the hungry pack. When he dozed despite himself, the whimpering and snarling of the dogs aroused him. Morning came, but for the first time the light of day failed to scatter the wolves. The man waited in vain for them to go. They remained in a circle about him and his fire, displaying an arrogance of possession that shook his courage born of the morning light.

He made one desperate attempt to pull out on the trail. But the moment he left the protection of the fire, the boldest wolf leaped for him, but leaped short. He saved himself by springing back, the jaws snapping together a scant six inches from his thigh. The rest of the pack was now up and surging upon him, and a throwing of firebrands right and left was necessary to drive them back to a respectful distance.

Even in the daylight he did not dare leave the fire to chop fresh wood. Twenty feet away towered a huge dead spruce. He spent half the day extending his campfire to the tree, at any moment a half dozen burning fagots ready at hand to fling at his enemies. Once at the tree, he studied the surrounding forest in order to fell the tree in the direction of the most firewood.

The night was a repetition of the night before, save that the need for sleep was becoming overpowering. The snarling of his dogs was losing its efficacy. Besides, they were snarling all the time, and his benumbed and drowsy senses no longer took note of changing pitch and intensity. He awoke with a start. The she-wolf was less than a yard from him. Mechanically, at short range, without letting go of it, he thrust a brand full into her open and snarling mouth. She sprang away, yelling with pain, and while he took delight in the smell of burning flesh and hair, he watched her shaking her head and growling wrathfully a score of feet away.

But this time, before he dozed again, he tied a burning pine-knot to his right hand. His eyes were closed but a few minutes when the burn of the flame on his flesh awakened him. For several hours he adhered to this programme. Every time he was thus awakened he drove back the wolves with flying brands, replenished the fire, and rearranged the pine-knot on his hand. All worked well, but there came a time when he fastened the pine-knot insecurely. As his eyes closed it fell away from his hand.

He dreamed. It seemed to him that he was in Fort McGurry. It was warm and comfortable, and he was playing cribbage with the Factor. Also, it seemed to him that the fort was besieged by wolves. They were howling at the very gates, and sometimes he and the Factor paused from the game to listen and laugh at the futile efforts of the wolves to get in. And then, so strange was the dream, there was a crash. The door was burst open. He could see the wolves flooding into the big living-room of the fort. They were leaping straight for him and the Factor. With the bursting open of the door, the noise of their howling had increased tremendously. This howling now bothered him. His dream was merging into something else—he knew not what; but through it all, following him, persisted the howling.

And then he awoke to find the howling real. There was a great snarling and yelping. The wolves were rushing him. They were all about him and upon him. The teeth of one had closed upon his arm. Instinctively he leaped into the fire, and as he leaped, he felt the sharp slash of teeth that tore through the flesh of his leg. Then began a fire fight. His stout mittens temporarily protected his hands, and he scooped live coals into the air in all directions, until the camp-fire took on the semblance of a volcano.

But it could not last long. His face was blistering in the heat, his eyebrows and lashes were singed off, and the heat was becoming unbearable to his feet. With a flaming brand in each hand, he sprang to the edge of the fire. The wolves had been driven back. On every side, wherever the live coals had fallen, the snow was sizzling, and every little while a retiring wolf, with wild leap and snort and snarl, announced that one such live coal had been stepped upon.

Flinging his brands at the nearest of his enemies, the

man thrust his smouldering mittens into the snow and stamped about to cool his feet. His two dogs were missing, and he well knew that they had served as a course in the protracted meal which had begun days before with Fatty, the last course of which would likely be himself in the days to follow.

"You ain't got me yet!" he cried, savagely shaking his fist at the hungry beasts; and at the sound of his voice the whole circle was agitated, there was a general snarl, and the she-wolf slid up close to him across the snow and watched him with hungry wistfulness.

He set to work to carry out a new idea that had come to him. He extended the fire into a large circle. Inside this circle he crouched, his sleeping outfit under him as a protection against the melting snow. When he had thus disappeared within his shelter of flame, the whole pack came curiously to the rim of the fire to see what had become of him. Hitherto they had been denied access to the fire, and they now settled down in a close-drawn circle, like so many dogs, blinking and yawning and stretching their lean bodies in the unaccustomed warmth. Then the she-wolf sat down, pointed her nose at a star, and began to howl. One by one the wolves joined her, till the whole pack, on haunches, with noses pointed skyward, was howling its hunger cry.

Dawn came, and daylight. The fire was burning low. The fuel had run out, and there was need to get more. The man attempted to step out of his circle of flame, but the wolves surged to meet him. Burning brands made them spring aside, but they no longer sprang back. In vain he strove to drive them back. As he gave up and stumbled inside his circle, a wolf leaped for him, missed, and landed with all four feet in the coals. It cried out with terror, at the same time snarling, and scrambled back to cool its paws in the snow.

The man sat down on his blankets in a crouching

position. His body leaned forward from the hips. His shoulders, relaxed and drooping, and his head on his knees advertised that he had given up the struggle. Now and again he raised his head to note the dying down of the fire. The circle of flame and coals was breaking into segments with openings in between. These openings grew in size, the segments diminished.

"I guess you can come an' get me any time," he mumbled. "Anyway, I'm goin' to sleep."

Once he wakened, and in an opening in the circle, directly in front of him, he saw the she-wolf gazing at him.

Again he awakened, a little later, though it seemed hours to him. A mysterious change had taken place—so mysterious a change that he was shocked wider awake. Something had happened. He could not understand at first. Then he discovered it. The wolves were gone. Remained only the trampled snow to show how closely they had pressed him. Sleep was welling up and gripping him again, his head was sinking down upon his knees, when he roused with a sudden start.

There were cries of men, the churn of sleds, the creaking of harnesses, and the eager whimpering of straining dogs. Four sleds pulled in from the river bed to the camp among the trees. Half a dozen men were about the man who crouched in the centre of the dying fire. They were shaking and prodding him into consciousness. He looked at them like a drunken man and maundered in strange, sleepy speech:

"Red she-wolf. . . . Come in with the dogs at feedin' time. . . . First she ate the dog-food. . . . Then she ate the dogs. . . . An' after that she ate Bill. . . ."

"Where's Lord Alfred?" one of the men bellowed in his ear, shaking him roughly.

He shook his head slowly. "No, she didn't eat him. . . . He's roostin' in a tree at the last camp."

"Dead?" the man shouted.

"An' in a box," Henry answered. He jerked his shoulder petulantly away from the grip of his questioner. "Say, you lemme alone. . . . I'm jes' plumb tuckered out. . . . Goo' night, everybody."

His eyes fluttered and went shut. His chin fell forward on his chest. And even as they eased him down upon the blankets his snores were rising on the frosty air.

But there was another sound. Far and faint it was, in the remote distance, the cry of the hungry wolf-pack as it took the trail of other meat than the man it had just missed.

PART TWO: BORN OF THE WILD

❧❧

CHAPTER I

The Battle of the Fangs

It was the she-wolf who had first caught the sound of men's voices and the whining of the sled-dogs; and it was the she-wolf who was first to spring away from the cornered man in his circle of dying flame. The pack had been loath to forego the kill it had hunted down, and it lingered for several minutes, making sure of the sounds; and then it, too, sprang away on the trail made by the she-wolf.

Running at the forefront of the pack was a large gray wolf—one of its several leaders. It was he who directed the pack's course on the heels of the she-wolf. It was he who snarled warningly at the younger members of the pack or slashed at them with his fangs when they ambitiously tried to pass him. And it was he who increased the pace when he sighted the she-wolf, now trotting slowly across the snow.

She dropped in alongside by him, as though it were her appointed position, and took the pace of the pack. He did not snarl at her, nor show his teeth, when any leap of hers chanced to put her in advance of him. On the contrary, he seemed kindly disposed toward her—too kindly to suit her, for he was prone to run near to her, and when he ran too near it was she who snarled and showed her teeth. Nor was she above slashing his shoulder sharply on occasion. At such times he betrayed no anger. He merely sprang to the side and ran stiffly ahead for several awkward leaps, in carriage and conduct resembling an abashed country swain.

This was his one trouble in the running of the pack; but she had other troubles. On her other side ran a gaunt old wolf, grizzled and marked with the scars of many battles. He ran always on her right side. The fact that he had but one eye, and that the left eye, might account for this. He, also, was addicted to crowding her, to veering toward her till his scarred muzzle touched her body, or shoulder, or neck. As with the running mate on the left, she repelled these attentions with her teeth; but when both bestowed their attentions at the same time she was roughly jostled, being compelled, with quick snaps to either side, to drive both lovers away and at the same time to maintain her forward leap with the pack and see the way of her feet before her. At such times her running mates flashed their teeth and growled threateningly across at each other. They might have fought, but even wooing and its rivalry waited upon the more pressing hunger-need of the pack.

After each repulse, when the old wolf sheered abruptly away from the sharp-toothed object of his desire, he shouldered against a young three-year-old that ran on his blind right side. This young wolf had attained his full size; and, considering the weak and famished condition of the pack, he possessed more than the average vigor and spirit. Nevertheless, he ran with his head even with the shoulder of his one-eyed elder. When he ventured to run abreast of the older wolf, (which was seldom), a snarl and a snap sent him back even with the shoulder again. Sometimes, however, he dropped cautiously and slowly behind and edged in between the old leader and the she-wolf. This was doubly resented, even triply resented. When she snarled her displeasure, the old leader would whirl on the three-

year-old. Sometimes she whirled with him. And sometimes the young leader on the left whirled, too.

At such times, confronted by three sets of savage
teeth, the young wolf stopped precipitately, throwing
himself back on his haunches, with fore-legs stiff,
mouth menacing, and mane bristling. This confusion in
the front of the moving pack always caused confusion
in the rear. The wolves behind collided with the young
wolf and expressed their displeasure by administering
sharp nips on his hind-legs and flanks. He was laying
up trouble for himself, for lack of food and short tempers went together; but with the boundless faith of
youth he persisted in repeating the manœuvre every
little while, though it never succeeded in gaining anything for him but discomfiture.

Had there been food, love-making and fighting
would have gone on apace, and the pack-formation
would have been broken up. But the situation of the
pack was desperate. It was lean with long-standing
hunger. It ran below its ordinary speed. At the rear
limped the weak members, the very young and the
very old. At the front were the strongest. Yet all were
more like skeletons than full-bodied wolves. Nevertheless, with the exception of the ones that limped, the
movements of the animals were effortless and tireless.
Their stringy muscles seemed founts of inexhaustible
energy. Behind every steel-like contraction of a muscle, lay another steel-like contraction, and another, and
another, apparently without end.

They ran many miles that day. They ran through
the night. And the next day found them still running.
They were running over the surface of a world frozen
and dead. No life stirred. They alone moved through
the vast inertness. They alone were alive, and they
sought for other things that were alive in order that
they might devour them and continue to live.

They crossed low divides and ranged a dozen small

streams in a lower-lying country before their quest was rewarded. Then they came upon moose. It was a big bull they first found. Here was meat and life, and it was guarded by no mysterious fires nor flying missiles of flame. Splay hoofs and palmated antlers they knew, and they flung their customary patience and caution to the wind. It was a brief fight and fierce. The big bull was beset on every side. He ripped them open or split their skulls with shrewdly driven blows of his great hoofs. He crushed them and broke them on his large horns. He stamped them into the snow under him in the wallowing struggle. But he was foredoomed, and he went down with the she-wolf tearing savagely at his throat, and with other teeth fixed everywhere upon him, devouring him alive, before ever his last struggles ceased or his last damage had been wrought.

There was food in plenty. The bull weighed over eight hundred pounds—fully twenty pounds of meat per mouth for the forty-odd wolves of the pack. But if they could fast prodigiously, they could feed prodigiously, and soon a few scattered bones were all that remained of the splendid live brute that had faced the pack a few hours before.

There was now much resting and sleeping. With full stomachs, bickering and quarrelling began among the younger males, and this continued through the few days that followed before the breaking-up of the pack. The famine was over. The wolves were now in the country of game, and though they still hunted in pack, they hunted more cautiously, cutting out heavy cows or crippled old bulls from the small moose-herds they ran across.

There came a day, in this land of plenty, when the wolf-pack split in half and went in different directions. The she-wolf, the young leader on her left, and the one-eyed elder on her right, led their half of the pack down to the Mackenzie River and across into the lake country to the east. Each day this remnant of the pack dwindled. Two by two, male and female, the wolves were deserting. Occasionally a solitary male was driven out by the sharp teeth of his rivals. In the end there remained only four: the she-wolf, the young leader, the one-eyed one, and the ambitious three-year-old.

The she-wolf had by now developed a ferocious temper. Her three suitors all bore the marks of her teeth. Yet they never replied in kind, never defended themselves against her. They turned their shoulders to her most savage slashes, and with wagging tails and mincing steps strove to placate her wrath. But if they were all mildness toward her, they were all fierceness toward one another. The three-year-old grew too ambitious in his fierceness. He caught the one-eyed elder on his blind side and ripped his ear into ribbons. Though the grizzled old fellow could see only on one side, against the youth and vigor of the other he brought into play the wisdom of long years of experience. His lost eye and his scarred muzzle bore evidence to the nature of his experience. He had survived too many battles to be in doubt for a moment about what to do.

The battle began fairly, but it did not end fairly. There was no telling what the outcome would have been, for the third wolf joined the elder, and together, old leader and young leader, they attacked the ambitious three-year-old and proceeded to destroy him. He was beset on either side by the merciless fangs of his erstwhile comrades. Forgotten were the days they had hunted together, the game they had pulled down, the famine they had suffered. That business was a thing of the past. The business of love was at hand—ever a sterner and crueler business than that of food-getting.

And in the meanwhile, the she-wolf, the cause of it all, sat down contentedly on her haunches and watched. She was even pleased. This was her day,—and it came not often,—when manes bristled, and fang smote fang or ripped and tore the yielding flesh, all for the possession of her.

And in the business of love the three-year-old, who had made this his first adventure upon it, yielded up his life. On either side of his body stood his two rivals. They were gazing at the she-wolf, who sat smiling in the snow. But the elder leader was wise, very wise, in love even as in battle. The younger leader turned his head to lick a wound on his shoulder. The curve of his neck was turned toward his rival. With his one eye the elder saw the opportunity. He darted in low and closed with his fangs. It was a long, ripping slash, and deep as well. His teeth, in passing, burst the wall of the great vein of the throat. Then he leaped clear.

The young leader snarled terribly, but his snarl broke midmost into a tickling cough. Bleeding and coughing, already stricken, he sprang at the elder and fought while life faded from him, his legs going weak beneath him, the light of day dulling on his eyes, his blows and springs falling shorter and shorter.

And all the while the she-wolf sat on her haunches and smiled. She was made glad in vague ways by the battle, for this was the love-making of the Wild, the sex-tragedy of the natural world that was tragedy only to those that died. To those that survived it was not tragedy, but realization and achievement.

When the young leader lay in the snow and moved no more, One Eye stalked over to the she-wolf. His carriage was one of mingled triumph and caution. He was plainly expectant of a rebuff, and he was just as plainly surprised when her teeth did not flash out at him in anger. For the first time she met him with a kindly manner. She sniffed noses with him, and even condescended to leap about and frisk and play with him in quite puppyish fashion. And he, for all his gray years and sage experience, behaved quite as puppyishly and even a little more foolishly.

Forgotten already were the vanquished rivals and the love-tale red-written on the snow. Forgotten, save once, when old One Eye stopped for a moment to lick his stiffening wounds. Then it was that his lips half writhed into a snarl, and the hair of his neck and shoulders involuntarily bristled, while he half crouched for a spring, his claws spasmodically clutching into the snow-surface for firmer footing. But it was all forgotten the next moment, as he sprang after the she-wolf, who was coyly leading him a chase through the woods.

After that they ran side by side, like good friends who have come to an understanding. The days passed by, and they kept together, hunting their meat and killing and eating it in common. After a time the she-wolf began to grow restless. She seemed to be searching for something that she could not find. The hollows under fallen trees seemed to attract her, and she spent much time nosing about among the larger snow-piled crevices in the rocks and in the caves of overhanging banks. Old One Eye was not interested at all, but he followed her good-naturedly in her quest, and when her investigations in particular places were unusually protracted, he would lie down and wait until she was ready to go on.

They did not remain in one place, but travelled across country until they regained the Mackenzie River, down which they slowly went, leaving it often to hunt game along the small streams that entered it, but always returning to it again. Sometimes they chanced upon other wolves, usually in pairs; but there was no friendliness of intercourse displayed on either side, no gladness at meeting, no desire to return to the pack-formation. Several times they encountered solitary wolves. These were always males, and they were pressingly insistent on joining with One Eye and his mate. This he resented, and when she stood shoulder to shoulder with him, bristling and showing her teeth, the aspiring solitary ones would back off, turn tail, and continue on their lonely way.

One moonlight night, running through the quiet forest, One Eye suddenly halted. His muzzle went up, his tail stiffened, and his nostrils dilated as he scented the air. One foot also he held up, after the manner of a dog. He was not satisfied, and he continued to smell the air, striving to understand the message borne upon it to him. One careless sniff had satisfied his mate, and she trotted on to reassure him. Though he followed her, he was still dubious, and he could not forbear an occasional halt in order more carefully to study the warning.

She crept out cautiously on the edge of a large open space in the midst of the trees. For some time she stood alone. Then One Eye, creeping and crawling, every sense on the alert, every hair radiating infinite suspicion, joined her. They stood side by side, watching and listening and smelling.

To their ears came the sounds of dogs wrangling and scuffling, the guttural cries of men, the sharper voices of scolding women, and once the shrill and plaintive cry of a child. With the exception of the huge bulks of the skin lodges, little could be seen save the flames of the fire, broken by the movements of intervening bodies, and the smoke rising slowly on the quiet air. But to their nostrils came the myriad smells of an Indian camp, carrying a story that was largely incomprehensible to One Eye, but every detail of which the she-wolf knew.

She was strangely stirred, and sniffed and sniffed with an increasing delight. But old One Eye was doubtful. He betrayed his apprehension, and started tentatively to go. She turned and touched his neck with her muzzle in a reassuring way, then regarded the camp again. A new wistfulness was in her face, but it was not the wistfulness of hunger. She was thrilling to a desire that urged her to go forward, to be in closer to that fire, to be squabbling with the dogs, and to be avoiding and dodging the stumbling feet of men.

One Eye moved impatiently beside her; her unrest came back upon her, and she knew again her pressing need to find the thing for which she searched. She turned and trotted back into the forest, to the great relief of One Eye, who trotted a little to the fore until they were well within the shelter of the trees.

As they slid along, noiseless as shadows, in the moonlight, they came upon a run-way. Both noses went down to the footprints in the snow. These footprints were very fresh. One Eye ran ahead cautiously, his mate at his heels. The broad pads of their feet were spread wide and in contact with the snow were like velvet. One Eye caught sight of a dim movement of white in the midst of the white. His sliding gait had been deceptively swift, but it was as nothing to the speed at which he now ran. Before him was bounding the faint patch of white he had discovered.

They were running along a narrow alley flanked on either side by a growth of young spruce. Through the trees the mouth of the alley could be seen, opening out on a moonlit glade. Old One Eye was rapidly overhauling the fleeing shape of white. Bound by bound he gained. Now he was upon it. One leap more and his teeth would be sinking into it. But that leap was never made. High in the air, and straight up, soared the shape of white, now a struggling snowshoe rabbit that leaped and bounded, executing a fantastic dance there above him in the air and never once returning to earth.

One Eye sprang back with a snort of sudden fright, then shrank down to the snow and crouched, snarling threats at this thing of fear he did not understand. But the she-wolf coolly thrust past him. She poised for a moment, than sprang for the dancing rabbit. She, too, soared high, but not so high as the quarry, and her teeth clipped emptily together with a metallic snap. She made another leap, and another.

Her mate had slowly relaxed from his crouch and was watching her. He now evinced displeasure at her repeated failures, and himself made a mighty spring upward. His teeth closed upon the rabbit, and he bore it back to earth with him. But at the same time there was a suspicious crackling movement beside him, and his astonished eye saw a young spruce sapling bending down above him to strike him. His jaws let go their grip, and he leaped backward to escape this strange danger, his lips drawn back from his fangs, his throat snarling, every hair bristling with rage and fright. And in that moment the sapling reared its slender length upright and the rabbit soared dancing in the air again.

The she-wolf was angry. She sank her fangs into her mate's shoulder in reproof; and he, frightened, unaware of what constituted this new onslaught, struck back ferociously and in still greater fright, ripping down the side of the she-wolf's muzzle. For him to resent such reproof was equally unexpected to her, and she sprang upon him in snarling indignation. Then he discovered his mistake and tried to placate her. But she proceeded to punish him roundly, until he gave over all attempts at placation, and whirled in a circle, his head away from her, his shoulders receiving the punishment of her teeth.

In the meantime the rabbit danced above them in the air. The she-wolf sat down in the snow, and old One Eye, now more in fear of his mate than of the mysterious sapling, again sprang for the rabbit. As he sank back with it between his teeth, he kept his eye on the sapling. As before, it followed him back to earth. He crouched down under the impending blow, his hair bristling, but his teeth still keeping tight hold of the rabbit. But the blow did not fall. The sapling remained bent above him. When he moved it moved, and he

growled at it through his clenched jaws; when he remained still, it remained still, and he concluded it was
safer to continue remaining still. Yet the warm blood of
the rabbit tasted good in his mouth.

It was his mate who relieved him from the quandary
in which he found himself. She took the rabbit from
him, and while the sapling swayed and teetered threateningly above her she calmly gnawed off the rabbit's
head. At once the sapling shot up, and after that gave
no more trouble, remaining in the decorous and perpendicular position in which nature had intended it to
grow. Then, between them, the she-wolf and One Eye
devoured the game which the mysterious sapling had
caught for them.

There were other run-ways and alleys where rabbits
were hanging in the air, and the wolf-pair prospected
them all, the she-wolf leading the way, old One Eye
following and observant, learning the method of robbing snares—a knowledge destined to stand him in
good stead in the days to come.

CHAPTER II

The Lair

For two days the she-wolf and One Eye hung about the Indian camp. He was worried and apprehensive, yet the camp lured his mate and she was loath to depart. But when, one morning, the air was rent with the report of a rifle close at hand, and a bullet smashed against a tree trunk several inches from One Eye's head, they hesitated no more, but went off on a long, swinging lope that put quick miles between them and the danger.

They did not go far—a couple of days' journey. The she-wolf's need to find the thing for which she searched had now become imperative. She was getting very heavy, and could run but slowly. Once, in the pursuit of a rabbit, which she ordinarily would have caught with ease, she gave over and lay down and rested. One Eye came to her; but when he touched her neck gently with his muzzle she snapped at him with such quick fierceness that he tumbled over backward and cut a ridiculous figure in his effort to escape her teeth. Her temper was now shorter than ever; but he had become more patient than ever and more solicitous.

And then she found the thing for which she sought. It was a few miles up a small stream that in the summer time flowed into the Mackenzie, but that then was fro-

zen over and frozen down to its rocky bottom—a dead
stream of solid white from source to mouth. The she-
wolf was trotting wearily along, her mate well in advance, when she came upon the overhanging, high
clay-bank. She turned aside and trotted over to it. The
wear and tear of spring storms and melting snows had
underwashed the bank and in one place had made a
small cave out of a narrow fissure.

She paused at the mouth of the cave and looked the
wall over carefully. Then, on one side and the other,
she ran along the base of the wall to where its abrupt
bulk merged from the softer-lined landscape. Returning to the cave, she entered its narrow mouth. For a
short three feet she was compelled to crouch; then the
walls widened and rose higher in a little round chamber
nearly six feet in diameter. The roof barely cleared her
head. It was dry and cosey. She inspected it with painstaking care, while One Eye, who had returned, stood
in the entrance and patiently watched her. She dropped
her head, with her nose to the ground and directed toward a point near to her closely bunched feet, and
around this point she circled several times; then, with a
tired sigh that was almost a grunt, she curled her body
in, relaxed her legs, and dropped down, her head toward the entrance. One Eye, with pointed, interested
ears, laughed at her, and beyond, outlined against the
white light, she could see the brush of his tail waving
good-naturedly. Her own ears, with a snuggling movement, laid their sharp points backward and down
against the head for a moment, while her mouth
opened and her tongue lolled peaceably out, and in this
way she expressed that she was pleased and satisfied.

One Eye was hungry. Though he lay down in the
entrance and slept, his sleep was fitful. He kept awak-
ing and cocking his ears at the bright world without,
where the April sun was blazing across the snow.
When he dozed, upon his ears would steal the faint

whispers of hidden trickles of running water, and he would rouse and listen intently. The sun had come back, and all the awakening Northland world was calling to him. Life was stirring. The feel of spring was in the air, the feel of growing life under the snow, of sap ascending in the trees, of buds bursting the shackles of the frost.

He cast anxious glances at his mate, but she showed no desire to get up. He looked outside, and half a dozen snow-birds fluttered across his field of vision. He started to get up, then looked back to his mate again, and settled down and dozed. A shrill and minute singing stole upon his hearing. Once, and twice, he sleepily brushed his nose with his paw. Then he woke up. There, buzzing in the air at the tip of his nose, was a lone mosquito. It was a full-grown mosquito, one that had lain frozen in a dry log all winter and that had now been thawed out by the sun. He could resist the call of the world no longer. Besides, he was hungry.

He crawled over to his mate and tried to persuade her to get up. But she only snarled at him, and he walked out alone into the bright sunshine to find the snow-surface soft underfoot and the travelling difficult. He went up the frozen bed of the stream, where the snow, shaded by the trees, was yet hard and crystalline. He was gone eight hours, and he came back through the darkness hungrier than when he had started. He had found game, but he had not caught it. He had broken through the melting snow-crust, and wallowed, while the snowshoe rabbits had skimmed along on top lightly as ever.

He paused at the mouth of the cave with a sudden shock of suspicion. Faint, strange sounds came from within. They were sounds not made by his mate, and yet they were remotely familiar. He bellied cautiously inside and was met by a warning snarl from the she-wolf. This he received without perturbation, though he obeyed it by keeping his distance; but he remained interested in the other sounds—faint, muffled sobbings and slubberings.

His mate warned him irritably away, and he curled up and slept in the entrance. When morning came and a dim light pervaded the lair, he again sought after the source of the remotely familiar sounds. There was a new note in his mate's warning snarl. It was a jealous note, and he was very careful in keeping a respectful distance. Nevertheless, he made out, sheltering between her legs against the length of her body, five strange little bundles of life, very feeble, very helpless, making tiny whimpering noises, with eyes that did not open to the light. He was surprised. It was not the first time in his long and successful life that this thing had happened. It had happened many times, yet each time it was as fresh a surprise as ever to him.

His mate looked at him anxiously. Every little while she emitted a low growl, and at times, when it seemed to her he approached too near, the growl shot up in her throat to a sharp snarl. Of her own experience she had no memory of the thing happening; but in her instinct, which was the experience of all the mothers of wolves, there lurked a memory of fathers that had eaten their new-born and helpless progeny. It manifested itself as a fear strong within her, that made her prevent One Eye from more closely inspecting the cubs he had fathered.

But there was no danger. Old One Eye was feeling the urge of an impulse, that was, in turn, an instinct that had come down to him from all the fathers of wolves. He did not question it, nor puzzle over it. It was there, in the fibre of his being; and it was the most natural thing in the world that he should obey it by turning his back on his new-born family and by trotting out and away on the meat-trail whereby he lived.

Five or six miles from the lair, the stream divided, its forks going off among the mountains at a right angle.

Here, leading up the left fork, he came upon a fresh track. He smelled it and found it so recent that he crouched swiftly, and looked in the direction in which it disappeared. Then he turned deliberately and took the right fork. The footprint was much larger than the one his own feet made, and he knew that in the wake of such a trail there was little meat for him.

Half a mile up the right fork, his quick ears caught the sound of gnawing teeth. He stalked the quarry and found it to be a porcupine, standing upright against a tree and trying his teeth on the bark. One Eye approached carefully but hopelessly. He knew the breed, though he had never met it so far north before; and never in his long life had porcupine served him for a meal. But he had long since learned that there was such a thing as Chance, or Opportunity, and he continued to draw near. There was never any telling what might happen, for with live things events were somehow always happening differently.

The porcupine rolled itself into a ball, radiating long, sharp needles in all directions that defied attack. In his youth One Eye had once sniffed too near a similar, apparently inert ball of quills, and had the tail flick out suddenly in his face. One quill he had carried away in his muzzle, where it had remained for weeks, a rankling flame, until it finally worked out. So he lay down, in a comfortable crouching position, his nose fully a foot away, and out of the line of the tail. Thus he waited, keeping perfectly quiet. There was no telling. Something might happen. The porcupine might unroll. There might be opportunity for a deft and ripping thrust of paw into the tender, unguarded belly.

But at the end of half an hour he arose, growled wrathfully at the motionless ball, and trotted on. He had waited too often and futilely in the past for porcupines to unroll, to waste any more time. He continued up the right fork. The day wore along, and nothing rewarded his hunt.

The urge of his awakened instinct of fatherhood was strong upon him. He must find meat. In the afternoon he blundered upon a ptarmigan. He came out of a thicket and found himself face to face with the slow-witted bird. It was sitting on a log, not a foot beyond the end of his nose. Each saw the other. The bird made a startled rise, but he struck it with his paw, and smashed it down to earth, then pounced upon it, and caught it in his teeth as it scuttled across the snow trying to rise in the air again. As his teeth crunched through the tender flesh and fragile bones, he began naturally to eat. Then he remembered, and, turning on the back-track, started for home, carrying the ptarmigan in his mouth.

A mile above the forks, running velvet-footed as was his custom, a gliding shadow that cautiously prospected each new vista of the trail, he came upon later imprints of the large tracks he had discovered in the early morning. As the track led his way, he followed, prepared to meet the maker of it at every turn of the stream.

He slid his head around a corner of rock, where began an unusually large bend in the stream, and his quick eyes made out something that sent him crouching swiftly down. It was the maker of the track, a large female lynx. She was crouching as he had crouched once that day, in front of her the tight-rolled ball of quills. If he had been a gliding shadow before, he now became the ghost of such a shadow, as he crept and circled around, and came up well to leeward of the silent, motionless pair.

He lay down in the snow, depositing the ptarmigan beside him, and with eyes peering through the needles of a low-growing spruce he watched the play of life before him—the waiting lynx and the waiting porcupine, each intent on life; and, such was the curiousness of the game, the way of life for one lay in the eating of the other, and the way of life for the other lay in being not eaten. While old One Eye, the wolf, crouching in the covert, played his part, too, in the game, waiting for some strange freak of Chance, that might help him on the meat-trail which was his way of life.

Half an hour passed, an hour; and nothing happened. The ball of quills might have been a stone for all it moved; the lynx might have been frozen to marble, and old One Eye might have been dead. Yet all three animals were keyed to a tenseness of living that was almost painful, and scarcely ever would it come to them to be more alive than they were in their seeming petrifaction.

One Eye moved slightly and peered forth with increased eagerness. Something was happening. The porcupine had at last decided that its enemy had gone away. Slowly, cautiously, it was unrolling its ball of impregnable armor. It was agitated by no tremor of anticipation. Slowly, slowly, the bristling ball straightened out and lengthened. One Eye, watching, felt a sudden moistness in his mouth and a drooling of saliva, involuntary, excited by the living meat that was spreading itself like a repast before him.

Not quite entirely had the porcupine unrolled when it discovered its enemy. In that instant the lynx struck. The blow was like a flash of light. The paw, with rigid claws curving like talons, shot under the tender belly and came back with a swift ripping movement. Had the porcupine been entirely unrolled, or had it not discovered its enemy a fraction of a second before the blow was struck, the paw would have escaped unscathed; but a side flick of the tail sank sharp quills into it as it was withdrawn.

Everything had happened at once,—the blow, the counter-blow, the squeal of agony from the porcupine, the big cat's squall of sudden hurt and astonishment. One Eye half arose in his excitement, his ears up, his tail straight out and quivering behind him. The lynx's

bad temper got the best of her. She sprang savagely at
the thing that had hurt her. But the porcupine, squealing and grunting, with disrupted anatomy trying feebly
to roll up into its ball-protection, flicked out its tail
again, and again the big cat squalled with hurt and astonishment. Then she fell to backing away and sneez-
ing, her nose bristling with quills like a monstrous pin-
cushion. She brushed her nose with her paws, trying to
dislodge the fiery darts, thrust it into the snow, and
rubbed it against twigs and branches, all the time leaping about, ahead, sidewise, up and down, in a frenzy of
pain and fright.

She sneezed continually, and her stub of a tail was
doing its best toward lashing about by giving quick,
violent jerks. She quit her antics, and quieted down for
a long minute. One Eye watched. And even he could
not repress a start and an involuntary bristling of hair
along his back when she suddenly leaped, without
warning, straight up in the air, at the same time emit-
ting a long and most terrible squall. Then she sprang
away, up the trail, squalling with every leap she made.

It was not until her racket had faded away in the
distance and died out that One Eye ventured forth. He
walked as delicately as though all the snow were car-
peted with porcupine quills, erect and ready to pierce
the soft pads of his feet. The porcupine met his approach with a furious squealing and a clashing of its
long teeth. It had managed to roll up in a ball again,
but it was not quite the old compact ball; its muscles
were too much torn for that. It had been ripped almost
in half, and was still bleeding profusely.

One Eye scooped out mouthfuls of the blood-soaked
snow, and chewed and tasted and swallowed. This
served as a relish, and his hunger increased mightily;
but he was too old in the world to forget his caution.
He waited. He lay down and waited, while the porcupine grated its teeth and uttered grunts and sobs and

occasional sharp little squeals. In a little while, One Eye noticed that the quills were drooping and that a great quivering had set up. The quivering came to an end suddenly. There was a final defiant clash of the long teeth. Then all the quills drooped quite down, and the body relaxed and moved no more.

With a nervous, shrinking paw, One Eye stretched out the porcupine to its full length and turned it over on its back. Nothing had happened. It was surely dead. He studied it intently for a moment, then took a careful grip with his teeth and started off down the stream, partly carrying, partly dragging the porcupine, with head turned to the side so as to avoid stepping on the prickly mass. He recollected something, dropped the burden, and trotted back to where he had left the ptarmigan. He did not hesitate a moment. He knew clearly what was to be done, and this he did by promptly eating the ptarmigan. Then he returned and took up his burden.

When he dragged the result of his day's hunt into the cave, the she-wolf inspected it, turned her muzzle to him, and lightly licked him on the neck. But the next instant she was warning him away from the cubs with a snarl that was less harsh than usual and that was more apologetic than menacing. Her instinctive fear of the father of her progeny was toning down. He was behaving as a wolf father should, and manifesting no unholy desire to devour the young lives she had brought into the world.

CHAPTER III

The Gray Cub

He was different from his brothers and sisters. Their hair already betrayed the reddish hue inherited from their mother, the she-wolf; while he alone, in this particular, took after his father. He was the one little gray cub of the litter. He had bred true to the straight wolf-stock—in fact, he had bred true, physically, to old One Eye himself, with but a single exception, and that was that he had two eyes to his father's one.

The gray cub's eyes had not been open long, yet already he could see with steady clearness. And while his eyes were still closed, he had felt, tasted, and smelled. He knew his two brothers and his two sisters very well. He had begun to romp with them in a feeble, awkward way, and even to squabble, his little throat vibrating with a queer rasping noise, (the forerunner of the growl), as he worked himself into a passion. And long before his eyes had opened, he had learned by touch, taste, and smell to know his mother—a fount of warmth and liquid food and tenderness. She possessed a gentle, caressing tongue that soothed him when it passed over his soft little body, and that impelled him to snuggle close against her and to doze off to sleep.

Most of the first month of his life had been passed thus in sleeping; but now he could see quite well, and he stayed awake for longer periods of time, and he was coming to learn his world quite well. His world was gloomy; but he did not know that, for he knew no other world. It was dim-lighted; but his eyes had never had to adjust themselves to any other light. His world was very small. Its limits were the walls of the lair; but as he had no knowledge of the wide world outside, he was never oppressed by the narrow confines of his existence.

But he had early discovered that one wall of his world was different from the rest. This was the mouth of the cave and the source of light. He had discovered that it was different from the other walls long before he had any thoughts of his own, any conscious volitions. It had been an irresistible attraction before ever his eyes opened and looked upon it. The light from it had beat upon his sealed lids, and the eyes and the optic nerves had pulsated to little, sparklike flashes, warm-colored and strangely pleasing. The life of his body, and of every fibre of his body, the life that was the very substance of his body and that was apart from his own personal life, had yearned toward this light and urged his body toward it in the same way that the cunning chemistry of a plant urges it toward the sun.

Always, in the beginning, before his conscious life dawned, he had crawled toward the mouth of the cave. And in this his brothers and sisters were one with him. Never, in that period, did any of them crawl toward the dark corners of the back-wall. The light drew them as if they were plants; the chemistry of the life that composed them demanded the light as a necessity of being; and their little puppet-bodies crawled blindly and chemically, like the tendrils of a vine. Later on, when each developed individuality and became personally conscious of impulsions and desires, the attraction of the light increased. They were always crawling and sprawling toward it, and being driven back from it by their mother.

It was in this way that the gray cub learned other attributes of his mother than the soft, soothing tongue. In his insistent crawling toward the light, he discovered in her a nose that with a sharp nudge administered rebuke, and later, a paw, that crushed him down or rolled him over and over with swift, calculating stroke. Thus he learned hurt; and on top of it he learned to avoid hurt, first, by not incurring the risk of it; and second, when he had incurred the risk, by dodging and by retreating. These were conscious actions, and were the results of his first generalizations upon the world. Before that he had recoiled automatically from hurt, as he had crawled automatically toward the light. After that he recoiled from hurt because he *knew* that it was hurt.

He was a fierce little cub. So were his brothers and sisters. It was to be expected. He was a carnivorous animal. He came of a breed of meat-killers and meat-eaters. His father and mother lived wholly upon meat. The milk he had sucked with his first flickering life was milk transformed directly from meat, and now, at a month old, when his eyes had been open for but a week, he was beginning himself to eat meat—meat half-digested by the she-wolf and disgorged for the five growing cubs that already made too great demand upon her breast.

But he was, further, the fiercest of the litter. He could make a louder rasping growl than any of them. His tiny rages were much more terrible than theirs. It was he that first learned the trick of rolling a fellow-cub over with a cunning paw-stroke. And it was he that first gripped another cub by the ear and pulled and tugged and growled through jaws tight-clenched. And certainly it was he that caused the mother the most trouble in keeping her litter from the mouth of the cave.

The fascination of the light for the gray cub increased from day to day. He was perpetually departing on yard-long adventures toward the cave's entrance, and as perpetually being driven back. Only he did not know it for an entrance. He did not know anything about entrances—passages whereby one goes from one place to another place. He did not know any other place, much less of a way to get there. So to him the entrance of the cave was a wall—a wall of light. As the sun was to the outside dweller, this wall was to him the sun of his world. It attracted him as a candle attracts a moth. He was always striving to attain it. The life that was so swiftly expanding within him, urged him continually toward the wall of light. The life that was within him knew that it was the one way out, the way he was predestined to tread. But he himself did not know anything about it. He did not know there was any outside at all.

There was one strange thing about this wall of light. His father (he had already come to recognize his father as the one other dweller in the world, a creature like his mother, who slept near the light and was a bringer of meat)—his father had a way of walking right into the white far wall and disappearing. The gray cub could not understand this. Though never permitted by his mother to approach that wall, he had approached the other walls, and encountered hard obstruction on the end of his tender nose. This hurt. And after several such adventures, he left the walls alone. Without thinking about it, he accepted this disappearing into the wall as a peculiarity of his father, as milk and half-digested meat were peculiarities of his mother.

In fact, the gray cub was not given to thinking—at least, to the kind of thinking customary of men. His brain worked in dim ways. Yet his conclusions were as sharp and distinct as those achieved by men. He had a method of accepting things, without questioning the why and wherefore. In reality, this was the act of classification. He was never disturbed over *why* a thing happened. *How* it happened was sufficient for him. Thus, when he had bumped his nose on the back-wall a few times, he accepted that he would not disappear into walls. In the same way he accepted that his father could disappear into walls. But he was not in the least disturbed by desire to find out the reason for the difference between his father and himself. Logic and physics were no part of his mental make-up.

Like most creatures of the Wild, he early experienced famine. There came a time when not only did the meat-supply cease, but the milk no longer came from his mother's breast. At first, the cubs whimpered and cried, but for the most part they slept. It was not long before they were reduced to a coma of hunger. There were no more spats and squabbles, no more tiny rages nor attempts at growling; while the adventures toward the far white wall ceased altogether. The cubs slept, while the life that was in them flickered and died down.

One Eye was desperate. He ranged far and wide, and slept but little in the lair that had now become cheerless and miserable. The she-wolf, too, left her litter and went out in search of meat. In the first days after the birth of the cubs, One Eye had journeyed several times back to the Indian camp and robbed the rabbit snares; but, with the melting of the snow and the opening of the streams, the Indian camp had moved away, and that source of supply was closed to him.

When the gray cub came back to life and again took interest in the far white wall, he found that the population of his world had been reduced. Only one sister remained to him. The rest were gone. As he grew stronger, he found himself compelled to play alone, for the sister no longer lifted her head nor moved about. His little body rounded out with the meat he now ate; but the food had come too late for her. She slept continuously, a tiny skeleton flung round with skin in which the flame flickered lower and lower and at last went out.

Then there came a time when the gray cub no

longer saw his father appearing and disappearing in the wall nor lying down asleep in the entrance. This had happened at the end of a second and less severe famine. The she-wolf knew why One Eye never came back, but there was no way by which she could tell what she had seen to the gray cub. Hunting herself for meat, up the left fork of the stream where lived the lynx, she had followed a day-old trail of One Eye. And she had found him, or what remained of him, at the end of the trail. There were many signs of the battle that had been fought, and of the lynx's withdrawal to her lair after having won the victory. Before she went away, the she-wolf had found this lair, but the signs told her that the lynx was inside, and she had not dared to venture in.

After that, the she-wolf in her hunting avoided the left fork. For she knew that in the lynx's lair was a litter of kittens, and she knew the lynx for a fierce, bad-tempered creature and a terrible fighter. It was all very well for half a dozen wolves to drive a lynx, spitting and bristling, up a tree; but it was quite a different matter for a lone wolf to encounter a lynx—especially when the lynx was known to have a litter of hungry kittens at her back.

But the Wild is the Wild, and motherhood is motherhood, at all times fiercely protective whether in the Wild or out of it; and the time was to come when the she-wolf, for her gray cub's sake, would venture the left fork, and the lair in the rocks, and the lynx's wrath.

CHAPTER IV

The Wall of the World

By the time his mother began leaving the cave on hunting expeditions, the cub had learned well the law that forbade his approaching the entrance. Not only had this law been forcibly and many times impressed on him by his mother's nose and paw, but in him the instinct of fear was developing. Never, in his brief cave-life, had he encountered anything of which to be afraid. Yet fear was in him. It had come down to him from a remote ancestry through a thousand thousand lives. It was a heritage he had received directly from One Eye and the she-wolf; but to them, in turn, it had been passed down through all the generations of wolves that had gone before. Fear!—that legacy of the Wild which no animal may escape nor exchange for pottage.

So the gray cub knew fear, though he knew not the stuff of which fear was made. Possibly he accepted it as one of the restrictions of life. For he had already learned that there were such restrictions. Hunger he had known; and when he could not appease his hunger he had felt restriction. The hard obstruction of the cave-wall, the sharp nudge of his mother's nose, the smashing stroke of her paw, the hunger unappeased of several famines, had borne in upon him that all was not freedom in the world, that to life there were limitations and restraints. These limitations and restraints were laws. To be obedient to them was to escape hurt and make for happiness.

He did not reason the question out in this man-fashion. He merely classified the things that hurt and the things that did not hurt. And after such classification he avoided the things that hurt, the restrictions and restraints, in order to enjoy the satisfactions and remunerations of life.

Thus it was that in obedience to the law laid down by his mother, and in obedience to the law of that unknown and nameless thing, fear, he kept away from the mouth of the cave. It remained to him a white wall of light. When his mother was absent, he slept most of the time, while during the intervals that he was awake he kept very quiet, suppressing the whimpering cries that tickled in his throat and strove for noise.

Once, lying awake, he heard a strange sound in the white wall. He did not know that it was a wolverine, standing outside, all a-tremble with its own daring, and cautiously scenting out the contents of the cave. The cub knew only that the sniff was strange, a something unclassified, therefore unknown and terrible—for the unknown was one of the chief elements that went into the making of fear.

The hair bristled up on the gray cub's back, but it bristled silently. How was he to know that this thing that sniffed was a thing at which to bristle? It was not born of any knowledge of his, yet it was the visible expression of the fear that was in him, and for which, in his own life, there was no accounting. But fear was accompanied by another instinct—that of concealment. The cub was in a frenzy of terror, yet he lay without movement or sound, frozen, petrified into immobility, to all appearances dead. His mother, coming home, growled as she smelt the wolverine's track, and bounded into the cave and licked and nuzzled him with undue vehemence of affection. And the cub felt that somehow he had escaped a great hurt.

But there were other forces at work in the cub, the greatest of which was growth. Instinct and law demanded of him obedience. But growth demanded disobedience. His mother and fear impelled him to keep away from the white wall. Growth is life, and life is forever destined to make for light. So there was no damming up the tide of life that was rising within him— rising with every mouthful of meat he swallowed, with every breath he drew. In the end, one day, fear and obedience were swept away by the rush of life, and the cub straddled and sprawled toward the entrance.

Unlike any other wall with which he had had experience, this wall seemed to recede from him as he approached. No hard surface collided with the tender little nose he thrust out tentatively before him. The substance of the wall seemed as permeable and yielding as light. And as condition, in his eyes, had the seeming of form, so he entered into what had been wall to him and bathed in the substance that composed it.

It was bewildering. He was sprawling through solidity. And ever the light grew brighter. Fear urged him to go back, but growth drove him on. Suddenly he found himself at the mouth of the cave. The wall, inside which he had thought himself, as suddenly leaped back before him to an immeasurable distance. The light had become painfully bright. He was dazzled by it. Likewise he was made dizzy by this abrupt and tremendous extension of space. Automatically, his eyes were adjusting themselves to the brightness, focussing themselves to meet the increased distance of objects. At first, the wall had leaped beyond his vision. He now saw it again; but it had taken upon itself a remarkable remoteness. Also, its appearance had changed. It was now a variegated wall, composed of the trees that fringed the stream, the opposing mountain that towered above the trees, and the sky that out-towered the mountain.

A great fear came upon him. This was more of the terrible unknown. He crouched down on the lip of the cave and gazed out on the world. He was very much afraid. Because it was unknown, it was hostile to him. Therefore the hair stood up on end along his back and his lips wrinkled weakly in an attempt at a ferocious and intimidating snarl. Out of his puniness and fright he challenged and menaced the whole wide world.

Nothing happened. He continued to gaze, and in his interest he forgot to snarl. Also, he forgot to be afraid. For the time, fear had been routed by growth, while growth had assumed the guise of curiosity. He began to notice near objects—an open portion of the stream that flashed in the sun, the blasted pine tree that stood at the base of the slope, and the slope itself, that ran right up to him and ceased two feet beneath the lip of the cave on which he crouched.

Now the gray cub had lived all his days on a level floor. He had never experienced the hurt of a fall. He did not know what a fall was. So he stepped boldly out upon the air. His hind-legs still rested on the cave-lip, so he fell forward head downward. The earth struck him a harsh blow on the nose that made him yelp. Then he began rolling down the slope, over and over. He was in a panic of terror. The unknown had caught him at last. It had gripped savagely hold of him and was about to wreak upon him some terrific hurt. Growth was now routed by fear, and he ki-yi'd like any frightened puppy.

The unknown bore him on he knew not to what frightful hurt, and he yelped and ki-yi'd unceasingly. This was a different proposition from crouching in frozen fear while the unknown lurked just alongside. Now the unknown had caught tight hold of him. Silence would do no good. Besides, it was not fear, but terror, that convulsed him.

But the slope grew more gradual, and its base was grass-covered. Here the cub lost momentum. When at last he came to a stop, he gave one last agonized yelp and then a long, whimpering wail. Also, and quite as a matter of course, as though in his life he had already made a thousand toilets, he proceeded to lick away the dry clay that soiled him.

After that he sat up and gazed about him, as might the first man of the earth who landed upon Mars. The cub had broken through the wall of the world, the unknown had let go its hold of him, and here he was without hurt. But the first man on Mars would have experienced less unfamiliarity than did he. Without any antecedent knowledge, without any warning whatever that such existed, he found himself an explorer in a totally new world.

Now that the terrible unknown had let go of him, he forgot that the unknown had any terrors. He was aware only of curiosity in all the things about him. He inspected the grass beneath him, the mossberry plant just beyond, and the dead trunk of the blasted pine that stood on the edge of an open space among the trees. A squirrel, running around the base of the trunk, came full upon him, and gave him a great fright. He cowered down and snarled. But the squirrel was as badly scared. It ran up the tree, and from a point of safety chattered back savagely.

This helped the cub's courage, and though the woodpecker he next encountered gave him a start, he proceeded confidently on his way. Such was his confidence, that when a moose-bird impudently hopped up to him, he reached out at it with a playful paw. The result was a sharp peck on the end of his nose that made him cower down and ki-yi. The noise he made was too much for the moose-bird, who sought safety in flight.

But the cub was learning. His misty little mind had already made an unconscious classification. There were live things and things not alive. Also, he must watch out for the live things. The things not alive remained always in one place; but the live things moved about, and there was no telling what they might do. The thing to expect of them was the unexpected, and for this he must be prepared.

He travelled very clumsily. He ran into sticks and things. A twig that he thought a long way off, would the next instant hit him on the nose or rake along his ribs. There were inequalities of surface. Sometimes he overstepped and stubbed his nose. Quite as often he understepped and stubbed his feet. Then there were the pebbles and stones that turned under him when he trod upon them; and from them he came to know that the things not alive were not all in the same state of stable equilibrium as was his cave; also, that small things not alive were more liable than large things to fall down or turn over. But with every mishap he was learning. The longer he walked, the better he walked. He was adjusting himself. He was learning to calculate his own muscular movements, to know his physical limitations, to measure distances between objects, and between objects and himself.

His was the luck of the beginner. Born to be a hunter of meat (though he did not know it), he blundered upon meat just outside his own cave-door on his first foray into the world. It was by sheer blundering that he chanced upon the shrewdly hidden ptarmigan nest. He fell into it. He had essayed to walk along the trunk of a fallen pine. The rotten bark gave way under his feet, and with a despairing yelp he pitched down the rounded descent, smashed through the leafage and stalks of a small bush, and in the heart of the bush, on the ground, fetched up amongst seven ptarmigan chicks.

They made noises, and at first he was frightened at them. Then he perceived that they were very little, and he became bolder. They moved. He placed his paw on one, and its movements were accelerated. This was a source of enjoyment to him. He smelled it. He picked it up in his mouth. It struggled and tickled his tongue. At the same time he was made aware of a sensation of hunger. His jaws closed together. There was a crunching of fragile bones, and warm blood ran in his mouth. The taste of it was good. This was meat, the same as his mother gave him, only it was alive between his teeth and therefore better. So he ate the ptarmigan. Nor did he stop till he had devoured the whole brood. Then he licked his chops in quite the same way his mother did, and began to crawl out of the bush.

He encountered a feathered whirlwind. He was confused and blinded by the rush of it and the beat of angry wings. He hid his head between his paws and yelped. The blows increased. The mother-ptarmigan was in a fury. Then he became angry. He rose up, snarling, striking out with his paws. He sank his tiny teeth into one of the wings and pulled and tugged sturdily. The ptarmigan struggled against him, showering blows upon him with her free wing. It was his first battle. He was elated. He forgot all about the unknown. He no longer was afraid of anything. He was fighting, tearing at a live thing that was striking at him. Also, this live thing was meat. The lust to kill was on him. He had just destroyed little live things. He would now destroy a big live thing. He was too busy and happy to know that he was happy. He was thrilling and exulting in ways new to him and greater to him than any he had known before.

He held on to the wing and growled between his tight-clenched teeth. The ptarmigan dragged him out of the bush. When she turned and tried to drag him back into the bush's shelter, he pulled her away from it and on into the open. And all the time she was making outcry and striking with her wing, while feathers were flying like a snow-fall. The pitch to which he was aroused was tremendous. All the fighting blood of his breed was up in him and surging through him. This was living, though he did not know it. He was realizing his own meaning in the world; he was doing that for which he was made—killing meat and battling to kill it. He was justifying his existence, than which life can do no greater; for life achieves its summit when it does to the uttermost that which it was equipped to do.

After a time, the ptarmigan ceased her struggling. He still held her by the wing, and they lay on the ground and looked at each other. He tried to growl threateningly, ferociously. She pecked on his nose, which by now, what of previous adventures, was sore. He winced but held on. She pecked him again and again. From wincing he went to whimpering. He tried to back away from her, oblivious of the fact that by his hold on her he dragged her after him. A rain of pecks fell on his ill-used nose. The flood of fight ebbed down in him, and, releasing his prey, he turned tail and scampered off across the open in inglorious retreat.

He lay down to rest on the other side of the open, near the edge of the bushes, his tongue lolling out, his chest heaving and panting, his nose still hurting him and causing him to continue his whimper. But as he lay there, suddenly there came to him a feeling as of something terrible impending. The unknown with all its terrors rushed upon him, and he shrank back instinctively into the shelter of the bush. As he did so, a draught of air fanned him, and a large, winged body swept ominously and silently past. A hawk, driving down out of the blue, had barely missed him.

While he lay in the bush, recovering from this fright and peering fearfully out, the mother-ptarmigan on the other side of the open space fluttered out of the ravaged nest. It was because of her loss that she paid no attention to the winged bolt of the sky. But the cub saw, and it was a warning and a lesson to him—the swift downward swoop of the hawk, the short skim of its body just above the ground, the strike of its talons in the body of the ptarmigan, the ptarmigan's squawk of agony and fright, and the hawk's rush upward into the blue, carrying the ptarmigan away with it.

It was a long time before the cub left his shelter. He had learned much. Live things were meat. They were good to eat. Also, live things when they were large enough, could give hurt. It was better to eat small live things like ptarmigan chicks, and to let alone large live things like ptarmigan hens. Nevertheless he felt a little prick of ambition, a sneaking desire to have another battle with that ptarmigan hen—only the hawk had carried her away. Maybe there were other ptarmigan hens. He would go and see.

He came down a shelving bank to the stream. He had never seen water before. The footing looked good. There were no inequalities of surface. He stepped boldly out on it; and went down, crying with fear, into the embrace of the unknown. It was cold, and he gasped, breathing quickly. The water rushed into his lungs instead of the air that had always accompanied his act of breathing. The suffocation he experienced was like the pang of death. To him it signified death. He had no conscious knowledge of death, but like every animal of the Wild, he possessed the instinct of death. To him it stood as the greatest of hurts. It was the very essence of the unknown; it was the sum of the terrors of the unknown, the one culminating and un-thinkable catastrophe that could happen to him, about which he knew nothing and about which he feared everything.

He came to the surface, and the sweet air rushed into his open mouth. He did not go down again. Quite as though it had been a long-established custom of his, he struck out with all his legs and began to swim. The near bank was a yard away; but he had come up with his back to it, and the first thing his eyes rested upon was the opposite bank, toward which he immediately began to swim. The stream was a small one, but in the pool it widened out to a score of feet.

Midway in the passage, the current picked up the cub and swept him down-stream. He was caught in the miniature rapid at the bottom of the pool. Here was little chance for swimming. The quiet water had become suddenly angry. Sometimes he was under, sometimes on top. At all times he was in violent motion, now being turned over or around, and again, being smashed against a rock. And with every rock he struck, he yelped. His progress was a series of yelps, from which might have been adduced the number of rocks he encountered.

Below the rapid was a second pool, and here, captured by the eddy, he was gently borne to the bank and as gently deposited on a bed of gravel. He crawled frantically clear of the water and lay down. He had learned some more about the world. Water was not alive. Yet it moved. Also, it looked as solid as the earth, but was without any solidity at all. His conclusion was that things were not always what they appeared to be. The cub's fear of the unknown was an inherited distrust, and it had now been strengthened by experience. Thenceforth, in the nature of things, he would possess an abiding distrust of appearances. He would have to learn the reality of a thing before he could put his faith into it.

One other adventure was destined for him that day. He had recollected that there was such a thing in the world as his mother. And then there came to him a feeling that he wanted her more than all the rest of the things in the world. Not only was his body tired with the adventures it had undergone, but his little brain was equally tired. In all the days he had lived it had not worked so hard as on this one day. Furthermore, he was sleepy. So he started out to look for the cave and his mother, feeling at the same time an overwhelming rush of loneliness and helplessness.

He was sprawling along between some bushes, when he heard a sharp, intimidating cry. There was a flash of yellow before his eyes. He saw a weasel leaping swiftly away from him. It was a small live thing, and he had no fear. Then, before him, at his feet, he saw an extremely small live thing, only several inches long—a young weasel, that, like himself, had disobediently gone out adventuring. It tried to retreat before him. He turned it over with his paw. It made a queer, grating noise. The next moment the flash of yellow reappeared before his eyes. He heard again the intimidating cry, and at the same instant received a severe blow on the side of the neck and felt the sharp teeth of the mother-weasel cut into his flesh.

While he yelped and ki-yi'd and scrambled backward, he saw the mother-weasel leap upon her young one and disappear with it into the neighboring thicket. The cut of her teeth in his neck still hurt, but his feelings were hurt more grievously, and he sat down and weakly whimpered. This mother-weasel was so small and so savage! He was yet to learn that for size and weight the weasel was the most ferocious, vindictive, and terrible of all the killers of the Wild. But a portion of this knowledge was quickly to be his.

He was still whimpering when the mother-weasel reappeared. She did not rush him, now that her young one was safe. She approached more cautiously, and the cub had full opportunity to observe her lean, snakelike body, and her head, erect, eager, and snakelike itself. Her sharp, menacing cry sent the hair bristling along his back, and he snarled warningly at her. She came closer and closer. There was a leap, swifter than his unpractised sight, and the lean, yellow body disappeared for a moment out of the field of his vision. The next moment she was at his throat, her teeth buried in his hair and flesh.

At first he snarled and tried to fight; but he was very young, and this was only his first day in the world, and his snarl became a whimper, his fight a struggle to escape. The weasel never relaxed her hold. She hung on, striving to press down with her teeth to the great vein where his life-blood bubbled. The weasel was a drinker of blood, and it was ever her preference to drink from the throat of life itself.

The gray cub would have died, and there would have been no story to write about him, had not the she-wolf come bounding through the bushes. The weasel let go the cub and flashed at the she-wolf's throat, missing, but getting a hold on the jaw instead. The she-wolf flirted her head like the snap of a whip, breaking the weasel's hold and flinging it high in the air. And, still in the air, the she-wolf's jaws closed on the lean, yellow body, and the weasel knew death between the crunching teeth.

The cub experienced another access of affection on the part of his mother. Her joy at finding him seemed greater even than his joy at being found. She nuzzled him and caressed him and licked the cuts made in him by the weasel's teeth. Then, between them, mother and cub, they ate the blood-drinker, and after that went back to the cave and slept.

CHAPTER V

The Law of Meat

The cub's development was rapid. He rested for two days, and then ventured forth from the cave again. It was on this adventure that he found the young weasel whose mother he had helped eat, and he saw to it that the young weasel went the way of its mother. But on this trip he did not get lost. When he grew tired, he found his way back to the cave and slept. And every day thereafter found him out and ranging a wider area.

He began to get an accurate measurement of his strength and his weakness, and to know when to be bold and when to be cautious. He found it expedient to be cautious all the time, except for the rare moments, when, assured of his own intrepidity, he abandoned himself to petty rages and lusts.

He was always a little demon of fury when he chanced upon a stray ptarmigan. Never did he fail to respond savagely to the chatter of the squirrel he had first met on the blasted pine. While the sight of a moose-bird almost invariably put him into the wildest of rages; for he never forgot the peck on the nose he had received from the first of that ilk he encountered.

But there were times when even a moose-bird failed to affect him, and those were times when he felt himself to be in danger from some other prowling meat-hunter. He never forgot the hawk, and its moving shadow always sent him crouching into the nearest thicket. He no longer sprawled and straddled, and already he was developing the gait of his mother, slinking and furtive, apparently without exertion, yet sliding along with a swiftness that was as deceptive as it was imperceptible.

In the matter of meat, his luck had been all in the beginning. The seven ptarmigan chicks and the baby weasel represented the sum of his killings. His desire to kill strengthened with the days, and he cherished hungry ambitions for the squirrel that chattered so volubly and always informed all wild creatures that the wolf-cub was approaching. But as birds flew in the air, squirrels could climb trees, and the cub could only try to crawl unobserved upon the squirrel when it was on the ground.

The cub entertained a great respect for his mother. She could get meat, and she never failed to bring him his share. Further, she was unafraid of things. It did not occur to him that this fearlessness was founded upon experience and knowledge. Its effect on him was that of an impression of power. His mother represented power; and as he grew older he felt this power in the sharper admonition of her paw; while the reproving nudge of her nose gave place to the slash of her fangs. For this, likewise, he respected his mother. She compelled obedience from him, and the older he grew the shorter grew her temper.

Famine came again, and the cub with clearer consciousness knew once more the bite of hunger. The she-wolf ran herself thin in the quest for meat. She rarely slept any more in the cave, spending most of her time on the meat-trail and spending it vainly. This famine was not a long one, but it was severe while it lasted. The cub found no more milk in his mother's breast, nor did he get one mouthful of meat for himself.

Before, he had hunted in play, for the sheer joyousness of it; now he hunted in deadly earnestness, and found nothing. Yet the failure of it accelerated his development. He studied the habits of the squirrel with greater carefulness, and strove with greater craft to steal upon it and surprise it. He studied the wood-mice and tried to dig them out of their burrows; and he learned much about the ways of moose-birds and woodpeckers. And there came a day when the hawk's shadow did not drive him crouching into the bushes. He had grown stronger, and wiser, and more confident. Also, he was desperate. So he sat on his haunches, conspicuously, in an open space, and challenged the hawk down out of the sky. For he knew that there, floating in the blue above him, was meat, the meat his stomach yearned after so insistently. But the hawk refused to come down and give battle, and the cub crawled away into a thicket and whimpered his disappointment and hunger.

The famine broke. The she-wolf brought home meat. It was strange meat, different from any she had ever brought before. It was a lynx kitten, partly grown, like the cub, but not so large. And it was all for him. His mother had satisfied her hunger elsewhere; though he did not know that it was the rest of the lynx litter that had gone to satisfy her. Nor did he know the desperateness of her deed. He knew only that the velvet-furred kitten was meat, and he ate and waxed happier with every mouthful.

A full stomach conduces to inaction, and the cub lay in the cave, sleeping against his mother's side. He was aroused by her snarling. Never had he heard her snarl so terribly. Possibly in her whole life it was the most terrible snarl she ever gave. There was reason for it, and none knew it better than she. A lynx's lair is not despoiled with impunity. In the full glare of the afternoon light, crouching in the entrance of the cave, the cub saw the lynx-mother. The hair rippled up all along his back at the sight. Here was fear, and it did not require his instinct to tell him of it. And if sight alone were not sufficient, the cry of rage the intruder gave, beginning with a snarl and rushing abruptly upward into a hoarse screech, was convincing enough in itself.

The cub felt the prod of the life that was in him, and stood up and snarled valiantly by his mother's side. But she thrust him ignominiously away and behind her. Because of the low-roofed entrance the lynx could not leap in, and when she made a crawling rush of it the she-wolf sprang upon her and pinned her down. The cub saw little of the battle. There was a tremendous snarling and spitting and screeching. The two animals threshed about, the lynx ripping and tearing with her claws and using her teeth as well, while the she-wolf used her teeth alone.

Once, the cub sprang in and sank his teeth into the hind leg of the lynx. He clung on, growling savagely. Though he did not know it, by the weight of his body he clogged the action of the leg and thereby saved his mother much damage. A change in the battle crushed him under both their bodies and wrenched loose his hold. The next moment the two mothers separated, and, before they rushed together again, the lynx lashed out at the cub with a huge fore-paw that ripped his shoulder open to the bone and sent him hurtling sidewise against the wall. Then was added to the uproar the cub's shrill yelp of pain and fright. But the fight lasted so long that he had time to cry himself out and to experience a second burst of courage; and the end of the battle found him again clinging to a hind-leg and furiously growling between his teeth.

The lynx was dead. But the she-wolf was very weak and sick. At first she caressed the cub and licked his wounded shoulder; but the blood she had lost had taken with it her strength, and for all of a day and a night she lay by her dead foe's side, without movement, scarcely breathing. For a week she never left the cave, except for water, and then her movements were slow and painful. At the end of that time the lynx was devoured, while the she-wolf's wounds had healed sufficiently to permit her to take the meat-trail again.

The cub's shoulder was stiff and sore, and for some time he limped from the terrible slash he had received. But the world now seemed changed. He went about in it with greater confidence, with a feeling of prowess that had not been his in the days before the battle with the lynx. He had looked upon life in a more ferocious aspect; he had fought; he had buried his teeth in the flesh of a foe; and he had survived. And because of all this, he carried himself more boldly, with a touch of defiance that was new in him. He was no longer afraid of minor things, and much of his timidity had vanished, though the unknown never ceased to press upon him with its mysteries and terrors, intangible and ever-menacing.

He began to accompany his mother on the meat-trail, and he saw much of the killing of meat and began to play his part in it. And in his own dim way he learned the law of meat. There were two kinds of life,—his own kind and the other kind. His own kind included his mother and himself. The other kind included all live things that moved. But the other kind was divided. One portion was what his own kind killed and ate. This portion was composed of the non-killers and the small killers. The other portion killed and ate his own kind, or was killed and eaten by his own kind. And out of this classification arose the law. The aim of life was meat. Life itself was meat. Life lived on life. There were the eaters and the eaten. The law was: EAT OR BE EATEN. He did not formulate the law in clear, set terms and moralize about it. He did not even think the law; he merely lived the law without thinking about it at all.

He saw the law operating around him on every side.

He had eaten the ptarmigan chicks. The hawk had eaten the ptarmigan-mother. The hawk would also have eaten him. Later, when he had grown more formidable, he wanted to eat the hawk. He had eaten the lynx kitten. The lynx-mother would have eaten him had she not herself been killed and eaten. And so it went. The law was being lived about him by all live things, and he himself was part and parcel of the law. He was a killer. His only food was meat, live meat, that ran away swiftly before him, or flew into the air, or climbed trees, or hid in the ground, or faced him and fought with him, or turned the tables and ran after him.

Had the cub thought in man-fashion, he might have epitomized life as a voracious appetite, and the world as a place wherein ranged a multitude of appetites, pursuing and being pursued, hunting and being hunted, eating and being eaten, all in blindness and confusion, with violence and disorder, a chaos of gluttony and slaughter, ruled over by chance, merciless, planless, endless.

But the cub did not think in man-fashion. He did not look at things with wide vision. He was single-purposed, and entertained but one thought or desire at a time. Besides the law of meat, there was a myriad other and lesser laws for him to learn and obey. The world was filled with surprise. The stir of the life that was in him, the play of his muscles, was an unending happiness. To run down meat was to experience thrills and elations. His rages and battles were pleasures. Terror itself, and the mystery of the unknown, lent to his living.

And there were easements and satisfactions. To have a full stomach, to doze lazily in the sunshine— such things were remuneration in full for his ardors and toils, while his ardors and toils were in themselves self-remunerative. They were expressions of life, and life is always happy when it is expressing itself. So the cub had no quarrel with his hostile environment. He was very much alive, very happy, and very proud of himself.

PART THREE: THE GODS OF THE WILD

❧

CHAPTER I

The Makers of Fire

The cub came upon it suddenly. It was his own fault. He had been careless. He had left the cave and run down to the stream to drink. It might have been that he took no notice because he was heavy with sleep. (He had been out all night on the meat-trail, and had but just then awakened.) And his carelessness might have been due to the familiarity of the trail to the pool. He had travelled it often, and nothing had ever happened on it.

He went down past the blasted pine, crossed the open space, and trotted in amongst the trees. Then, at the same instant, he saw and smelt. Before him, sitting silently on their haunches, were five live things, the like of which he had never seen before. It was his first glimpse of mankind. But at the sight of him the five men did not spring to their feet, nor show their teeth, nor snarl. They did not move, but sat there, silent and ominous.

Nor did the cub move. Every instinct of his nature would have impelled him to dash wildly away, had there not suddenly and for the first time arisen in him another and counter instinct. A great awe descended upon him. He was beaten down to movelessness by an overwhelming sense of his own weakness and littleness. Here was mastery and power, something far and away beyond him.

The cub had never seen man, yet the instinct concerning man was his. In dim ways he recognized in man the animal that had fought itself to primacy over the other animals of the Wild. Not alone out of his own eyes, but out of the eyes of all his ancestors was the cub now looking upon man—out of eyes that had circled in the darkness around countless winter campfires, that had peered from safe distances and from the hearts of thickets at the strange, two-legged animal that was lord over living things. The spell of the cub's heritage was upon him, the fear and the respect born of the centuries of struggle and the accumulated experience of the generations. The heritage was too compelling for a wolf that was only a cub. Had he been full-grown, he would have run away. As it was, he cowered down in a paralysis of fear, already half proffering the submission that his kind had proffered from the first time a wolf came in to sit by man's fire and be made warm.

One of the Indians arose and walked over to him and stooped above him. The cub cowered closer to the ground. It was the unknown, objectified at last, in concrete flesh and blood, bending over him and reaching down to seize hold of him. His hair bristled involuntarily; his lips writhed back and his little fangs were bared. The hand, poised like doom above him, hesitated, and the man spoke, laughing, *"Wabam wabisca ip pit tah."* ("Look! The white fangs!")

The other Indians laughed loudly, and urged the man on to pick up the cub. As the hand descended closer and closer, there raged within the cub a battle of the instincts. He experienced two great impulsions,— to yield and to fight. The resulting action was a compromise. He did both. He yielded till the hand almost touched him. Then he fought, his teeth flashing in a snap that sank them into the hand. The next moment he received a clout alongside the head that knocked him over on his side. Then all fight fled out of him. His puppyhood and the instinct of submission took charge of him. He sat up on his haunches and ki-yi'd. But the man whose hand he had bitten was angry. The cub received a clout on the other side of his head. Whereupon he sat up and ki-yi'd louder than ever.

The four Indians laughed more loudly, while even the man who had been bitten began to laugh. They surrounded the cub and laughed at him, while he wailed out his terror and his hurt. In the midst of it, he heard something. The Indians heard it, too. But the cub knew what it was, and with a last, long wail that had in it more of triumph than grief, he ceased his noise and waited for the coming of his mother, of his ferocious and indomitable mother who fought and killed all things and was never afraid. She was snarling as she ran. She had heard the cry of her cub and was dashing to save him.

She bounded in amongst them, her anxious and militant motherhood making her anything but a pretty sight. But to the cub the spectacle of her protective rage was pleasing. He uttered a glad little cry and bounded to meet her, while the man-animals went back hastily several steps. The she-wolf stood over against her cub, facing the men, with bristling hair, a snarl rumbling deep in her throat. Her face was distorted and malignant with menace, even the bridge of the nose wrinkling from tip to eyes so prodigious was her snarl.

Then it was that a cry went up from one of the men. "Kiche!" was what he uttered. It was an exclamation of surprise. The cub felt his mother wilting at the sound.

"Kiche!" the man cried again, this time with sharpness and authority.

And then the cub saw his mother, the she-wolf, the fearless one, crouching down till her belly touched the ground, whimpering, wagging her tail, making peace signs. The cub could not understand. He was appalled. The awe of man rushed over him again. His instinct had been true. His mother verified it. She, too, rendered submission to the man-animals.

The man who had spoken came over to her. He put his hand upon her head, and she only crouched closer. She did not snap, nor threaten to snap. The other men came up, and surrounded her, and felt her, and pawed her, which actions she made no attempt to resent. They were greatly excited, and made many noises with their mouths. These noises were not indications of danger, the cub decided, as he crouched near his mother, still bristling from time to time but doing his best to submit.

"It is not strange," an Indian was saying. "Her father was a wolf. It is true, her mother was a dog; but did not my brother tie her out in the woods all of three nights in the mating season? Therefore was the father of Kiche a wolf."

"It is a year, Gray Beaver, since she ran away," spoke a second Indian.

"It is not strange, Salmon Tongue," Gray Beaver answered. "It was the time of the famine, and there was no meat for the dogs."

"She has lived with the wolves," said a third Indian.

"So it would seem, Three Eagles," Gray Beaver answered, laying his hand on the cub; "and this be the sign of it."

The cub snarled a little at the touch of the hand, and the hand flew back to administer a clout. Whereupon the cub covered its fangs and sank down submissively, while the hand, returning, rubbed behind his ears, and up and down his back.

"This be the sign of it," Gray Beaver went on. "It is plain that his mother is Kiche. But his father was a wolf. Wherefore is there in him little dog and much wolf. His fangs be white, and White Fang shall be his name. I have spoken. He is my dog. For was not Kiche my brother's dog? And is not my brother dead?"

The cub, who had thus received a name in the

world, lay and watched. For a time the man-animals continued to make their mouth-noises. Then Gray Beaver took a knife from a sheath that hung around his neck, and went into the thicket and cut a stick. White Fang watched him. He notched the stick at each end and in the notches fastened strings of raw-hide. One string he tied around the throat of Kiche. Then he led her to a small pine, around which he tied the other string.

White Fang followed and lay down beside her. Salmon Tongue's hand reached out to him and rolled him over on his back. Kiche looked on anxiously. White Fang felt fear mounting in him again. He could not quite suppress a snarl, but he made no offer to snap. The hand, with fingers crooked and spread apart, rubbed his stomach in a playful way and rolled him from side to side. It was ridiculous and ungainly, lying there on his back with legs sprawling in the air. Besides, it was a position of such utter helplessness that White Fang's whole nature revolted against it. He could do nothing to defend himself. If this man-animal intended harm, White Fang knew that he could not escape it. How could he spring away with his four legs in the air above him? Yet submission made him master his fear, and he only growled softly. This growl he could not suppress; nor did the man-animal resent it by giving him a blow on the head. And furthermore, such was the strangeness of it, White Fang experienced an unaccountable sensation of pleasure as the hand rubbed back and forth. When he was rolled on his side he ceased the growl; when the fingers pressed and prodded at the base of his ears the pleasurable sensation increased; and when, with a final rub and scratch, the man left him alone and went away, all fear had died out of White Fang. He was to know fear many times in his dealings with man; yet it was a token of the fearless companionship with man that was ultimately to be his.

After a time, White Fang heard strange noises approaching. He was quick in his classification, for he knew them at once for man-animal noises. A few minutes later the remainder of the tribe, strung out as it was on the march, trailed in. There were more men and many women and children, forty souls of them, and all heavily burdened with camp equipage and outfit. Also there were many dogs; and these, with the exception of the part-grown puppies, were likewise burdened with camp outfit. On their backs, in bags that fastened tightly around underneath, the dogs carried from twenty to thirty pounds of weight.

White Fang had never seen dogs before, but at sight of them he felt that they were his own kind, only somehow different. But they displayed little difference from the wolf when they discovered the cub and his mother. There was a rush. White Fang bristled and snarled and snapped in the face of the open-mouthed oncoming wave of dogs, and went down and under them, feeling the sharp slash of teeth in his body, himself biting and tearing at the legs and bellies above him. There was a great uproar. He could hear the snarl of Kiche as she fought for him; and he could hear the cries of the man-animals, the sound of clubs striking upon bodies, and the yelps of pain from the dogs so struck.

Only a few seconds elapsed before he was on his feet again. He could now see the man-animals driving back the dogs with clubs and stones, defending him, saving him from the savage teeth of his kind that somehow was not his kind. And though there was no reason in his brain for a clear conception of so abstract a thing as justice, nevertheless, in his own way, he felt the justice of the man-animals, and he knew them for what they were—makers of law and executors of law. Also, he appreciated the power with which they administered the law. Unlike any animals he had ever encountered, they did not bite nor claw. They enforced their live strength with the power of dead things. Dead things did their bidding. Thus, sticks and stones, directed by these strange creatures, leaped through the air like living things, inflicting grievous hurts upon the dogs.

To his mind this was power unusual, power inconceivable and beyond the natural, power that was godlike. White Fang, in the very nature of him, could never know anything about gods; at the best he could know only things that were beyond knowing; but the wonder and awe that he had of these man-animals in ways resembled what would be the wonder and awe of man at sight of some celestial creature, on a mountain top, hurling thunderbolts from either hand at an astonished world.

The last dog had been driven back. The hubbub died down. And White Fang licked his hurts and meditated upon this, his first taste of pack-cruelty and his introduction to the pack. He had never dreamed that his own kind consisted of more than One Eye, his mother, and himself. They had constituted a kind apart, and here, abruptly, he had discovered many more creatures apparently of his own kind. And there was a subconscious resentment that these, his kind, at first sight had pitched upon him and tried to destroy him. In the same way he resented his mother being tied with a stick, even though it was done by the superior man-animals. It savored of the trap, of bondage. Yet of the trap and of bondage he knew nothing. Freedom to roam and run and lie down at will had been his heritage; and here it was being infringed upon. His mother's movements were restricted to the length of a stick, and by the length of that same stick was he restricted, for he had not yet got beyond the need of his mother's side.

He did not like it. Nor did he like it when the man-animals arose and went on with their march; for a tiny man-animal took the other end of the stick and led

Kiche captive behind him, and behind Kiche followed White Fang, greatly perturbed and worried by this new adventure he had entered upon.

They went down the valley of the stream, far beyond White Fang's widest ranging, until they came to the end of the valley, where the stream ran into the Mackenzie River. Here, where canoes were cached on poles high in the air and where stood fish-racks for the drying of fish, camp was made; and White Fang looked on with wondering eyes. The superiority of these man-animals increased with every moment. There was their mastery over all these sharp-fanged dogs. It breathed of power. But greater than that, to the wolf-cub, was their mastery over things not alive; their capacity to communicate motion to unmoving things; their capacity to change the very face of the world.

It was this last that especially affected him. The elevation of frames of poles caught his eye; yet this in itself was not so remarkable, being done by the same creatures that flung sticks and stones to great distances. But when the frames of poles were made into tepees by being covered with cloth and skins, White Fang was astounded. It was the colossal bulk of them that impressed him. They arose around him, on every side, like some monstrous quick-growing form of life. They occupied nearly the whole circumference of his field of vision. He was afraid of them. They loomed ominously above him; and when the breeze stirred them into huge movements, he cowered down in fear, keeping his eyes warily upon them, and prepared to spring away if they attempted to precipitate themselves upon him.

But in a short while his fear of the tepees passed away. He saw the women and children passing in and out of them without harm, and he saw the dogs trying often to get into them, and being driven away with sharp words and flying stones. After a time he left Kiche's side and crawled cautiously toward the wall of the nearest tepee. It was the curiosity of growth that urged him on—the necessity of learning and living and doing that brings experience. The last few inches to the wall of the tepee were crawled with painful slowness and precaution. The day's events had prepared him for the unknown to manifest itself in most stupendous and unthinkable ways. At last his nose touched the canvas. He waited. Nothing happened. Then he smelled the strange fabric, saturated with the man-smell. He closed on the canvas with his teeth and gave a gentle tug. Nothing happened, though the adjacent portions of the tepee moved. He tugged harder. There was a greater movement. It was delightful. He tugged still harder, and repeatedly, until the whole tepee was in motion. Then the sharp cry of a squaw inside sent him scampering back to Kiche. But after that he was afraid no more of the looming bulks of the tepees.

A moment later he was straying away again from his mother. Her stick was tied to a peg in the ground and she could not follow him. A part-grown puppy, somewhat larger and older than he, came toward him slowly, with ostentatious and belligerent importance. The puppy's name, as White Fang was afterward to hear him called, was Lip-lip. He had had experience in puppy fights and was already something of a bully.

Lip-lip was White Fang's own kind, and, being only a puppy, did not seem dangerous; so White Fang prepared to meet him in friendly spirit. But when the stranger's walk became stiff-legged and his lips lifted clear of his teeth, White Fang stiffened, too, and answered with lifted lips. They half circled about each other, tentatively, snarling and bristling. This lasted several minutes, and White Fang was beginning to enjoy it, as a sort of game. But suddenly, with remarkable swiftness, Lip-lip leaped in, delivered a slashing snap, and leaped away again. The snap had taken effect on the shoulder that had been hurt by the lynx and that was still sore deep down near the bone. The surprise and hurt of it brought a yelp out of White Fang; but the next moment, in a rush of anger, he was upon Lip-lip and snapping viciously.

But Lip-lip had lived his life in camp and had fought many puppy fights. Three times, four times, and half a dozen times, his sharp little teeth scored on the new-comer, until White Fang, yelping shamelessly, fled to the protection of his mother. It was the first of the many fights he was to have with Lip-lip, for they were enemies from the start, born so, with natures destined perpetually to clash.

Kiche licked White Fang soothingly with her tongue, and tried to prevail upon him to remain with her. But his curiosity was rampant, and several minutes later he was venturing forth on a new quest. He came upon one of the man-animals, Gray Beaver, who was squatting on his hams and doing something with sticks and dry moss spread before him on the ground. White Fang came near to him and watched. Gray Beaver made mouth-noises which White Fang interpreted as not hostile, so he came still nearer.

Women and children were carrying more sticks and branches to Gray Beaver. It was evidently an affair of moment. White Fang came in until he touched Gray Beaver's knee, so curious was he, and already forgetful that this was a terrible man-animal. Suddenly he saw a strange thing like mist beginning to arise from the sticks and moss beneath Gray Beaver's hands. Then, amongst the sticks themselves, appeared a live thing, twisting and turning, of a color like the color of the sun in the sky. White Fang knew nothing about fire. It drew him as the light in the mouth of the cave had drawn him in his early puppyhood. He crawled the sev-eral steps toward the flame. He heard Gray Beaver chuckle above him, and he knew the sound was not hostile. Then his nose touched the flame, and at the same instant his little tongue went out to it.

For a moment he was paralyzed. The unknown,

lurking in the midst of the sticks and moss, was savagely clutching him by the nose. He scrambled backward, bursting out in an astonished explosion of ki-yi's. At the sound, Kiche leaped snarling to the end of her stick, and there raged terribly because she could not come to his aid. But Gray Beaver laughed loudly, and slapped his thighs, and told the happening to all the rest of the camp, till everybody was laughing uproariously. But White Fang sat on his haunches and ki-yi'd and ki-yi'd, a forlorn and pitiable little figure in the midst of the man-animals.

It was the worst hurt he had ever known. Both nose and tongue had been scorched by the live thing, suncolored, that had grown up under Gray Beaver's hands. He cried and cried interminably, and every fresh wail was greeted by bursts of laughter on the part of the man-animals. He tried to soothe his nose with his tongue, but the tongue was burnt too, and the two hurts coming together produced greater hurt; whereupon he cried more hopelessly and helplessly than ever.

And then shame came to him. He knew laughter and the meaning of it. It is not given us to know how some animals know laughter, and know when they are being laughed at; but it was this same way that White Fang knew it. And he felt shame that the man-animals should be laughing at him. He turned and fled away, not from the hurt of the fire, but from the laughter that sank even deeper, and hurt in the spirit of him. And he fled to Kiche, raging at the end of her stick like an animal gone mad—to Kiche, the one creature in the world who was not laughing at him.

Twilight drew down and night came on, and White Fang lay by his mother's side. His nose and tongue still hurt, but he was perplexed by a greater trouble. He was homesick. He felt a vacancy in him, a need for the hush and quietude of the stream and the cave in the cliff. Life had become too populous. There were so many of the man-animals, men, women, and children, all making noises and irritations. And there were the dogs, ever squabbling and bickering, bursting into uproars and creating confusions. The restful loneliness of the only life he had known was gone. Here the very air was palpitant with life. It hummed and buzzed unceasingly. Continually changing its intensity and abruptly variant in pitch, it impinged on his nerves and senses, made him nervous and restless and worried him with a perpetual imminence of happening.

He watched the man-animals coming and going and moving about the camp. In fashion distantly resembling the way men look upon the gods they create, so looked White Fang upon the man-animals before him. They were superior creatures, of a verity, gods. To his dim comprehension they were as much wonderworkers as gods are to men. They were creatures of mastery, possessing all manner of unknown and impossible potencies, overlords of the alive and the not alive,—making obey that which moved, imparting movement to that which did not move, and making life, sun-colored and biting life, to grow out of dead moss and wood. They were fire-makers! They were gods!

CHAPTER II

The Bondage

The days were thronged with experience for White Fang. During the time that Kiche was tied by the stick, he ran about over all the camp, inquiring, investigating, learning. He quickly came to know much of the ways of the man-animals, but familiarity did not breed contempt. The more he came to know them, the more they vindicated their superiority, the more they displayed their mysterious powers, the greater loomed their god-likeness.

To man has been given the grief, often, of seeing his gods overthrown and his altars crumbling; but to the wolf and the wild dog that have come in to crouch at man's feet, this grief has never come. Unlike man, whose gods are of the unseen and the overguessed, vapors and mists of fancy eluding the garmenture of reality, wandering wraiths of desired goodness and power, intangible outcroppings of self into the realm of spirit—unlike man, the wolf and the wild dog that have come in to the fire find their gods in the living flesh, solid to the touch, occupying earth-space and requiring time for the accomplishment of their ends and their existence. No effort of faith is necessary to believe in such a god; no effort of will can possibly induce disbelief in such a god. There is no getting away from it. There it stands, on its two hind-legs, club in hand, immensely potential, passionate and wrathful and loving, god and mystery and power all wrapped up and around by flesh that bleeds when it is torn and that is good to eat like any flesh.

And so it was with White Fang. The man-animals were gods unmistakable and unescapable. As his mother, Kiche, had rendered her allegiance to them at the first cry of her name, so he was beginning to render his allegiance. He gave them the trail as a privilege indubitably theirs. When they walked, he got out of their way. When they called, he came. When they threatened, he cowered down. When they commanded him to go, he went away hurriedly. For behind any wish of theirs was power to enforce that wish, power that hurt, power that expressed itself in clouts and clubs, in flying stones and stinging lashes of whips.

He belonged to them as all dogs belonged to them. His actions were theirs to command. His body was theirs to maul, to stamp upon, to tolerate. Such was the lesson that was quickly borne in upon him. It came hard, going as it did, counter to much that was strong and dominant in his own nature; and, while he disliked it in the learning of it, unknown to himself he was learning to like it. It was a placing of his destiny in another's hands, a shifting of the responsibilities of existence. This in itself was compensation, for it is always easier to lean upon another than to stand alone.

But it did not all happen in a day, this giving over of himself, body and soul, to the man-animals. He could not immediately forego his wild heritage and his memories of the Wild. There were days when he crept to the edge of the forest and stood and listened to something calling him far and away. And always he returned, restless and uncomfortable, to whimper softly and wistfully at Kiche's side and to lick her face with eager, questioning tongue.

White Fang learned rapidly the ways of the camp.

He knew the injustice and greediness of the older dogs when meat or fish was thrown out to be eaten. He came to know that men were more just, children more cruel, and women more kindly and more likely to toss him a bit of meat or bone. And after two or three painful adventures with the mothers of part-grown puppies, he came into the knowledge that it was always good policy to let such mothers alone, to keep away from them as far as possible, and to avoid them when he saw them coming.

But the bane of his life was Lip-lip. Larger, older, and stronger, Lip-lip had selected White Fang for his special object of persecution. White Fang fought willingly enough, but he was outclassed. His enemy was too big. Lip-lip became a nightmare to him. Whenever he ventured away from his mother, the bully was sure to appear, trailing at his heels, snarling at him, picking upon him, and watchful of an opportunity, when no man-animal was near, to spring upon him and force a fight. As Lip-lip invariably won, he enjoyed it hugely. It became his chief delight in life, as it became White Fang's chief torment.

But the effect upon White Fang was not to cow him. Though he suffered most of the damage and was always defeated, his spirit remained unsubdued. Yet a bad effect was produced. He became malignant and morose. His temper had been savage by birth, but it became more savage under this unending persecution. The genial, playful, puppyish side of him found little expression. He never played and gambolled about with the other puppies of the camp. Lip-lip would not permit it. The moment White Fang appeared near them, Lip-lip was upon him, bullying and hectoring him, or fighting with him until he had driven him away.

The effect of all this was to rob White Fang of much of his puppyhood and to make him in his comportment older than his age. Denied the outlet, through play, of his energies, he recoiled upon himself and developed his mental processes. He became cunning; he had idle time in which to devote himself to thoughts of trickery. Prevented from obtaining his share of meat and fish when a general feed was given to the camp-dogs, he became a clever thief. He had to forage for himself, and he foraged well, though he was ofttimes a plague to the squaws in consequence. He learned to sneak about camp, to be crafty, to know what was going on everywhere, to see and to hear everything and to reason accordingly, and successfully to devise ways and means of avoiding his implacable persecutor.

It was early in the days of his persecution that he played his first really big crafty game and got therefrom his first taste of revenge. As Kiche, when with the wolves, had lured out to destruction dogs from the camps of men, so White Fang, in manner somewhat similar, lured Lip-lip into Kiche's avenging jaws. Retreating before Lip-lip, White Fang made an indirect flight that led in and out and around the various tepees of the camp. He was a good runner, swifter than any other puppy of his size, and swifter than Lip-lip. But he did not run his best in this chase. He barely held his own, one leap ahead of his pursuer.

Lip-lip, excited by the chase and by the persistent nearness of his victim, forgot caution and locality. When he remembered locality, it was too late. Dashing at top speed around a tepee, he ran full tilt into Kiche lying at the end of her stick. He gave one yelp of consternation, and then her punishing jaws closed upon him. She was tied, but he could not get away from her easily. She rolled him off his legs so that he could not run, while she repeatedly ripped and slashed him with her fangs.

When at last he succeeded in rolling clear of her, he crawled to his feet, badly dishevelled, hurt both in body and in spirit. His hair was standing out all over him in tufts where her teeth had mauled. He stood where he had arisen, opened his mouth, and broke out the long, heart-broken puppy wail. But even this he was not allowed to complete. In the middle of it, White Fang, rushing in, sank his teeth into Lip-lip's hind leg. There was no fight left in Lip-lip, and he ran away shamelessly, his victim hot on his heels and worrying him all the way back to his own tepee. Here the squaws came to his aid, and White Fang, transformed into a raging demon, was finally driven off only by a fusillade of stones.

Came the day when Gray Beaver, deciding that the liability of her running away was past, released Kiche. White Fang was delighted with his mother's freedom. He accompanied her joyfully about the camp; and, so long as he remained close by her side, Lip-lip kept a respectful distance. White Fang even bristled up to him and walked stiff-legged, but Lip-lip ignored the challenge. He was no fool himself, and whatever vengeance he desired to wreak, he could wait until he caught White Fang alone.

Later on that day, Kiche and White Fang strayed into the edge of the woods next to the camp. He had led his mother there, step by step, and now, when she stopped, he tried to inveigle her farther. The stream, the lair, and the quiet woods were calling to him, and he wanted her to come. He ran on a few steps, stopped, and looked back. She had not moved. He whined pleadingly, and scurried playfully in and out of the underbrush. He ran back to her, licked her face, and ran on again. And still she did not move. He stopped and regarded her, all of an intentness and eagerness, physically expressed, that slowly faded out of him as she turned her head and gazed back at the camp.

There was something calling to him out there in the open. His mother heard it, too. But she heard also that other and louder call, the call of the fire and of man— the call which it has been given alone of all animals to the wolf to answer, to the wolf and the wild-dog, who are brothers.

Kiche turned and slowly trotted back toward camp. Stronger than the physical restraint of the stick was the clutch of the camp upon her. Unseen and occultly, the gods still gripped with their power and would not let her go. White Fang sat down in the shadow of a birch and whimpered softly. There was a strong smell of pine, and subtle woods fragrances filled the air, reminding him of his old life of freedom before the days of his bondage. But he was still only a part-grown puppy, and stronger than the call either of man or of the Wild was the call of his mother. All the hours of his short life he had depended upon her. The time was yet to come for independence. So he arose and trotted forlornly back to camp, pausing once, and twice, to sit down and whimper and to listen to the call that still sounded in the depths of the forest.

In the Wild the time of a mother with her young is short; but under the dominion of man it is sometimes even shorter. Thus it was with White Fang. Gray Beaver was in the debt of Three Eagles. Three Eagles was going away on a trip up the Mackenzie to the Great Slave Lake. A strip of scarlet cloth, a bearskin, twenty cartridges, and Kiche, went to pay the debt. White Fang saw his mother taken aboard Three Eagles' canoe, and tried to follow her. A blow from Three Eagles knocked him backward to the land. The canoe shoved off. He sprang into the water and swam after it, deaf to the sharp cries of Gray Beaver to return. Even a man-animal, a god, White Fang ignored, such was the terror he was in of losing his mother.

But gods are accustomed to being obeyed, and Gray Beaver wrathfully launched a canoe in pursuit. When he overtook White Fang, he reached down and by the nape of the neck lifted him clear of the water. He did not deposit him at once in the bottom of the canoe. Holding him suspended with one hand, with the other hand he proceeded to give him a beating. And it *was* a beating. His hand was heavy. Every blow was shrewd to hurt; and he delivered a multitude of blows.

Impelled by the blows that rained upon him, now from this side, now from that, White Fang swung back and forth like an erratic and jerky pendulum. Varying were the emotions that surged through him. At first, he had known surprise. Then came a momentary fear, when he yelped several times to the impact of the hand. But this was quickly followed by anger. His free nature asserted itself, and he showed his teeth and snarled fearlessly in the face of the wrathful god. This but served to make the god more wrathful. The blows came faster, heavier, more shrewd to hurt.

Gray Beaver continued to beat. White Fang continued to snarl. But this could not last forever. One or the other must give over, and that one was White Fang. Fear surged through him again. For the first time he was being really man-handled. The occasional blows of sticks and stones he had previously experienced were as caresses compared with this. He broke down and began to cry and yelp. For a time each blow brought a yelp from him; but fear passed into terror, until finally his yelps were voiced in unbroken succession, unconnected with the rhythm of the punishment.

At last Gray Beaver withheld his hand. White Fang, hanging limply, continued to cry. This seemed to satisfy his master, who flung him down roughly in the bottom of the canoe. In the meantime the canoe had drifted down the stream. Gray Beaver picked up the paddle. White Fang was in his way. He spurned him savagely with his foot. In that moment White Fang's free nature flashed forth again, and he sank his teeth into the moccasined foot.

The beating that had gone before was as nothing compared with the beating he now received. Gray Beaver's wrath was terrible; likewise was White Fang's fright. Not only the hand, but the hard wooden paddle was used upon him; and he was bruised and sore in all his small body when he was again flung down in the canoe. Again, and this time with purpose, did Gray Beaver kick him. White Fang did not repeat his attack on the foot. He had learned another lesson of his bondage. Never, no matter what the circumstance, must he dare to bite the god who was lord and master over him; the body of the lord and master was sacred, not to be defiled by the teeth of such as he. That was evidently the crime of crimes, the one offence there was no condoning nor overlooking.

When the canoe touched the shore, White Fang lay whimpering and motionless, waiting the will of Gray Beaver. It was Gray Beaver's will that he should go ashore, for ashore he was flung, striking heavily on his side and hurting his bruises afresh. He crawled tremblingly to his feet and stood whimpering. Lip-lip, who had watched the whole proceeding from the bank, now rushed upon him, knocking him over and sinking his teeth into him. White Fang was too helpless to defend himself, and it would have gone hard with him had not Gray Beaver's foot shot out, lifting Lip-lip into the air with its violence so that he smashed down to earth a dozen feet away. This was the man-animal's justice; and even then, in his own pitiable plight, White Fang experienced a little grateful thrill. At Gray Beaver's heels he limped obediently through the village to the tepee. And so it came that White Fang learned that the right to punish was something the gods reserved for themselves and denied to the lesser creatures under them.

That night, when all was still, White Fang remembered his mother and sorrowed for her. He sorrowed too loudly and woke up Gray Beaver, who beat him. After that he mourned gently when the gods were around. But sometimes, straying off to the edge of the woods by himself, he gave vent to his grief, and cried it out with loud whimperings and wailings.

It was during this period that he might have hearkened to the memories of the lair and the stream and run back into the Wild. But the memory of his mother held him. As the hunting man-animals went out and came back, so she would come back to the village sometime. So he remained in his bondage waiting for her.

But it was not altogether an unhappy bondage. There was much to interest him. Something was always happening. There was no end to the strange things these gods did, and he was always curious to see. Besides, he was learning how to get along with Gray Beaver. Obedience, rigid, undeviating obedience, was what was expected of him; and in return he escaped beatings and his existence was tolerated.

Nay, Gray Beaver himself sometimes tossed him a piece of meat, and defended him against the other dogs in the eating of it. And such a piece of meat was of value. It was worth more, in some strange way, than a dozen pieces of meat from the hand of a squaw. Gray Beaver never petted nor caressed. Perhaps it was the weight of his hand, perhaps his justice, perhaps the sheer power of him, and perhaps it was all these things that influenced White Fang; for a certain tie of attachment was forming between him and his surly lord.

Insidiously, and by remote ways, as well as by the power of stick and stone and clout of hand, were the shackles of White Fang's bondage being riveted upon him. The qualities in his kind that in the beginning made it possible for them to come in to the fires of men, were qualities capable of development. They were developing in him, and the camp-life, replete with misery as it was, was secretly endearing itself to him all the time. But White Fang was unaware of it. He knew only grief for the loss of Kiche, hope for her return, and a hungry yearning for the free life that had been his.

CHAPTER III

The Outcast

Lip-lip continued so to darken his days that White Fang became wickeder and more ferocious than it was his natural right to be. Savageness was a part of his make-up, but the savageness thus developed exceeded his make-up. He acquired a reputation for wickedness amongst the man-animals themselves. Wherever there was trouble and uproar in camp, fighting and squabbling or the outcry of a squaw over a bit of stolen meat, they were sure to find White Fang mixed up in it and usually at the bottom of it. They did not bother to look after the causes of his conduct. They saw only the effects, and the effects were bad. He was a sneak and a thief, a mischief-maker, a fomenter of trouble; and irate squaws told him to his face, the while he eyed them alert and ready to dodge any quick-flung missile, that he was a wolf and worthless and bound to come to an evil end.

He found himself an outcast in the midst of the populous camp. All the young dogs followed Lip-lip's lead. There was a difference between White Fang and them. Perhaps they sensed his wild-wood breed, and instinctively felt for him the enmity that the domestic dog feels for the wolf. But be that as it may, they joined with Lip-lip in the persecution. And, once declared against him, they found good reason to continue declared against him. One and all, from time to time, they felt his teeth; and to his credit, he gave more than he received. Many of them he could whip in a single fight; but single fight was denied him. The beginning of such a fight was a signal for all the young dogs in camp to come running and pitch upon him.

Out of this pack-persecution he learned two important things: how to take care of himself in a mass-fight against him; and how, on a single dog, to inflict the greatest amount of damage in the briefest space of time. To keep one's feet in the midst of the hostile mass meant life, and this he learned well. He became catlike in his ability to stay on his feet. Even grown dogs might hurtle him backward or sideways with the impact of their heavy bodies; and backward or sideways he would go, in the air or sliding on the ground, but always with his legs under him and his feet downward to the mother earth.

When dogs fight, there are usually preliminaries to the actual combat—snarlings and bristlings and stiff-legged struttings. But White Fang learned to omit these preliminaries. Delay meant the coming against him of all the young dogs. He must do his work quickly and get away. So he learned to give no warning of his intention. He rushed in and snapped and slashed on the instant, without notice, before his foe could prepare to meet him. Thus he learned how to inflict quick and severe damage. Also he learned the value of surprise. A dog, taken off its guard, its shoulder slashed open or its ear ripped in ribbons before it knew what was happening, was a dog half whipped.

Furthermore, it was remarkably easy to overthrow a dog taken by surprise; while a dog, thus overthrown, invariably exposed for a moment the soft underside of its neck—the vulnerable point at which to strike for its life. White Fang knew this point. It was a knowledge bequeathed to him directly from the hunting generations of wolves. So it was that White Fang's method, when he took the offensive, was: first, to find a young dog alone; second, to surprise it and knock it off its feet; and third, to drive in with his teeth at the soft throat.

Being but partly grown, his jaws had not yet become large enough nor strong enough to make his throat-attack deadly; but many a young dog went around camp with a lacerated throat in token of White Fang's intention. And one day, catching one of his enemies alone on the edge of the woods, he managed, by repeatedly overthrowing him and attacking the throat, to cut the great vein and let out the life. There had been a great row that night. He had been observed, the news had been carried to the dead dog's master, the squaws remembered all the instances of the stolen meat, and Gray Beaver was beset by many angry voices. But he resolutely held the door of his tepee, inside which he had placed the culprit, and refused to permit the vengeance for which his tribespeople clamored.

White Fang became hated by man and dog. During this period of his development he never knew a moment's security. The tooth of every dog was against him, the hand of every man. He was greeted with snarls by his kind, with curses and stones by his gods. He lived tensely. He was always keyed up, alert for attack, wary of being attacked, with an eye for sudden and unexpected missiles, prepared to act precipitately and coolly, to leap in with a flash of teeth, or to leap away with a menacing snarl.

As for snarling, he could snarl more terribly than any dog, young or old, in camp. The intent of the snarl is to warn or frighten, and judgment is required to know when it should be used. White Fang knew how to make it and when to make it. Into his snarl he incorporated all that was vicious, malignant, and horrible. With nose serrulated by continuous spasms, hair bris-

tling in recurrent waves, tongue whipping out like a
red snake and whipping back again, ears flattened
down, eyes gleaming hatred, lips wrinkled back, and
fangs exposed and dripping, he could compel a pause
on the part of almost any assailant. A temporary pause,
when taken off his guard, gave him the vital moment in
which to think and determine his action. But often a
pause so gained lengthened out until it evolved into a
complete cessation from the attack. And before more
than one of the grown dogs White Fang's snarl enabled him to beat an honorable retreat.

An outcast himself from the pack of the part-grown
dogs, his sanguinary methods and remarkable efficiency made the pack pay for its persecution of him.
Not permitted himself to run with the pack, the curious state of affairs obtained that no member of the pack
could run outside the pack. White Fang would not
permit it. What of his bushwhacking and waylaying
tactics, the young dogs were afraid to run by themselves. With the exception of Lip-lip, they were compelled to bunch together for mutual protection against
the terrible enemy they had made. A puppy alone by
the river bank meant a puppy dead or a puppy that
aroused the camp with its shrill pain and terror as it
fled back from the wolf-cub that had waylaid it.

But White Fang's reprisals did not ease, even when
the young dogs had learned thoroughly that they must
stay together. He attacked them when he caught them
alone, and they attacked him when they were bunched.
The sight of him was sufficient to start them rushing
after him, at which times his swiftness usually carried
him into safety. But woe to the dog that outran his fellows in such pursuit! White Fang had learned to turn
suddenly upon the pursuer that was ahead of the pack
and thoroughly to rip him up before the pack could arrive. This occurred with great frequency, for, once in
full cry, the dogs were prone to forget themselves in

the excitement of the chase, while White Fang never forgot himself. Stealing backward glances as he ran, he was always ready to whirl around and down the over-zealous pursuer that outran his fellows.

Young dogs are bound to play, and out of the exigencies of the situation they realized their play in this mimic warfare. Thus it was that the hunt of White Fang became their chief game—a deadly game, withal, and at all times a serious game. He, on the other hand, being the fastest-footed, was unafraid to venture anywhere. During the period that he waited vainly for his mother to come back, he led the pack many a wild chase through the adjacent woods. But the pack invariably lost him. Its noise and outcry warned him of its presence, while he ran alone, velvet-footed, silently, a moving shadow among the trees after the manner of his father and mother before him. Further, he was more directly connected with the Wild than they; and he knew more of its secrets and stratagems. A favorite trick of his was to lose his trail in running water and then lie quietly in a near-by thicket while their baffled cries arose around him.

Hated by his kind and by mankind, indomitable, perpetually warred upon and himself waging perpetual war, his development was rapid and one-sided. This was no soil for kindliness and affection to blossom in. Of such things he had not the faintest glimmering. The code he learned was to obey the strong and to oppress the weak. Gray Beaver was a god, and strong. Therefore White Fang obeyed him. But the dog younger or smaller than himself was weak, a thing to be destroyed. His development was in the direction of power. In order to face the constant danger of hurt and even of destruction, his predatory and protective faculties were unduly developed. He became quicker of movement than the other dogs, swifter of foot, craftier, deadlier, more lithe, more lean with ironlike muscle and sinew, more enduring, more cruel, more ferocious, and more intelligent. He had to become all these things, else he would not have held his own nor survived the hostile environment in which he found himself.

CHAPTER IV

The Trail of the Gods

I n the fall of the year, when the days were shortening and the bite of the frost was coming into the air, White Fang got his chance for liberty. For several days there had been a great hubbub in the village. The summer camp was being dismantled, and the tribe, bag and baggage, was preparing to go off to the fall hunting. White Fang watched it all with eager eyes, and when the tepees began to come down and the canoes were loading at the bank, he understood. Already the canoes were departing, and some had disappeared down the river.

Quite deliberately he determined to stay behind. He waited his opportunity to slink out of camp to the woods. Here in the running stream where ice was beginning to form, he hid his trail. Then he crawled into the heart of a dense thicket and waited. The time passed by, and he slept intermittently for hours. Then he was aroused by Gray Beaver's voice calling him by name. There were other voices. White Fang could hear Gray Beaver's squaw taking part in the search, and Mit-sah, who was Gray Beaver's son.

White Fang trembled with fear, and though the impulse came to crawl out of his hiding-place, he resisted it. After a time the voices died away, and some time after that he crept out to enjoy the success of his undertaking. Darkness was coming on, and for a while he played about among the trees, pleasuring his freedom. Then, and quite suddenly, he became aware of loneliness. He sat down to consider, listening to the silence of the forest and perturbed by it. That nothing moved nor sounded, seemed ominous. He felt the lurking of danger, unseen and unguessed. He was suspicious of the looming bulks of the trees and of the dark shadows that might conceal all manner of perilous things.

Then it was cold. Here was no warm side of a tepee against which to snuggle. The frost was in his feet, and he kept lifting first one fore-foot and then the other. He curved his bushy tail around to cover them, and at the same time he saw a vision. There was nothing strange about it. Upon his inward sight was impressed a succession of memory-pictures. He saw the camp again, the tepees, and the blaze of the fires. He heard the shrill voices of the women, the gruff basses of the men, and the snarling of the dogs. He was hungry, and he remembered pieces of meat and fish that had been thrown him. Here was no meat, nothing but a threatening and inedible silence.

His bondage had softened him. Irresponsibility had weakened him. He had forgotten how to shift for himself. The night yawned about him. His senses, accustomed to the hum and bustle of the camp, used to the continuous impact of sights and sounds, were now left idle. There was nothing to do, nothing to see nor hear. They strained to catch some interruption of the silence and immobility of nature. They were appalled by inaction and by the feel of something terrible impending.

He gave a great start of fright. A colossal and formless something was rushing across the field of his vision. It was a tree-shadow flung by the moon, from whose face the clouds had been brushed away. Reassured, he whimpered softly; then he suppressed the whimper for fear that it might attract the attention of the lurking dangers.

A tree, contracting in the cool of the night, made a loud noise. It was directly above him. He yelped in his fright. A panic seized him, and he ran madly toward the village. He knew an overpowering desire for the protection and companionship of man. In his nostrils was the smell of the camp-smoke. In his ears the camp sounds and cries were ringing loud. He passed out of the forest and into the moonlit open where were no shadows nor darknesses. But no village greeted his eyes. He had forgotten. The village had gone away.

His wild flight ceased abruptly. There was no place to which to flee. He slunk forlornly through the deserted camp, smelling the rubbish-heaps and the discarded rags and tags of the gods. He would have been glad for the rattle of the stones about him, flung by an angry squaw, glad for the hand of Gray Beaver descending upon him in wrath; while he would have welcomed with delight Lip-lip and the whole snarling, cowardly pack.

He came to where Gray Beaver's tepee had stood. In the centre of the space it had occupied, he sat down. He pointed his nose at the moon. His throat was afflicted with rigid spasms, his mouth opened, and in a heart-broken cry bubbled up his loneliness and fear, his grief for Kiche, all his past sorrows and miseries as well as his apprehension of sufferings and dangers to come. It was the long wolf-howl, full-throated and mournful, the first howl he had ever uttered.

The coming of daylight dispelled his fears, but increased his loneliness. The naked earth, which so shortly before had been so populous, thrust his loneliness more forcibly upon him. It did not take him long to make up his mind. He plunged into the forest and followed the river bank down the stream. All day he ran. He did not rest. He seemed made to run on forever. His ironlike body ignored fatigue. And even after fatigue came, his heritage of endurance braced him to endless endeavor and enabled him to drive his complaining body onward.

Where the river swung in against precipitous bluffs, he climbed the high mountains behind. Rivers and streams that entered the main river he forded or swam. Often he took to the rim-ice that was beginning to form, and more than once he crashed through and struggled for life in the icy current. Always he was on the lookout for the trail of the gods where it might leave the river and proceed inland.

White Fang was intelligent beyond the average of his kind; yet his mental vision was not wide enough to embrace the other bank of the Mackenzie. What if the trail of the gods led out on that side? It never entered his head. Later on, when he had travelled more and grown older and wiser and come to know more of trails and rivers, it might be that he could grasp and apprehend such a possibility. But that mental power was yet in the future. Just now he ran blindly, his own bank of the Mackenzie alone entering into his calculations.

All night he ran, blundering in the darkness into mishaps and obstacles that delayed but did not daunt. By the middle of the second day he had been running continuously for thirty hours, and the iron of his flesh was giving out. It was the endurance of his mind that kept him going. He had not eaten in forty hours, and he was weak with hunger. The repeated drenchings in the icy water had likewise had their effect on him. His handsome coat was draggled. The broad pads of his feet were bruised and bleeding. He had begun to limp and this limp increased with the hours. To make it worse, the light of the sky was obscured and snow began to fall—a raw, moist, melting, clinging snow, slippery under foot, that hid him from the landscape he traversed, and that covered over the inequalities of the ground so that the way of his feet was more difficult and painful.

Gray Beaver had intended camping that night on the far bank of the Mackenzie, for it was in that direction that the hunting lay. But on the near bank, shortly before dark, a moose, coming down to drink, had been espied by Kloo-kooch, who was Gray Beaver's squaw. Now, had not the moose come down to drink, had not Mit-sah been steering out of the course because of the snow, had not Kloo-kooch sighted the moose, and had not Gray Beaver killed it with a lucky shot from his rifle, all subsequent things would have happened differently. Gray Beaver would not have camped on the near side of the Mackenzie, and White Fang would have passed by and gone on, either to die or to find his way to his wild brothers and become one of them,—a wolf to the end of his days.

Night had fallen. The snow was flying more thickly, and White Fang, whimpering softly to himself as he stumbled and limped along, came upon a fresh trail in the snow. So fresh was it that he knew it immediately for what it was. Whining with eagerness, he followed back from the river bank and in among the trees. The camp-sounds came to his ears. He saw the blaze of the fire, Kloo-kooch cooking, and Gray Beaver squatting on his hams and mumbling a chunk of raw tallow. There was fresh meat in camp!

White Fang expected a beating. He crouched and bristled a little at the thought of it. Then he went forward again. He feared and disliked the beating he knew to be waiting for him. But he knew, further, that the comfort of the fire would be his, the protection of the gods, the companionship of the dogs—the last, a companionship of enmity, but nonetheless a companionship and satisfying to his gregarious needs.

He came cringing and crawling into the firelight. Gray Beaver saw him, and stopped munching his tallow. White Fang crawled slowly, cringing and grovelling in the abjectness of his abasement and submission.

He crawled straight toward Gray Beaver, every inch of his progress becoming slower and more painful. At last he lay at the master's feet, into whose possession he now surrendered himself, voluntarily, body and soul. Of his own choice, he came in to sit by man's fire and to be ruled by him. White Fang trembled, waiting for the punishment to fall upon him. There was a movement of the hand above him. He cringed involuntarily under the expected blow. It did not fall. He stole a glance upward. Gray Beaver was breaking the lump of tallow in half! Gray Beaver was offering him one piece of the tallow! Very gently and somewhat suspiciously, he first smelled the tallow and then proceeded to eat it. Gray Beaver ordered meat to be brought to him, and guarded him from the other dogs while he ate. After that, grateful and content, White Fang lay at Gray Beaver's feet, gazing at the fire that warmed him, blinking and dozing, secure in the knowledge that the morrow would find him, not wandering forlorn through bleak forest-stretches, but in the camp of the man-animals, with the gods to whom he had given himself and upon whom he was now dependent.

CHAPTER V

The Covenant

When December was well along, Gray Beaver went on a journey up the Mackenzie. Mit-sah and Kloo-kooch went with him. One sled he drove himself, drawn by dogs he had traded for or borrowed. A second and smaller sled was driven by Mit-sah, and to this was harnessed a team of puppies. It was more of a toy affair than anything else, yet it was the delight of Mit-sah, who felt that he was beginning to do a man's work in the world. Also, he was learning to drive dogs and to train dogs; while the puppies themselves were being broken in to the harness. Furthermore, the sled was of some service, for it carried nearly two hundred pounds of outfit and food.

White Fang had seen the camp-dogs toiling in the harness, so that he did not resent overmuch the first placing of the harness upon himself. About his neck was put a moss-stuffed collar, which was connected by two pulling-traces to a strap that passed around his chest and over his back. It was to this that was fastened the long rope by which he pulled at the sled.

There were seven puppies in the team. The others had been born earlier in the year and were nine and ten months old, while White Fang was only eight months old. Each dog was fastened to the sled by a single rope. No two ropes were of the same length, while the differ-

ence in length between any two ropes was at least that
of a dog's body. Every rope was brought to a ring at
the front end of the sled. The sled itself was without
runners, being a birch-bark toboggan, with upturned
forward end to keep it from ploughing under the snow.
This construction enabled the weight of the sled and
load to be distributed over the largest snow-surface; for
the snow was crystal-powder and very soft. Observing
the same principle of widest distribution of weight, the
dogs at the ends of their ropes radiated fan-fashion
from the nose of the sled, so that no dog trod in another's footsteps.

There was, furthermore, another virtue in the fan-
formation. The ropes of varying length prevented the
dogs' attacking from the rear those that ran in front of
them. For a dog to attack another, it would have to
turn upon one at a shorter rope. In which case it would
find itself face to face with the dog attacked, and also it
would find itself facing the whip of the driver. But the
most peculiar virtue of all lay in the fact that the dog
that strove to attack one in front of him must pull the
sled faster, and that the faster the sled travelled, the
faster could the dog attacked run away. Thus the dog
behind could never catch up with the one in front. The
faster he ran, the faster ran the one he was after, and
the faster ran all the dogs. Incidentally, the sled went
faster, and thus, by cunning indirection, did man increase his mastery over the beasts.

Mit-sah resembled his father, much of whose gray
wisdom he possessed. In the past he had observed Lip-
lip's persecution of White Fang; but at that time Lip-
lip was another man's dog, and Mit-sah had never
dared more than to shy an occasional stone at him. But
now Lip-lip was his dog, and he proceeded to wreak his
vengeance upon him by putting him at the end of the
longest rope. This made Lip-lip the leader, and was
apparently an honor; but in reality it took away from

him all honor, and instead of being bully and master of the pack, he now found himself hated and persecuted by the pack.

Because he ran at the end of the longest rope, the dogs had always the view of him running away before them. All that they saw of him was his bushy tail and fleeing hind legs—a view far less ferocious and intimidating than his bristling mane and gleaming fangs. Also, dogs being so constituted in their mental ways, the sight of him running away gave desire to run after him and a feeling that he ran away from them.

The moment the sled started, the team took after Lip-lip in a chase that extended throughout the day. At first he had been prone to turn upon his pursuers, jealous of his dignity and wrathful; but at such times Mit-sah would throw the stinging lash of the thirty-foot cariboo-gut whip into his face and compel him to turn tail and run on. Lip-lip might face the pack, but he could not face that whip, and all that was left him to do was to keep his long rope taut and his flanks ahead of the teeth of his mates.

But a still greater cunning lurked in the recesses of the Indian mind. To give point to unending pursuit of the leader, Mit-sah favored him over the other dogs. These favors aroused in them jealousy and hatred. In their presence Mit-sah would give him meat and would give it to him only. This was maddening to them. They would rage around just outside the throwing distance of the whip, while Lip-lip devoured the meat and Mit-sah protected him. And when there was no meat to give, Mit-sah would keep the team at a distance and make believe to give meat to Lip-lip.

White Fang took kindly to the work. He had travelled a greater distance than the other dogs in the yielding of himself to the rule of the gods, and he had learned more thoroughly the futility of opposing their will. In addition, the persecution he had suffered from the pack had made the pack less to him in the scheme of things, and man more. He had not learned to be dependent on his kind for companionship. Besides, Kiche was well-nigh forgotten; and the chief outlet of expression that remained to him was in the allegiance he tendered the gods he had accepted as masters. So he worked hard, learned discipline, and was obedient. Faithfulness and willingness characterized his toil. These are essential traits of the wolf and the wild-dog when they have become domesticated, and these traits White Fang possessed in unusual measure.

A companionship did exist between White Fang and the other dogs, but it was one of warfare and enmity. He had never learned to play with them. He knew only how to fight, and fight with them he did, returning to them a hundred-fold the snaps and slashes they had given him in the days when Lip-lip was leader of the pack. But Lip-lip was no longer leader—except when he fled away before his mates at the end of his rope, the sled bounding along behind. In camp he kept close to Mit-sah or Gray Beaver or Kloo-kooch. He did not dare venture away from the gods, for now the fangs of all dogs were against him, and he tasted to the dregs the persecution that had been White Fang's.

With the overthrow of Lip-lip, White Fang could have become leader of the pack. But he was too morose and solitary for that. He merely thrashed his teammates. Otherwise he ignored them. They got out of his way when he came along; nor did the boldest of them ever dare to rob him of his meat. On the contrary, they devoured their own meat hurriedly, for fear that he would take it away from them. White Fang knew the law well: *to oppress the weak and obey the strong.* He ate his share of meat as rapidly as he could. And then woe the dog that had not yet finished! A snarl and a flash of fangs, and that dog would wail his indignation to the uncomforting stars while White Fang finished his portion for him.

Every little while, however, one dog or another would flame up in revolt and be promptly subdued. Thus White Fang was kept in training. He was jealous of the isolation in which he kept himself in the midst of the pack, and he fought often to maintain it. But such fights were of brief duration. He was too quick for the others. They were slashed open and bleeding before they knew what had happened, were whipped almost before they had begun to fight.

As rigid as the sled-discipline of the gods, was the discipline maintained by White Fang amongst his fellows. He never allowed them any latitude. He compelled them to an unremitting respect for him. They might do as they pleased amongst themselves. That was no concern of his. But it *was* his concern that they leave him alone in his isolation, get out of his way when he elected to walk among them, and at all times acknowledge his mastery over them. A hint of stiff-leggedness on their part, a lifted lip or a bristle of hair, and he would be upon them, merciless and cruel, swiftly convincing them of the error of their way.

He was a monstrous tyrant. His mastery was rigid as steel. He oppressed the weak with a vengeance. Not for nothing had he been exposed to the pitiless struggle for life in the days of his cubhood, when his mother and he, alone and unaided, held their own and survived in the ferocious environment of the Wild. And not for nothing had he learned to walk softly when superior strength went by. He oppressed the weak, but he respected the strong. And in the course of the long journey with Gray Beaver he walked softly indeed amongst the full-grown dogs in the camps of the strange man-animals they encountered.

The months passed by. Still continued the journey of Gray Beaver. White Fang's strength was developed by the long hours on the trail and the steady toil at the sled; and it would have seemed that his mental development was well-nigh complete. He had come to know quite thoroughly the world in which he lived. His outlook was bleak and materialistic. The world as he saw it was a fierce and brutal world, a world without warmth, a world in which caresses and affection and the bright sweetnesses of the spirit did not exist.

He had no affection for Gray Beaver. True, he was a god, but a most savage god. White Fang was glad to acknowledge his lordship, but it was a lordship based upon superior intelligence and brute strength. There was something in the fibre of White Fang's being that made this lordship a thing to be desired, else he would not have come back from the Wild when he did to tender his allegiance. There were deeps in his nature which had never been sounded. A kind word, a caressing touch of the hand, on the part of Gray Beaver, might have sounded these deeps; but Gray Beaver did not caress nor speak kind words. It was not his way. His primacy was savage, and savagely he ruled, administering justice with a club, punishing transgression with the pain of a blow, and rewarding merit, not by kindness, but by withholding a blow.

So White Fang knew nothing of the heaven a man's hand might contain for him. Besides, he did not like the hands of the man-animals. He was suspicious of them. It was true that they sometimes gave meat, but more often they gave hurt. Hands were things to keep away from. They hurled stones, wielded sticks and clubs and whips, administered slaps and clouts, and, when they touched him, were cunning to hurt with pinch and twist and wrench. In strange villages he had encountered the hands of the children and learned that they were cruel to hurt. Also, he had once nearly had an eye poked out by a toddling papoose. From these experiences he became suspicious of all children. He could not tolerate them. When they came near with their ominous hands, he got up.

It was in a village at Great Slave Lake, that, in the

course of resenting the evil of the hands of the man-animals, he came to modify the law that he had learned from Gray Beaver; namely, that the unpardonable crime was to bite one of the gods. In this village, after the custom of all dogs in all villages, White Fang went foraging for food. A boy was chopping frozen moose-meat with an axe, and the chips were flying in the snow. White Fang, sliding by in quest of meat, stopped and began to eat the chips. He observed the boy lay down the axe and take up a stout club. White Fang sprang clear, just in time to escape the descending blow. The boy pursued him, and he, a stranger in the village, fled between two tepees, to find himself cornered against a high earth bank.

There was no escape for White Fang. The only way out was between the two tepees, and this the boy guarded. Holding the club prepared to strike, he drew in on his cornered quarry. White Fang was furious. He faced the boy, bristling and snarling, his sense of justice outraged. He knew the law of forage. All the wastage of meat, such as the frozen chips, belonged to the dog that found it. He had done no wrong, broken no law, yet here was this boy preparing to give him a beating. White Fang scarcely knew what happened. He did it in a surge of rage. And he did it so quickly that the boy did not know, either. All the boy knew was that he had in some unaccountable way been overturned into the snow, and that his club-hand had been ripped wide open by White Fang's teeth.

But White Fang knew that he had broken the law of the gods. He had driven his teeth into the sacred flesh of one of them, and could expect nothing but a most terrible punishment. He fled away to Gray Beaver, behind whose protecting legs he crouched when the bitten boy and the boy's family came, demanding vengeance. But they went away with vengeance unsatisfied. Gray Beaver defended White Fang. So did Mit-sah and Kloo-kooch. White Fang, listening to the wordy war and watching the angry gestures, knew that his act was justified. And so it came that he learned there were gods and gods. There were his gods, and there were other gods, and between them there was a difference. Justice or injustice, it was all the same, he must take all things from the hands of his own gods. But he was not compelled to take injustice from the other gods. It was his privilege to resent it with his teeth. And this also was a law of the gods.

Before the day was out, White Fang was to learn more about this law. Mit-sah, alone, gathering fire-wood in the forest, encountered the boy that had been bitten. With him were other boys. Hot words passed. Then all the boys attacked Mit-sah. It was going hard with him. Blows were raining upon him from all sides. White Fang looked on at first. This was an affair of the gods, and no concern of his. Then he realized that this was Mit-sah, one of his own particular gods, who was being maltreated. It was no reasoned impulse that made White Fang do what he then did. A mad rush of anger sent him leaping in amongst the combatants. Five minutes later the landscape was covered with flee-ing boys, many of whom dripped blood upon the snow in token that White Fang's teeth had not been idle. When Mit-sah told his story in camp, Gray Beaver ordered meat to be given to White Fang. He ordered much meat to be given, and White Fang, gorged and sleepy by the fire, knew that the law had received its verification.

It was in line with these experiences that White Fang came to learn the law of property and the duty of the defence of property. From the protection of his god's body to the protection of his god's possessions was a step, and this step he made. What was his god's was to be defended against all the world—even to the extent of biting other gods. Not only was such an act sacrilegious in its nature, but it was fraught with peril. The gods were all-powerful, and a dog was no match against them; yet White Fang learned to face them, fiercely belligerent and unafraid. Duty rose above fear, and thieving gods learned to leave Gray Beaver's property alone.

One thing, in this connection, White Fang quickly learned, and that was that a thieving god was usually a cowardly god and prone to run away at the sounding of the alarm. Also, he learned that but brief time elapsed between his sounding of the alarm and Gray Beaver's coming to his aid. He came to know that it was not fear of him that drove the thief away, but fear of Gray Beaver. White Fang did not give the alarm by barking. He never barked. His method was to drive straight at the intruder, and to sink his teeth in if he could. Because he was morose and solitary, having nothing to do with the other dogs, he was unusually fitted to guard his master's property; and in this he was encouraged and trained by Gray Beaver. One result of this was to make White Fang more ferocious and indomitable, and more solitary.

The months went by, binding stronger and stronger the covenant between dog and man. This was the ancient covenant that the first wolf that came in from the Wild entered into with man. And, like all succeeding wolves, and wild dogs that had done likewise, White Fang worked the covenant out for himself. The terms were simple. For the possession of a flesh-and-blood god, he exchanged his own liberty. Food and fire, protection and companionship, were some of the things he received from the god. In return, he guarded the god's property, defended his body, worked for him, and obeyed him.

The possession of a god implies service. White Fang's was a service of duty and awe, but not of love. He did not know what love was. He had no experience of love. Kiche was a remote memory. Besides, not only had he abandoned the Wild and his kind when he gave himself up to man, but the terms of the covenant were such that if he ever met Kiche again he would not desert his god to go with her. His allegiance to man seemed somehow a law of his being greater than the love of liberty, of kind and kin.

CHAPTER VI

The Famine

The spring of the year was at hand when Gray Beaver finished his long journey. It was April, and White Fang was a year old when he pulled into the home village and was loosed from the harness by Mitsah. Though a long way from his full growth, White Fang, next to Lip-lip, was the largest yearling in the village. Both from his father, the wolf, and from Kiche, he had inherited stature and strength, and already he was measuring up alongside the full-grown dogs. But he had not yet grown compact. His body was slender and rangy, and his strength more stringy than massive. His coat was the true wolf-gray, and to all appearances he was true wolf himself. The quarter-strain of dog he had inherited from Kiche had left no mark on him physically, though it played its part in his mental make-up.

He wandered through the village, recognizing with staid satisfaction the various gods he had known before the long journey. Then there were the dogs, puppies growing up like himself, and grown dogs that did not look so large and formidable as the memory-pictures he retained of them. Also, he stood less in fear of them than formerly, stalking among them with a certain careless ease that was as new to him as it was enjoyable.

There was Baseek, a grizzled old fellow that in his

younger days had but to uncover his fangs to send
White Fang cringing and crouching to the right-about.
From him White Fang had learned much of his own
insignificance; and from him he was now to learn much
of the change and development that had taken place in
himself. While Baseek had been growing weaker with
age, White Fang had been growing stronger with
youth.

It was at the cutting-up of a moose, fresh-killed, that
White Fang learned of the changed relations in which
he stood to the dog-world. He had got for himself a
hoof and part of the shin-bone, to which quite a bit of
meat was attached. Withdrawn from the immediate
scramble of the other dogs,—in fact, out of sight behind a thicket,—he was devouring his prize, when Baseek rushed in upon him. Before he knew what he was
doing, he had slashed the intruder twice and sprung
clear. Baseek was surprised by the other's temerity and
swiftness of attack. He stood, gazing stupidly across at
White Fang, the raw, red shin-bone between them.

Baseek was old, and already he had come to know
the increasing valor of the dogs it had been his wont to
bully. Bitter experiences these, which, perforce, he
swallowed, calling upon all his wisdom to cope with
them. In the old days, he would have sprung upon
White Fang in a fury of righteous wrath. But now his
waning powers would not permit such a course. He
bristled fiercely and looked ominously across the shin-
bone at White Fang. And White Fang, resurrecting
quite a deal of the old awe, seemed to wilt and to shrink
in upon himself and grow small, as he cast about in his
mind for a way to beat a retreat not too inglorious.

And right here Baseek erred. Had he contented
himself with looking fierce and ominous, all would have
been well. White Fang, on the verge of retreat, would
have retreated, leaving the meat to him. But Baseek
did not wait. He considered the victory already his and

stepped forward to the meat. As he bent his head carelessly to smell it, White Fang bristled slightly. Even then it was not too late for Baseek to retrieve the situation. Had he merely stood over the meat, head up and glowering, White Fang would ultimately have slunk away. But the fresh meat was strong in Baseek's nostrils, and greed urged him to take a bite of it.

This was too much for White Fang. Fresh upon his months of mastery over his own team-mates, it was beyond his self-control to stand idly by while another devoured the meat that belonged to him. He struck, after his custom, without warning. With the first slash, Baseek's right ear was ripped into ribbons. He was astounded at the suddenness of it. But more things, and most grievous ones, were happening with equal suddenness. He was knocked off his feet. His throat was bitten. While he was struggling to his feet the young dog sank teeth twice into his shoulder. The swiftness of it was bewildering. He made a futile rush at White Fang, clipping the empty air with an outraged snap. The next moment his nose was laid open and he was staggering backward away from the meat.

The situation was now reversed. White Fang stood over the shin-bone, bristling and menacing, while Baseek stood a little way off, preparing to retreat. He dared not risk a fight with this young lightning-flash, and again he knew, and more bitterly, the enfeeblement of oncoming age. His attempt to maintain his dignity was heroic. Calmly turning his back upon young dog and shin-bone, as though both were beneath his notice and unworthy of consideration, he stalked grandly away. Nor, until well out of sight, did he stop to lick his bleeding wounds.

The effect on White Fang was to give him a greater faith in himself, and a greater pride. He walked less softly among the grown dogs; his attitude toward them was less compromising. Not that he went out of his way looking for trouble. Far from it. But upon his way he demanded consideration. He stood upon his right to go his way unmolested and to give trail to no dog. He had to be taken into account, that was all. He was no longer to be disregarded and ignored, as was the lot of puppies and as continued to be the lot of the puppies that were his team-mates. They got out of the way, gave trail to the grown dogs, and gave up meat to them under compulsion. But White Fang, uncompanionable, solitary, morose, scarcely looking to right or left, re-doubtable, forbidding of aspect, remote and alien, was accepted as an equal by his puzzled elders. They quickly learned to leave him alone, neither venturing hostile acts nor making overtures of friendliness. If they left him alone, he left them alone—a state of af-fairs that they found, after a few encounters, to be preëminently desirable.

In midsummer White Fang had an experience. Trotting along in his silent way to investigate a new tepee which had been erected on the edge of the village while he was away with the hunters after moose, he came full upon Kiche. He paused and looked at her. He remembered her vaguely, but he *remembered* her, and that was more than could be said for her. She lifted her lip at him in the old snarl of menace, and his memory became clear. His forgotten cubhood, all that was asso-ciated with that familiar snarl, rushed back to him. Be-fore he had known the gods, she had been to him the centre-pin of the universe. The old familiar feelings of that time came back upon him, surged up within him. He bounded toward her joyously, and she met him with shrewd fangs that laid his cheek open to the bone. He did not understand. He backed away, bewildered and puzzled.

But it was not Kiche's fault. A wolf-mother was not made to remember her cubs of a year or so before. So she did not remember White Fang. He was a strange animal, an intruder; and her present litter of puppies gave her the right to resent such intrusion.

One of the puppies sprawled up to White Fang. They were half-brothers, only they did not know it. White Fang sniffed the puppy curiously, whereupon Kiche rushed upon him, gashing his face a second time. He backed farther away. All the old memories and associations died down again and passed into the grave from which they had been resurrected. He looked at Kiche licking her puppy and stopping now and then to snarl at him. She was without value to him. He had learned to get along without her. Her meaning was forgotten. There was no place for her in his scheme of things, as there was no place for him in hers.

He was still standing, stupid and bewildered, the memories forgotten, wondering what it was all about, when Kiche attacked him a third time, intent on driving him away altogether from the vicinity. And White Fang allowed himself to be driven away. This was a female of his kind, and it was a law of his kind that the males must not fight the females. He did not know anything about this law, for it was no generalization of the mind, not a something acquired by experience in the world. He knew it as a secret prompting, as an urge of instinct—of the same instinct that made him howl at the moon and stars of nights and that made him fear death and the unknown.

The months went by. White Fang grew stronger, heavier, and more compact, while his character was developing along the lines laid down by his heredity and his environment. His heredity was a life-stuff that may be likened to clay. It possessed many possibilities, was capable of being moulded into many different forms. Environment served to model the clay, to give it a particular form. Thus, had White Fang never come in to the fires of man, the Wild would have moulded him into a true wolf. But the gods had given him a different environment, and he was moulded into a dog that was rather wolfish, but that was a dog and not a wolf.

And so, according to the clay of his nature and the pressure of his surroundings, his character was being moulded into a certain particular shape. There was no escaping it. He was becoming more morose, more uncompanionable, more solitary, more ferocious; while the dogs were learning more and more that it was better to be at peace with him than at war, and Gray Beaver was coming to prize him more greatly with the passage of each day.

White Fang, seeming to sum up strength in all his qualities, nevertheless suffered from one besetting weakness. He could not stand being laughed at. The laughter of men was a hateful thing. They might laugh among themselves about anything they pleased except himself, and he did not mind. But the moment laughter was turned upon him he would fly into a most terrible rage. Grave, dignified, sombre, a laugh made him frantic to ridiculousness. It so outraged him and upset him that for hours he would behave like a demon. And woe to the dog that at such times ran foul of him. He knew the law too well to take it out on Gray Beaver; behind Gray Beaver were a club and a god-head. But behind the dogs there was nothing but space, and into this space they fled when White Fang came on the scene, made mad by laughter.

In the third year of his life there came a great famine to the Mackenzie Indians. In the summer the fish failed. In the winter the cariboo forsook their accustomed track. Moose were scarce, the rabbits almost disappeared, hunting and preying animals perished. Denied their usual food-supply, weakened by hunger, they fell upon and devoured one another. Only the strong survived. White Fang's gods were also hunting animals. The old and the weak of them died of hunger. There was wailing in the village, where the women and children went without in order that what little they had might go into the bellies of the lean and hollow-eyed hunters who trod the forest in the vain pursuit of meat.

To such extremity were the gods driven that they ate the soft-tanned leather of their moccasins and mittens, while the dogs ate the harnesses off their backs and the very whip-lashes. Also, the dogs ate one another, and also the gods ate the dogs. The weakest and the more worthless were eaten first. The dogs that still lived, looked on and understood. A few of the boldest and wisest forsook the fires of the gods, which had now become a shambles, and fled into the forest, where, in the end, they starved to death or were eaten by wolves.

In this time of misery, White Fang, too, stole away into the woods. He was better fitted for the life than the other dogs, for he had the training of his cubhood to guide him. Especially adept did he become in stalking small living things. He would lie concealed for hours, following every movement of a cautious tree-squirrel, waiting, with a patience as huge as the hunger he suffered from, until the squirrel ventured out upon the ground. Even then, White Fang was not premature. He waited until he was sure of striking before the squirrel could gain a tree-refuge. Then, and not until then, would he flash from his hiding-place, a gray projectile, incredibly swift, never failing its mark—the fleeing squirrel that fled not fast enough.

Successful as he was with squirrels, there was one difficulty that prevented him from living and growing fat on them. There were not enough squirrels. So he was driven to hunt still smaller things. So acute did his hunger become at times that he was not above rooting out wood-mice from their burrows in the ground. Nor did he scorn to do battle with a weasel as hungry as himself and many times more ferocious.

In the worst pinches of the famine he stole back to the fires of the gods. But he did not go in to the fires.

He lurked in the forest, avoiding discovery and robbing the snares at the rare intervals when game was caught. He even robbed Gray Beaver's snare of a rabbit at a time when Gray Beaver staggered and tottered through the forest, sitting down often to rest, what of weakness and of shortness of breath.

One day White Fang encountered a young wolf, gaunt and scrawny, loose-jointed with famine. Had he not been hungry himself, White Fang might have gone with him and eventually found his way into the pack amongst his wild brethren. As it was, he ran the young wolf down and killed and ate him.

Fortune seemed to favor him. Always, when hardest pressed for food, he found something to kill. Again, when he was weak, it was his luck that none of the larger preying animals chanced upon him. Thus, he was strong from the two days' eating a lynx had afforded him, when the hungry wolf-pack ran full tilt upon him. It was a long, cruel chase, but he was better nourished than they, and in the end outran them. And not only did he outrun them, but, circling widely back on his track, he gathered in one of his exhausted pursuers.

After that he left that part of the country and journeyed over to the valley wherein he had been born. Here, in the old lair, he encountered Kiche. Up to her old tricks, she, too, had fled the inhospitable fires of the gods and gone back to her old refuge to give birth to her young. Of this litter but one remained alive when White Fang came upon the scene, and this one was not destined to live long. Young life had little chance in such a famine.

Kiche's greeting of her grown son was anything but affectionate. But White Fang did not mind. He had outgrown his mother. So he turned tail philosophically and trotted on up the stream. At the forks he took the turning to the left, where he found the lair of the lynx with whom his mother and he had fought long before. Here, in the abandoned lair, he settled down and rested for a day.

During the early summer, in the last days of the famine, he met Lip-lip, who had likewise taken to the woods, where he had eked out a miserable existence. White Fang came upon him unexpectedly. Trotting in opposite directions along the base of a high bluff, they rounded a corner of rock and found themselves face to face. They paused with instant alarm, and looked at each other suspiciously.

White Fang was in splendid condition. His hunting had been good, and for a week he had eaten his fill. He was even gorged from his latest kill. But in the moment he looked at Lip-lip his hair rose on end all along his back. It was an involuntary bristling on his part, the physical state that in the past had always accompanied the mental state produced in him by Lip-lip's bullying and persecution. As in the past he had bristled and snarled at sight of Lip-lip, so now, and automatically, he bristled and snarled. He did not waste any time. The thing was done thoroughly and with despatch. Lip-lip essayed to back away, but White Fang struck him hard, shoulder to shoulder. Lip-lip was overthrown and rolled upon his back. White Fang's teeth drove into the scrawny throat. There was a death-struggle, during which White Fang walked around, stiff-legged and observant. Then he resumed his course and trotted on along the base of the bluff.

One day, not long after, he came to the edge of the forest, where a narrow stretch of open land sloped down to the Mackenzie. He had been over this ground before, when it was bare, but now a village occupied it. Still hidden amongst the trees, he paused to study the situation. Sights and sounds and scents were familiar to him. It was the old village changed to a new place. But sights and sounds and smells were different from those he had last had when he fled away from it. There was no whimpering nor wailing. Contented sounds saluted his ear, and when he heard the angry voice of a woman he knew it to be the anger that proceeds from a full stomach. And there was a smell in the air of fish. There was food. The famine was gone. He came out boldly from the forest and trotted into camp straight to Gray Beaver's tepee. Gray Beaver was not there; but Klookooch welcomed him with glad cries and the whole of a fresh-caught fish, and he lay down to wait Gray Beaver's coming.

PART FOUR: THE SUPERIOR GODS

CHAPTER I

The Enemy of His Kind

Had there been in White Fang's nature any possibility, no matter how remote, of his ever coming to fraternize with his kind, such possibility was irretrievably destroyed when he was made leader of the sled-team. For now the dogs hated him—hated him for the extra meat bestowed upon him by Mit-sah; hated him for all the real and fancied favors he received; hated him for that he fled always at the head of the team, his waving brush of a tail and his perpetually retreating hind-quarters forever maddening their eyes.

And White Fang just as bitterly hated them back. Being sled-leader was anything but gratifying to him. To be compelled to run away before the yelling pack, every dog of which, for three years, he had thrashed and mastered, was almost more than he could endure. But endure it he must, or perish, and the life that was in him had no desire to perish. The moment Mit-sah gave his order for the start, that moment the whole team, with eager, savage cries, sprang forward at White Fang.

There was no defence for him. If he turned upon them, Mit-sah would throw the stinging lash of the whip into his face. Only remained to him to run away. He could not encounter that howling horde with his tail and hind-quarters. These were scarcely fit weapons with which to meet the many merciless fangs. So run away he did, violating his own nature and pride with every leap he made, leaping all day long.

One cannot violate the promptings of one's nature without having that nature recoil upon itself. Such a recoil is like that of a hair, made to grow out from the body, turning unnaturally upon the direction of its growth and growing into the body—a rankling, festering thing of hurt. And so with White Fang. Every urge of his being impelled him to spring upon the pack that cried at his heels, but it was the will of the gods that this should not be; and behind the will, to enforce it, was the whip of cariboo-gut with its biting thirty-foot lash. So White Fang could only eat his heart in bitterness and develop a hatred and malice commensurate with the ferocity and indomitability of his nature.

If ever a creature was the enemy of its kind, White Fang was that creature. He asked no quarter, gave none. He was continually marred and scarred by the teeth of the pack, and as continually he left his own marks upon the pack. Unlike most leaders, who, when camp was made and the dogs were unhitched, huddled near to the gods for protection, White Fang disdained such protection. He walked boldly about the camp, inflicting punishment in the night for what he had suffered in the day. In the time before he was made leader of the team, the pack had learned to get out of his way. But now it was different. Excited by the day-long pursuit of him, swayed subconsciously by the insistent iteration on their brains of the sight of him fleeing away, mastered by the feeling of mastery enjoyed all day, the dogs could not bring themselves to give way to him. When he appeared amongst them, there was always a squabble. His progress was marked by snarl and snap and growl. The very atmosphere he breathed was surcharged with hatred and malice, and this but served to increase the hatred and malice within him.

When Mit-sah cried out his command for the team to stop, White Fang obeyed. At first this caused trouble for the other dogs. All of them would spring upon the hated leader, only to find the tables turned. Behind him would be Mit-sah, the great whip singing in his hand. So the dogs came to understand that when the team stopped by order, White Fang was to be let alone. But when White Fang stopped without orders, then it was allowed them to spring upon him and destroy him if they could. After several experiences, White Fang never stopped without orders. He learned quickly. It was in the nature of things that he must learn quickly, if he were to survive the unusually severe conditions under which life was vouchsafed him.

But the dogs could never learn the lesson to leave him alone in camp. Each day, pursuing him and crying defiance at him, the lesson of the previous night was erased, and that night would have to be learned over again, to be as immediately forgotten. Besides, there was a greater consistence in their dislike of him. They sensed between themselves and him a difference of kind—cause sufficient in itself for hostility. Like him, they were domesticated wolves. But they had been domesticated for generations. Much of the Wild had been lost, so that to them the Wild was the unknown, the terrible, the ever menacing and ever warring. But to him, in appearance and action and impulse, still clung the Wild. He symbolized it, was its personification; so that when they showed their teeth to him they were defending themselves against the powers of destruction that lurked in the shadows of the forest and in the dark beyond the camp-fire.

But there was one lesson the dogs did learn, and that was to keep together. White Fang was too terrible for any of them to face single-handed. They met him with the mass-formation, otherwise he would have killed them, one by one, in a night. As it was, he never had a chance to kill them. He might roll a dog off its feet, but the pack would be upon him before he could follow up and deliver the deadly throat-stroke. At the first hint of conflict, the whole team drew together and faced him. The dogs had quarrels among themselves, but these were forgotten when trouble was brewing with White Fang.

On the other hand, try as they would, they could not kill White Fang. He was too quick for them, too formidable, too wise. He avoided tight places and always backed out of it when they bade fair to surround him. While, as for getting him off his feet, there was no dog among them capable of doing the trick. His feet clung to the earth with the same tenacity that he clung to life. For that matter, life and footing were synonymous in this unending warfare with the pack, and none knew it better than White Fang.

So he became the enemy of his kind, domesticated wolves that they were, softened by the fires of man, weakened in the sheltering shadow of man's strength. White Fang was bitter and implacable. The clay of him was so moulded. He declared a vendetta against all dogs. And so terribly did he live this vendetta that Gray Beaver, fierce savage himself, could not but marvel at White Fang's ferocity. Never, he swore, had there been the like of this animal; and the Indians in strange villages swore likewise when they considered the tale of his killings amongst their dogs.

When White Fang was nearly five years old, Gray Beaver took him on another great journey, and long remembered was the havoc he worked amongst the dogs of the many villages along the Mackenzie, across the Rockies, and down the Porcupine to the Yukon. He revelled in the vengeance he wreaked upon his kind. They were ordinary, unsuspecting dogs. They were not prepared for his swiftness and directness, for his attack without warning. They did not know him for what he was, a lightning-flash of slaughter. They bristled up to him, stiff-legged and challenging, while he, wasting no time on elaborate preliminaries, snapping into action like a steel spring, was at their throats and destroying them before they knew what was happening and while they were yet in the throes of surprise.

He became an adept at fighting. He economized. He never wasted his strength, never tussled. He was in too quickly for that, and, if he missed, was out again too quickly. The dislike of the wolf for close quarters was his to an unusual degree. He could not endure a prolonged contact with another body. It smacked of danger. It made him frantic. He must be away, free, on his own legs, touching no living thing. It was the Wild still clinging to him, asserting itself through him. This feeling had been accentuated by the Ishmaelite life he had led from his puppyhood. Danger lurked in contacts. It was the trap, ever the trap, the fear of it lurking deep in the life of him, woven into the fibre of him.

In consequence, the strange dogs he encountered had no chance against him. He eluded their fangs. He got them, or got away, himself untouched in either event. In the natural course of things there were exceptions to this. There were times when several dogs, pitching on to him, punished him before he could get away; and there were times when a single dog scored deeply on him. But these were accidents. In the main, so efficient a fighter had he become, he went his way unscathed.

Another advantage he possessed was that of correctly judging time and distance. Not that he did this consciously, however. He did not calculate such things. It was all automatic. His eyes saw correctly, and the nerves carried the vision correctly to his brain. The parts of him were better adjusted than those of the average dog. They worked together more smoothly and steadily. His was a better, far better, nervous, mental, and muscular coördination. When his eyes conveyed to his brain the moving image of an action, his brain, without conscious effort, knew the space that limited that action and the time required for its completion. Thus, he could avoid the leap of another dog, or the drive of its fangs, and at the same moment could seize the infinitesimal fraction of time in which to deliver his own attack. Body and brain, his was a more perfected mechanism. Not that he was to be praised for it. Nature had been more generous to him than to the average animal, that was all.

It was in the summer that White Fang arrived at Fort Yukon. Gray Beaver had crossed the great watershed between the Mackenzie and the Yukon in the late winter, and spent the spring in hunting among the western outlying spurs of the Rockies. Then, after the break-up of the ice on the Porcupine, he had built a canoe and paddled down that stream to where it effected its junction with the Yukon just under the Arctic Circle. Here stood the old Hudson's Bay Company fort; and here were many Indians, much food, and unprecedented excitement. It was the summer of 1898, and thousands of gold-hunters were going up the Yukon to Dawson and the Klondike. Still hundreds of miles from their goal, nevertheless many of them had been on the way for a year, and the least any of them had traveled to get that far was five thousand miles, while some had come from the other side of the world.

Here Gray Beaver stopped. A whisper of the gold-rush had reached his ears, and he had come with several bales of furs, and another of gut-sewn mittens and moccasins. He would not have ventured so long a trip had he not expected generous profits. But what he had expected was nothing to what he realized. His wildest dream had not exceeded a hundred per cent. profit; he made a thousand per cent. And like a true Indian, he settled down to trade carefully and slowly, even if it took all summer and the rest of the winter to dispose of his goods.

It was at Fort Yukon that White Fang saw his first white men. As compared with the Indians he had known, they were to him another race of beings, a race of superior gods. They impressed him as possessing superior power, and it is on power that god-head rests. White Fang did not reason it out, did not in his mind make the sharp generalization that the white gods were more powerful. It was a feeling, nothing more, and yet none the less potent. As, in his puppyhood, the looming bulks of the tepees, man-reared, had affected him as manifestations of power, so was he affected now by the houses and the huge fort all of massive logs. Here was power. Those white gods were strong. They possessed greater mastery over matter than the gods he had known, most powerful among which was Gray Beaver. And yet Gray Beaver was as a child-god among these white-skinned ones.

To be sure, White Fang only felt these things. He was not conscious of them. Yet it is upon feeling, more often than thinking, that animals act; and every act White Fang now performed was based upon the feeling that the white men were the superior gods. In the first place he was very suspicious of them. There was no telling what unknown terrors were theirs, what unknown hurts they could administer. He was curious to observe them, fearful of being noticed by them. For the first few hours he was content with slinking around and watching them from a safe distance. Then he saw that no harm befell the dogs that were near to them, and he came in closer.

In turn, he was an object of great curiosity to them. His wolfish appearance caught their eyes at once, and they pointed him out to one another. This act of pointing put White Fang on his guard, and when they tried to approach him he showed his teeth and backed away.

Not one succeeded in laying a hand on him, and it was well that they did not.

White Fang soon learned that very few of these gods—not more than a dozen—lived at this place. Every two or three days a steamer (another and colossal manifestation of power) came in to the bank and stopped for several hours. The white men came from off these steamers and went away on them again. There seemed untold numbers of these white men. In the first day or so, he saw more of them than he had seen Indians in all his life; and as the days went by they continued to come up the river, stop, and then go on up the river and out of sight.

But if the white gods were all-powerful, their dogs did not amount to much. This White Fang quickly discovered by mixing with those that came ashore with their masters. They were of irregular shapes and sizes. Some were short-legged—too short; others were long-legged—too long. They had hair instead of fur, and a few had very little hair at that. And none of them knew how to fight.

As an enemy of his kind, it was in White Fang's province to fight with them. This he did, and he quickly achieved for them a mighty contempt. They were soft and helpless, made much noise, and floundered around clumsily, trying to accomplish by main strength what he accomplished by dexterity and cunning. They rushed bellowing at him. He sprang to the side. They did not know what had become of him; and in that moment he struck them on the shoulder, rolling them off their feet and delivering his stroke at the throat.

Sometimes this stroke was successful, and a stricken dog rolled in the dirt, to be pounced upon and torn to pieces by the pack of Indian dogs that waited. White Fang was wise. He had long since learned that the gods were made angry when their dogs were killed. The white men were no exception to this. So he was content, when he had overthrown and slashed wide the throat of one of their dogs, to drop back and let the pack go in and do the cruel finishing work. It was then that the white men rushed in, visiting their wrath heavily on the pack, while White Fang went free. He would stand off at a little distance and look on, while stones, clubs, axes, and all sorts of weapons fell upon his fellows. White Fang was very wise.

But his fellows grew wise, in their own way; and in this White Fang grew wise with them. They learned that it was when a steamer first tied to the bank that they had their fun. After the first two or three strange dogs had been downed and destroyed, the white men hustled their own animals back on board and wreaked savage vengeance on the offenders. One white man, having seen his dog, a setter, torn to pieces before his eyes, drew a revolver. He fired rapidly, six times, and six of the pack lay dead or dying—another manifestation of power that sank deep into White Fang's consciousness.

White Fang enjoyed it all. He did not love his kind, and he was shrewd enough to escape hurt himself. At first, the killing of the white men's dogs had been a diversion. After a time it became his occupation. There was no work for him to do. Gray Beaver was busy trading and getting wealthy. So White Fang hung around the landing with the disreputable gang of Indian dogs, waiting for steamers. With the arrival of a steamer the fun began. After a few minutes, by the time the white men had got over their surprise, the gang scattered. The fun was over until the next steamer should arrive.

But it can scarcely be said that White Fang was a member of the gang. He did not mingle with it, but remained aloof, always himself, and was even feared by it. It is true, he worked with it. He picked the quarrel

with the strange dog while the gang waited. And when
he had overthrown the strange dog the gang went in to
finish it. But it is equally true that he then withdrew,
leaving the gang to receive the punishment of the outraged gods.

It did not require much exertion to pick these quarrels. All he had to do, when the strange dogs came
ashore, was to show himself. When they saw him they
rushed for him. It was their instinct. He was the
Wild—the unknown, the terrible, the ever menacing,
the thing that prowled in the darkness around the fires
of the primeval world when they, cowering close to the
fires, were reshaping their instincts, learning to fear the
Wild out of which they had come, and which they had
deserted and betrayed. Generation by generation,
down all the generations, had this fear of the Wild
been stamped into their natures. For centuries the
Wild had stood for terror and destruction. And during
all this time free license had been theirs, from their
masters, to kill the things of the Wild. In doing this
they had protected both themselves and the gods
whose companionship they shared.

And so, fresh from the soft southern world, these
dogs, trotting down the gang-plank and out upon the
Yukon shore, had but to see White Fang to experience
the irresistible impulse to rush upon him and destroy
him. They might be town-reared dogs, but the instinctive fear of the Wild was theirs just the same. Not
alone with their own eyes did they see the wolfish creature in the clear light of the day, standing before them.
They saw him with the eyes of their ancestors, and by
their inherited memory they knew White Fang for the
wolf, and they remembered the ancient feud.

All of which served to make White Fang's days enjoyable. If the sight of him drove these strange dogs
upon him, so much the better for him, so much the
worse for them. They looked upon him as legitimate
prey, and as legitimate prey he looked upon them.

Not for nothing had he first seen the light of day in a lonely lair and fought his first fights with the ptarmigan, the weasel, and the lynx. And not for nothing had his puppyhood been made bitter by the persecution of Lip-lip and the whole puppy-pack. It might have been otherwise, and he would then have been otherwise. Had Lip-lip not existed, he would have passed his puppyhood with the other puppies and grown up more doglike and with more liking for dogs. Had Gray Beaver possessed the plummet of affection and love, he might have sounded the deeps of White Fang's nature and brought up to the surface all manner of kindly qualities. But these things had not been so. The clay of White Fang had been moulded until he became what he was, morose and lonely, unloving and ferocious, the enemy of all his kind.

CHAPTER II

The Mad God

A small number of white men lived in Fort Yukon. These men had been long in the country. They called themselves Sour-doughs, and took great pride in so classifying themselves. For other men, new in the land, they felt nothing but disdain. The men who came ashore from the steamers were newcomers. They were known as *chechaquos*, and they always wilted at the application of the name. They made their bread with baking-powder. This was the invidious distinction between them and the Sour-doughs, who, forsooth, made their bread from sour-dough because they had no baking-powder.

All of which is neither here nor there. The men in the fort disdained the newcomers and enjoyed seeing them come to grief. Especially did they enjoy the havoc worked amongst the newcomers' dogs by White Fang and his disreputable gang. When a steamer arrived, the men of the fort made it a point always to come down to the bank and see the fun. They looked forward to it with as much anticipation as did the Indian dogs, while they were not slow to appreciate the savage and crafty part played by White Fang.

But there was one man amongst them who particularly enjoyed the sport. He would come running at the first sound of a steamboat's whistle; and when the last fight was over and White Fang and the pack had scattered, he would return slowly to the fort, his face heavy with regret. Sometimes, when a soft Southland dog went down, shrieking its death-cry under the fangs of the pack, this man would be unable to contain himself, and would leap into the air and cry out with delight. And always he had a sharp and covetous eye for White Fang.

This man was called "Beauty" by the other men of the fort. No one knew his first name, and in general he was known in the country as Beauty Smith. But he was anything save a beauty. To antithesis was due his naming. He was preëminently unbeautiful. Nature had been niggardly with him. He was a small man to begin with; and upon his meagre frame was deposited an even more strikingly meagre head. Its apex might be likened to a point. In fact, in his boyhood, before he had been named Beauty by his fellows, he had been called "Pinhead."

Backward, from the apex, his head slanted down to his neck; and forward, it slanted uncompromisingly to meet a low and remarkably wide forehead. Beginning here, as though regretting her parsimony, Nature had spread his features with a lavish hand. His eyes were large, and between them was the distance of two eyes. His face, in relation to the rest of him, was prodigious. In order to discover the necessary area, Nature had given him an enormous prognathous jaw. It was wide and heavy, and protruded outward and down until it seemed to rest on his chest. Possibly this appearance was due to the weariness of the slender neck, unable properly to support so great a burden.

This jaw gave the impression of ferocious determination. But something lacked. Perhaps it was from excess. Perhaps the jaw was too large. At any rate, it was a lie. Beauty Smith was known far and wide as the weakest of weak-kneed and snivelling cowards. To complete his description, his teeth were large and yellow, while the two eye-teeth, larger than their fellows, showed under his lean lips like fangs. His eyes were yellow and muddy, as though Nature had run short on pigments and squeezed together the dregs of all her tubes. It was the same with his hair, sparse and irregular of growth, muddy-yellow and dirty-yellow, rising on his head and sprouting out of his face in unexpected tufts and bunches, in appearance like clumped and wind-blown grain.

In short, Beauty Smith was a monstrosity, and the blame of it lay elsewhere. He was not responsible. The clay of him had been so moulded in the making. He did the cooking for the other men in the fort, the dish-washing and the drudgery. They did not despise him. Rather did they tolerate him in a broad human way, as one tolerates any creature evilly treated in the making. Also, they feared him. His cowardly rages made them dread a shot in the back or poison in their coffee. But somebody had to do the cooking, and whatever else his shortcomings, Beauty Smith could cook.

This was the man that looked at White Fang, delighted in his ferocious prowess, and desired to possess him. He made overtures to White Fang from the first. White Fang began by ignoring him. Later on, when the overtures became more insistent, White Fang bristled and bared his teeth and backed away. He did not like the man. The feel of him was bad. He sensed the evil in him, and feared the extended hand and the attempts at soft-spoken speech. Because of all this, he hated the man.

With the simpler creatures, good and bad are things simply understood. The good stands for all things that bring easement and satisfaction and surcease from pain. Therefore, the good is liked. The bad stands for all things that are fraught with discomfort, menace, and hurt, and is hated accordingly. White Fang's feel of

Beauty Smith was bad. From the man's distorted body and twisted mind, in occult ways, like mists rising from malarial marshes, came emanations of the unhealth within. Not by reasoning, not by the five senses alone, but by other and remoter and uncharted senses, came the feeling to White Fang that the man was ominous with evil, pregnant with hurtfulness, and therefore a thing bad, and wisely to be hated.

White Fang was in Gray Beaver's camp when Beauty Smith first visited it. At the faint sound of his distant feet, before he came in sight, White Fang knew who was coming and began to bristle. He had been lying down in an abandon of comfort, but he arose quickly, and, as the man arrived, slid away in true wolf-fashion to the edge of the camp. He did not know what they said, but he could see the man and Gray Beaver talking together. Once, the man pointed at him, and White Fang snarled back as though the hand were just descending upon him instead of being, as it was, fifty feet away. The man laughed at this; and White Fang slunk away to the sheltering woods, his head turned to observe as he glided softly over the ground.

Gray Beaver refused to sell the dog. He had grown rich with his trading and stood in need of nothing. Besides, White Fang was a valuable animal, the strongest sled-dog he had ever owned, and the best leader. Furthermore, there was no dog like him on the Mackenzie nor the Yukon. He could fight. He killed other dogs as easily as men killed mosquitoes. (Beauty Smith's eyes lighted up at this, and he licked his thin lips with an eager tongue.) No, White Fang was not for sale at any price.

But Beauty Smith knew the ways of Indians. He visited Gray Beaver's camp often, and hidden under his coat was always a black bottle or so. One of the potencies of whiskey is the breeding of thirst. Gray Beaver got the thirst. His fevered membranes and burnt stomach began to clamor for more and more of the scorching fluid; while his brain, thrust all awry by the unwonted stimulant, permitted him to go any length to obtain it. The money he had received for his furs and mittens and moccasins began to go. It went faster and faster, and the shorter his money-sack grew, the shorter grew his temper.

In the end his money and goods and temper were all gone. Nothing remained to him but his thirst, a prodigious possession in itself that grew more prodigious with every sober breath he drew. Then it was that Beauty Smith had talk with him again about the sale of White Fang; but this time the price offered was in bottles, not dollars, and Gray Beaver's ears were more eager to hear.

"You ketch um dog you take um all right," was his last word.

The bottles were delivered, but after two days, "You ketch um dog," were Beauty Smith's words to Gray Beaver.

White Fang slunk into camp one evening and dropped down with a sigh of content. The dreaded white god was not there. For days his manifestations of desire to lay hands on him had been growing more insistent, and during that time White Fang had been compelled to avoid the camp. He did not know what evil was threatened by those insistent hands. He knew only that they did threaten evil of some sort, and that it was best for him to keep out of their reach.

But scarcely had he lain down when Gray Beaver staggered over to him and tied a leather thong around his neck. He sat down beside White Fang, holding the end of the thong in his hand. In the other hand he held a bottle, which, from time to time, was inverted above his head to the accompaniment of gurgling noises.

An hour of this passed, when the vibrations of feet in contact with the ground foreran the one who approached. White Fang heard it first, and he was bristling with recognition while Gray Beaver still nodded stupidly. White Fang tried to draw the thong softly out of his master's hand; but the relaxed fingers closed tightly and Gray Beaver roused himself.

Beauty Smith strode into camp and stood over White Fang. He snarled softly up at the thing of fear, watching keenly the deportment of the hands. One hand extended outward and began to descend upon his head. His soft snarl grew tense and harsh. The hand continued slowly to descend, while he crouched beneath it, eyeing it malignantly, his snarl growing shorter and shorter as, with quickening breath, it approached its culmination. Suddenly he snapped, striking with his fangs like a snake. The hand was jerked back, and the teeth came together emptily with a sharp click. Beauty Smith was frightened and angry. Gray Beaver clouted White Fang alongside the head, so that he cowered down close to the earth in respectful obedience.

White Fang's suspicious eyes followed every movement. He saw Beauty Smith go away and return with a stout club. Then the end of the thong was given over to him by Gray Beaver. Beauty Smith started to walk away. The thong grew taut. White Fang resisted it. Gray Beaver clouted him right and left to make him get up and follow. He obeyed, but with a rush, hurling himself upon the stranger who was dragging him away. Beauty Smith did not jump away. He had been waiting for this. He swung the club smartly, stopping the rush midway and smashing White Fang down upon the ground. Gray Beaver laughed and nodded approval. Beauty Smith tightened the thong again, and White Fang crawled limply and dizzily to his feet.

He did not rush a second time. One smash from the club was sufficient to convince him that the white god knew how to handle it, and he was too wise to fight the inevitable. So he followed morosely at Beauty Smith's heels, his tail between his legs, yet snarling softly under his breath. But Beauty Smith kept a wary eye on him, and the club was held always ready to strike.

At the fort Beauty Smith left him securely tied and went in to bed. White Fang waited an hour. Then he applied his teeth to the thong, and in the space of ten seconds was free. He had wasted no time with his teeth. There had been no useless gnawing. The thong was cut across, diagonally, almost as clean as though done by a knife. White Fang looked up at the fort, at the same time bristling and growling. Then he turned and trotted back to Gray Beaver's camp. He owed no allegiance to this strange and terrible god. He had given himself to Gray Beaver, and to Gray Beaver he considered he still belonged.

But what had occurred before was repeated—with a difference. Gray Beaver again made him fast with a thong, and in the morning turned him over to Beauty Smith. And here was where the difference came in. Beauty Smith gave him a beating. Tied securely, White Fang could only rage futilely and endure the punishment. Club and whip were both used upon him, and he experienced the worst beating he had ever received in his life. Even the big beating given him in his puppyhood by Gray Beaver was mild compared with this.

Beauty Smith enjoyed the task. He delighted in it. He gloated over his victim, and his eyes flamed dully, as he swung the whip or club and listened to White Fang's cries of pain and to his helpless bellows and snarls. For Beauty Smith was cruel in the way that cowards are cruel. Cringing and snivelling himself before the blows or angry speech of a man, he revenged himself, in turn, upon creatures weaker than he. All life likes power, and Beauty Smith was no exception. Denied the expression of power amongst his own kind, he fell back upon the lesser creatures and there vindicated the life that was in him. But Beauty Smith had not created himself, and no blame was to be attached to him. He had come into the world with a twisted body and a brute intelligence. This had constituted the clay of him, and it had not been kindly moulded by the world.

White Fang knew why he was being beaten. When Gray Beaver tied the thong around his neck, and passed the end of the thong into Beauty Smith's keeping, White Fang knew that it was his god's will for him to go with Beauty Smith. And when Beauty Smith left him tied outside the fort, he knew that it was Beauty Smith's will that he should remain there. Therefore, he had disobeyed the will of both the gods, and earned the consequent punishment. He had seen dogs change owners in the past, and he had seen the runaways beaten as he was being beaten. He was wise, and yet in the nature of him there were forces greater than wisdom. One of these was fidelity. He did not love Gray Beaver; yet, even in the face of his will and his anger, he was faithful to him. He could not help it. This faithfulness was a quality of the clay that composed him. It was the quality that was peculiarly the possession of his kind; the quality that set apart his species from all other species; the quality that had enabled the wolf and the wild dog to come in from the open and be the companions of man.

After the beating, White Fang was dragged back to the fort. But this time Beauty Smith left him tied with a stick. One does not give up a god easily, and so with White Fang. Gray Beaver was his own particular god, and, in spite of Gray Beaver's will, White Fang still clung to him and would not give him up. Gray Beaver had betrayed and forsaken him, but that had no effect upon him. Not for nothing had he surrendered himself body and soul to Gray Beaver. There had been no reservation on White Fang's part, and the bond was not to be broken easily.

So, in the night, when the men in the fort were asleep, White Fang applied his teeth to the stick that held him. The wood was seasoned and dry, and it was tied so closely to his neck that he could scarcely get his teeth to it. It was only by the severest muscular exertion and neck-arching that he succeeded in getting the wood between his teeth, and barely between his teeth at that; and it was only by the exercise of an immense patience, extending through many hours, that he succeeded in gnawing through the stick. This was something that dogs were not supposed to do. It was unprecedented. But White Fang did it, trotting away from the fort in the early morning with the end of the stick hanging to his neck.

He was wise. But had he been merely wise he would not have gone back to Gray Beaver, who had already twice betrayed him. But there was his faithfulness, and he went back to be betrayed yet a third time. Again he yielded to the tying of a thong around his neck by Gray Beaver, and again Beauty Smith came to claim him. And this time he was beaten even more severely than before.

Gray Beaver looked on stolidly while the white man wielded the whip. He gave no protection. It was no longer his dog. When the beating was over White Fang was sick. A soft Southland dog would have died under it, but not he. His school of life had been sterner, and he was himself of sterner stuff. He had too great vitality. His clutch on life was too strong. But he was very sick. At first he was unable to drag himself along, and Beauty Smith had to wait half an hour on him. And then, blind and reeling, he followed at Beauty Smith's heels back to the fort.

But now he was tied with a chain that defied his teeth, and he strove in vain, by lunging, to draw the staple from the timber into which it was driven. After a few days, sober and bankrupt, Gray Beaver departed up the Porcupine on his long journey to the Mackenzie. White Fang remained on the Yukon, the property of a man more than half mad and all brute. But what is a dog to know in its consciousness of madness? To White Fang, Beauty Smith was a veritable, if terrible, god. He was a mad god at best, but White Fang knew nothing of madness; he knew only that he must submit to the will of this new master, obey his every whim and fancy.

CHAPTER III

The Reign of Hate

Under the tutelage of the mad god, White Fang became a fiend. He was kept chained in a pen at the rear of the fort, and here Beauty Smith teased and irritated and drove him wild with petty torments. The man early discovered White Fang's susceptibility to laughter, and made it a point, after painfully tricking him, to laugh at him. This laughter was uproarious and scornful, and at the same time the god pointed his finger derisively at White Fang. At such times reason fled from White Fang, and in his transports of rage he was even more mad than Beauty Smith.

Formerly, White Fang had been merely the enemy of his kind, withal a ferocious enemy. He now became the enemy of all things, and more ferocious than ever. To such an extent was he tormented, that he hated blindly and without the faintest spark of reason. He hated the chain that bound him, the men who peered in at him through the slats of the pen, the dogs that accompanied the men and that snarled malignantly at him in his helplessness. He hated the very wood of the pen that confined him. And first, last, and most of all, he hated Beauty Smith.

But Beauty Smith had a purpose in all that he did to White Fang. One day a number of men gathered about the pen. Beauty Smith entered, club in hand, and took the chain from off White Fang's neck. When his master had gone out, White Fang turned loose and tore around the pen, trying to get at the men outside. He was magnificently terrible. Fully five feet in length, and standing two and one-half feet at the shoulder, he far outweighed a wolf of corresponding size. From his mother he had inherited the heavier proportions of the dog, so that he weighed, without any fat and without an ounce of superfluous flesh, over ninety pounds. It was all muscle, bone, and sinew—fighting flesh in the finest condition.

The door of the pen was being opened again. White Fang paused. Something unusual was happening. He waited. The door was opened wider. Then a huge dog was thrust inside, and the door was slammed shut behind him. White Fang had never seen such a dog (it was a mastiff); but the size and fierce aspect of the intruder did not deter him. Here was something, not wood nor iron, upon which to wreak his hate. He leaped in with a flash of fangs that ripped down the side of the mastiff's neck. The mastiff shook his head, growled hoarsely, and plunged at White Fang. But White Fang was here, there, and everywhere, always evading and eluding, and always leaping in and slashing with his fangs and leaping out again in time to escape punishment.

The men outside shouted and applauded, while Beauty Smith, in an ecstasy of delight, gloated over the ripping and mangling performed by White Fang. There was no hope for the mastiff from the first. He was too ponderous and slow. In the end, while Beauty Smith beat White Fang back with a club, the mastiff was dragged out by its owner. Then there was a payment of bets, and money clinked in Beauty Smith's hand.

White Fang came to look forward eagerly to the gathering of men around his pen. It meant a fight; and this was the only way that was now vouchsafed him of expressing the life that was in him. Tormented, incited to hate, he was kept a prisoner so that there was no way of satisfying that hate except at the times his master saw fit to put another dog against him. Beauty Smith had estimated his powers well, for he was invariably the victor. One day, three dogs were turned in upon him in succession. Another day, a full-grown wolf, fresh-caught from the Wild, was shoved in through the door of the pen. And on still another day two dogs were set against him at the same time. This was his severest fight, and although in the end he killed them both he was himself half killed in doing it.

In the fall of the year, when the first snows were falling and mush-ice was running in the river, Beauty Smith took passage for himself and White Fang on a steamboat bound up the Yukon to Dawson. White Fang had now achieved a reputation in the land. As "The Fighting Wolf" he was known far and wide, and the cage in which he was kept on the steamboat's deck was usually surrounded by curious men. He raged and snarled at them, or lay quietly and studied them with cold hatred. Why should he not hate them? He never asked himself the question. He knew only hate and lost himself in the passion of it. Life had become a hell to him. He had not been made for the close confinement wild beasts endure at the hands of men. And yet it was in precisely this way that he was treated. Men stared at him, poked sticks between the bars to make him snarl, and then laughed at him.

They were his environment, these men, and they were moulding the clay of him into a more ferocious thing than had been intended by Nature. Nevertheless, Nature had given him plasticity. Where many another animal would have died or had its spirit broken, he adjusted himself and lived, and at no expense of the spirit. Possibly Beauty Smith, arch-fiend and tormentor, was capable of breaking White Fang's spirit, but as yet there were no signs of his succeeding.

If Beauty Smith had in him a devil, White Fang had another; and the two of them raged against each other unceasingly. In the days before, White Fang had had the wisdom to cower down and submit to a man with a club in his hand; but this wisdom now left him. The mere sight of Beauty Smith was sufficient to send him into transports of fury. And when they came to close quarters, and he had been beaten back by the club, he went on growling and snarling and showing his fangs. The last growl could never be extracted from him. No matter how terribly he was beaten, he had always another growl; and when Beauty Smith gave up and withdrew, the defiant growl followed after him, or White Fang sprang at the bars of the cage bellowing his hatred.

When the steamboat arrived at Dawson, White Fang went ashore. But he still lived a public life, in a cage, surrounded by curious men. He was exhibited as "The Fighting Wolf," and men paid fifty cents in gold dust to see him. He was given no rest. Did he lie down to sleep, he was stirred up by a sharp stick—so that the audience might get its money's worth. In order to make the exhibition interesting, he was kept in a rage most of the time. But worse than all this, was the atmosphere in which he lived. He was regarded as the most fearful of wild beasts, and this was borne in to him through the bars of the cage. Every word, every cautious action, on the part of the men, impressed upon him his own terrible ferocity. It was so much added fuel to the flame of his fierceness. There could be but one result, and that was that his ferocity fed upon itself and increased. It was another instance of the plasticity of his clay, of his capacity for being moulded by the pressure of environment.

In addition to being exhibited, he was a professional

fighting animal. At irregular intervals, whenever a fight could be arranged, he was taken out of his cage and led off into the woods a few miles from town. Usually this occurred at night, so as to avoid interference from the mounted police of the Territory. After a few hours of waiting, when daylight had come, the audience and the dog with which he was to fight arrived. In this manner it came about that he fought all sizes and breeds of dogs. It was a savage land, the men were savage, and the fights were usually to the death.

Since White Fang continued to fight, it is obvious that it was the other dogs that died. He never knew defeat. His early training, when he fought with Lip-lip and the whole puppy-pack, stood him in good stead. There was the tenacity with which he clung to the earth. No dog could make him lose his footing. This was the favorite trick of the wolf breeds—to rush in upon him, either directly or with an unexpected swerve, in the hope of striking his shoulder and overthrowing him. Mackenzie hounds, Eskimo and Labrador dogs, huskies and Malemutes—all tried it on him, and all failed. He was never known to lose his footing. Men told this to one another, and looked each time to see it happen; but White Fang always disappointed them.

Then there was his lightning quickness. It gave him a tremendous advantage over his antagonists. No matter what their fighting experience, they had never encountered a dog that moved so swiftly as he. Also to be reckoned with, was the immediateness of his attack. The average dog was accustomed to the preliminaries of snarling and bristling and growling, and the average dog was knocked off his feet and finished before he had begun to fight or recovered from his surprise. So often did this happen, that it became the custom to hold White Fang until the other dog went through its preliminaries, was good and ready, and even made the first attack.

But greatest of all the advantages in White Fang's favor, was his experience. He knew more about fighting than did any of the dogs that faced him. He had fought more fights, knew how to meet more tricks and methods, and had more tricks himself, while his own method was scarcely to be improved upon.

As the time went by, he had fewer and fewer fights. Men despaired of matching him with an equal, and Beauty Smith was compelled to pit wolves against him. These were trapped by the Indians for the purpose, and a fight between White Fang and a wolf was always sure to draw a crowd. Once, a full-grown female lynx was secured, and this time White Fang fought for his life. Her quickness matched his; her ferocity equalled his; while he fought with his fangs alone, and she fought with her sharp-clawed feet as well.

But after the lynx, all fighting ceased for White Fang. There were no more animals with which to fight—at least, there was none considered worthy of fighting with him. So he remained on exhibition until spring, when one Tim Keenan, a faro-dealer, arrived in the land. With him came the first bulldog that had ever entered the Klondike. That this dog and White Fang should come together was inevitable, and for a week the anticipated fight was the mainspring of conversation in certain quarters of the town.

CHAPTER IV

The Clinging Death

B eauty Smith slipped the chain from his neck and stepped back.

For once White Fang did not make an immediate attack. He stood still, ears pricked forward, alert and curious, surveying the strange animal that faced him. He had never seen such a dog before. Tim Keenan shoved the bulldog forward with a muttered "Go to it." The animal waddled toward the centre of the circle, short and squat and ungainly. He came to a stop and blinked across at White Fang.

There were cries from the crowd of "Go to him, Cherokee!" "Sick 'm, Cherokee!" "Eat 'm up!"

But Cherokee did not seem anxious to fight. He turned his head and blinked at the men who shouted, at the same time wagging his stump of a tail good-naturedly. He was not afraid, but merely lazy. Besides, it did not seem to him that it was intended he should fight with the dog he saw before him. He was not used to fighting with that kind of dog, and he was waiting for them to bring on the real dog.

Tim Keenan stepped in and bent over Cherokee, fondling him on both sides of the shoulders with hands that rubbed against the grain of the hair and that made slight, pushing-forward movements. These were so many suggestions. Also, their effect was irritating, for Cherokee began to growl, very softly, deep down in his throat. There was a correspondence in rhythm between the growls and the movements of the man's hands. The growl rose in the throat with the culmination of each forward-pushing movement, and ebbed down to start up afresh with the beginning of the next movement. The end of each movement was the accent of the rhythm, the movement ending abruptly and the growling rising with a jerk.

This was not without its effect on White Fang. The hair began to rise on his neck and across the shoulders. Tim Keenan gave a final shove forward and stepped back again. As the impetus that carried Cherokee forward died down, he continued to go forward of his own volition, in a swift, bow-legged run. Then White Fang struck. A cry of startled admiration went up. He had covered the distance and gone in more like a cat than a dog; and with the same catlike swiftness he had slashed with his fangs and leaped clear.

The bulldog was bleeding back of one ear from a rip in his thick neck. He gave no sign, did not even snarl, but turned and followed after White Fang. The display on both sides, the quickness of the one and the steadiness of the other, had excited the partisan spirit of the crowd, and the men were making new bets and increasing original bets. Again, and yet again, White Fang sprang in, slashed, and got away untouched; and still his strange foe followed after him, without too great haste, not slowly, but deliberately and determinedly, in a businesslike sort of way. There was purpose in his method—something for him to do that he was intent upon doing and from which nothing could distract him.

His whole demeanor, every action, was stamped with this purpose. It puzzled White Fang. Never had he seen such a dog. It had no hair protection. It was soft, and bled easily. There was no thick mat of fur to baffle White Fang's teeth, as they were often baffled by dogs of his own breed. Each time that his teeth struck they sank easily into the yielding flesh, while the animal did not seem able to defend itself. Another disconcerting thing was that it made no outcry, such as he had been accustomed to with the other dogs he had fought. Beyond a growl or a grunt, the dog took its punishment silently. And never did it flag in its pursuit of him.

Not that Cherokee was slow. He could turn and whirl swiftly enough, but White Fang was never there. Cherokee was puzzled, too. He had never fought before with a dog with which he could not close. The desire to close had always been mutual. But here was a dog that kept at a distance, dancing and dodging here and there and all about. And when it did get its teeth into him, it did not hold on but let go instantly and darted away again.

But White Fang could not get at the soft underside of the throat. The bulldog stood too short, while its massive jaws were an added protection. White Fang darted in and out unscathed, while Cherokee's wounds increased. Both sides of his neck and head were ripped and slashed. He bled freely, but showed no signs of being disconcerted. He continued his plodding pursuit, though once, for the moment baffled, he came to a full stop and blinked at the men who looked on, at the same time wagging his stump of a tail as an expression of his willingness to fight.

In that moment White Fang was in upon him and out, in passing ripping his trimmed remnant of an ear. With a slight manifestation of anger, Cherokee took up the pursuit again, running on the inside of the circle White Fang was making, and striving to fasten his deadly grip on White Fang's throat. The bulldog missed by a hair's-breadth, and cries of praise went up as White Fang doubled suddenly out of danger in the opposite direction.

The time went by. White Fang still danced on,

dodging and doubling, leaping in and out, and ever inflicting damage. And still the bulldog, with grim certitude, toiled after him. Sooner or later he would accomplish his purpose, get the grip that would win the
battle. In the meantime he accepted all the punishment
the other could deal him. His tufts of ears had become
tassels, his neck and shoulders were slashed in a score
of places, and his very lips were cut and bleeding—all
from those lightning snaps that were beyond his fore-
seeing and guarding.

Time and again White Fang had attempted to
knock Cherokee off his feet; but the difference in their
height was too great. Cherokee was too squat, too close
to the ground. White Fang tried the trick once too
often. The chance came in one of his quick doublings
and counter-circlings. He caught Cherokee with head
turned away as he whirled more slowly. His shoulder
was exposed. White Fang drove in upon it; but his own
shoulder was high above, while he struck with such
force that his momentum carried him on across over
the other's body. For the first time in his fighting history, men saw White Fang lose his footing. His body
turned a half-somersault in the air, and he would have
landed on his back had he not twisted, catlike, still in
the air, in the effort to bring his feet to the earth. As it
was, he struck heavily on his side. The next instant he
was on his feet, but in that instant Cherokee's teeth
closed on his throat.

It was not a good grip, being too low down toward
the chest; but Cherokee held on. White Fang sprang to
his feet and tore wildly around, trying to shake off the
bulldog's body. It made him frantic, this clinging,
dragging weight. It bound his movements, restricted
his freedom. It was like a trap, and all his instinct resented it and revolted against it. It was a mad revolt.
For several minutes he was to all intents insane. The
basic life that was in him took charge of him. The will

to exist of his body surged over him. He was dominated by this mere flesh-love of life. All intelligence was gone. It was as though he had no brain. His reason was unseated by the blind yearning of the flesh to exist and move, at all hazards to move, to continue to move, for movement was the expression of its existence.

Round and round he went, whirling and turning and reversing, trying to shake off the fifty-pound weight that dragged at his throat. The bulldog did little but keep his grip. Sometimes, and rarely, he managed to get his feet to the earth and for a moment to brace himself against White Fang. But the next moment his footing would be lost and he would be dragging around in the whirl of one of White Fang's mad gyrations. Cherokee identified himself with his instinct. He knew he was doing the right thing by holding on, and there came to him certain blissful thrills of satisfaction. At such moments he even closed his eyes and allowed his body to be hurled hither and thither, willy-nilly, careless of any hurt that might thereby come to it. That did not count. The grip was the thing, and the grip he kept.

White Fang ceased only when he had tired himself out. He could do nothing, and he could not understand. Never, in all his fighting, had this thing happened. The dogs he had fought with did not fight that way. With them it was snap and slash and get away, snap and slash and get away. He lay partly on his side, panting for breath. Cherokee, still holding his grip, urged against him, trying to get him over entirely on his side. White Fang resisted, and he could feel the jaws shifting their grip, slightly relaxing and coming together again in a chewing movement. Each shift brought the grip closer in to his throat. The bulldog's method was to hold what he had, and when opportunity favored to work in for more. Opportunity favored when White Fang remained quiet. When White Fang struggled, Cherokee was content merely to hold on.

The bulging back of Cherokee's neck was the only portion of his body that White Fang's teeth could reach. He got hold toward the base where the neck comes out from the shoulders; but he did not know the chewing method of fighting, nor were his jaws adapted to it. He spasmodically ripped and tore with his fangs for a space. Then a change in their position diverted him. The bulldog had managed to roll him over on his back, and still hanging on to his throat, was on top of him. Like a cat, White Fang bowed his hind-quarters in, and, with the feet digging into his enemy's abdomen above him, he began to claw with long, tearing strokes. Cherokee might well have been disembowelled had he not quickly pivoted on his grip and got his body off of White Fang's and at right angles to it.

There was no escaping that grip. It was like Fate itself, and as inexorable. Slowly it shifted up along the jugular. All that saved White Fang from death was the loose skin of his neck and the thick fur that covered it. This served to form a large roll in Cherokee's mouth, the fur of which well-nigh defied his teeth. But bit by bit, whenever the chance offered, he was getting more of the loose skin and fur in his mouth. The result was that he was slowly throttling White Fang. The latter's breath was drawn with greater and greater difficulty as the moments went by.

It began to look as though the battle were over. The backers of Cherokee waxed jubilant and offered ridiculous odds. White Fang's backers were correspondingly depressed, and refused bets of ten to one and twenty to one, though one man was rash enough to close a wager of fifty to one. This man was Beauty Smith. He took a step into the ring and pointed his finger at White Fang. Then he began to laugh derisively and scornfully. This produced the desired effect. White Fang went wild with rage. He called up his reserves of strength and gained his feet. As he struggled around the ring, the fifty pounds of his foe ever dragging on his throat, his anger passed on into panic. The basic life of him dominated him again, and his intelligence fled before the will of his flesh to live. Round and round and back again, stumbling and falling and rising, even uprearing at times on his hind-legs and lifting his foe clear of the earth, he struggled vainly to shake off the clinging death.

At last he fell, toppling backward, exhausted; and the bulldog promptly shifted his grip, getting in closer, mangling more and more of the fur-folded flesh, throttling White Fang more severely than ever. Shouts of applause went up for the victor, and there were many cries of "Cherokee!" "Cherokee!" To this Cherokee responded by vigorous wagging of the stump of his tail. But the clamor of approval did not distract him. There was no sympathetic relation between his tail and his massive jaws. The one might wag, but the others held their terrible grip on White Fang's throat.

It was at this time that a diversion came to the spectators. There was a jingle of bells. Dog-mushers' cries were heard. Everybody, save Beauty Smith, looked apprehensively, the fear of the police strong upon them. But they saw, up the trail, and not down, two men running with sled and dogs. They were evidently coming down the creek from some prospecting trip. At sight of the crowd they stopped their dogs and came over and joined it, curious to see the cause of the excitement. The dog-musher wore a mustache, but the other, a taller and younger man, was smooth-shaven, his skin rosy from the pounding of his blood and the running in the frosty air.

White Fang had practically ceased struggling. Now and again he resisted spasmodically and to no purpose. He could get little air, and that little grew less and less under the merciless grip that ever tightened. In spite of his armor of fur, the great vein of his throat would have long since been torn open, had not the first grip of the bulldog been so low down as to be practically on the chest. It had taken Cherokee a long time to shift that grip upward, and this had also tended further to clog his jaws with fur and skin-fold.

In the meantime, the abysmal brute in Beauty Smith had been rising up into his brain and mastering the small bit of sanity that he possessed at best. When he saw White Fang's eyes beginning to glaze, he knew beyond doubt that the fight was lost. Then he broke loose. He sprang upon White Fang and began savagely to kick him. There were hisses from the crowd and cries of protest, but that was all. While this went on, and Beauty Smith continued to kick White Fang, there was a commotion in the crowd. The tall young newcomer was forcing his way through, shouldering men right and left without ceremony or gentleness. When he broke through into the ring, Beauty Smith was just in the act of delivering another kick. All his weight was on one foot, and he was in a state of unstable equilibrium. At that moment the newcomer's fist landed a smashing blow full in his face. Beauty Smith's remaining leg left the ground, and his whole body seemed to lift into the air as he turned over backward and struck the snow. The newcomer turned upon the crowd.

"You cowards!" he cried. "You beasts!"

He was in a rage himself—a sane rage. His gray eyes seemed metallic and steellike as they flashed upon the crowd. Beauty Smith regained his feet and came toward him, sniffling and cowardly. The newcomer did not understand. He did not know how abject a coward the other was, and thought he was coming back intent on fighting. So, with a "You beast!" he smashed Beauty Smith over backward with a second blow in the face. Beauty Smith decided that the snow was the safest place for him, and lay where he had fallen, making no effort to get up.

"Come on, Matt, lend a hand," the newcomer called to the dog-musher, who had followed him into the ring.

Both men bent over the dogs. Matt took hold of

White Fang, ready to pull when Cherokee's jaws should be loosened. This the younger man endeavored to accomplish by clutching the bulldog's jaws in his hands and trying to spread them. It was a vain undertaking. As he pulled and tugged and wrenched, he kept exclaiming with every expulsion of breath, "Beasts!"

The crowd began to grow unruly, and some of the men were protesting against the spoiling of the sport; but they were silenced when the newcomer lifted his head from his work for a moment and glared at them.

"You damn beasts!" he finally exploded, and went back to his task.

"It's no use, Mr. Scott, you can't break 'm apart that way," Matt said at last.

The pair paused and surveyed the locked dogs.

"Ain't bleedin' much," Matt announced. "Ain't got all the way in yet."

"But he's liable to any moment," Scott answered. "There, did you see that! He shifted his grip in a bit."

The younger man's excitement and apprehension for White Fang was growing. He struck Cherokee about the head savagely again and again. But that did not loosen the jaw. Cherokee wagged the stump of his tail in advertisement that he understood the meaning of the blows, but that he knew he was himself in the right and only doing his duty by keeping his grip.

"Won't some of you help?" Scott cried desperately at the crowd.

But no help was offered. Instead, the crowd began sarcastically to cheer him on and showered him with facetious advice.

"You'll have to get a pry," Matt counselled.

The other reached into the holster at his hip, drew his revolver, and tried to thrust its muzzle between the bulldog's jaws. He shoved, and shoved hard, till the grating of the steel against the locked teeth could be distinctly heard. Both men were on their knees, bending over the dogs. Tim Keenan strode into the ring.

He paused beside Scott and touched him on the shoulder, saying ominously:

"Don't break them teeth, stranger."

"Then I'll break his neck," Scott retorted, continuing his shoving and wedging with the revolver muzzle.

"I said don't break them teeth," the faro-dealer repeated more ominously than before.

But if it was a bluff he intended, it did not work. Scott never desisted in his efforts, though he looked up coolly and asked:

"Your dog?"

The faro-dealer grunted.

"Then get in here and break this grip."

"Well, stranger," the other drawled irritatingly, "I don't mind telling you that's something I ain't worked out for myself. I don't know how to turn the trick."

"Then get out of the way," was the reply, "and don't bother me. I'm busy."

Tim Keenan continued standing over him, but Scott took no further notice of his presence. He had managed to get the muzzle in between the jaws on one side and was trying to get it out between the jaws on the other side. This accomplished, he pried gently and carefully, loosening the jaws a bit at a time, while Matt, a bit at a time, extricated White Fang's mangled neck.

"Stand by to receive your dog," was Scott's peremptory order to Cherokee's owner.

The faro-dealer stooped down obediently and got a firm hold on Cherokee.

"Now," Scott warned, giving the final pry.

The dogs were drawn apart, the bulldog struggling vigorously.

"Take him away," Scott commanded, and Tim Keenan dragged Cherokee back into the crowd.

White Fang made several ineffectual efforts to get up. Once he gained his feet, but his legs were too weak to sustain him, and he slowly wilted and sank back into the snow. His eyes were half closed, and the surface of them was glassy. His jaws were apart, and through them the tongue protruded, draggled and limp. To all appearances he looked like a dog that had been strangled to death. Matt examined him.

"Just about all in," he announced; "but he's breathin' all right."

Beauty Smith had regained his feet and come over to look at White Fang.

"Matt, how much is a good sled-dog worth?" Scott asked.

The dog-musher, still on his knees and stooped over White Fang, calculated for a moment.

"Three hundred dollars," he answered.

"And how much for one that's all chewed up like this one?" Scott asked, nudging White Fang with his foot.

"Half of that," was the dog-musher's judgment.

Scott turned upon Beauty Smith.

"Did you hear, Mr. Beast? I'm going to take your dog from you, and I'm going to give you a hundred and fifty for him."

He opened his pocket-book and counted out the bills.

Beauty Smith put his hands behind his back, refusing to touch the proffered money.

"I ain't a-sellin'," he said.

"Oh, yes you are," the other assured him. "Because I'm buying. Here's your money. The dog's mine."

Beauty Smith, his hands still behind him, began to back away.

Scott sprang toward him, drawing his fist back to strike. Beauty Smith cowered down in anticipation of the blow.

"I've got my rights," he whimpered.

"You've forfeited your rights to own that dog," was the rejoinder. "Are you going to take the money? or do I have to hit you again?"

"All right," Beauty Smith spoke up with the alacrity of fear. "But I take the money under protest," he added. "The dog's a mint. I ain't a-goin' to be robbed. A man's got his rights."

"Correct," Scott answered, passing the money over to him. "A man's got his rights. But you're not a man. You're a beast."

"Wait till I get back to Dawson," Beauty Smith threatened. "I'll have the law on you."

"If you open your mouth when you get back to Dawson, I'll have you run out of town. Understand?"

Beauty Smith replied with a grunt.

"Understand?" the other thundered with abrupt fierceness.

"Yes," Beauty Smith grunted, shrinking away.

"Yes what?"

"Yes, sir," Beauty Smith snarled.

"Look out! He'll bite!" some one shouted, and a guffaw of laughter went up.

Scott turned his back on him, and returned to help the dog-musher, who was working over White Fang.

Some of the men were already departing; others stood in groups, looking on and talking. Tim Keenan joined one of the groups.

"Who's that mug?" he asked.

"Weedon Scott," some one answered.

"And who in hell is Weedon Scott?" the faro-dealer demanded.

"Oh, one of them crack-a-jack minin' experts. He's in with all the big bugs. If you want to keep out of trouble, you'll steer clear of him, that's my talk. He's all hunky with the officials. The Gold Commissioner's a special pal of his."

"I thought he must be somebody," was the faro-dealer's comment. "That's why I kept my hands offen him at the start."

CHAPTER V

The Indomitable

"It's hopeless," Weedon Scott confessed.

He sat on the step of his cabin and stared at the dog-musher, who responded with a shrug that was equally hopeless.

Together they looked at White Fang at the end of his stretched chain, bristling, snarling, ferocious, straining to get at the sled-dogs. Having received sundry lessons from Matt, said lessons being imparted by means of a club, the sled-dogs had learned to leave White Fang alone; and even then they were lying down at a distance, apparently oblivious of his existence.

"It's a wolf and there's no taming it," Weedon Scott announced.

"Oh, I don't know about that," Matt objected. "Might be a lot of dog in 'm, for all you can tell. But there's one thing I know sure, an' that there's no gettin' away from."

The dog-musher paused and nodded his head confidently at Moosehide Mountain.

"Well, don't be a miser with what you know," Scott said sharply, after waiting a suitable length of time. "Spit it out. What is it?"

The dog-musher indicated White Fang with a backward thrust of his thumb.

"Wolf or dog, it's all the same—he's ben tamed a'ready."

"No!"

"I tell you yes, an' broke to harness. Look close there. D'ye see them marks across the chest?"

"You're right, Matt. He was a sled-dog before Beauty Smith got hold of him."

"An' there's not much reason against his bein a sled-dog again."

"What d'ye think?" Scott queried eagerly. Then the hope died down as he added, shaking his head, "We've had him two weeks now, and if anything, he's wilder than ever at the present moment."

"Give 'm a chance," Matt counselled. "Turn 'm loose for a spell."

The other looked at him incredulously.

"Yes," Matt went on, "I know you've tried to, but you didn't take a club."

"You try it then."

The dog-musher secured a club and went over to the chained animal. White Fang watched the club after the manner of a caged lion watching the whip of its trainer.

"See 'm keep his eye on that club," Matt said. "That's a good sign. He's no fool. Don't dast tackle me so long as I got that club handy. He's not clean crazy, sure."

As the man's hand approached his neck, White Fang bristled and snarled and crouched down. But while he eyed the approaching hand, he at the same time contrived to keep track of the club in the other hand, suspended threateningly above him. Matt unsnapped the chain from the collar and stepped back.

White Fang could scarcely realize that he was free. Many months had gone by since he passed into the possession of Beauty Smith, and in all that period he had never known a moment of freedom except at the times he had been loosed to fight with other dogs. Immediately after such fights he had been imprisoned again.

He did not know what to make of it. Perhaps some new deviltry of the gods was about to be perpetrated on him. He walked slowly and cautiously, prepared to be assailed at any moment. He did not know what to do, it was all so unprecedented. He took the precaution to sheer off from the two watching gods, and walked carefully to the corner of the cabin. Nothing happened. He was plainly perplexed, and he came back again, pausing a dozen feet away and regarding the two men intently.

"Won't he run away?" his new owner asked.

Matt shrugged his shoulders. "Got to take a gamble. Only way to find out is to find out."

"Poor devil," Scott murmured pityingly. "What he needs is some show of human kindness," he added, turning and going into the cabin.

He came out with a piece of meat, which he tossed to White Fang. He sprang away from it, and from a distance studied it suspiciously.

"Hi-yu, Major!" Matt shouted warningly, but too late.

Major had made a spring for the meat. At the instant his jaws closed on it, White Fang struck him. He was overthrown. Matt rushed in, but quicker than he was White Fang. Major staggered to his feet, but the blood spouting from his throat reddened the snow in a widening path.

"It's too bad, but it served him right," Scott said hastily.

But Matt's foot had already started on its way to kick White Fang. There was a leap, a flash of teeth, a sharp exclamation. White Fang, snarling fiercely, scrambled backward for several yards, while Matt stooped and investigated his leg.

"He got me all right," he announced, pointing to the torn trousers and underclothes, and the growing stain of red.

"I told you it was hopeless, Matt," Scott said in a

discouraged voice. "I've thought about it off and on, while not wanting to think of it. But we've come to it now. It's the only thing to do."

As he talked, with reluctant movements he drew his revolver, threw open the cylinder, and assured himself of its contents.

"Look here, Mr. Scott," Matt objected; "that dog's ben through hell. You can't expect 'm to come out a white an' shinin' angel. Give 'm time."

"Look at Major," the other rejoined.

The dog-musher surveyed the stricken dog. He had sunk down on the snow in the circle of his blood, and was plainly in the last gasp.

"Served 'm right. You said so yourself, Mr. Scott. He tried to take White Fang's meat, an' he's dead-O. That was to be expected. I wouldn't give two whoops in hell for a dog that wouldn't fight for his own meat."

"But look at yourself, Matt. It's all right about the dogs, but we must draw the line somewhere."

"Served me right," Matt argued stubbornly. "What'd I want to kick 'm for? You said yourself he'd done right. Then I had no right to kick 'm."

"It would be a mercy to kill him," Scott insisted. "He's untamable."

"Now look here, Mr. Scott, give the poor devil a fightin' chance. He ain't had no chance yet. He's just come through hell, an' this is the first time he's ben loose. Give 'm a fair chance, an' if he don't deliver the goods, I'll kill 'm myself. There!"

"God knows I don't want to kill him or have him killed," Scott answered, putting away the revolver. "We'll let him run loose and see what kindness can do for him. And here's a try at it."

He walked over to White Fang and began talking to him gently and soothingly.

"Better have a club handy," Matt warned.

Scott shook his head and went on trying to win White Fang's confidence.

White Fang was suspicious. Something was impending. He had killed this god's dog, bitten his companion god, and what else was to be expected than some terrible punishment? But in the face of it he was indomitable. He bristled and showed his teeth, his eyes vigilant, his whole body wary and prepared for anything. The god had no club, so he suffered him to approach quite near. The god's hand had come out and was descending on his head. White Fang shrank together and grew tense as he crouched under it. Here was danger, some treachery or something. He knew the hands of the gods, their proved mastery, their cunning to hurt. Besides, there was his old antipathy to being touched. He snarled more menacingly, crouched still lower, and still the hand descended. He did not want to bite the hand, and he endured the peril of it until his instinct surged up in him, mastering him with its insatiable yearning for life.

Weedon Scott had believed that he was quick enough to avoid any snap or slash. But he had yet to learn the remarkable quickness of White Fang, who struck with the certainty and swiftness of a coiled snake.

Scott cried out sharply with surprise, catching his torn hand and holding it tightly in his other hand. Matt uttered a great oath and sprang to his side. White Fang crouched down and backed away, bristling, showing his fangs, his eyes malignant with menace. Now he could expect a beating as fearful as any he had received from Beauty Smith.

"Here! What are you doing?" Scott cried suddenly.

Matt had dashed into the cabin and come out with a rifle.

"Nothin'," he said slowly, with a careless calmness that was assumed; "only goin' to keep that promise I made. I reckon it's up to me to kill 'm as I said I'd do."

"No you don't!"

"Yes I do. Watch me."

As Matt had pleaded for White Fang when he had been bitten, it was now Weedon Scott's turn to plead.

"You said to give him a chance. Well, give it to him. We've only just started, and we can't quit at the beginning. It served me right, this time. And—look at him!"

White Fang, near the corner of the cabin and forty feet away, was snarling with blood-curdling viciousness, not at Scott, but at the dog-musher.

"Well, I'll be everlastin'ly gosh-swoggled!" was the dog-musher's expression of astonishment.

"Look at the intelligence of him," Scott went on hastily. "He knows the meaning of firearms as well as you do. He's got intelligence, and we've got to give that intelligence a chance. Put up that gun."

"All right, I'm willin'," Matt agreed, leaning the rifle against the woodpile.

"But will you look at that!" he exclaimed the next moment.

White Fang had quieted down and ceased snarling.

"This is worth investigatin'. Watch."

Matt reached for the rifle, and at the same moment White Fang snarled. He stepped away from the rifle, and White Fang's lifted lips descended, covering his teeth.

"Now, just for fun."

Matt took the rifle and began slowly to raise it to his shoulder. White Fang's snarling began with the movement, and increased as the movement approached its culmination. But the moment before the rifle came to a level on him, he leaped sidewise behind the corner of the cabin. Matt stood staring along the sights at the empty space of snow which had been occupied by White Fang.

The dog-musher put the rifle down solemnly, then turned and looked at his employer.

"I agree with you, Mr. Scott. That dog's too intelligent to kill."

CHAPTER VI

The Love-Master

As White Fang watched Weedon Scott approach, he bristled and snarled to advertise that he would not submit to punishment. Twenty-four hours had passed since he had slashed open the hand that was now bandaged and held up by a sling to keep the blood out of it. In the past White Fang had experienced delayed punishments, and he apprehended that such a one was about to befall him. How could it be otherwise? He had committed what was to him sacrilege, sunk his fangs into the holy flesh of a god, and of a white-skinned superior god at that. In the nature of things, and of intercourse with gods, something terrible awaited him.

The god sat down several feet away. White Fang could see nothing dangerous in that. When the gods administered punishment they stood on their legs. Besides, this god had no club, no whip, no firearm. And furthermore, he himself was free. No chain nor stick bound him. He could escape into safety while the god was scrambling to his feet. In the meantime he would wait and see.

The god remained quiet, made no movement; and White Fang's snarl slowly dwindled to a growl that ebbed down in his throat and ceased. Then the god spoke, and at the first sound of his voice, the hair rose on White Fang's neck and the growl rushed up in his throat. But the god made no hostile movement and went on calmly talking. For a time White Fang growled in unison with him, a correspondence of rhythm being established between growl and voice. But the god talked on interminably. He talked to White Fang as White Fang had never been talked to before. He talked softly and soothingly, with a gentleness that somehow, somewhere, touched White Fang. In spite of himself and all the pricking warnings of his instinct, White Fang began to have confidence in this god. He had a feeling of security that was belied by all his experience with men.

After a long time, the god got up and went into the cabin. White Fang scanned him apprehensively when he came out. He had neither whip nor club nor weapon. Nor was his injured hand behind his back hiding something. He sat down as before, in the same spot, several feet away. He held out a small piece of meat. White Fang pricked his ears and investigated it suspiciously, managing to look at the same time both at the meat and the god, alert for any overt act, his body tense and ready to spring away at the first sign of hostility.

Still the punishment delayed. The god merely held near to his nose a piece of meat. And about the meat there seemed nothing wrong. Still White Fang suspected; and though the meat was proffered to him with short inviting thrusts of the hand, he refused to touch it. The gods were all-wise, and there was no telling what masterful treachery lurked behind that apparently harmless piece of meat. In past experience, especially in dealing with squaws, meat and punishment had often been disastrously related.

In the end, the god tossed the meat on the snow at White Fang's feet. He smelled the meat carefully; but he did not look at it. While he smelled it he kept his eyes on the god. Nothing happened. He took the meat into his mouth and swallowed it. Still nothing happened. The god was actually offering him another piece of meat. Again he refused to take it from the hand, and again it was tossed to him. This was repeated a number of times. But there came a time when the god refused to toss it. He kept it in his hand and steadfastly proffered it.

The meat was good meat, and White Fang was hungry. Bit by bit, infinitely cautious, he approached the hand. At last the time came that he decided to eat the meat from the hand. He never took his eyes from the god, thrusting his head forward with ears flattened back and hair involuntarily rising and cresting on his neck. Also a low growl rumbled in his throat as warning that he was not to be trifled with. He ate the meat, and nothing happened. Piece by piece, he ate all the meat, and nothing happened. Still the punishment delayed.

He licked his chops and waited. The god went on talking. In his voice was kindness—something of which White Fang had no experience whatever. And within him it aroused feelings which he had likewise never experienced before. He was aware of a certain strange satisfaction, as though some need were being gratified, as though some void in his being were being filled. Then again came the prod of his instinct and the warning of past experience. The gods were ever crafty, and they had unguessed ways of attaining their ends.

Ah, he had thought so! There it came now, the god's hand, cunning to hurt, thrusting out at him, descending upon his head. But the god went on talking. His voice was soft and soothing. In spite of the menacing hand, the voice inspired confidence. And in spite of the assuring voice, the hand inspired distrust. White Fang was torn by conflicting feelings, impulses. It seemed he would fly to pieces, so terrible was the control he was exerting, holding together by an unwonted indecision the counter-forces that struggled within him for mastery.

He compromised. He snarled and bristled and flattened his ears. But he neither snapped nor sprang away. The hand descended. Nearer and nearer it came. It touched the ends of his upstanding hair. He shrank down under it. It followed down after him, pressing more closely against him. Shrinking, almost shivering, he still managed to hold himself together. It was a torment, this hand that touched him and violated his instinct. He could not forget in a day all the evil that had been wrought him at the hands of men. But it was the will of the god, and he strove to submit.

The hand lifted and descended again in a patting, caressing movement. This continued, but every time the hand lifted, the hair lifted under it. And every time the hand descended, the ears flattened down and a cavernous growl surged in his throat. White Fang growled and growled with insistent warning. By this means he announced that he was prepared to retaliate for any hurt he might receive. There was no telling when the god's ulterior motive might be disclosed. At any moment that soft, confidence-inspiring voice might break forth in a roar of wrath, that gentle and caressing hand transform itself into a viselike grip to hold him helpless and administer punishment.

But the god talked on softly, and ever the hand rose and fell with non-hostile pats. White Fang experienced dual feelings. It was distasteful to his instinct. It restrained him, opposed the will of him toward personal liberty. And yet it was not physically painful. On the contrary, it was even pleasant, in a physical way. The patting movement slowly and carefully changed to a rubbing of the ears about their bases, and the physical pleasure even increased a little. Yet he continued to fear, and he stood on guard, expectant of unguessed evil, alternately suffering and enjoying as one feeling or the other came uppermost and swayed him.

"Well, I'll be gosh-swoggled!"

So spoke Matt, coming out of the cabin, his sleeves rolled up, a pan of dirty dish-water in his hands, arrested in the act of emptying the pan by the sight of Weedon Scott patting White Fang.

At the instant his voice broke the silence, White Fang leaped back, snarling savagely at him.

Matt regarded his employer with grieved disapproval.

"If you don't mind my expressin' my feelin's, Mr. Scott, I'll make free to say you're seventeen kinds of a damn fool an' all of 'em different, and then some."

Weedon Scott smiled with a superior air, gained his feet, and walked over to White Fang. He talked soothingly to him, but not for long, then slowly put out his hand, rested it on White Fang's head, and resumed the interrupted patting. White Fang endured it, keeping his eyes fixed suspiciously, not upon the man that petted him, but upon the man that stood in the doorway.

"You may be a number one, tip-top minin' expert, all right all right," the dog-musher delivered himself oracularly, "but you missed the chance of your life when you was a boy, an' didn't run off an' join a circus."

White Fang snarled at the sound of his voice, but this time did not leap away from under the hand that was caressing his head and the back of his neck with long, soothing strokes.

It was the beginning of the end for White Fang— the ending of the old life and the reign of hate. A new and incomprehensibly fairer life was dawning. It required much thinking and endless patience on the part of Weedon Scott to accomplish this. And on the part of White Fang it required nothing less than a revolution. He had to ignore the urges and promptings of instinct and reason, defy experience, give the lie to life itself.

Life, as he had known it, not only had had no place in it for much that he now did; but all the currents had gone counter to those to which he now abandoned himself. In short, when all things were considered, he had to achieve an orientation far vaster than the one he had achieved at the time he came voluntarily in from the Wild and accepted Gray Beaver as his lord. At that time he was a mere puppy, soft from the making, without form, ready for the thumb of circumstance to begin its work upon him. But now it was different. The thumb of circumstance had done its work only too well. By it he had been formed and hardened into the Fighting Wolf, fierce and implacable, unloving and unlovable. To accomplish the change was like a reflux of being, and this when the plasticity of youth was no longer his; when the fibre of him had become tough and knotty; when the warp and the woof of him had made of him an adamantine texture, harsh and unyielding; when the face of his spirit had become iron and all his instincts and axioms had crystallized into set rules, cautions, dislikes, and desires.

Yet again, in this new orientation, it was the thumb of circumstance that pressed and prodded him, softening that which had become hard and remoulding it into fairer form. Weedon Scott was in truth this thumb. He had gone to the roots of White Fang's nature, and with kindness touched to life potencies that had languished and well-nigh perished. One such potency was *love.* It took the place of *like,* which latter had been the highest feeling that thrilled him in his intercourse with the gods.

But this love did not come in a day. It began with *like* and out of it slowly developed. White Fang did not run away, though he was allowed to remain loose, because he liked this new god. This was certainly better than the life he had lived in the cage of Beauty Smith, and it was necessary that he should have some god. The lordship of man was a need of his nature. The seal of his dependence on man had been set upon him in that early day when he turned his back on the Wild and crawled to Gray Beaver's feet to receive the expected beating. This seal had been stamped upon him again, and ineradicably, on his second return from the Wild, when the long famine was over and there was fish once more in the village of Gray Beaver.

And so, because he needed a god and because he preferred Weedon Scott to Beauty Smith, White Fang remained. In acknowledgment of fealty, he proceeded to take upon himself the guardianship of his master's property. He prowled about the cabin while the sled-dogs slept, and the first night-visitor to the cabin fought him off with a club until Weedon Scott came to the rescue. But White Fang soon learned to differentiate between thieves and honest men, to appraise the true value of step and carriage. The man who travelled, loud-stepping, the direct line to the cabin door, he let alone—though he watched him vigilantly until the door opened and he received the indorsement of the master. But the man who went softly, by circuitous ways, peering with caution, seeking after secrecy—that was the man who received no suspension of judgment from White Fang, and who went away abruptly hurriedly, and without dignity.

Weedon Scott had set himself the task of redeeming White Fang—or rather, of redeeming mankind from the wrong it had done White Fang. It was a matter of principle and conscience. He felt that the ill done White Fang was a debt incurred by man and that it must be paid. So he went out of his way to be especially kind to the Fighting Wolf. Each day he made it a point to caress and pet White Fang, and to do it at length.

At first suspicious and hostile, White Fang grew to like this petting. But there was one thing that he never outgrew—his growling. Growl he would, from the moment the petting began until it ended. But it was a growl with a new note in it. A stranger could not hear this note, and to such a stranger the growling of White Fang was an exhibition of primordial savagery, nerve-racking and blood-curdling. But White Fang's throat had become harsh-fibred from the making of ferocious sounds through the many years since his first little rasp of anger in the lair of his cubhood, and he could not soften the sounds of that throat now to express the gentleness he felt. Nevertheless, Weedon Scott's ear and sympathy were fine enough to catch the new note all but drowned in the fierceness—the note that was the faintest hint of a croon of content and that none but he could hear.

As the days went by, the evolution of *like* into *love* was accelerated. White Fang himself began to grow aware of it, though in his consciousness he knew not what love was. It manifested itself to him as a void in his being—a hungry, aching, yearning void that clamored to be filled. It was a pain and an unrest; and it received easement only by the touch of the new god's presence. At such times love was a joy to him, a wild, keen-thrilling satisfaction. But when away from his god, the pain and the unrest returned; the void in him sprang up and pressed against him with its emptiness, and the hunger gnawed and gnawed unceasingly.

White Fang was in the process of finding himself. In spite of the maturity of his years and of the savage rigidity of the mould that had formed him, his nature was undergoing an expansion. There was a burgeoning within him of strange feelings and unwonted impulses. His old code of conduct was changing. In the past he had liked comfort and surcease from pain, disliked discomfort and pain, and he had adjusted his actions accordingly. But now it was different. Because of this new feeling within him, he ofttimes elected discomfort and pain for the sake of his god. Thus, in the early morning, instead of roaming and foraging, or lying in a sheltered nook, he would wait for hours on the cheer less cabin-stoop for a sight of the god's face. At night, when the god returned home, White Fang would leave the warm sleeping-place he had burrowed in the snow in order to receive the friendly snap of fingers and the word of greeting. Meat, even meat itself, he would forego to be with his god, to receive a caress from him or to accompany him down into the town.

Like had been replaced by *love*. And love was the plummet dropped down into the deeps of him where like had never gone. And responsive, out of his deeps had come the new thing—love. That which was given unto him did he return. This was a god indeed, a love-god, a warm and radiant god, in whose light White Fang's nature expanded as a flower expands under the sun.

But White Fang was not demonstrative. He was too old, too firmly moulded, to become adept at expressing himself in new ways. He was too self-possessed, too strongly poised in his own isolation. Too long had he cultivated reticence, aloofness, and moroseness. He had never barked in his life, and he could not now learn to bark a welcome when his god approached. He was never in the way, never extravagant nor foolish in the expression of his love. He never ran to meet his god. He waited at a distance, but he always waited, was always there. His love partook of the nature of worship, dumb, inarticulate, a silent adoration. Only by the steady regard of his eyes did he express his love, and by the unceasing following with his eyes of his god's every movement. Also, at times, when his god looked at him and spoke to him, he betrayed an awkward self-consciousness, caused by the struggle of his love to express itself and his physical inability to express it.

He learned to adjust himself in many ways to his new mode of life. It was borne in upon him that he must let his master's dogs alone. Yet his dominant nature asserted itself, and he had first to thrash them into an acknowledgment of his superiority and leadership. This accomplished, he had little trouble with them. They gave trail to him when he came and went or walked among them, and when he asserted his will they obeyed.

In the same way, he came to tolerate Matt—as a possession of his master. His master rarely fed him; Matt did that, it was his business; yet White Fang divined that it was his master's food he ate and that it was his master who thus fed him vicariously. Matt it was who tried to put him into the harness and make him haul sled with the other dogs. But Matt failed. It was not until Weedon Scott put the harness on White Fang and worked him, that he understood. He took it as his master's will that Matt should drive him and work him just as he drove and worked his master's other dogs.

Different from the Mackenzie toboggans were the Klondike sleds with runners under them. And different was the method of driving the dogs. There was no fan-formation of the team. The dogs worked in single file, one behind another, hauling on double traces. And here, in the Klondike, the leader was indeed the leader. The wisest as well as strongest dog was the leader, and the team obeyed him and feared him. That White Fang should quickly gain the post was inevitable. He could not be satisfied with less, as Matt learned after much inconvenience and trouble. White Fang picked out the post for himself, and Matt backed his judgment with strong language after the experiment had been tried. But, though he worked in the sled in the day, White Fang did not forego the guarding of his master's property in the night. Thus he was on duty all the time, ever vigilant and faithful, the most valuable of all the dogs.

"Makin' free to spit out what's in me," Matt said, one day, "I beg to state that you was a wise guy all right when you paid the price you did for that dog. You clean swindled Beauty Smith on top of pushin' his face in with your fist."

A recrudescence of anger glinted in Weedon Scott's gray eyes, and he muttered savagely, "The beast!"

In the late spring a great trouble came to White Fang. Without warning, the love-master disappeared. There had been warning, but White Fang was unversed in such things and did not understand the packing of a grip. He remembered afterward that this packing had preceded the master's disappearance; but at the time he suspected nothing. That night he waited for the master to return. At midnight the chill wind that blew drove him to shelter at the rear of the cabin. There he drowsed, only half asleep, his ears keyed for the first sound of the familiar step. But, at two in the morning, his anxiety drove him out to the cold front stoop, where he crouched and waited.

But no master came. In the morning the door opened and Matt stepped outside. White Fang gazed at him wistfully. There was no common speech by which he might learn what he wanted to know. The days came and went, but never the master. White Fang, who had never known sickness in his life, became sick. He became very sick, so sick that Matt was finally compelled to bring him inside the cabin. Also, in writing to his employer, Matt devoted a postscript to White Fang.

Weedon Scott, reading the letter down in Circle City, came upon the following:

"That dam wolf wont work. Wont eat. Aint got no spunk left. All the dogs is licking him. Wants to know what has become of you, and I dont know how to tell him. Mebbe he is going to die."

It was as Matt had said. White Fang had ceased eating, lost heart, and allowed every dog of the team to thrash him. In the cabin he lay on the floor near the stove, without interest in food, in Matt, nor in life.

Matt might talk gently to him or swear at him, it was all the same; he never did more than turn his dull eyes upon the man, then drop his head back to its customary position on his fore-paws.

And then, one night, Matt, reading to himself with moving lips and mumbled sounds, was startled by a low whine from White Fang. He had got upon his feet, his ears cocked toward the door, and he was listening intently. A moment later, Matt heard a footstep. The door opened, and Weedon Scott stepped in. The two men shook hands. Then Scott looked around the room.

"Where's the wolf?" he asked.

Then he discovered him, standing where he had been lying, near to the stove. He had not rushed forward after the manner of other dogs. He stood, watching and waiting.

"Holy smoke!" Matt exclaimed. "Look at 'm wag his tail!"

Weedon Scott strode half across the room toward him, at the same time calling him. White Fang came to him, not with a great bound, yet quickly. He was awkward from self-consciousness, but as he drew near, his eyes took on a strange expression. Something, an incommunicable vastness of feeling, rose up into his eyes as a light and shone forth.

"He never looked at me that way all the time you was gone," Matt commented.

Weedon Scott did not hear. He was squatting down on his heels, face to face with White Fang and petting him—rubbing at the roots of the ears, making long, caressing strokes down the neck to the shoulders, tapping the spine gently with the balls of his fingers. And White Fang was growling responsively, the crooning note of the growl more pronounced than ever.

But that was not all. What of his joy, the great love in him, ever surging and struggling to express itself, succeeded in finding a new mode of expression. He suddenly thrust his head forward and nudged his way in between the master's arm and body. And here, confined, hidden from view all except his ears, no longer growling, he continued to nudge and snuggle.

The two men looked at each other. Scott's eyes were shining.

"Gosh!" said Matt in an awe-stricken voice.

A moment later, when he had recovered himself, he said, "I always insisted that wolf was a dog. Look at 'm!"

With the return of the love-master, White Fang's recovery was rapid. Two nights and a day he spent in the cabin. Then he sallied forth. The sled-dogs had forgotten his prowess. They remembered only the latest, which was his weakness and sickness. At the sight of him as he came out of the cabin, they sprang upon him.

"Talk about your rough-houses," Matt murmured gleefully, standing in the doorway and looking on. "Give 'm hell, you wolf! Give 'm hell!—and then some!"

White Fang did not need the encouragement. The return of the love-master was enough. Life was flowing through him again, splendid and indomitable. He fought from sheer joy, finding in it an expression of much that he felt and that otherwise was without speech. There could be but one ending. The team dispersed in ignominious defeat, and it was not until after dark that the dogs came sneaking back, one by one, by meekness and humility signifying their fealty to White Fang.

Having learned to snuggle, White Fang was guilty of it often. It was the final word. He could not go beyond it. The one thing of which he had always been particularly jealous, was his head. He had always disliked to have it touched. It was the Wild in him, the fear of hurt and of the trap, that had given rise to the panicky impulses to avoid contacts. It was the mandate of his instinct that that head must be free. And now, with the love-master, his snuggling was the deliberate act of putting himself into a position of hopeless helplessness. It was an expression of perfect confidence, of absolute self-surrender, as though he said: "I put myself into thy hands. Work thou thy will with me."

One night, not long after the return, Scott and Matt sat at a game of cribbage preliminary to going to bed. "Fifteen-two, fifteen-four, an' a pair makes six," Matt was pegging up, when there was an outcry and sound of snarling without. They looked at each other as they started to rise to their feet.

"The wolf's nailed somebody," Matt said.

A wild scream of fear and anguish hastened them.

"Bring a light!" Scott shouted, as he sprang outside.

Matt followed with the lamp, and by its light they saw a man lying on his back in the snow. His arms were folded, one above the other, across his face and throat. Thus he was trying to shield himself from White Fang's teeth. And there was need for it. White Fang was in a rage, wickedly making his attack on the most vulnerable spot. From shoulder to wrist of the crossed arms, the coat-sleeve, blue flannel shirt and undershirt were ripped in rags, while the arms themselves were terribly slashed and streaming blood.

All this the two men saw in the first instant. The next instant Weedon Scott had White Fang by the throat and was dragging him clear. White Fang struggled and snarled, but made no attempt to bite, while he quickly quieted down at a sharp word from the master.

Matt helped the man to his feet. As he arose he lowered his crossed arms, exposing the bestial face of Beauty Smith. The dog-musher let go of him precipitately, with action similar to that of a man who has picked up live fire. Beauty Smith blinked in the lamp-light and looked about him. He caught sight of White Fang and terror rushed into his face.

At the same moment Matt noticed two objects lying

in the snow. He held the lamp close to them, indicating them with his toe for his employer's benefit—a steel dog-chain and a stout club.

Weedon Scott saw and nodded. Not a word was spoken. The dog-musher laid his hand on Beauty Smith's shoulder and faced him to the right-about. No word needed to be spoken. Beauty Smith started.

In the meantime the love-master was patting White Fang and talking to him.

"Tried to steal you, eh? And you wouldn't have it! Well, well, he made a mistake, didn't he?"

"Must 'a' thought he had hold of seventeen devils," the dog-musher sniggered.

White Fang, still wrought up and bristling, growled and growled, the hair slowly lying down, the crooning note remote and dim, but growing in his throat.

PART FIVE: THE TAME

CHAPTER I

The Long Trail

It was in the air. White Fang sensed the coming calamity, even before there was tangible evidence of it. In vague ways it was borne in upon him that a change was impending. He knew not how nor why, yet he got his feel of the oncoming event from the gods themselves. In ways subtler than they knew, they betrayed their intentions to the wolf-dog that haunted the cabin-stoop, and that, though he never came inside the cabin, knew what went on inside their brains.

"Listen to that, will you!" the dog-musher exclaimed at supper one night.

Weedon Scott listened. Through the door came a low, anxious whine, like a sobbing under the breath that has just grown audible. Then came the long sniff, as White Fang reassured himself that his god was still inside and had not yet taken himself off in mysterious and solitary flight.

"I do believe that wolf's on to you," the dog-musher said.

Weedon Scott looked across at his companion with eyes that almost pleaded, though this was given the lie by his words.

"What the devil can I do with a wolf in California?" he demanded.

"That's what I say," Matt answered. "What the devil can you do with a wolf in California?"

But this did not satisfy Weedon Scott. The other seemed to be judging him in a non-committal sort of way.

"White-man's dogs would have no show against him," Scott went on. "He'd kill them on sight. If he didn't bankrupt me with damage suits, the authorities would take him away from me and electrocute him."

"He's a downright murderer, I know," was the dog-musher's comment.

Weedon Scott looked at him suspiciously.

"It would never do," he said decisively.

"It would never do," Matt concurred. "Why, you'd have to hire a man 'specially to take care of 'm."

The other's suspicion was allayed. He nodded cheerfully. In the silence that followed, the low, half-sobbing whine was heard at the door and then the long, questing sniff.

"There's no denyin' he thinks a hell of a lot of you," Matt said.

The other glared at him in sudden wrath. "Damn it all, man! I know my own mind and what's best!"

"I'm agreein' with you, only . . ."

"Only what?" Scott snapped out.

"Only . . ." the dog-musher began softly, then changed his mind and betrayed a rising anger of his own. "Well, you needn't get so all-fired het up about it. Judgin' by your actions one'd think you didn't know your own mind."

Weedon Scott debated with himself for a while, and then said more gently: "You are right, Matt. I don't know my own mind, and that's what's the trouble."

"Why, it would be rank ridiculousness for me to take that dog along," he broke out after another pause.

"I'm agreein' with you," was Matt's answer, and again his employer was not quite satisfied with him.

"But how in the name of the great Sardanapalus he knows you're goin' is what gets me," the dog-musher continued innocently.

"It's beyond me, Matt," Scott answered, with a mournful shake of the head.

Then came the day when, through the open cabin door, White Fang saw the fatal grip on the floor and the love-master packing things into it. Also, there were comings and goings, and the erstwhile placid atmosphere of the cabin was vexed with strange perturbations and unrest. Here was indubitable evidence. White Fang had already sensed it. He now reasoned it. His god was preparing for another flight. And since he had not taken him with him before, so, now, he could look to be left behind.

That night he lifted the long wolf-howl. As he had howled, in his puppy days, when he fled back from the Wild to the village to find it vanished and naught but a rubbish-heap to mark the site of Gray Beaver's tepee, so now he pointed his muzzle to the cold stars and told to them his woe.

Inside the cabin the two men had just gone to bed.

"He's gone off his food again," Matt remarked from his bunk.

There was a grunt from Weedon Scott's bunk, and a stir of blankets.

"From the way he cut up the other time you went away, I wouldn't wonder this time but what he died."

The blankets in the other bunk stirred irritably.

"Oh, shut up!" Scott cried out through the darkness. "You nag worse than a woman."

"I'm agreein' with you," the dog-musher answered, and Weedon Scott was not quite sure whether or not the other had snickered.

The next day White Fang's anxiety and restlessness were even more pronounced. He dogged his master's heels whenever he left the cabin, and haunted the front stoop when he remained inside. Through the open door he could catch glimpses of the luggage on the floor. The grip had been joined by two large canvas bags and a box. Matt was rolling the master's blankets and fur robe inside a small tarpaulin. White Fang whined as he watched the operation.

Later on, two Indians arrived. He watched them closely as they shouldered the luggage and were led off down the hill by Màtt, who carried the bedding and the grip. But White Fang did not follow them. The master was still in the cabin. After a time, Matt returned. The master came to the door and called White Fang inside.

"You poor devil," he said gently, rubbing White Fang's ears and tapping his spine. "I'm hitting the long trail, old man, where you cannot follow. Now give me a growl—the last, good, good-by growl."

But White Fang refused to growl. Instead, and after a wistful, searching look, he snuggled in, burrowing his head out of sight between the master's arm and body.

"There she blows!" Matt cried. From the Yukon arose the hoarse bellowing of a river steamboat. "You've got to cut it short. Be sure and lock the front door. I'll go out the back. Get a move on!"

The two doors slammed at the same moment, and Weedon Scott waited for Matt to come around to the front. From inside the door came a low whining and sobbing. Then there were long, deep-drawn sniffs.

"You must take good care of him, Matt," Scott said, as they started down the hill. "Write and let me know how he gets along."

"Sure," the dog-musher answered. "But listen to that, will you!"

Both men stopped. White Fang was howling as dogs howl when their masters lie dead. He was voicing an utter woe, his cry bursting upward in great, heart-breaking rushes, dying down into quivering misery, and bursting upward again with rush upon rush of grief.

The *Aurora* was the first steamboat of the year for the Outside, and her decks were jammed with prosperous adventurers and broken gold seekers, all equally as mad to get to the Outside as they had been originally to get to the Inside. Near the gang-plank, Scott was shaking hands with Matt, who was preparing to go ashore. But Matt's hand went limp in the other's grasp as his gaze shot past and remained fixed on something behind him. Scott turned to see. Sitting on the deck several feet away and watching wistfully was White Fang.

The dog-musher swore softly, in awe-stricken accents. Scott could only look in wonder.

"Did you lock the front door?" Matt demanded.

The other nodded, and asked, "How about the back?"

"You just bet I did," was the fervent reply

White Fang flattened his ears ingratiatingly, but remained where he was, making no attempt to approach.

"I'll have to take 'm ashore with me."

Matt made a couple of steps toward White Fang, but the latter slid away from him. The dog-musher made a rush of it, and White Fang dodged between the legs of a group of men. Ducking, turning, doubling, he slid about the deck, eluding the other's efforts to capture him.

But when the love-master spoke, White Fang came to him with prompt obedience.

"Won't come to the hand that's fed 'm all these months," the dog-musher muttered resentfully. "And you—you ain't never fed 'm after them first days of gettin' acquainted. I'm blamed if I can see how he works it out that you're the boss."

Scott, who had been patting White Fang, suddenly bent closer and pointed out fresh-made cuts on his muzzle, and a gash between the eyes.

Matt bent over and passed his hand along White Fang's belly.

"We plumb forgot the window. He's all cut an' gouged underneath. Must 'a' butted clean through it, b'gosh!"

But Weedon Scott was not listening. He was thinking rapidly. The *Aurora*'s whistle hooted a final announcement of departure. Men were scurrying down the gang-plank to the shore. Matt loosened the bandana from his own neck and started to put it around White Fang's. Scott grasped the dog-musher's hand.

"Good-by, Matt, old man. About the wolf—you needn't write. You see, I've . . . !"

"What!" the dog-musher exploded. "You don't mean to say . . . ?"

"The very thing I mean. Here's your bandana. *I'll* write to *you* about him."

Matt paused halfway down the gang-plank.

"He'll never stand the climate!" he shouted back. "Unless you clip 'm in warm weather!"

The gang-plank was hauled in, and the *Aurora* swung out from the bank. Weedon Scott waved a last good-by. Then he turned and bent over White Fang, standing by his side.

"Now growl, damn you, growl," he said, as he patted the responsive head and rubbed the flattening ears.

CHAPTER II

The Southland

White Fang landed from the steamer in San Francisco. He was appalled. Deep in him, below any reasoning process or act of consciousness, he had associated power with godhead. And never had the white men seemed such marvellous gods as now, when he trod the slimy pavement of San Francisco. The log cabins he had known were replaced by towering buildings. The streets were crowded with perils—wagons, carts, automobiles; great, straining horses pulling huge trucks; and monstrous cable and electric cars hooting and clanging through the midst, screeching their insistent menace after the manner of the lynxes he had known in the northern woods.

All this was the manifestation of power. Through it all, behind it all, was man, governing and controlling, expressing himself, as of old, by his mastery over matter. It was colossal, stunning. White Fang was awed. Fear sat upon him. As in his cubhood he had been made to feel his smallness and puniness on the day he first came in from the Wild to the village of Gray Beaver, so now, in his full-grown stature and pride of strength, he was made to feel small and puny. And there were so many gods! He was made dizzy by the swarming of them. The thunder of the streets smote upon his ears. He was bewildered by the tremendous and endless rush and movement of things. As never before, he felt his dependence on the love-master, close at whose heels he followed, no matter what happened never losing sight of him.

But White Fang was to have no more than a nightmare vision of the city—an experience that was like a bad dream, unreal and terrible, that haunted him for long after in his dreams. He was put into a baggage-car by the master, chained in a corner in the midst of heaped trunks and valises. Here a squat and brawny god held sway, with much noise, hurling trunks and boxes about, dragging them in through the door and tossing them into the piles, or flinging them out of the door, smashing and crashing, to other gods who awaited them.

And here, in this inferno of luggage, was White Fang deserted by the master. Or at least White Fang thought he was deserted, until he smelled out the master's canvas clothes-bags alongside of him and proceeded to mount guard over them.

" 'Bout time you come," growled the god of the car, an hour later, when Weedon Scott appeared at the door. "That dog of yourn won't let me lay a finger on your stuff."

White Fang emerged from the car. He was astonished. The nightmare city was gone. The car had been to him no more than a room in a house, and when he had entered it the city had been all around him. In the interval the city had disappeared. The roar of it no longer dinned upon his ears. Before him was smiling country, streaming with sunshine, lazy with quietude. But he had little time to marvel at the transformation. He accepted it as he accepted all the unaccountable doings and manifestations of the gods. It was their way.

There was a carriage waiting. A man and a woman approached the master. The woman's arms went out and clutched the master around the neck—a hostile act! The next moment Weedon Scott had torn loose from the embrace and closed with White Fang, who had become a snarling, raging demon.

"It's all right, mother," Scott was saying as he kept tight hold of White Fang and placated him. "He thought you were going to injure me, and he wouldn't stand for it. It's all right. It's all right. He'll learn soon enough."

"And in the meantime I may be permitted to love my son when his dog is not around," she laughed, though she was pale and weak from the fright.

She looked at White Fang, who snarled and bristled and glared malevolently.

"He'll have to learn, and he shall, without postponement," Scott said.

He spoke softly to White Fang until he had quieted him, then his voice became firm.

"Down, sir! Down with you!"

This had been one of the things taught him by the master, and White Fang obeyed, though he lay down reluctantly and sullenly.

"Now, mother."

Scott opened his arms to her, but kept his eyes on White Fang.

"Down!" he warned. "Down!"

White Fang, bristling silently, half-crouching as he rose, sank back and watched the hostile act repeated. But no harm came of it, nor of the embrace from the strange man-god that followed. Then the clothes-bags were taken into the carriage, the strange gods and the love-master followed, and White Fang pursued, now running vigilantly behind, now bristling up to the running horses and warning them that he was there to see that no harm befell the god they dragged so swiftly across the earth.

At the end of fifteen minutes, the carriage swung in through a stone gateway and on between a double row of arched and interlacing walnut trees. On either side stretched lawns, their broad sweep broken, here and there, by great, sturdy-limbed oaks. In the near distance, in contrast with the young green of the tended grass, sunburnt hay-fields showed tan and gold; while beyond were the tawny hills and upland pastures. From the head of the lawn, on the first soft swell from the valley-level, looked down the deep-porched, many-windowed house.

Little opportunity was given White Fang to see all this. Hardly had the carriage entered the grounds, when he was set upon by a sheep-dog, bright-eyed, sharp-muzzled, righteously indignant and angry. It was between him and the master, cutting him off. White Fang snarled no warning, but his hair bristled as he made his silent and deadly rush. This rush was never completed. He halted with awkward abruptness, with stiff fore-legs bracing himself against his momentum, almost sitting down on his haunches, so desirous was he of avoiding contact with the dog he was in the act of attacking. It was a female, and the law of his kind thrust a barrier between. For him to attack her would require nothing less than a violation of his instinct.

But with the sheep-dog it was otherwise. Being a female, she possessed no such instinct. On the other hand, being a sheep-dog, her instinctive fear of the Wild, and especially of the wolf, was unusually keen. White Fang was to her a wolf, the hereditary marauder who had preyed upon her flocks from the time sheep were first herded and guarded by some dim ancestor of hers. And so, as he abandoned his rush at her and braced himself to avoid the contact, she sprang upon him. He snarled involuntarily as he felt her teeth in his shoulder, but beyond this made no offer to hurt her. He backed away, stiff-legged with self-consciousness, and tried to go around her. He dodged this way and that, and curved and turned, but to no purpose. She remained always between him and the way he wanted to go.

"Here, Collie!" called the strange man in the carriage.

Weedon Scott laughed.

"Never mind, father. It is good discipline. White Fang will have to learn many things, and it's just as well that he begins now. He'll adjust himself all right."

The carriage drove on, and still Collie blocked White Fang's way. He tried to outrun her by leaving the drive and circling across the lawn; but she ran on the inner and smaller circle, and was always there, facing him with her two rows of gleaming teeth. Back he circled, across the drive to the other lawn, and again she headed him off.

The carriage was bearing the master away. White Fang caught glimpses of it disappearing amongst the trees. The situation was desperate. He essayed another circle. She followed, running swiftly. And then, suddenly, he turned upon her. It was his old fighting trick. Shoulder to shoulder, he struck her squarely. Not only was she overthrown. So fast had she been running that she rolled along, now on her back, now on her side, as she struggled to stop, clawing gravel with her feet and crying shrilly her hurt pride and indignation.

White Fang did not wait. The way was clear, and that was all he had wanted. She took after him, never ceasing her outcry. It was the straightaway now, and when it came to real running, White Fang could teach her things. She ran frantically, hysterically, straining to the utmost, advertising the effort she was making with every leap; and all the time White Fang slid smoothly away from her, silently, without effort, gliding like a ghost over the ground.

As he rounded the house to the *porte-cochère,* he came upon the carriage. It had stopped, and the master was alighting. At this moment, still running at top speed, White Fang became suddenly aware of an attack from the side. It was a deer-hound rushing upon him. White Fang tried to face it. But he was going too fast, and the hound was too close. It struck him on the side; and such was his forward momentum and the unexpectedness of it, White Fang was hurled to the ground and rolled clear over. He came out of the tangle a spectacle of malignancy, ears flattened back, lips writhing, nose wrinkling, his teeth clipping together as the fangs barely missed the hound's soft throat.

The master was running up, but was too far away; and it was Collie that saved the hound's life. Before White Fang could spring in and deliver the fatal stroke, and just as he was in the act of springing in, Collie arrived. She had been out-manœuvred and out-run, to say nothing of her having been unceremoniously tumbled in the gravel, and her arrival was like that of a tornado—made up of offended dignity, justifiable wrath, and instinctive hatred for this marauder from the Wild. She struck White Fang at right angles in the midst of his spring, and again he was knocked off his feet and rolled over.

The next moment the master arrived, and with one hand held White Fang, while the father called off the dogs.

"I say, this is a pretty warm reception for a poor lone wolf from the Arctic," the master said, while White Fang calmed down under his caressing hand. "In all his life he's only been known once to go off his feet, and here he's been rolled twice in thirty seconds."

The carriage had driven away, and other strange gods had appeared from out the house. Some of these stood respectfully at a distance; but two of them, women, perpetrated the hostile act of clutching the master around the neck. White Fang, however, was beginning to tolerate this act. No harm seemed to come of it, while the noises the gods made were certainly not threatening. These gods also made overtures to White Fang, but he warned them off with a snarl, and the master did likewise with word of mouth. At such times White Fang leaned in close against the master's legs and received reassuring pats on the head.

The hound, under the command, "Dick! Lie down, sir!" had gone up the steps and lain down to one side on the porch, still growling and keeping a sullen watch on the intruder. Collie had been taken in charge by one of the woman-gods, who held arms around her neck and petted and caressed her; but Collie was very much perplexed and worried, whining and restless, outraged by the permitted presence of this wolf and confident that the gods were making a mistake.

All the gods started up the steps to enter the house. White Fang followed closely at the master's heels. Dick, on the porch, growled, and White Fang, on the steps, bristled and growled back.

"Take Collie inside and leave the two of them to fight it out," suggested Scott's father. "After that they'll be friends."

"Then White Fang, to show his friendship, will have to be chief mourner at the funeral," laughed the master.

The elder Scott looked incredulously, first at White Fang, then at Dick, and finally at his son.

"You mean that . . . ?"

Weedon nodded his head. "I mean just that. You'd have a dead Dick inside one minute—two minutes at the farthest."

He turned to White Fang. "Come on, you wolf. It's you that'll have to come inside."

White Fang walked stiff-legged up the steps and across the porch, with tail rigidly erect, keeping his eyes on Dick to guard against a flank attack, and at the same time prepared for whatever fierce manifestation of the unknown that might pounce out upon him from the interior of the house. But no thing of fear pounced out, and when he had gained the inside he scouted carefully around, looking for it and finding it not. Then he lay down with a contented grunt at the master's feet, observing all that went on, ever ready to spring to his feet and fight for life with the terrors he felt must lurk under the trap-roof of the dwelling.

CHAPTER III

The God's Domain

Not only was White Fang adaptable by nature, but he had travelled much, and knew the meaning and necessity of adjustment. Here, in Sierra Vista, which was the name of Judge Scott's place, White Fang quickly began to make himself at home. He had no further serious trouble with the dogs. They knew more about the ways of the Southland gods than did he, and in their eyes he had qualified when he accompanied the gods inside the house. Wolf that he was, and unprecedented as it was, the gods had sanctioned his presence, and they, the dogs of the gods, could only recognize this sanction.

Dick, perforce, had to go through a few stiff formalities at first, after which he calmly accepted White Fang as an addition to the premises. Had Dick had his way, they would have been good friends; but White Fang was averse to friendship. All he asked of other dogs was to be let alone. His whole life he had kept aloof from his kind, and he still desired to keep aloof. Dick's overtures bothered him, so he snarled Dick away. In the north he had learned the lesson that he must let the master's dogs alone, and he did not forget that lesson now. But he insisted on his own privacy and self-seclusion, and so thoroughly ignored Dick that that good-natured creature finally gave him up and scarcely took as much interest in him as in the hitching-post near the stable.

Not so with Collie. While she accepted him because it was the mandate of the gods, that was no reason that she should leave him in peace. Woven into her being was the memory of countless crimes he and his had perpetrated against her ancestry. Not in a day nor a generation were the ravaged sheepfolds to be forgotten. All this was a spur to her, pricking her to retaliation. She could not fly in the face of the gods who permitted him, but that did not prevent her from making life miserable for him in petty ways. A feud, ages old, was between them, and she, for one, would see to it that he was reminded.

So Collie took advantage of her sex to pick upon White Fang and maltreat him. His instinct would not permit him to attack her, while her persistence would not permit him to ignore her. When she rushed at him he turned his fur-protected shoulder to her sharp teeth and walked away stiff-legged and stately. When she forced him too hard, he was compelled to go about in a circle, his shoulder presented to her, his head turned from her, and on his face and in his eyes a patient and bored expression. Sometimes, however, a nip on his hind-quarters hastened his retreat and made it anything but stately. But as a rule he managed to maintain a dignity that was almost solemnity. He ignored her existence whenever it was possible, and made it a point to keep out of her way. When he saw or heard her coming, he got up and walked off.

There was much in other matters for White Fang to learn. Life in the Northland was simplicity itself when compared with the complicated affairs of Sierra Vista. First of all, he had to learn the family of the master. In a way he was prepared to do this. As Mit-sah and Kloo-kooch had belonged to Gray Beaver, sharing his food, his fire, and his blankets, so now, at Sierra Vista, belonged to the love-master all the denizens of the house.

But in this matter there was a difference, and many differences. Sierra Vista was a far vaster affair than the tepee of Gray Beaver. There were many persons to be considered. There was Judge Scott, and there was his wife. There were the master's two sisters, Beth and Mary. There was his wife, Alice, and then there were his children, Weedon and Maud, toddlers of four and six. There was no way for anybody to tell him about all these people, and of blood-ties and relationship he knew nothing whatever and never would be capable of knowing. Yet he quickly worked it out that all of them belonged to the master. Then, by observation, whenever opportunity offered, by study of action, speech, and the very intonations of the voice, he slowly learned the intimacy and the degree of favor they enjoyed with the master. And by this ascertained standard, White Fang treated them accordingly. What was of value to the master he valued; what was dear to the master was to be cherished by White Fang and guarded carefully.

Thus it was with the two children. All his life he had disliked children. He hated and feared their hands. The lessons were not tender that he had learned of their tyranny and cruelty in the days of the Indian villages. When Weedon and Maud had first approached him, he growled warningly and looked malignant. A cuff from the master and a sharp word had then compelled him to permit their caresses, though he growled and growled under their tiny hands, and in the growl there was no crooning note. Later, he observed that the boy and girl were of great value in the master's eyes. Then it was that no cuff nor sharp word was necessary before they could pat him.

Yet White Fang was never effusively affectionate. He yielded to the master's children with an ill but honest grace, and endured their fooling as one would endure a painful operation. When he could no longer endure, he would get up and stalk determinedly away from them. But after a time, he grew even to like the children. Still he was not demonstrative. He would not go up to them. On the other hand, instead of walking away at sight of them, he waited for them to come to him. And still later, it was noticed that a pleased light came into his eyes when he saw them approaching, and that he looked after them with an appearance of curious regret when they left him for other amusements.

All this was a matter of development, and took time. Next in his regard, after the children, was Judge Scott. There were two reasons, possibly, for this. First, he was evidently a valuable possession of the master's, and next, he was undemonstrative. White Fang liked to lie at his feet on the wide porch when he read the newspaper, from time to time favoring White Fang with a look or a word—untroublesome tokens that he recognized White Fang's presence and existence. But this was only when the master was not around. When the master appeared, all other beings ceased to exist so far as White Fang was concerned.

White Fang allowed all the members of the family to pet him and make much of him; but he never gave to them what he gave to the master. No caress of theirs could put the love-croon into his throat, and, try as they would, they could never persuade him into snuggling against them. This expression of abandon and surrender, of absolute trust, he reserved for the master alone. In fact, he never regarded the members of the family in any other light than possessions of the love-master.

Also White Fang had early come to differentiate between the family and the servants of the household. The latter were afraid of him, while he merely refrained from attacking them. This because he considered that they were likewise possessions of the master.

Between White Fang and them existed a neutrality and no more. They cooked for the master and washed the dishes and did other things, just as Matt had done up in the Klondike. They were, in short, appurtenances of the household.

Outside the household there was even more for White Fang to learn. The master's domain was wide and complex, yet it had its metes and bounds. The land itself ceased at the county road. Outside was the common domain of all gods—the roads and streets. Then inside other fences were the particular domains of other gods. A myriad laws governed all these things and determined conduct; yet he did not know the speech of the gods, nor was there any way for him to learn save by experience. He obeyed his natural impulses until they ran him counter to some law. When this had been done a few times, he learned the law and after that observed it.

But most potent in his education were the cuff of the master's hand, the censure of the master's voice. Because of White Fang's very great love, a cuff from the master hurt him far more than any beating Gray Beaver or Beauty Smith had ever given him. They had hurt only the flesh of him; beneath the flesh the spirit had still raged, splendid and invincible. But with the master the cuff was always too light to hurt the flesh. Yet it went deeper. It was an expression of the master's disapproval, and White Fang's spirit wilted under it.

In point of fact, the cuff was rarely administered. The master's voice was sufficient. By it White Fang knew whether he did right or not. By it he trimmed his conduct and adjusted his actions. It was the compass by which he steered and learned to chart the manners of a new land and life.

In the Northland, the only domesticated animal was the dog. All other animals lived in the Wild, and were, when not too formidable, lawful spoil for any dog. All his days White Fang had foraged among the live things for food. It did not enter his head that in the Southland it was otherwise. But this he was to learn early in his residence in Santa Clara Valley. Sauntering around the corner of the house in the early morning, he came upon a chicken that had escaped from the chicken-yard. White Fang's natural impulse was to eat it. A couple of bounds, a flash of teeth and a frightened squawk, and he had scooped in the adventurous fowl. It was farmbred and fat and tender; and White Fang licked his chops and decided that such fare was good.

Later in the day, he chanced upon another stray chicken near the stables. One of the grooms ran to the rescue. He did not know White Fang's breed, so for weapon he took a light buggy-whip. At the first cut of the whip, White Fang left the chicken for the man. A club might have stopped White Fang, but not a whip. Silently, without flinching, he took a second cut in his forward rush, and as he leaped for the throat the groom cried out, "My God!" and staggered backward. He dropped the whip and shielded his throat with his arms. In consequence, his forearm was ripped open to the bone.

The man was badly frightened. It was not so much White Fang's ferocity as it was his silence that unnerved the groom. Still protecting his throat and face with his torn and bleeding arm, he tried to retreat to the barn. And it would have gone hard with him had not Collie appeared on the scene. As she had saved Dick's life, she now saved the groom's. She rushed upon White Fang in frenzied wrath. She had been right. She had known better than the blundering gods. All her suspicions were justified. Here was the ancient marauder up to his old tricks again.

The groom escaped into the stables, and White Fang backed away before Collie's wicked teeth, or presented his shoulder to them and circled round and round. But Collie did not give over, as was her wont, after a decent interval of chastisement. On the contrary, she grew more excited and angry every moment, until, in the end, White Fang flung dignity to the winds and frankly fled away from her across the fields.

"He'll learn to leave chickens alone," the master said. "But I can't give him the lesson until I catch him in the act."

Two nights later came the act, but on a more generous scale than the master had anticipated. White Fang had observed closely the chicken-yards and the habits of the chickens. In the night-time, after they had gone to roost, he climbed to the top of a pile of newly hauled lumber. From there he gained the roof of a chicken-house, passed over the ridgepole and dropped to the ground inside. A moment later he was inside the house, and the slaughter began.

In the morning, when the master came out on to the porch, fifty white Leghorn hens, laid out in a row by the groom, greeted his eyes. He whistled to himself, softly, first with surprise, and then, at the end, with admiration. His eyes were likewise greeted by White Fang, but about the latter there were no signs of shame nor guilt. He carried himself with pride, as though, forsooth, he had achieved a deed praiseworthy and meritorious. There was about him no consciousness of sin. The master's lips tightened as he faced the disagreeable task. Then he talked harshly to the unwitting culprit, and in his voice there was nothing but godlike wrath. Also, he held White Fang's nose down to the slain hens, and at the same time cuffed him soundly.

White Fang never raided a chicken-roost again. It was against the law, and he had learned it. Then the master took him into the chicken-yards. White Fang's natural impulse, when he saw the live food fluttering about him and under his very nose, was to spring upon it. He obeyed the impulse, but was checked by his master's voice. They continued in the yards for half an hour. Time and again the impulse surged over White Fang, and each time, as he yielded to it, he was checked by the master's voice. Thus it was he learned the law, and ere he left the domain of the chickens, he had learned to ignore their existence.

"You can never cure a chicken-killer." Judge Scott shook his head sadly at the luncheon table, when his son narrated the lesson he had given White Fang. "Once they've got the habit and the taste of blood . . ." Again he shook his head sadly.

But Weedon Scott did not agree with his father.

"I'll tell you what I'll do," he challenged finally. "I'll lock White Fang in with the chickens all afternoon."

"But think of the chickens," objected the Judge.

"And furthermore," the son went on, "for every chicken he kills, I'll pay you one dollar gold coin of the realm."

"But you should penalize father, too," interposed Beth.

Her sister seconded her, and a chorus of approval arose from around the table. Judge Scott nodded his head in agreement.

"All right." Weedon Scott pondered for a moment. "And if, at the end of the afternoon, White Fang hasn't harmed a chicken, for every ten minutes of the time he has spent in the yard, you will have to say to him, gravely and with deliberation, just as if you were sitting on the bench and solemnly passing judgment, 'White Fang, you are smarter than I thought.'"

From hidden points of vantage the family watched the performance. But it was a fizzle. Locked in the yard and there deserted by the master, White Fang lay down and went to sleep. Once he got up and walked over to the trough for a drink of water. The chickens he calmly ignored. So far as he was concerned they did not exist. At four o'clock he executed a running jump, gained the roof of the chicken house and leaped to the ground outside, whence he sauntered gravely to the house. He had learned the law. And on the porch, before the delighted family, Judge Scott, face to face with White Fang, said slowly and solemnly, sixteen times, "White Fang, you are smarter than I thought."

But it was the multiplicity of laws that befuddled White Fang and often brought him into disgrace. He had to learn that he must not touch the chickens that belonged to other gods. Then there were cats, and rabbits, and turkeys; all these he must let alone. In fact, when he had but partly learned the law, his impression was that he must leave all live things alone. Out in the back-pasture, a quail could flutter up under his nose unharmed. All tense and trembling with eagerness and desire, he mastered his instinct and stood still. He was obeying the will of the gods.

And then, one day, again out in the back-pasture, he saw Dick start a jackrabbit and run it. The master himself was looking on and did not interfere. Nay, he encouraged White Fang to join in the chase. And thus he learned that there was no taboo on jackrabbits. In the end he worked out the complete law. Between him and all domestic animals there must be no hostilities. If not amity, at least neutrality must obtain. But the other animals—the squirrels, and quail, and cottontails, were creatures of the Wild who had never yielded allegiance to man. They were the lawful prey of any dog. It was only the tame that the gods protected and between the tame deadly strife was not permitted. The gods held the power of life and death over their subjects, and the gods were jealous of their power.

Life was complex in the Santa Clara Valley after the simplicities of the Northland. And the chief thing demanded by these intricacies of civilization was control, restraint—a poise of self that was as delicate as the fluttering of gossamer wings and at the same time as rigid as steel. Life had a thousand faces, and White Fang found he must meet them all—thus, when he went to town, in to San Jose, running behind the carriage or loafing about the streets when the carriage stopped. Life flowed past him, deep and wide and varied, continually impinging upon his senses, demanding of him instant and endless adjustments and correspondences, and compelling him, almost always, to suppress his natural impulses.

There were butcher-shops where meat hung within reach. This meat he must not touch. There were cats at the houses the master visited that must be let alone. And there were dogs everywhere that snarled at him and that he must not attack. And then, on the crowded sidewalks, there were persons innumerable whose attention he attracted. They would stop and look at him, point him out to one another, examine him, talk to him, and, worst of all, pat him. And these perilous contacts from all these strange hands he must endure. Yet this endurance he achieved. Furthermore he got over being awkward and self-conscious. In a lofty way he received the attentions of the multitudes of strange gods. With condescension he accepted their condescension. On the other hand, there was something about him that prevented great familiarity. They patted him on the head and passed on, contented and pleased with their own daring.

But it was not all easy for White Fang. Running behind the carriage in the outskirts of San Jose, he encountered certain small boys who made a practice of flinging stones at him. Yet he knew that it was not permitted him to pursue and drag them down. Here he was compelled to violate his instinct of self-preservation, and violate it he did, for he was becoming tame and qualifying himself for civilization.

Nevertheless, White Fang was not quite satisfied

with the arrangement. He had no abstract ideas about justice and fair play. But there is a certain sense of equity that resides in life, and it was this sense in him that resented the unfairness of his being permitted no defence against the stone-throwers. He forgot that in the covenant entered into between him and the gods they were pledged to care for him and defend him. But one day the master sprang from the carriage, whip in hand, and gave the stone-throwers a thrashing. After that they threw stones no more, and White Fang understood and was satisfied.

One other experience of similar nature was his. On the way to town, hanging around the saloon at the cross-roads, were three dogs that made a practice of rushing out upon him when he went by. Knowing his deadly method of fighting, the master had never ceased impressing upon White Fang the law that he must not fight. As a result, having learned the lesson well, White Fang was hard put whenever he passed the cross-roads saloon. After the first rush, each time, his snarl kept the three dogs at a distance, but they trailed along behind, yelping and bickering and insulting him. This endured for some time. The men at the saloon even urged the dogs on to attack White Fang. One day they openly sicked the dogs on him. The master stopped the carriage.

"Go to it," he said to White Fang.

But White Fang could not believe. He looked at the master, and he looked at the dogs. Then he looked back eagerly and questioningly at the master.

The master nodded his head. "Go to them, old fellow. Eat them up."

White Fang no longer hesitated. He turned and leaped silently among his enemies. All three faced him. There was a great snarling and growling, a clashing of teeth and a flurry of bodies. The dust of the road arose in a cloud and screened the battle. But at the end of several minutes two dogs were struggling in the dirt and the third was in full flight. He leaped a ditch, went through a rail fence, and fled across a field. White Fang followed, sliding over the ground in wolf fashion and with wolf speed, swiftly and without noise, and in the centre of the field he dragged down and slew the dog.

With this triple killing his main troubles with dogs ceased. The word went up and down the valley, and men saw to it that their dogs did not molest the Fighting Wolf.

CHAPTER IV

The Call of Kind

The months came and went. There was plenty of food and no work in the Southland, and White Fang lived fat and prosperous and happy. Not alone was he in the geographical Southland, for he was in the Southland of life. Human kindness was like a sun shining upon him, and he flourished like a flower planted in good soil.

And yet he remained somehow different from other dogs. He knew the law even better than did the dogs that had known no other life, and he observed the law more punctiliously; but still there was about him a suggestion of lurking ferocity, as though the Wild still lingered in him and the wolf in him merely slept.

He never chummed with other dogs. Lonely he had lived, so far as his kind was concerned, and lonely he would continue to live. In his puppyhood, under the persecution of Lip-lip and the puppy-pack, and in his fighting days with Beauty Smith, he had acquired a fixed aversion for dogs. The natural course of his life had been diverted, and, recoiling from his kind, he had clung to the human.

Besides, all Southland dogs looked upon him with suspicion. He aroused in them their instinctive fear of the Wild, and they greeted him always with snarl and growl and belligerent hatred. He, on the other hand, learned that it was not necessary to use his teeth upon them. His naked fangs and writhing lips were uniformly efficacious, rarely failing to send a bellowing on-rushing dog back on its haunches.

But there was one trial in White Fang's life—Collie. She never gave him a moment's peace. She was not so amenable to the law as he. She defied all efforts of the master to make her become friends with White Fang. Ever in his ears was sounding her sharp and nervous snarl. She had never forgiven him the chicken-killing episode, and persistently held to the belief that his intentions were bad. She found him guilty before the act, and treated him accordingly. She became a pest to him, like a policeman following him around the stable and the grounds, and, if he even so much as glanced curiously at a pigeon or chicken, bursting into an outcry of indignation and wrath. His favorite way of ignoring her was to lie down, with his head on his forepaws, and pretend sleep. This always dumfounded and silenced her.

With the exception of Collie, all things went well with White Fang. He had learned control and poise, and he knew the law. He achieved a staidness, and calmness, and philosophic tolerance. He no longer lived in a hostile environment. Danger and hurt and death did not lurk everywhere about him. In time, the unknown, as a thing of terror and menace ever impending, faded away. Life was soft and easy. It flowed along smoothly, and neither fear nor foe lurked by the way.

He missed the snow without being aware of it. "An unduly long summer" would have been his thought had he thought about it; as it was, he merely missed the snow in a vague, subconscious way. In the same fashion, especially in the heat of summer when he suffered from the sun, he experienced faint longings for the Northland. Their only effect upon him, however, was to make him uneasy and restless without his knowing what was the matter.

White Fang had never been demonstrative. Beyond his snuggling and the throwing of a crooning note into his love-growl, he had no way of expressing his love. Yet it was given him to discover a third way. He had always been susceptible to the laughter of the gods. Laughter had affected him with madness, made him frantic with rage. But he did not have it in him to be angry with the love-master, and when that god elected to laugh at him in a good-natured, bantering way, he was nonplussed. He could feel the pricking and stinging of the old anger as it strove to rise up in him, but it strove against love. He could not be angry; yet he had to do something. At first he was dignified and the master laughed the harder. Then he tried to be more dignified, and the master laughed harder than before. In the end, the master laughed him out of his dignity. His jaws slightly parted, his lips lifted a little, a quizzical expression that was more love than humor came into his eyes. He had learned to laugh.

Likewise he learned to romp with the master, to be tumbled down and rolled over, and be the victim of innumerable rough tricks. In return he feigned anger, bristling and growling ferociously, and clipping his teeth together in snaps that had all the seeming of deadly intention. But he never forgot himself. Those snaps were always delivered on the empty air. At the end of such a romp, when blow and cuff and snap and snarl were fast and furious, they would break off suddenly and stand several feet apart, glaring at each other. And then, just as suddenly, like the sun rising on a stormy sea, they would begin to laugh. This would always culminate with the master's arms going around White Fang's neck and shoulders while the latter crooned and growled his love-song.

But nobody else ever romped with White Fang. He

did not permit it. He stood on his dignity, and when they attempted it, his warning snarl and bristling mane were anything but playful. That he allowed the master these liberties was no reason that he should be a common dog, loving here and loving there, everybody's property for a romp and good time. He loved with single heart and refused to cheapen himself or his love.

The master went out on horseback a great deal, and to accompany him was one of White Fang's chief duties in life. In the Northland he had evidenced his fealty by toiling in the harness; but there were no sleds in the Southland, nor did dogs pack burdens on their backs. So he rendered fealty in the new way, by running with the master's horse. The longest day never played White Fang out. His was the gait of the wolf, smooth, tireless, and effortless, and at the end of fifty miles he would come in jauntily ahead of the horse.

It was in connection with the riding, that White Fang achieved one other mode of expression—remarkable in that he did it but twice in all his life. The first time occurred when the master was trying to teach a spirited thoroughbred the method of opening and closing gates without the rider's dismounting. Time and again and many times he ranged the horse up to the gate in the effort to close it, and each time the horse became frightened and backed and plunged away. It grew more nervous and excited every moment. When it reared, the master put the spurs to it and made it drop its fore-legs back to earth, whereupon it would begin kicking with its hind-legs. White Fang watched the performance with increasing anxiety until he could contain himself no longer, when he sprang in front of the horse and barked savagely and warningly.

Though he often tried to bark thereafter, and the master encouraged him, he succeeded only once, and then it was not in the master's presence. A scamper across the pasture, a jackrabbit rising suddenly under the horse's feet, a violent sheer, a stumble, a fall to earth, and a broken leg for the master were the cause of it. White Fang sprang in a rage at the throat of the offending horse, but was checked by the master's voice.

"Home! Go home!" the master commanded, when he had ascertained his injury.

White Fang was disinclined to desert him. The master thought of writing a note, but searched his pockets vainly for pencil and paper. Again he commanded White Fang to go home.

The latter regarded him wistfully, started away, then returned and whined softly. The master talked to him gently but seriously, and he cocked his ears and listened with painful intentness.

"That's all right, old fellow, you just run along home," ran the talk. "Go home and tell them what's happened to me. Home with you, you wolf. Get along home!"

White Fang knew the meaning of "home," and though he did not understand the remainder of the master's language, he knew it was his will that he should go home. He turned and trotted reluctantly away. Then he stopped, undecided, and looked back over his shoulder.

"Go home!" came the sharp command, and this time he obeyed.

The family was on the porch, taking the cool of the afternoon, when White Fang arrived. He came in among them, panting, covered with dust.

"Weedon's back," Weedon's mother announced.

The children welcomed White Fang with glad cries and ran to meet him. He avoided them and passed down the porch, but they cornered him against a rocking-chair and the railing. He growled and tried to push by them. Their mother looked apprehensively in their direction.

"I confess he makes me nervous around the children," she said. "I have a dread that he will turn upon them unexpectedly some day."

Growling savagely, White Fang sprang out of the corner, overturning the boy and the girl. The mother called them to her and comforted them, telling them not to bother White Fang.

"A wolf is a wolf," commented Judge Scott. "There is no trusting one."

"But he is not all wolf," interposed Beth, standing for her brother in his absence.

"You have only Weedon's opinion for that," rejoined the Judge. "He merely surmises that there is some strain of dog in White Fang; but as he will tell you himself, he knows nothing about it. As for his appearance——"

He did not finish the sentence. White Fang stood before him, growling fiercely.

"Go away! Lie down, sir!" Judge Scott commanded.

White Fang turned to the love-master's wife. She screamed with fright as he seized her dress in his teeth and dragged on it till the frail fabric tore away. By this time he had become the centre of interest. He had ceased from his growling and stood, head up, looking into their faces. His throat worked spasmodically, but made no sound, while he struggled with all his body, convulsed with the effort to rid himself of the incommunicable something that strained for utterance.

"I hope he is not going mad," said Weedon's mother. "I told Weedon that I was afraid the warm climate would not agree with an Arctic animal."

"He's trying to speak, I do believe," Beth announced.

At this moment speech came to White Fang, rushing up in a great burst of barking.

"Something has happened to Weedon," his wife said decisively.

They were all on their feet, now, and White Fang ran down the steps, looking back for them to follow. For the second and last time in his life he had barked and made himself understood.

After this event he found a warmer place in the hearts of the Sierra Vista people, and even the groom whose arm he had slashed admitted that he was a wise dog even if he was a wolf. Judge Scott still held to the same opinion, and proved it to everybody's dissatisfaction by measurements and descriptions taken from the encyclopædia and various works on natural history.

The days came and went, streaming their unbroken sunshine over the Santa Clara Valley. But as they grew shorter and White Fang's second winter in the Southland came on, he made a strange discovery. Collie's teeth were no longer sharp. There was a playfulness about her nips and a gentleness that prevented them from really hurting him. He forgot that she had made life a burden to him, and when she disported herself around him he responded solemnly, striving to be playful and becoming no more than ridiculous.

One day she led him off on a long chase through the back-pasture and into the woods. It was the afternoon that the master was to ride, and White Fang knew it. The horse stood saddled and waiting at the door. White Fang hesitated. But there was that in him deeper than all the law he had learned, than the customs that had moulded him, than his love for the master, than the very will to live of himself; and when, in the moment of his indecision, Collie nipped him and scampered off, he turned and followed after. The master rode alone that day; and in the woods, side by side, White Fang ran with Collie, as his mother, Kiche, and old One Eye had run long years before in the silent Northland forest.

CHAPTER V

The Sleeping Wolf

It was about this time that the newspapers were full of the daring escape of a convict from San Quentin prison. He was a ferocious man. He had been ill-made in the making. He had not been born right, and he had not been helped any by the moulding he had received at the hands of society. The hands of society are harsh, and this man was a striking sample of its handiwork. He was a beast—a human beast, it is true, but nevertheless so terrible a beast that he can best be characterized as carnivorous.

In San Quentin prison he had proved incorrigible. Punishment failed to break his spirit. He could die dumb-mad and fighting to the last, but he could not live and be beaten. The more fiercely he fought, the more harshly society handled him, and the only effect of harshness was to make him fiercer. Straitjackets, starvation, and beatings and clubbings were the wrong treatment for Jim Hall; but it was the treatment he received. It was the treatment he had received from the time he was a little pulpy boy in a San Francisco slum—soft clay in the hands of society and ready to be formed into something.

It was during Jim Hall's third term in prison that he encountered a guard that was almost as great a beast as he. The guard treated him unfairly, lied about him to the warden, lost him his credits, persecuted him. The difference between them was that the guard carried a bunch of keys and a revolver. Jim Hall had only his naked hands and his teeth. But he sprang upon the guard one day and used his teeth on the other's throat just like any jungle animal.

After this, Jim Hall went to live in the incorrigible cell. He lived there three years. The cell was of iron, the floor, the walls, the roof. He never left this cell. He never saw the sky nor the sunshine. Day was a twilight and night was a black silence. He was in an iron tomb, buried alive. He saw no human face, spoke to no human thing. When his food was shoved in to him, he growled like a wild animal. He hated all things. For days and nights he bellowed his rage at the universe. For weeks and months he never made a sound, in the black silence eating his very soul. He was a man and a monstrosity, as fearful a thing of fear as ever gibbered in the visions of a maddened brain.

And then, one night, he escaped. The warden said it was impossible, but nevertheless the cell was empty, and half in half out of it lay the body of a dead guard. Two other dead guards marked his trail through the prison to the outer walls, and he had killed with his hands to avoid noise.

He was armed with the weapons of the slain guards—a live arsenal that fled through the hills pursued by the organized might of society. A heavy price of gold was upon his head. Avaricious farmers hunted him with shot-guns. His blood might pay off a mortgage or send a son to college. Public-spirited citizens took down their rifles and went out after him. A pack of bloodhounds followed the way of his bleeding feet. And the sleuth-hounds of the law, the paid fighting animals of society, with telephone, and telegraph, and special train, clung to his trail night and day.

Sometimes they came upon him, and men faced him like heroes, or stampeded through barb-wire fences to the delight of the commonwealth reading the account at the breakfast table. It was after such encounters that the dead and wounded were carted back to the towns, and their places filled by men eager for the man-hunt.

And then Jim Hall disappeared. The bloodhounds vainly quested on the lost trail. Inoffensive ranchers in remote valleys were held up by armed men and compelled to identify themselves; while the remains of Jim Hall were discovered on a dozen mountainsides by greedy claimants for blood-money.

In the meantime the newspapers were read at Sierra Vista, not so much with interest as with anxiety. The women were afraid. Judge Scott pooh-poohed and laughed, but not with reason, for it was in his last days on the bench that Jim Hall had stood before him and received sentence. And in open courtroom, before all men, Jim Hall had proclaimed that the day would come when he would wreak vengeance on the Judge that sentenced him.

For once, Jim Hall was right. He was innocent of the crime for which he was sentenced. It was a case, in the parlance of thieves and police, of "railroading." Jim Hall was being "railroaded" to prison for a crime he had not committed. Because of the two prior convictions against him, Judge Scott imposed upon him a sentence of fifty years.

Judge Scott did not know all things, and he did not know that he was party to a police conspiracy, that the evidence was hatched and perjured, that Jim Hall was guiltless of the crime charged. And Jim Hall, on the other hand, did not know that Judge Scott was merely ignorant. Jim Hall believed that the Judge knew all about it and was hand in glove with the police in the perpetration of the monstrous injustice. So it was, when the doom of fifty years of living death was uttered by Judge Scott, that Jim Hall, hating all things in the society that misused him, rose up and raged in the courtroom until dragged down by half a dozen of his blue-coated enemies. To him, Judge Scott was the keystone in the arch of injustice, and upon Judge Scott he emptied the vials of his wrath and hurled the threats of his revenge yet to come. Then Jim Hall went to his living death . . . and escaped.

Of all this White Fang knew nothing. But between him and Alice, the master's wife, there existed a secret. Each night, after Sierra Vista had gone to bed, she arose and let in White Fang to sleep in the big hall. Now White Fang was not a house-dog, nor was he permitted to sleep in the house; so each morning, early, she slipped down and let him out before the family was awake.

On one such night, while all the house slept, White Fang awoke and lay very quietly. And very quietly he smelled the air and read the message it bore of a strange god's presence. And to his ears came sounds of the strange god's movements. White Fang burst into no furious outcry. It was not his way. The strange god walked softly, but more softly walked White Fang, for he had no clothes to rub against the flesh of his body. He followed silently. In the Wild he had hunted live meat that was infinitely timid, and he knew the advantage of surprise.

The strange god paused at the foot of the great staircase and listened, and White Fang was as dead, so without movement was he as he watched and waited. Up that staircase the way led to the love-master and to the love-master's dearest possessions. White Fang bristled, but waited. The strange god's foot lifted. He was beginning the ascent.

Then it was that White Fang struck. He gave no warning, with no snarl anticipated his own action. Into the air he lifted his body in the spring that landed him on the strange god's back. White Fang clung with his fore-paws to the man's shoulders, at the same time burying his fangs into the back of the man's neck. He clung on for a moment, long enough to drag the god over backward. Together they crashed to the floor. White Fang leaped clear, and, as the man struggled to rise, was in again with the slashing fangs.

Sierra Vista awoke in alarm. The noise from downstairs was as that of a score of battling fiends. There were revolver shots. A man's voice screamed once in horror and anguish. There was a great snarling and growling, and over all arose a smashing and crashing of furniture and glass.

But almost as quickly as it had arisen, the commotion died away. The struggle had not lasted more than three minutes. The frightened household clustered at the top of the stairway. From below, as from out an abyss of blackness, came up a gurgling sound, as of air bubbling through water. Sometimes this gurgle became sibilant, almost a whistle. But this, too, quickly died down and ceased. Then naught came up out of the blackness save a heavy panting of some creature struggling sorely for air.

Weedon Scott pressed a button, and the staircase and downstairs hall were flooded with light. Then he and Judge Scott, revolvers in hand, cautiously descended. There was no need for this caution. White Fang had done his work. In the midst of the wreckage of overthrown and smashed furniture, partly on his side, his face hidden by an arm, lay a man. Weedon Scott bent over, removed the arm, and turned the man's face upward. A gaping throat explained the manner of his death.

"Jim Hall," said Judge Scott, and father and son looked significantly at each other.

Then they turned to White Fang. He, too, was lying on his side. His eyes were closed, but the lids slightly lifted in an effort to look at them as they bent over him, and the tail was perceptibly agitated in a vain effort to wag. Weedon Scott patted him, and his throat rumbled an acknowledging growl. But it was a weak growl at best, and it quickly ceased. His eyelids drooped and went shut, and his whole body seemed to relax and flatten out upon the floor.

"He's all in, poor devil," muttered the master.

"We'll see about that," asserted the Judge, as he started for the telephone.

"Frankly, he has one chance in a thousand," announced the surgeon, after he had worked an hour and a half on White Fang.

Dawn was breaking through the windows and dimming the electric lights. With the exception of the children, the whole family was gathered about the surgeon to hear his verdict.

"One broken hind-leg," he went on. "Three broken ribs, one at least of which has pierced the lungs. He has lost nearly all the blood in his body. There is a large likelihood of internal injuries. He must have been jumped upon. To say nothing of three bullet holes clear through him. One chance in a thousand is really optimistic. He hasn't a chance in ten thousand."

"But he mustn't lose any chance that might be of help to him," Judge Scott exclaimed. "Never mind expense. Put him under the X-ray—anything. Weedon, telegraph at once to San Francisco for Doctor Nichols. No reflection on you, doctor, you understand; but he must have the advantage of every chance."

The surgeon smiled indulgently. "Of course I understand. He deserves all that can be done for him. He must be nursed as you would nurse a human being, a sick child. And don't forget what I told you about temperature. I'll be back at ten o'clock again."

White Fang received the nursing. Judge Scott's suggestion of a trained nurse was indignantly clamored

down by the girls, who themselves undertook the task.
And White Fang won out on the one chance in ten
thousand denied him by the surgeon.

The latter was not to be censured for his misjudg-
ment. All his life he had tended and operated on the
soft humans of civilization, who lived sheltered lives
and had descended out of many sheltered generations.
Compared with White Fang, they were frail and
flabby, and clutched life without any strength in their
grip. White Fang had come straight from the Wild,
where the weak perish early and shelter is vouchsafed
to none. In neither his father nor his mother was there
any weakness, nor in the generations before them. A
constitution of iron and the vitality of the Wild were
White Fang's inheritance, and he clung to life, the
whole of him and every part of him, in spirit and in
flesh, with the tenacity that of old belonged to all creatures.

Bound down a prisoner, denied even movement by
the plaster casts and bandages, White Fang lingered
out the weeks. He slept long hours and dreamed much,
and through his mind passed an unending pageant of
Northland visions. All the ghosts of the past arose and
were with him. Once again he lived in the lair with
Kiche, crept trembling to the knees of Gray Beaver to
tender his allegiance, ran for his life before Lip-lip and
all the howling bedlam of the puppy-pack.

He ran again through the silence, hunting his living
food through the months of famine; and again he ran at
the head of the team, the gut-whips of Mit-sah and
Gray Beaver snapping behind, their voices crying
"Raa! Raa!" when they came to a narrow passage and
the team closed together like a fan to go through. He
lived again all his days with Beauty Smith and the
fights he had fought. At such times he whimpered and
snarled in his sleep, and they that looked on said that
his dreams were bad.

But there was one particular nightmare from which he suffered—the clanking, clanging monsters of electric cars that were to him colossal screaming lynxes. He would lie in a screen of bushes, watching for a squirrel to venture far enough out on the ground from its tree-refuge. Then, when he sprang out upon it, it would transform itself into an electric car, menacing and terrible, towering over him like a mountain, screaming and clanging and spitting fire at him. It was the same when he challenged the hawk down out of the sky. Down out of the blue it would rush, as it dropped upon him changing itself into the ubiquitous electric car. Or again, he would be in the pen of Beauty Smith. Outside the pen, men would be gathering, and he knew that a fight was on. He watched the door for his antagonist to enter. The door would open, and thrust in upon him would come the awful electric car. A thousand times this occurred, and each time the terror it inspired was as vivid and great as ever.

Then came the day when the last bandage and the last plaster cast were taken off. It was a gala day. All Sierra Vista was gathered around. The master rubbed his ears, and he crooned his love-growl. The master's wife called him the Blessed Wolf, which name was taken up with acclaim and all the women called him the Blessed Wolf.

He tried to rise to his feet, and after several attempts fell down from weakness. He had lain so long that his muscles had lost their cunning, and all the strength had gone out of them. He felt a little shame because of his weakness, as though, forsooth, he were failing the gods in the service he owed them. Because of this he made heroic efforts to arise, and at last he stood on his four legs, tottering and swaying back and forth.

"The Blessed Wolf!" chorused the women.

Judge Scott surveyed them triumphantly.

"Out of your own mouths be it," he said. "Just as I

contended right along. No mere dog could have done what he did. He's a wolf."

"A Blessed Wolf," amended the Judge's wife.

"Yes, Blessed Wolf," agreed the Judge. "And henceforth that shall be my name for him."

"He'll have to learn to walk again," said the surgeon; "so he might as well start in right now. It won't hurt him. Take him outside."

And outside he went, like a king, with all Sierra Vista about him and tending on him. He was very weak, and when he reached the lawn he lay down and rested for a while.

Then the procession started on, little spurts of strength coming into White Fang's muscles as he used them and the blood began to surge through them. The stables were reached, and there in the doorway lay Collie, a half-dozen pudgy puppies playing about her in the sun.

White Fang looked on with a wondering eye. Collie snarled warningly at him, and he was careful to keep his distance. The master with his toe helped one sprawling puppy toward him. He bristled suspiciously, but the master warned him that all was well. Collie, clasped in the arms of one of the women, watched him jealously and with a snarl warned him that all was not well.

The puppy sprawled in front of him. He cocked his ears and watched it curiously. Then their noses touched, and he felt the warm little tongue of the puppy on his jowl. White Fang's tongue went out, he knew not why, and he licked the puppy's face.

Hand-clapping and pleased cries from the gods greeted the performance. He was surprised, and looked at them in a puzzled way. Then his weakness asserted itself, and he lay down, his ears cocked, his head on one side, as he watched the puppy. The other puppies came sprawling toward him, to Collie's great disgust; and he gravely permitted them to clamber and tumble over him. At first, amid the applause of the gods, he betrayed a trifle of his old self-consciousness and awkwardness. This passed away as the puppies' antics and mauling continued, and he lay with half-shut, patient eyes, drowsing in the sun.

A Note on Jack London's Life and Works

J ack London was born on January 12, 1876, in San
Francisco, the only child of a spiritualist and music
teacher, Flora Wellman. His father was probably a
wandering astrologer called William Henry Chaney.
His mother was soon married to a widower and Civil
War veteran, John London, who had two young
daughters with him, Eliza and Ida. Flora's son was
given his stepfather's name, John Griffith London.

Jack London's boyhood was spent in Oakland and
on small farms near San Francisco Bay. His parents'
schemes for making money failed and the family returned to live in a succession of poorhouses in Oakland.
To earn a few dollars, Jack worked as a newsboy and in
a skittle alley, and later in a cannery. He had an early
love of books and of sailing in a skiff on the bay. By the
age of fifteen, he was a delinquent and an oyster pi-
rate—a time which he was to romanticize in a book for
boys, *The Cruise of the Dazzler* (1902). He also briefly
joined the side of the law against his old comrades and
later wrote of his adventures in *Tales of the Fish Patrol*
(1905).

In 1893, he set off for a seven·month sealing voyage
on the schooner *Sophia Sutherland*. This hard life
among sailors engaged in a bloody task gave him the
experience to write and publish his first story, about a

typhoon off Japan—and the material for his best novel about the struggle of men against nature and each other, *The Sea-Wolf* (1904).

The nex⁺ year, 1894, he joined Kelly's detachment of Coxey's Army of the unemployed, which tried to march on Washington. His experiences as a Road Kid and a vagrant are recounted in *The Road* (1907), the forerunner of the work of Dos Passos and Kerouac. The thirty days he spent in jail in the Erie County Penitentiary marked him all his life. He became determined to use his brains to keep out of the degradation forced on the jobless.

He returned to high school in Oakland, became a radical, joined the Socialist Labor Party, and spent one semester at the University of California at Berkeley. He fell deeply under the influence of Spencer's social Darwinism and also Marxism, as preached by the Oakland socialists and the circle gathering round Anna Strunsky, one of his early loves.

In 1897, Jack London went on the Klondike Gold Rush, caught scurvy, and returned to California after a two-thousand-mile voyage down the Yukon River. He applied himself to writing as a profession, nearly starving and working incessantly. A partly autobiographical account of these harsh years can be found in his novel *Martin Eden* (1909).

His Klondike stories soon attracted attention. After publishing his first three collections of them, *The Son of the Wolf* (1900), *The God of His Fathers* (1901), and *Children of the Frost* (1902), he found himself famous. If his first novel, *A Daughter of the Snows,* was a failure, *The Call of the Wild* (1903) was his masterpiece as a short novel and gave him international recognition, enhanced by another collection of Alaskan stories, *The ˥aith of Men* (1904).

In 1900, he had married Elizabeth (Bess) Maddern, mainly for biological reasons, as he declared in his collaboration with Anna Strunsky, *The Kempton-Wace Letters* (1903). His wife bore him two daughters, Joan and Becky. In 1902, he fell in love with Anna Strunsky, but lost her when he left for London, where he wrote his emotional account of the poor in the East End, *The People of the Abyss*. Reconciled with his wife on his return, he soon left her for the older Charmian Kittredge, an emancipated and courageous Californian.

In 1904, he became a correspondent for the Hearst newspapers in the Russo-Japanese war, and recognized the threat of Asia to the world dominance of Europe. The Russian revolution of 1905 inflamed his radicalism, so that he gave a series of socialist lectures, later published in two important collections of essays, *War of the Classes* and *Revolution*. His divorce and his instant remarriage, to Charmian Kittredge, put him even more in the news.

He continued to write intensively, inventing the American boxing novel in *The Game* (1905), recreating primitive existence in *Before Adam* (1907), and continuing to mine his lucrative Klondike vein with *Moon-Face* and *Love of Life and Other Stories*. His greatest success after *The Sea-Wolf* was another short novel, *White Fang* (1906), which told the story of a wild dog tamed by civilization, the reverse of *The Call of the Wild*. Yet his most original contribution was *The Iron Heel* (1908), a chilling prophecy of the Fascist period to come.

At the peak of his influence and powers, Jack London decided to build his own sailing boat, the *Snark*, and to cruise round the world with Charmian as his "mate." The San Francisco earthquake of 1906 doubled the costs and delayed the start of the voyage, so that Jack was nearly bankrupt when he sailed to Hawaii, the Marquesas, Tahiti, Samoa, and the Solomon Islands. The two-year voyage, interrupted by a short return home to rescue his finances, was a saga of acci

dents and diseases ending in the complete collapse of
Jack's health. He abandoned the *Snark* and started
some disastrous arsenic treatments in Australia, which
damaged his nerves and kidneys. He sailed back to California in 1909. It was the first public defeat of a man
who had created the image of a superman and now was
trapped within it.

During the last seven years of his life, Jack lived in
deteriorating health and devoted his energies to developing his ranch near Glen Ellen in Northern California
and to building his stone "Wolf House." Always short
of money for his increasing expenses, he lived a disci-
plined life, writing every day. He returned to the prof-
itable theme of Alaska in *Lost Face* and *Burning Daylight* (1910) and *Smoke Bellew* (1912). His long sea
voyage produced the autobiographical *The Cruise of the
Snark* and, between 1911 and 1913, a succession of Pacific stories and novels: *When God Laughs, Adventure,
South Sea Tales, A Son of the Sun,* and *The House of
Pride.* If the quality of his work deteriorated with his
health, yet his style and professionalism kept him popular and respected.

In 1912, he sailed round Cape Horn on the *Dirigo,*
the basis of his grisly novel *The Mutiny of the Elsinore.*
Charmian miscarried for the second time, removing
any chance of his having a male child. He had quar-
reled with his first wife and two daughters, and his last
misfortune was to lose the completed Wolf House by
fire. His story of his own problems with alcohol, *John
Barleycorn* (1913), showed his writing and his self-
awareness at their best, while his new devotion to the
land and life on his ranch was portrayed in two novels,
The Valley of the Moon (1913) and *The Little Lady of
the Big House* (1916). His life at Glen Ellen had truly
become the center of his existence, devotedly run by
Charmian and his stepsister Eliza, who acted as his
ranch manager.

Some of his best short stories were written in his declining years, particularly those in *The Strength of the Strong* (1914), which contains "South of the Slot," "The Dream of Debs," "The Sea Farmer," and "Samuel." Other collections of stories were *The Night Born* and *The Turtles of Tasman.* He continued his boxing novels with *The Abysmal Brute* and his science fiction with *The Scarlet Plague* (1915) and the haunting *The Red One* (1918). Yet his most extraordinary feat of imagination was his novel of prison life and time travel, *The Star Rover* (1915).

His physical condition was made even worse by a severe attack of dysentery while he was reporting the Mexican Revolution in 1914. Hardly alive and existing on huge quantities of fluid and pain-killing drugs, Jack spent the last two years of his life becoming conscious of the many contradictions of his character. His animal novels *Jerry of the Islands* and *Michael, Brother of Jerry* were run-of-the-mill, but his psychological stories, after his reading of Freud and Jung, proved to be some of his finer work, published in *On the Makaloa Mat* (1919). His notes for a projected novel on his dead Shire stallion and for "Farthest Distant: The Last Novel of Them All" promised great works to come.

Unfortunately, long stays in Hawaii could not help his internal maladies and increasing sense of disgust with life. He resigned from the Socialist Party in 1916 and shortly afterward took an overdose of the drugs prescribed for his kidney and bladder problems. He had done this many times before, but this time his weakened body could not take the strain. He lapsed into a coma and died on November 22, 1916.

He died at the age of forty. He had written more than fifty books in twenty years and had lived nine lives. He was the archetype of the American hero who tried to live what he wrote. He was also the Californian Pilgrim, in search of the new at all costs, as if life would go on forever. He made himself a myth in his own time and for ours.

ANDREW SINCLAIR

For a full life of Jack London, see my own *Jack: A Biography of Jack London* (New York, London and Paris, 1977).

Selected Bibliography

BOOKS

Kingman, R. *A Pictorial Life of Jack London.* Crown: New York, 1979.

Labor, E. *Jack London.* Twayne: New York, 1974.

London, C. K. *The Book of Jack London,* 2 vols. Century: New York, 1921.

London, J. *Jack London and His Times: An Unconventional Biography.* University of Washington Press: Seattle, 1968.

McClintock, J. I. *White Logic: Jack London's Short Stories.* Wolf House: Grand Rapids, Mich., 1975.

Ownbey, R. W., ed. *Jack London: Essays in Criticism.* Peregrine Smith: Layton, Utah, 1978.

Sherman, J. *Jack London: A Reference Guide.* G. K. Hall: Boston, 1977.

Sinclair, A. *Jack: A Biography of Jack London.* Harper and Row: New York, 1977.

Stone, I. *Sailor on Horseback.* Houghton Mifflin: Boston, 1938.

Walcutt, C. C. *Jack London.* University of Minnesota Press: Minneapolis, 1966.

Walker, D. L., ed. *Jack London: No Mentor But Myself:* A Collection of Articles, Essays, Reviews, and Letters on Writing and Writers. Kennikat: Port Washington, N.Y., 1979.

Walker, D. L., ed., *The Fiction of Jack London: A Chronological Bibliography.* Tex Western: El Paso, Tex., 1972.

Walker, F. *Jack London and the Klondike.* Huntington Library: San Marino, Calif., 1966.

409

ARTICLES

Benoit, R. "Jack London's *The Call of the Wild*," *American Quarterly* XX (1968).

Etulain, R. "The Lives of Jack London," *Western American Literature* XI (1976).

Flink, A. *"Call of the Wild:* Jack London's Catharsis," *Jack London Newsletter* XI (1978).

Geismar, M. "Jack London: The Short Cut," in *Rebels and Ancestors: The American Novel, 1890–1915*. Boston, 1953.

Labor, E. Introduction to *Great Short Works of Jack London*. New York, 1970.

Noto, S. "Jack London's Dawson: Past and Present," *The Pacific Historian* XXIV (1980).

Pattee, F. L. "The Prophet of the Last Frontier," in *Sidelights on American Literature*. New York, 1922.

Peterson, C. T. "Jack London's Alaskan Stories," *American Book Collector* IX (1959).

Shivers, A. S. "The Romantic in Jack London," *Alaska Review* I (1963).

Walcutt, C. C. "Jack London: Blond Beasts and Supermen," in *American Literary Naturalism: A Divided Stream*. Minneapolis, 1956.

Wilcox, E. "Le Milieu, Le Moment, La Race: Literary Naturalism in *White Fang*," *Jack London Newsletter* III (1970).

A comprehensive checklist of critical writings about London's works has been compiled by H. L. Lachtman for the Jack London special number of *Modern Fiction Studies* XXII (1976).